Also by Richard Hawke

SPEAK OF THE DEVIL
COLD DAY IN HELL

HOUSE
OF
SECRETS

HOUSE OF SECRETS

OF

SECRETS

A NOVEL

• • •

RICHARD HAWKE

RANDOM HOUSE NEW YORK

Copyright © 2010 by Richard Hawke

All rights reserved.
Published in the United States by Random House,
an imprint of The Random House Publishing Group,
a division of Random House, Inc., New York.

RANDOM HOUSE and colophon are registered trademarks of Random House, Inc.

Library of Congress Cataloging-in-Publication Data

Hawke, Richard.
House of secrets : a novel / Richard Hawke.
p. cm.
ISBN 978-1-4000-6608-7
eBook ISBN 978-0-679-60357-3
I. Legislators—United States—Fiction.   2. Family secrets—Fiction.   I. Title.
PS3608.A886H68 2010
813´.6—dc22   2009033151

Printed in the United States of America on acid-free paper

www.atrandom.com

2 4 6 8 9 7 5 3 1

First Edition

For Jules
. . . throughout the three times

PART **ONE**

CHAPTER 1

Christine Foster sat with her stepfather at the bar in Denver International Airport, her eyes trained on the hideous swirls of snow having their way with the terminal's large slanted windows. Her stepfather was watching them as well. For the better part of the past hour, Ben Turner had been digging his thumbnail into the label of his beer bottle, rendering it a shredded mess. Anyone watching the two would have thought that *he* was the one waiting to hear the status of *his* night flight from Denver to New York.

Ben looked up from his mutilation project. "Are you getting a signal?"

Christine's cell was pressed to her ear. The strap of her camera had ridden up on her neck, catching some of her hair. She twisted her body slightly on the barstool in a vain attempt to escape the music—Steely Dan's "Reeling in the Years"—pumping relentlessly from the low ceiling speakers. She ignored Ben's question as her husband's outgoing message gave over to the beep.

"Hi, honey," Christine said loudly. She bent further into her phone. "Mrs. Miniver here. I'm at the airport. It's my guess we're about to be officially socked in, but I haven't heard for sure yet. This snow is intense. If I come home with frostbite and you're all tanned and yummy, I'm going to kill you, I swear. You have been warned."

She aimed a smile over at her mother's husband. "Ben's here with me. We're getting plastered at the bar. You'd be so ashamed of me. Listen, I'll call you later when I know something. I hope your talk went well. I can't wait to see you. Mother sends her worst, ha ha."

As Christine tucked the phone back into her purse, Ben asked, "He wasn't there?"

Christine took a beat. The question was classic Ben. For reasons that Christine was certain she would never fully fathom, her mother had decided to take as Spouse Number Two the type of person who would watch a person leaving a message for someone over the phone and then ask, "He wasn't there?" Sweet man, but only nominally more vibrant than a paper clip. He and Lillian had now been married for just over six years. For someone like Lillian, Ben had been an astonishing plunge into meekness, about as far from Christine's father—who was still very much alive—as she could have gone. But then, Lillian lived to astonish.

Christine confirmed Ben's deduction. "No. He wasn't there."

"What's 'Mrs. Miniver'?"

Christine was readjusting the strap of her camera. "That? It's just silliness. Andy's in eternal love with Greer Garson, the movie actress from the forties. The very first time we met, he went through his whole Greer Garson song and dance. She's so beautiful, she's so warm, she's so spunky. And of course he said I reminded him of *her,* thank you muchly. Though I guess that's not such a bad pickup line. 'You remind me of someone I absolutely adore.' " She laughed. "I was certainly not immune."

Outside the window, furious gusts were whipping the snow about, as if the night was determined to beat down the glass and roar right into the terminal. From the blackness, a large bloblike shape appeared and smacked hard against the window. Christine and Ben started. It was a tarp of some sort, possibly torn loose from one of the luggage wagons. The tarp rotated slowly on the glass—it too looked as if it wanted in—then peeled back along one corner and was flung back into the night.

Christine's milky skin had gone a shade sour. She turned to Ben.

"News flash. Mrs. Miniver is *not* climbing into any goddamned airplane tonight, no matter what anybody says. Just how dumb do I look?"

Dimitri Bulakov twisted the cap from the wet bottle and tossed it in a high arc toward the black plastic trash can. It hit the television set atop the dresser, bounced off Barbra Streisand as she was charming the great Louis Armstrong with her invisible trombone, and fell to the carpet.

Dimitri could not understand what it was about this woman on the television that had made her such a big American star in her day. *She is pushy. Her eyes are too small and too close together. And the nose, it is more like a joke than a nose. It is the nose of a camel.* Dimitri supposed that if he and this pushy woman were stranded together on a deserted island, okay, that was one thing. But otherwise . . .

In just under an hour—according to the cardboard triangle on top of the television—the next movie would be starting. It starred the actress Angelina Jolie. *This,* Dimitri thought, *makes sense.* He could imagine spending many many *many* months on the island with someone like this. Dimitri glanced around the wood-paneled confines of his motel room and imagined Angelina Jolie coming in from the tiny bathroom wrapped in a small towel, her big hair falling down past her shoulders like wet snakes, and looking at him with those mean sexy eyes of hers. Dimitri slid his free hand down the front of his boxers. As he did, his gaze drifted to the mirror that sat behind the television set. Reflected in the glass was a puffy-faced, forty-one-year-old man sporting an impressive beer gut and a nest of wiry black hair all over his torso, holding a beer bottle in one hand, and with his other hand shoved down the front of his faded plaid boxers. On the TV, Camel Nose and Louis Armstrong were making goo-goo eyes at each other and laughing uproariously.

Dimitri withdrew his hand from his boxers.

His cell phone rang.

Dimitri hit the mute button on the television and scooped the phone off the pillow next to him. The accent on the other end of the line was the same as Dimitri's.

"They're on their way."

Dimitri scooted up in the bed. "Yes."

"Everything is set?"

Dimitri answered. "Good to go." Dimitri liked this expression, though he wasn't happy with the way it had sounded just now. Two or three times recently in front of the bathroom mirror, he had gotten it pretty good. Good. To. Go.

There was a pause on the other end of the phone. Then, "You'll call me once it's done."

It was not a question.

"Yes."

"The sound quality is good? We will be able to hear everything?"

Dimitri scowled. "I told you. It's all good. It's ready. I know what I am doing."

On the silent television screen the actress whose popularity Dimitri could not fathom was sauntering away from the camera spinning a parasol over her shoulder. Her dress came all the way to her feet and was nice and tight across her body. Nice rump, Dimitri thought. *This* he could fathom.

"Call me," the man said again, and the phone went dead.

Dimitri hit the remote and the hourglass figure vanished. He rolled off the bed and carried his beer bottle to the window, where he tweezered open the curtains to peer out into the night. Across the narrow road in front of the motel was the small beach, a crescent of sand bordering the inlet. The beach was empty: a lifeguard chair, a tangle of braided white cord pocked with red oval floats, an overturned rowboat. It was only April. In another few months, the renters and second-home owners from the city would be flooding the small island. But right now it was Deadtown.

At the far end of the beach—to Dimitri's right—a steep wooded hill rose up from the inlet. Dimitri turned from the window and knuckled the ENTER key on the laptop that was lying open on the second bed. He leaned past the computer to fetch his cigarettes and matches from the bedside table, shook one loose, and lit it. As a ghostlike rectangle burned into view on the computer's screen, Dimitri set down his beer bottle and took up a pair of binoculars from the bed. Scratching his belly, he returned to the window.

On the nearby hill Dimitri sighted the staccato illumination from a pair of headlights as a car passed among the trees. He trained the binoculars on an area near the highest part of the hill, where the front portion of a modest-sized house was somewhat visible. Several seconds passed, then a light-colored sports car came into view and pulled to a stop in front of the house.

Smoke from Dimitri's cigarette was stinging his eyes, but he ignored it as he toggled the binoculars' focus wheel. The driver's side door opened, and a woman stepped out of the car. She paused, raking both her hands through her hair. The passenger's side door opened, and a man emerged. Dimitri lowered the binoculars.

"Hello, Dolly," he intoned thickly. "Good to go."

And he turned to his computer.

Robert Smallwood sat hunched in the wooden lifeguard chair, hugging his long, slightly chubby legs against his chest and gazing intently up at the stars.

Rather, he was staring *back* at them.

It was Smallwood's contention that every single puckered star dotting the vast black bowl overhead was an eye—an actual, glimmering, data-collecting eye—and that from the moment he had clambered up into the wooden chair those countless eyes peering down from the dark had all turned their attention to *him.* They were watching *him.* They were mesmerized by *him.*

The eyes had it.

While sitting motionless in the wooden chair, Smallwood had also deduced that just as the human eye is attached to a human consciousness, this extraordinary collection of eye-stars must be linked to a Supreme Sage Consciousness. And that Consciousness—of this he was positive—was fully aware of what it was Robert Smallwood was planning to do in just under an hour's time. It *knew.* It was aware of his motivations and it was aware of his intentions. And it approved wholeheartedly.

Of course it did. It couldn't *not.*

The rope of muscles along Smallwood's shoulders ached wonderfully from the strenuous rowing across the choppy sound to the island beach earlier in the evening. Once settled in the wooden chair he had made a vow to remain completely still and to simply wait, to keep all his energy balled up, hugging his knees to his chest and bringing forth his Prodigious Patience. The only part of his body to which he had granted permission to move was his glorious head, which swiveled slowly, like a methodical owl's: a perfect calibration of ball bearings in the neck. Smallwood scanned the calm inlet, taking in the black sound just beyond it, as well as the phosphorescent haze hovering over sleepy Greenport Harbor, some half mile distant. This sublime level of stillness—his oscillating head notwithstanding—enthralled Smallwood. Such contained and sustained energy, he couldn't explain. He found it so *exciting.* Smallwood felt that had he chosen to, he could have detonated the energy gathered at his very core and propelled himself out into the sky *exactly* like a rocket or a missile. In fact, when at one point a shooting star grazed the edge of his peripheral vision, a Mona Lisa smile tugged at the corners of Smallwood's mouth.

That's me. There I go. Faster than a blazing motherfucker.

All flights were canceled. The midsection of the country was taking too hard a pounding. Ben and Christine were moving briskly through the terminal. Ben implored Christine as they stepped onto the moving walkway: "But Lillian will insist that I bring you back home."

Christine was adamant. "It doesn't make any sense, Ben. I've had my visit. I'm just going to get a room in one of the hotels here. I'll fly out as soon as the weather clears. I tried to tell you both it wasn't necessary for you to drive me out here in the first place."

"I know. But . . ." Ben gave up the fight.

"If you want me to call Lillian myself and tell her, I will."

"No. It's okay, Chrissie. I'll explain it to her. Don't worry about it."

As they reached the end of the moving walkway Christine spotted an airport bookstore. She brushed Ben's elbow.

"Hold on a second."

Pulling her roller bag behind her, she veered off the carpeted hallway and into the store. A round table just inside the entrance held a pyramid display of the current bestseller by the latest spiritual health guru, a seven-figure smile beaming from the book's cover. Christine moved past the guru's pyramid to a second display table, this one featuring several titles in more modest stacks. Christine picked a book off one of the stacks. Even three weeks into the whole thing, the funny feeling still came to Christine's stomach when she saw Andy's book.

A SENSE OF URGENCY
SENATOR ANDREW P. FOSTER

Christine still considered the photograph on the cover essentially shameless: her and Andy's daughter, Michelle (six years old in the photograph; seven and a half years old now), whispering something into her daddy's ear and Andy responding with a huge burst of laughter. Part of what was so special about the photograph was the knowing expression on Michelle's face, the little girl's awareness that what she was whispering to Daddy would definitely trigger his funny bone. The striking family similarity in the two faces lent an additional power to the photograph. *Little Wizard, Big Wizard.* Neither Andy nor Christine could recall precisely when the paired nicknames had first surfaced, but Michelle and her father had been employing them on each other now for several years at least. Christine had thrown a small fit during Andy's recent reelection campaign when Andy had allowed the media (*invited,* had been Christine's assertion) to catch Michelle on tape using the nickname. Michelle had subsequently been referred to as "the Wiz Kid" in most of the news outlets, a development that had done little to stem Christine's irritation with her husband.

"The next time you want to exploit our child, why don't you put her on your payroll first?" Christine had told him pointedly. "There's one public figure in this household, okay? And it's not the kid with the pink back-pack."

As she gazed at the cover of her husband's book, Christine was seized by twin twinges of guilt and hypocrisy, hardly the first of either. The truth was, she had not only been the one to tell Michelle what to whisper into Daddy's ear, she had been the one aiming the camera, nailing the compo-sition perfectly. It's what she did. She took pictures. What was worse was that ultimately she had allowed Andy and his editor to convince her that the photograph absolutely had to be used for the cover of Andy's book. The sense of hypocrisy Christine felt whenever she fielded compliments on the photograph was due in no small part to the fact that for all that it irked her to have given in to the use of her daughter's image for the fur-thering of Andy's career, she couldn't help but take pride in the photo-graph itself. In the end, it had been on *that* basis as much as anything else that Christine had given her blessings for its use.

Ben appeared next to her. "You know, I've been dying to ask. Just what is she saying to Andy that's so funny?"

Christine lied. "Oh, who knows? It's just those two. They're always goofing together."

The two exited the bookstore, Ben insisting on commandeering Christine's roller bag. Christine granted the man his chivalry, and as the two continued down the terminal hub, Ben asked yet another question whose answer he already knew.

"So, when does Andy get back from Florida?"

"He flies into D.C. tomorrow morning," Christine said. "Then home for the weekend, and we'll spend Easter with my dad and Jenny."

"And the book? It's selling well?"

"It's looking pretty good so far. Everybody seems to be pleased. Andy's been getting more-than-decent turnouts at the bookstores." She let out a gently mocking laugh. "The publisher's hoping that all the retired New Yorkers down in Florida will flock to see the great man."

An electric cart carrying half a dozen elderly passengers was trundling down the center of the wide aisle, beeping as it approached. As Ben and Christine skirted to the side to let it pass, Christine noted the anxious ex-pression on her stepfather's face. "Is everything okay, Ben?"

Ben's gaze trailed after the receding cart. "I probably shouldn't be bringing this up. But . . . I just wanted to say that it was really good of you to visit, Chrissie. Seriously. I know your mother can be a handful some-times."

"Sometimes?" Christine could not contain her laugh. "Good Lord, Ben, *you* should be the one in politics. You said that with a completely straight face! Yeah. I most certainly do know how she is."

"Your mother misses the East. Denver is just not Lillian's speed."

Christine scoffed. "Neither was Albany. And apparently neither was Greenwich. In fact, even London didn't seem to float her boat. I'm not sure that anywhere is Miss Lillian's speed. You're amazingly sweet to put up with her, Ben. Daddy used to say that governing the state of New York was the simple part. It was governing his wife that took all his real skills."

Ben's nervous laugh betrayed his discomfort. The poor man, Christine thought. I'm not telling him anything he doesn't know.

Smallwood spotted the ferry carrying his cousin Joy within a minute of its leaving Greenport.

He watched as it crossed the bay and disappeared from sight on the other side of the wooded point that jutted into the water. Smallwood's in-sights about Cousin Joy had been surging through his mind for months now, his large brain gathering and processing and gathering and process-ing with prodigious efficiency. He had her nailed, pegged, analyzed, dis-sected. Gone was the sweet little girl with whom he used to spend summers out on the island. In her place was a creature Smallwood barely recognized and had come to despise.

Smallwood had taken the train out from the city and then "borrowed" the rowboat to travel over to the island. He had come to confront his cousin with the results of his analyses. There could be no more avoiding it. Lately Joy had been refusing to even answer the phone when he called. It had been a pure fluke that she had refused his most recent request to get together by letting him know—angrily—that she was heading out that night to the house on Shelter Island.

Or possibly not a fluke. Possibly it was all in the stars.

The temperature had dropped in the past hour. Some fifteen minutes after the ferry docked, a car's headlights had appeared on the hill, stopping at the very last house. Through the magic of sound on water, Smallwood had heard a pair of doors closing, followed by the tiny buzzing sounds of conversation. A man. A woman.

Smallwood rose. Stretching his arms out from his sides for balance, he stepped from the lifeguard chair and landed softly in the sand, cushioning the drop with his knees. Lifting his feet decorously—like a slow prancing Andalusian horse—large and determined Robert Smallwood marched along the sand toward the road, feeling extremely goddamned noble.

As Christine stepped onto the down escalator, her attention was drawn to an elderly man standing at the bottom, edging onto the moving stairs using a wooden cane. He was dressed in a plaid jacket and a red bow tie, and was stooped with age. His hair was wavy and cotton white, with salt-and-pepper eyebrows that flared at the ends. He looked like a lost vaude-villian.

Instinctively, Christine reached for her camera and began firing off shots of the man, at the same time taking methodical steps backward so that she might stay in place near the top of the escalator. Each foot landed seamlessly on the next descending stair. Ben continued down toward the bottom.

The man in the bow tie was hesitating at the bottom of the escalator, poking tremulously at the moving stairs with the tip of his cane, but finally he committed. Christine captured a dozen images in the space of five seconds. Then she paused, ceasing her backpedaling, and squeezed the zoom. An elegant face of thin rubbery folds filled the viewfinder. Christine tightened the frame even more. It was only the precise instant that the white-haired man looked directly over into her camera that Christine became aware of the tears of humiliation glistening on his cheeks.

The two passed in the middle. As she reached the bottom, Christine wanted nothing else but for a second escalator to open up in front of her and take her down, down, down. She stepped over to a row of chairs and dropped into the first one she reached. The pitiable man's mournful face filled her mind and she had an urge to go racing up the escalator, to find the man, to do . . . *something.* She didn't budge. Her eyes fell blindly on two women seated across from her. It took the better part of a minute for it to dawn on her what book one of the two women was reading. The teary old man dissolved from Christine's mind. She realized she was staring at the photograph of her handsome laughing husband and her mildly exploited daughter.

Something felt terribly, terribly wrong.

To avoid the crunching sound of gravel underfoot, Smallwood kept off the driveway. His breathing was labored, from walking up the steep road as well as from the adrenaline rushing powerfully through his system.

The trees surrounding the house created an additional canopy of darkness. Smallwood felt as if he could swipe his hand through the air in front of him and come up with a smear of black on his fingers. The vision further suggested to him that were he to circle the house several dozen times before entering it, he could render himself an unseeable shadow form, as invisible as a gathering of wind.

The black wind of night.

Joy's Miata was parked on the gravel drive. Smallwood stepped daintily over the gravel to the car and peered into the window. He was curious about the keys. The family habit when coming out to stay in the house was to forgo locks, forgo keys. The house had always been that sort of refuge from the otherwise restrictive and wary world. A place to let down your guard.

Yes. The keys were in the car.

As Smallwood turned to confront the house, echoes of the long-ago voices of his cousins and himself swirled deliciously in his head, and with no difficulty at all he could see Cousin Joy making one of those explosive leaps they all enjoyed making from the front porch, her ponytail rising behind her like an Indian's feather, her bare skinny limbs flying in their four directions.

Smallwood froze the image: Cousin Joy suspended in the air, with her little pretty face open in a shriek of delight. Smallwood stepped over to where his mind had fixed her in space. He remained there, Black Wind of the Night, wholly motionless for a full minute . . . two . . . three . . . gazing at his own imagination. Inches from little Joy's face. Studying the tiny gap between her Chiclet teeth. Breathing in her imagined scent.

Presently, Smallwood became aware of sounds. For a moment he thought the soft cooing sounds were coming from him, from his own sweet nostalgia. Then he recognized them for what they were. Not his pathetic pigeon sounds at all. Anything but. They were coming from the house.

From Joy.

No longer worried in the slightest about making noise, Smallwood marched to the side of the house and around toward the back. Off at the edge of the property, beyond the trees, floated the black pool of the inlet down below. As he neared the rear of the house the sounds became louder. Unmistakable.

His . . . hers . . . his . . . hers . . .

Theirs.

Smallwood's shin banged against a hard object that was sticking out of the ground. The white flash of pain fueled his surging anger. Smallwood knew what he'd hit, and he reached down and wrenched it from the ground. It made no difference to him that the metal horseshoes on the ground clanked. The couple inside the house couldn't hear a goddamned thing other than their own animal *grunts.* Smallwood flipped the iron horseshoe pole deftly, catching it just at the base.

In ten seconds he was on the back patio.

Through the sliding glass door he could now see what he had been hearing. His breath was pouring furiously from his nostrils like that of an enraged dragon as he tried the door. It was locked. The ghostlike figures on the bed didn't seem to notice a damn thing except themselves.

The *crash* of the horseshoe pole breaking through the glass changed all that.

Smallwood brought the iron rod down on the glass door in a swift series of blows, sweeping it in a circular motion to snap away the hanging shards. Joy was screaming. The two bodies scrambled in place, kicking the white sheets into a pile.

Smallwood reached inside the broken glass to flip the lock. Jerking the door open, he charged forward, the iron bar lifted over his head. His naked targets were stranded on the bed. Joy the Disappointment and some irrelevant quivering dark-haired man.

Robert Smallwood had never felt more alive or more important than he did as his arm—itself feeling long and liquid and, in such a peculiar way, sublime—began its powerful descent.

He hoped the stars were watching.

CHAPTER 2

"**H**oly Josef!"

Dimitri Bulakov's beer bottle fell from the bedside table and glug-glug-glugged its contents onto the floor.

"Child of Jesus," Dimitri muttered, lurching closer to the laptop. His hands went to the headset, pressing the miniature speakers hard to his ears.

The laptop showed a split screen. Earlier in the day, Dimitri Bulakov had planted three fiber-optic cameras in the bedroom of the house atop the nearby hill. Two of the slender devices were located in the brass casing on the overhead fan, spaced in such a fashion that should one of the fan blades come to a stop beneath one camera, the second camera would still have a clear view of the bed below. The third filament had been run along the power cord leading from the wall outlet to the bedside clock radio and secured against the bottom of the appliance by good old-fashioned chewing gum, Dimitri's proud marriage of high and low tech. He had learned this trick at the last full-time job he had held, that is if two and a half months could be considered full-time. Dimitri Bulakov knew electronics, but what he did not know was cooperation and playing well with others. It was the temper thing, and the drinking thing. One thing or another. Often both.

The bedside filament also collected the audio. Both the images and audio routed wirelessly through a feeder MacBook that Dimitri had hidden under the shoes on the floor in the bedroom's closet, and from there to Dimitri's laptop in Room 5 of the Sunset Motel, half a mile's distance away. With a sequence of keystrokes, Dimitri could bring to his screen either the image of the entire bed as seen from the overhead fan locations, or the tight bedside close-up on the pair of pillows. Or both images at once—hence the split screen.

This was the configuration on Dimitri's monitor—on the left side, two pale bodies as seen from above, contorting, and the woman's face on the right side—when the jarring sound of breaking glass abruptly sounded.

The woman's screams assaulted Dimitri's eardrums as the couple on the bed swiftly separated. A figure moved into the frame of the overhead shot.

Which was when Dimitri's beer bottle fell.

The figure could have been a bear, it seemed so large. A white blur bled across the screen as limbs and torsos scrambled crablike up against the wall. Dimitri watched as the naked man lurched toward the intruder. But the intruder swung his arm, and the man pitched sideways and fell from the bed. The woman's screams intensified.

"No! Please! Robbie! No!"

The intruder was holding something long and thin in his hand. In the dreamlike image on the screen, it looked to Dimitri like a wand. With a *crack* that Dimitri could plainly hear, the weapon landed on the woman's face. Her screams died instantly. The man continued swinging his weapon furiously, bringing it down over and over. At one point, the woman's arms seemed to float upward—it almost looked as if she were beckoning her attacker to accept her embrace—then she fell backward onto the pillows, still as a stone. On the left-hand screen, the naked man appeared, rising partway to his knees. The attacker gave an almost nonchalant backhand swing, landing his weapon on the side of the man's head. The man dropped once more from view.

Dimitri glanced at the computer's toolbar: INPUT DOWNLOADING. He was getting it all. On-screen, the intruder turned back to the woman, and Dimitri tore off the headphones. He swung his feet to the carpet and lurched over to the window. Behind him, the grunting sounds were rendered cheap and tinny in the headset's tiny speakers. Dimitri ripped the curtains aside.

The partly hidden house on the hill was black. No suggestion of the brutality that was playing out inside its walls. Dimitri was hyperventilating, unaware of the tears that were streaming down his face.

He waited. He was impotent to do anything else.

Dimitri could not have said how long it took for the noises coming from the laptop to subside and then finally cease altogether. Not long. But still, too long. In its way, the silence that replaced the horrible noises was just as ugly.

Dimitri released the curtain and picked up his binoculars. He was sweating furiously. At first he saw nothing. But then, from the rear of the house, a shadowy form appeared. It moved swiftly around to the front of the house, where it paused, its hands on its hips, stretching backward, working out a kink. The figure pulled open the driver's side door of the sports car and squeezed in behind the wheel. Seconds later the headlights lit up a corner of the house as the car swung a tight turn to aim itself back down the driveway.

Dimitri lowered the binoculars and watched the twin cones of light flicker deftly along the woods and disappear from sight.

Christine Foster stood nose to nose with her reflection in the black glass of her hotel room. The snow had not let up, although now it was mixed with an icy slush, lending a sense that chunky pieces of the sky were being propelled to earth.

Christine wanted to be back in New York. Although she hadn't appreciated just how difficult three and a half days—now to be a full four—away from Michelle would prove, she *had* anticipated the challenge of spending those days with her own mother.

She was drained.

Twelve years distant from her marriage to Christine's father and Lillian was still fully capable of casting herself as a person tossed blithely into exile. This was the role she relished. Sufficiently lubricated—as it seemed she'd been for much of Christine's visit—Lillian showed no compunction about prattling away to anyone within earshot about all the charms and excitements of her former life, beginning with accounts of her fairy-tale life as New York's First Lady and then moving on to her time as an ambassador's wife in London. Although Lillian's manic reminiscences gave the impression—initially—that the woman had actually *enjoyed* these heady days, nothing could have been further from the truth. Even in Lillian's legendarily vivacious early years in Manhattan there had already existed a certain dark-eyed danger lingering in the young woman's shadows. By the time Christine was a child her mother's eccentric charms had begun to devolve into the tedium of erratic behavior and social hostage-taking. The seductive honey of Lillian's tongue had transformed into something decidedly more acidic. The black moods had begun appearing with greater frequency. Especially after the move to London, when Christine was sixteen, Lillian blew ever hotter and colder, and Christine and her brother came to wonder whenever they heard their mother approaching just which Lillian would be walking through the door.

Of the two siblings, it was Peter who had been more adept at accommodating his mother's growing instability. Being more naturally possessed of an instinct about fragility, Christine's older brother had displayed the sort of caring and forgiveness for their mother that Christine had been much less inclined to generate. Christine resented the upheaval that her mother's petulant whirlwinds brought to the household. Peter argued that their father's ungenerous response to Lillian's behavior was contributing enormously to the discord.

Christine raised a hand and placed her fingers on her reflection in the window. It was impossible for her to recall her father's years as ambassador—nine in all—without the stinging memory of his and Lillian's wretched return to the States. Christine had long since fled the nest, married for several years to Andy. There was general agreement that it was Peter's tragic death, only months after Whitney and Lillian's return from London, that had provided the final tipping point for Lillian's crack-up. Though in Lillian's telling of the tale, her son's sad fate played no part. She would always contend that her collapse had everything to do with her husband's coldness and meanness and eagerness to cast her off.

Lillian still prized the pain. Or at least she enjoyed letting it out of its cage and taking it about for a walk. Fortunately, she now employed more serpentine ways of making her feelings known than in the past, and so her digs at Christine and Whitney and his current wife, Jenny, and pretty much the entirety of the East Coast came more in viper's bites. Sharp and quick. The relative mellowing had come in part from her surprise move to Denver and her marriage to the eminently squishable Ben. But partly the change was in Christine herself, who learned over time to adopt some of her late brother's benevolence toward the challenging woman. Lillian was not unaware of her daughter's increased patience, and in her own way she was willing to declare her gratitude on that front.

"You're the real diplomat in the family, sweetheart. I understand that it's partly because you can't stand the thought of people not liking you. But you try. I see that."

Only from her mother's tongue could a word like *diplomat* take on such a sour taste. Christine leaned her head against the cold glass. She wanted to be home.

The chirping cell phone nearly made Dimitri wet his boxers. He plodded to the second bed. It was Irena.

"I cannot talk now, I am busy," he said into the phone, eyeing his chunky form in the dresser mirror.

"When do you come home?"

Dimitri always felt that his wife's voice sounded like a mouse. When they first began seeing each other, he had loved that funny sound.

"Tomorrow," he said thickly. "Like I said."

"Dimitri, Leonard is in the hospital. It is to do with his heart again. How early can you be home?"

Leonard was Dimitri's brother. The two of them owned and operated a Ping-Pong parlor and tavern in the Brighton Beach section of Brooklyn. Only thirty-seven and Leonard was already having heart problems. Partly it was the business, Dimitri was convinced. The business was not doing well. He and his brother were hemorrhaging money.

"How is he?" Dimitri asked.

But the little mouse insisted. "When?"

Dimitri exploded, in Russian. *Tell me how my brother is! You do not order me around! I am home when I am home! Tell me where he is and how he is doing!*

Irena held her ground. "Where are you? Why are you so secret, Dimitri?"

Dimitri looked down at the laptop. The scene on the screen nearly made him gag.

He snarled into the phone. "I am somewhere to make us money, okay? I work! I make you happy. That is all you need to know, Irena. I am work-ing!"

He glanced down at the laptop again. There had been a movement. Not from the bloodied form on the bed, but from the naked man on the floor. The man was rising unsteadily to his feet and turning to look at the bed. His long, gruesome moan was easily audible to Dimitri. Irena began to speak, but Dimitri cut her off.

"Wait! Hold on."

The man on the screen made his way haltingly around to the far side of the bed. A black trickle ran from the side of his head all the way down onto his chest. He paused and then bent down slowly, placing his ear gently against the woman's chest. Dimitri stared fiercely at the close-up image.

I know this man!

Over the phone, Irena was calling his name. "Dimitri? Dimitri, are you still there?"

Dimitri leaned down so close to the computer that his nose was nearly touching the screen.

"Dimitri?"

He jerked upright.

"Irena! Listen to me. Do not ask me any questions, but listen to me. This is *very* important. I will explain to you. Later."

"What is—"

"No! Leave the apartment! Leave it, Irena. Right now. As soon as you hang up. Do not tell anyone where you are going. Are you listening? Pack a suitcase and go to a hotel. Not in Brighton Beach. Somewhere else. Do this now."

"But Dimitri—"

The veins in his neck bulged. *"Now, Irena!* You will call me tomorrow. At noon. Twelve o'clock. You will tell me where are you, and I will go there."

"But I am going to see Leonard in the—"

"No! Do not see Leonard. Do you understand? Do not see *anyone,* Irena! This is more important than I can tell you. You must do this. Tell me."

There was a pause. "You're scaring me, Dimitri."

"Good. Be scared. Now do what I tell you. Go to a hotel. Pay with cash. Stay off the street. Do not let anyone see you. Call me tomorrow."

"Hotels are—"

"Just do this!" The man on the computer had lifted his face from the woman's chest. Unknowing, he was staring directly into the camera. "I must go. I am hanging up."

Dimitri broke the connection and tossed the phone onto the bed.

I know this man.

Dimitri took up his pack of cigarettes, but his hands were working as if they were thumbless. The pack was ravaged by the time he managed to extract a cigarette. The match trembled as it neared his face.

Everybody knows this man.

The phone on the bed chirped again, and Dimitri squeezed his eyes closed. He had exactly three seconds to think. Answer? Don't answer? He wanted to bellow at the top of his lungs.

One second.

He reached for the phone. "It's me," he said.

"Well? Let's hear it. Did we get a good show?"

CHAPTER 3

The face looking out from Andy Foster's mirror was a wreck, the mask of a man who had just passed a sleepless and bewildering night. At the moment, Andy could not envision where the next possibility of sleep would be fitting into his schedule—he was due over on the Hill in less than two hours—but even when it did finally arrive, he knew that no lurid concoctions of his own subconscious would be even remotely capable of rivaling the events of the past twelve hours.

And any nightmare would be preferable to this.

The man in the mirror touched his fingers tenderly against the right side of his head. The gash above the ear had stopped its active bleeding hours ago, but the wound remained spongy and had not stopped its intermittent seeping. Andy knew that the injury was too large for him to trust its closing up on its own. He would need to have it looked at. Likely there would be stitches. He prayed that no infection had already started during the twelve hours required to make his way first off the island and then all the way back down to Washington.

Even without his touching the wound, it felt to Andy as if hot knives were being thrust into his head. It hurt to blink. It hurt not to blink. There was no middle ground. Blink and bear it, Andy told himself grimly. Or not. It's a free country.

Andy cranked on the shower water, then stepped into the kitchen. The nickname for the apartment complex where Andy stayed when he was in D.C. was Boxtown, so named for the aesthetics-free efficiency of its architecture. Cellblock Six was Christine's designation for her husband's home away from home. When Andy signed his lease on the apartment, Christine had declared a zero-intervention policy concerning the furnishing and decorating of the several small rooms. Her own trips down to D.C. were rare, and when she did visit, she and Andy always took a room in a Georgetown guesthouse that Christine was particularly fond of. By her own admission, Christine was not immune to a little pampering touch now and then. And Andy Foster was all too happy to pamper.

He did love his wife.

Andy was ravenous, though he was not convinced that food would actually stay down. He tried a few bites of a banana, followed by some orange juice. He checked the wall clock. It was nine thirty. According to the set of misdirections he had fed his wife and his staff, his morning flight from Miami would have landed several minutes ago at Reagan National and he would be on his way into the city, well rested after a good long sleep in his Miami hotel room.

Andy felt like a shit.

Pouring himself another glass of juice, he turned on the radio to take in the news. The lead story, predictably enough, concerned the growing troubles of the new vice president. A whispering campaign that had begun earlier in the month over alleged shell companies and kickbacks purportedly connected with Vice President Wyeth, back in his days as New York's attorney general, was growing noticeably louder. Although President Hyland had issued a statement overnight declaring "complete trust and faith" in his vice president, the new president's statement of confidence was so boilerplate as to be laughable. Andy happened to know from completely reliable sources that John Hyland held no such fuzzy feelings toward his veep. Prior to his party's convention the previous summer, Hyland had been pressured to include Chris Wyeth on the ticket, due as much as anything else to Wyeth's inside-the-Beltway experience. Andy had known Wyeth for well over a decade, himself having come up under the veteran pol's shadow in the Empire State. The two had a standing tennis date every Tuesday night at the East Potomac Tennis Center. Even prior to the current media dustup, Wyeth had grumbled to Andy about the chief executive's coolness toward him.

"I understand the man's position. Nobody likes being on the receiving end of a shotgun proposal. It's a reminder that you've been *given* power, which is a reminder that there are forces out there who have the power to take it back. Which means your hot shit ain't really the hottest shit in town after all."

Political discourse: Andy couldn't get enough of it.

For his part, Chris Wyeth had yet to reply publicly to the allegations. And his failure to do so was beginning to make some party stalwarts nervous, especially those who had crowbarred Chris Wyeth onto Hyland's ticket. The news spot concluded with a former secretary of state remarking that as the administration was not even three months old, "it can ill afford to shoot itself in the foot while it's still coming out of the gate."

Right, Andy thought. *And we'll cross that bridge when that dog don't hunt because it takes two to tango.*

In other news, China was still showing belligerence in response to the latest calls that it curb its aggressive release of contaminants into the atmosphere. A tornado had ripped through parts of Nashville overnight, killing two and blowing out several stained-glass windows of the Ryman Auditorium but otherwise sparing the fabled structure. A child actor from one of the seventies sitcoms had been found dead in his Glendale apartment. The Nikkei was up in modest trading and the dollar was taking a hammering in London.

Nothing about Joy Resnick.

Andy got up from the table and turned off the radio. Holding on to the counter for support, he bowed his head and allowed his heavy eyelids to lower.

Think.

Had he tried hard enough to defend Joy Resnick? Yes. No. Somewhat. He didn't know. It had all happened so fast the question had no real meaning. Andy remembered lunging at the attacker, but being swept aside like a piddling pest when the intruder landed his weapon against Andy's skull. He'd tried a second time to intervene, but this time the weapon had come down with full force, and Andy had remained on the bedroom floor, semiconscious, while the intruder delivered his full butchery to Joy. By the time Andy had finally pulled himself to his feet and made the too-easy determination that Joy was dead, the killer was long gone. The thought of phoning 911 had passed in an instant. Anonymous or not, the risk was too great. And the gain at that point was minimal. For Joy, it was nonexistent.

Steam was misting out from the bathroom as Andy made his way into the bedroom, carrying a white plastic kitchen garbage bag. The clothes he had been wearing the night before were folded on the bed and neatly stacked atop his shoes. Andy deposited the clothes into the plastic bag, but he paused a moment before including the shoes. From one viewpoint, this level of precaution was ridiculous. If circumstances were to unravel to the point where someone was even considering pressuring Andy to produce *any* sample of his wardrobe to be tested for DNA evidence with connection to the events at the Resnick family beach house, then his goose was already cooked. In the world Andy moved in, mere suspicion spelled total calamity.

Andy dropped the shoes into the bag. Imagining himself lurking around a dumpster behind some Safeway store in some Maryland suburb, he had to lower himself shakily onto the edge of the bed.

Think!

After determining that Joy was beyond rescue, what Andy had felt most of all was the basic need to *get away*. The smashing of the sliding glass door, Joy's screams, and who-knows-what-other sounds must have carried through the night air and reached *someone*. At the very instant that Andy had been determining that Joy Resnick was dead, somebody might have been making their way up to the house. New York's junior senator had certainly not wanted to be found standing naked next to the bloodied bed when the lights came on. Not to mention that he didn't relish the idea of being there should the attacker decide to return, thank you muchly.

Andy had dressed quickly, panicking a moment when he couldn't find his overnight bag. Then he recalled Joy taking the bag from him after they'd entered the house and dropping it onto a bamboo chair in the living room. He'd fetched the bag, filled a dish towel with ice from the freezer, then made a frantic stab at wiping clean anyplace he might have left his fingerprints. He exited the house through the destroyed glass door, crossed the moist grass, and plunged into the trees behind the house. Stumbling through the woods, Andy had remained mindful of protecting his face from nicks and cuts from the low branches. Instinctively, he knew that the fewer lies required down the line to explain his appearance— should it come to that—the better. Finally, he fell forward into a small clearing of dead leaves, and it was there that he had collected himself and focused on the task of building a plan. Commiseration. Regret. Self-loathing. All that could wait. If ever there was a time to be solution-oriented, this was it. Every single person who was in a position to know Andy's declared itinerary for that day and evening assumed that the senator was spending the night in a comfortable Miami hotel after his book-store appearance and then flying first thing in the morning up to Reagan National. The fact that the oyster moon rising over Shelter Island was sending its soft glow down onto the results of an alternate itinerary gone horrifically wrong was something that Andy had to confront, and confront quickly. He couldn't undo the foolish escapade. Simple fact. There was no undoing the clandestine flight he'd made from Miami to JFK, nor his rendezvous with the woman who had helped to mastermind his most recent reelection campaign. He could not un-dead Joy Resnick. He could certainly not un-make love to her. And the fact he had dared not dwell on: He could not un-cheat on his wife.

Seated gurulike on the dead leaves, Andy had known that if he could just keep his focus out ahead of his panic, he could damn well get himself off that damn little island. He could somehow travel the several hundred miles down to D.C. and pick up from where he should have been all along. Only at that point would he let himself turn his prayers to a thousand gods that his involvement with Joy Resnick go completely unsuspected and undiscovered. But until then he had needed a plan, a definitive plan, something to successfully reposition himself from the whole ungainly, surreal mess. The blood loss from his head wound had enfeebled his faculties, which required Andy to muster extraordinary concentration. But eventually he had managed to move all the pieces around in his mind and come up with the plan. Once that was done—conceived, reviewed, tweaked, and approved—he had pulled his cell phone from his pocket and made the one call he had determined could start things rolling.

And it had. Thank sweet Jesus and his retinue of saints.

As he started into the bathroom, Andy pushed his fingers gently against the gash on his head. This next part of his plan—he prayed it would prove to be the final part—was grim business. But the injury to his head had to be tended to. There was no thought of attempting to let the wound go untreated. The very first person he encountered would drag him bodily off to the nearest doctor.

But first he had to give the injury a story; he had to give it a lie. Andy rubbed a circle into the steamy mirror. The man in the reflection looked contrite. Authentically so. He did not look conniving, or in any way proud of himself for his deft maneuverings. He looked sad and shaken and brimming with genuine remorse. Although his mind was swirling with lies, both the ones already decided on as well as the ones still being auditioned, a sharp truth sliced through them all. This one glinted with certainty. In a hoarse whisper, Andy gave it voice.

"You don't deserve to get away with this."

The statement wasn't even completed before the steam from the shower blurred his reflection completely. Andy stepped into the tub. He moved into the searing stream and turned his face up into the water, tilting his head slightly to keep the water from pummeling his wound. Andy balled his fists as tight as he could.

I am a fool.

I love my wife.

I am an idiot.

I love my wife.

I will never, ever, ever do something so goddamned boneheaded again.

I love my wife.

He took a deep breath and closed his eyes. He got the cry of pain under way even before he started his head toward the tiles.

Christine limped into the JFK arrivals terminal. The slender architect from San Diego who had chatted her up nearly the entire flight from Denver was insisting on steering her roller bag for her. It was his Hugo Boss, after all, that had come down on Christine's ankle and pinned it to the cabin floor as the two had been jostling against other passengers to extract their bags from the overhead bin.

Christine wanted nothing but to get to ground transportation and grab a cab into the city and be home. As the thin joke had it, flying was for the birds.

But walking was for the capable-of-foot, and as she cleared the departures desk Christine had no choice but to hobble painfully to the nearest seat and slide onto it. Her architect-assailant rolled her bag over and parked it at her feet.

"You need to elevate it. Just stay put, I'll go get you some ice."

The man insisted on helping her ferry the injured limb up onto the roller bag. The slight elevation seemed inconsequential to Christine, but she said nothing about it. The man was as fussy now about trying to help her as he had been blunt with his flirting during the flight.

While the quasi Good Samaritan headed off in the direction of the food court, Christine pulled out her phone to call her daughter. Michelle wouldn't be home from school yet—Rosa would be fetching her—but Christine wanted to leave a message to let her daughter know that she was on her way.

There was a message on her phone from Andy. Christine called home first.

"Hey, darling, it's Mommy. I'm back now. I just got off the plane. I'll be home soon. Tell Rosa not to start any dinner. I thought the two of us could get some takeout from Mama Buddha, does that sound nice? Don't forget we're going to Grandpa and Jenny's this weekend. We've got some eggs to color! I'll see you soon, goofy. I love you, sweetheart."

Christine played her messages. By the time the architect returned with a plastic baggy of crushed ice, she was already clambering out of her seat.

"Hey. Whoa. You've really got to ice that—"

Christine cut him off, gesturing with her phone. "That was my husband. I've got to go. He slipped in the shower this morning. The fool man has got six stitches in his head!"

Andy and Christine Foster lived on the top floor of an apartment building on Greenwich Avenue, overlooking the Hudson River. Their view to the west took in the river, and beyond that, the stretch of New Jersey towns bordering the river. Most important, it included the large empty expanse that overtopped both the river and the far shore, the luxury craved by all New Yorkers: sky.

Christine's father had not exactly given the couple the apartment when they got married. But nearly. Although he'd no longer been in office at the time, the former governor's spheres of influence had remained expansive, and as construction of the apartment building on Greenwich neared completion, remarkably generous financing for one of the top-floor apartments had fallen into place for then congressman Andrew Foster and his pretty fiancée, bolstered by a sizable down payment that had been wired directly from the Bermuda-based account of Ambassador Hoyt. The card from Whitney and Lillian—which Andy had insisted be framed and displayed in the front hallway—showed an Appalachian lean-to tilting perilously close to an equally dilapidated outhouse.

YOU'VE GOT TO START SOMEWHERE
With our blessings.
Whit & Lil

Seven years after they moved in, Christine and Andy's enviable expanse of sky had suffered the incursion of black smoke moving northward from the cruelly bludgeoned tip of the island. Christine's particular cries on that horrible day—quite piercing at their peak—had been for vastly different reasons than those of so many of her fellow citizens. Far from being a response to the swift shuttering of so many lives, Christine's cries had sounded the requisite agony accompanying the miracle of new life. A daughter. Barred from their home those first weeks after the cataclysm,

Christine and Andy had given their newborn her first taste of true luxury living, taking her up to the other Greenwich—not the street but the town, Greenwich, Connecticut—and the rambling family estate where Christine and her brother, Peter, had spent their childhoods. The sprawling house was also where Michelle Foster's parents had legally linked their fates in matrimony some years previous, for better or worse, for richer or for poorer, in sickness and in health, for as long as they both shall live.

So far so good. At least, so it seemed.

Rosa had left a phone message that she and Michelle were going to head over to Hudson River Park for a while after school, so Christine puttered the afternoon away on her own. She wasn't able to get Andy on the phone until several hours after her return home. He'd been tied up in closed-door hearings all day over the situation in Athens (what the situation was, she didn't even know) and she'd managed to catch him during a brief recess. She had grabbed the *Times* and pulled a chair up to the large picture window, elevating her foot on a stack of magazines. Out on the water, a large brown barge was being nudged upriver by a comparably tiny tugboat. Michelle called them pushboats, a logical enough renaming. Seven and a half years and counting and the little girl had never seen any of the cartoon-looking craft actually tugging anything. It was all push and nudge.

Christine opted not to share with Andy her own injury. It could wait. Instead, she scolded her husband. "What do you think you're doing running around with fresh stitches in your head? Are you a nut? You should be taking it easy. I think you can put off saving the world for one day."

"Tell that to the Greek defense minister."

"Gladly. Put him on the line."

A red balloon trailing a long white ribbon appeared in the window, moving diagonally across Christine's vision, buffeted by minor gusts. Christine swiveled her foot gingerly.

"Seriously, Andy. Are you all right? How in the world did you manage to fall down in a shower of all things?"

"I didn't mention the banana peel?"

Christine ignored the joke. "Seriously, though. You're okay?"

"I'm fine," Andy said. "Except for my pride. I do feel pretty stupid."

Christine laughed. "If I know you, your pride will heal up a lot quicker than your head."

"Ouch."

"Suck it up, Senator. But listen. I'm serious about you taking it easy. You're not a hundred percent. I can hear it in your voice."

Christine's gaze landed on the newspaper on her lap. She winced as she shifted her foot again. "Andy, what's all this noise about Chris Wyeth? I thought you told me it was just politics as usual. But it sounds to me like this VP thing is actually heating up. We're not actually talking anything serious here, are we?"

"I don't think so," Andy said. "You know how it goes. Something's got to bring the president's honeymoon to a close. Too much good cheer makes people nervous."

"So, it's just political spitballs." The term was a favorite of her father's.

"Exactly. It'll pass."

The two chatted for another few minutes. Andy informed his wife that on orders from the doctor who had stitched him up, he was planning on taking the Amtrak back to New York the next day instead of flying.

"We don't have anything planned until Sunday, right?"

Christine switched the phone to her other ear. "Not much. Some charity dinners. Dancing at the Rainbow Room. I think you're giving a speech to the Aardvark Society. And, oh yes. You're supposed to go down to the seaport and christen a boat or two and kiss a whole bunch of babies."

"So, basically we're just laying low until Sunday."

"Basically."

"Good. I'll sign off on that plan."

"Okay then, sweetie," Christine said. "You'd better get back and patch things up for the Greeks. Otherwise everything will be in ruins, ha ha. I'll see you tomorrow. I promise we'll do absolutely nothing together. It'll be nice. I love you."

"I love you, too," Andy said. He added, "Seriously."

Five minutes later, the front door opened and Michelle bounded into the apartment.

"Mommy!"

Mommy was still seated by the window with her foot up on a stack of magazines. She was still gazing out at the sky. Still musing on her husband's sign-off.

Seriously?

What the hell was that all about?

CHAPTER 5

Dimitri tossed the last empty mussel shell onto the plate. He tore a chunk of bread from the small loaf in the wicker basket and dabbed it among the shells, saturating it with garlic butter. The waiter was passing by the next table, and Dimitri waved the chunk of bread to get his attention.

"Hey! Another beer." He shoved the piece of bread in his mouth.

Acknowledging the order with a nod, the waiter addressed the woman seated across from Dimitri.

"Would you like another Chablis?"

Irena Bulakov had been nursing her glass of wine throughout dinner. Over an inch remained. "No, thank you." Her intention to smile fell short. She was nervous; she couldn't help herself.

After the waiter left, Dimitri spoke through his chewing. "What is it, are you pissing in your pants over there? Why don't you enjoy yourself? Here. Have some of this butter."

As he slid the oval plate across the table, a few of the slick black shells spilled onto the floor. An elderly couple was coming through the front door to the restaurant, and Irena glanced over to see the Coney Island Cyclone a block away, silhouetted against the ghostly dusk.

"I don't want the butter," Irena said.

"You only ate half your fish."

"I am not hungry, Dimitri. The butter is too rich."

"The food is good here," Dimitri said, scowling. "You see what it costs."

"I'm sorry." Irena leaned over and retrieved the empty shells from the floor and returned them to the plate. She hesitated, then lapped at her fingers. "There. Very tasty. Thank you."

The beer arrived, and the waiter swapped it for Dimitri's latest empty. Dimitri took a large swig, internalized the belch, and looked around at the nearly full dining room. A somewhat older crowd, many of the men wearing coats and ties. The pimply boy at the hotel across the street had recommended the restaurant.

Irena placed her hands in her lap. Her small shoulders were hunched forward. She had a narrow face with a small thick mouth and a long narrow nose. Her eyes these days generally knew two modes: weary and wearier. Tonight was the latter.

"Dimitri?" It was almost a mew. "Why don't you talk to me? Please tell me. What happened yesterday? Why are we in a hotel? I am so confused."

Dimitri had been drinking beer ever since meeting up with his wife. That was three hours ago. She had done as he asked on the phone the night before and packed a bag and located a hotel. She had phoned Dimitri at noon, as instructed, and told him where she was. When he arrived he was full of energy, but still grumpy and nonresponsive. All he would say to Irena's questions was, "Not now. I have to think."

Irena hadn't dared to say it out loud. *But you don't think, Dimitri. You drink.*

Dimitri had not been quite so round-bellied when Irena met him nine years before. He had shown her his smile more often back then. Soon after their marriage, however, she had come to discover that her husband's good moods had a distressingly short shelf life. The same could be said concerning Dimitri's employment. If he arrived home stinking of beer and ranting about how stupid his coworkers or his boss were, Irena could be pretty sure that her husband was out of work again. Just under two years ago, Irena had prayed to Jesus and crossed her fingers when Dimitri and his brother, Leonard, signed the lease for the building they were planning to convert into their Ping-Pong center. The brothers had been so excited. Dimitri had come to Irena with dollar signs in his blurry eyes.

"Look at what people do with the pool halls and the bowling alleys. Leonard and I can create a demand, and soon we will have to open up a second center. This is how it is done. You attract the best players. You become tournament level! You have no limit to what can happen."

While working on his dream, Dimitri had wearied of trying to work for other people and had gotten his hack license. He calculated that within months of his and Leonard's Ping-Pong parlor opening he would be able to quit his taxi job. This had proved an ambitious calculation. Before the first year was out, Dimitri had *added* a number of shifts. Dimitri and Leonard had lined up several silent partners to help with their initial financing. There were several bank loans as well, but the preference—mainly Dimitri's—had been to accept the services of certain "community leaders," as the local newspaper liked to call them, men whose philosophy was that countrymen should look out for countrymen. One such person in particular, a mobster named Aleksey Titov, had taken a special interest in Dimitri and his brother. Against Leonard's protests, Titov had arranged for the brothers to procure a liquor license for their establishment. The original plans had not called for the serving of alcohol, or even much food beyond light snacks. But Titov had convinced Dimitri otherwise, even arranging free of charge for a set of plans to be drawn up that would include a full-service tavern in the rear of the parlor. Titov arranged for the extra loans to cover the additional costs. He brought in some people who, he told Dimitri and Leonard, could do the construction work in half the usual time. An exaggerated claim, as it turned out. In fact, a second loan had been required—this one also choreographed by Aleksey Titov—to help finance the unfortunate overages.

Dimitri's smile had made fewer and fewer appearances as the construction and the money hemorrhaging had dragged on. The grueling schedule of his taxi shifts and his time spent overseeing matters at the parlor—he and Leonard had come up with the name, Paddles—left him punchy and increasingly irritable. The balance on the loans never seemed to be budging. Equally discouraging, the quality of play at the tables was hardly screaming "tournament!" People came to play, yes, but mostly it was just for fun. They were not taking the game seriously. The night that Dimitri and Leonard had their first really ugly argument, Dimitri stormed out and went home confused and angry, and before he knew it he had slapped Irena in the face. Then he cried. He also cried the next time it happened, though not any of the times after that. Irena took to telling herself, *Dimitri does not hit me. He loves me. It is his beer. His beer hits me.*

Irena loved her husband. She knew that the real Dimitri was in there somewhere. Irena had miscarried three times over the past five years, and Dimitri had not handled the incidents well. Irena knew that her husband was taking their failure to have children as his failure: yet another of Dimitri's forestalled visions. The fault, of course, if that was the correct word to use, resided in Irena's nervous body. But then, Dimitri had chosen her for his wife, so perhaps it was for this reason that he took the blame onto himself. How else to explain his irrationality and his sullenness after each of the miscarriages? Irena worried for him. He was under so much pressure. If only the pressure could just lift a little, maybe the old Dimitri would return. She had faith. She prayed daily for his return.

After dinner, Irena convinced Dimitri to take a walk with her along the boardwalk. First, he bought a baseball cap from a souvenir shop, pulling it down low over his face. Dimitri had ordered too many beers at dinner, and his feet shuffled somewhat. But the air seemed to revive him. Studying him closely ever since he had arrived at the hotel and again through dinner, Irena knew that the secrets he was withholding from her were something new, something different from the usual pressures that had become so commonplace over the past several years. What alarmed Irena the most was that Dimitri was not asking about Leonard. His brother had been admitted to the hospital the day before with chest pains, yet the topic didn't seem to find any space in Dimitri's mind. Other thoughts were crowding it out. They could not be good thoughts.

The breeze was coming in briskly off the water. The night was cool and briny. Irena hooked her arm in Dimitri's elbow and set her head lightly against his shoulder as they walked. She hummed a made-up tune in the slow rhythm of their steps. A volleyball game was under way on the sand, the ball barely visible in the night air, just a faint little moon arcing through the air. Laughter carried over from the sand, and Irena became sad. Spring and summer had not proven to be nearly as good a time for business as Dimitri and Leonard had once predicted. People wanted to remain outdoors, not come inside to hit the Ping-Pong balls. The sound of laughter on the beach was not always something that lifted her husband's spirits.

Dimitri and Irena took a seat on a bench, facing the water. Dimitri was still lost in his private thoughts.

"Wait here," Irena said, and she backtracked over to a pizza place and bought a pair of coffees. When she returned, Dimitri was on his cell phone. Irena slowed and then stopped altogether some twenty feet from the bench.

Dimitri's voice was harsh and more than a little slurred.

"No! This is what I am trying to tell you! It is no longer enough money, no way. I am thinking of you, too. Do you understand? You are also being cheated. This deal must be renegotiated, Aleksey. I am telling you, *everything* has changed."

Irena's heart sank. Aleksey Titov. Of course. It was always Aleksey Titov, the man who owned her husband and her brother-in-law. Aleksey

Titov was in the business of owning people. Once upon a time, Irena had prayed for Aleksey Titov's soul, but no longer. If God wanted to work with Aleksey Titov, that was his business. But the man was destroying Irena and Dimitri's happiness. He was an evil man with a heart of coal who rejoiced in the miseries of others. That was the mark of evil. There was no more to be said on the matter.

Irena inched closer to the bench. Dimitri had risen to his feet. He was still facing the water.

"No, you must listen to me, Aleksey. You will understand when you see what I saw. A man making love with a woman is a small potato. But a man like *this*? Excuse my opinion, Aleksey, but two thousand dollars for me is ridiculous. You do not know who this man is. But I know. It is all different now. Your client does not have this man by the balls. *I* have your *client* by the balls. You see? I have this file, Aleksey. I am putting it on the flash drive, where it is safe. And I tell you, no stupid two thousand dollars will do. Not now. Not for this!"

The anger in his voice was beginning to spike. Irena worried that Dimitri would turn around and see her standing there listening in on his side of the conversation. Dimitri continued.

"Aleksey, I risked my *life* to go back into that house to get my equipment. This crazy man, he could have come back. So, now you listen to me. I am not just a person to push around here. I need you to understand this. This is too big. I am dying in that fucking taxicab. I am dying in that fucking *hole* that my brother and I should have never climbed into. That is all over now. When I tell you who is this man, Aleksey, you will see. You will have your client by the balls. But what I am saying is that right now I have *you* by the balls."

Irena started. *No! Oh Lord. Please, no. Do not say such words. Not to Aleksey Titov. Please. No.*

But people did not call Dimitri Bulakov stupid for nothing.

Dimitri was yelling now. "You tell him this! One. Million. Dollars! Nothing less! It comes from *him* or it comes from the man himself, I do not care which it is. You and I will get this money, Aleksey, and you and I will shake hands and drink a toast, and we will go home and make love to our wives. It will all be good."

Dimitri turned his head abruptly and saw Irena standing there holding two cups of coffee. To Irena's surprise, he did not scowl at her.

"I am hanging up now," Dimitri said into the phone. "You will thank me when you hear who this man is. We will laugh, and we will all be rich."

Dimitri flipped the phone closed. Behind him, the ocean and the sky had become an identical midnight blue. Indistinguishable.

Irena's knees were shaking. "Dimitri. Please do not play around with Aleksey Titov. He is dangerous."

Dimitri started toward her. "I have something he wants."

"Give it to him!" The cry choked in her throat.

Dimitri reached her and lifted one of the coffees from her. The glow of neon lights from the amusement park rides were playing over his face. He looked like a mad clown.

"I have Aleksey Titov by the *balls,* Irena. This is our chance!"

The shaking moved its way through the rest of Irena's frail body. Coffee splashed onto her wrist.

"Oh, no. Dimitri. Do not say that. Please. Do not do this thing."

CHAPTER 6

All through the weekend, the drumbeat grew louder: the vice president needed to make a clear accounting of his activities while he'd been serving as New York's attorney general. On Saturday, traditionally a slow news day, a new story had emerged concerning the renovation of a severely fire-damaged theater in Ithaca and possible links between Chris Wyeth and the contractor who had been awarded the project. A sweetheart deal involving one of Wyeth's financial supporters. The Republicans smelled blood, and on the Sunday talk shows the thirstiest of them showed off their gleaming incisors.

"*I think maybe the vice president of the United States has reached his expiration date. Chris Wyeth owes it to the country to step aside.*"

"*Look. President Hyland's honeymoon has already been undermined. That's over, folks. Sorry. The only question now is, will he let blind loyalty do the same to his presidency?*"

"*Vice President Wyeth is a heartbeat away from the presidency and a heartbeat away from indictment. It's not Chris Wyeth anymore, George. It's Crisis Wyeth.*"

Andy monitored the news programs from the study in his apartment. Dressed in gray sweatpants and his faded navy blue sweatshirt, he sat in his swiveling black leather chair, his chin planted on his two thumbs. Christine had fashioned a less intrusive bandage for the wound over his ear, but there was nothing she could do about the headaches. And certainly nothing she could do about the pulsing pangs of guilt and anxiety that were inhabiting her husband's gut. These he was keeping to himself.

Christine and Michelle were in the kitchen, making brownies. Forty-plus hours essentially off her feet, and her ankle was sufficiently functional again. To be safe, it was wrapped in a small Ace bandage. Michelle had enjoyed the game of "taking care of the invalids" all day Saturday.

The smell of the brownies wafted down the narrow hallway and into Andy's study. Christine and Michelle were singing a silly song, or attempting to. Peals of laughter kept interrupting snatches of the actual melody. Normally Andy might have eased the door closed or simply turned up the volume on the TV. The Sunday chatter was required listening. But this morning he wasn't really focusing on the particulars. The general tone was clear enough. The specifics themselves were either talking points that would be repeated ad nauseam by the loyal foot soldiers over the coming days or else predictable personal hyperbole. Andy wasn't in the mood to hear either. The TV simply gave him cover for not conversing with his family.

Doc lay in a heap at his feet. The old boy was snoring and twitching lightly every several seconds. Probably dreaming of a younger and pre-arthritic Doc, chasing cute cocker spaniels or comely collies. Doc was a cross between a Great Dane and a German Shepherd, which essentially meant a German Shepherd the size of a small horse. He was only several months older than Michelle. In dog years—at least for a hybrid mutt of this size—AARP time. His hips were going, and when he walked, his rear end traced painful circles. Andy and Christine both knew that an irretrievable layer of their daughter's innocence was poised to be peeled back any time now. The Death Discussion was looming. Doc in Dog Heaven, and all that. Andy and Christine had discussed the matter. Michelle had a lively imagination. Already she sent the dog postcards whenever the family traveled. The two had no doubt that soon after Doc's inevitable demise, their daughter would be asking them for the zip code for heaven.

Michelle came into the study holding a plate stacked high with brownies. Even though the plate wasn't hot, Michelle was wearing a pair of oven mitts that came halfway to her elbows. Doc raised his head, and a thin line of drool fell onto one of his paws.

Michelle announced, "I made brownies."

Andy straightened in his chair. "I see that. You made the brown kind."

"They're *brownies.*"

"I see that," Andy said again, the smile tugging at the corners of his mouth. "You made the brown kind."

Michelle turned her head and yelled back toward the kitchen. "*Mommy!*" She turned back to her father. "You can't have any."

"Oh? And why is that?"

Christine came into the room, wiping her hands on her thighs.

"Mommy. Tell Daddy why he can't have any brownies."

"Because they're for Grandpa and Jenny," Christine said. She placed a hand on her daughter's head and lightly stroked her hair. She addressed Andy. "Are you sure you're up for it, sweetie?"

Andy reached for the remote. "I'm fine. Plus I gather it's the only way I'm going to get one of these hot-to-trot brownies that some elf pulled out of the ground."

Michelle puckered up her face. "*You're* an elf!"

Footage of Chris Wyeth being sworn in as vice president came onto the screen. Andy thumbed the off button and the screen went blank.

Christine frowned. "Is that any way to treat a friend?"

"I guess I'm just a mean old backstabbing bastard kind of friend," Andy said. He'd intended to sound more jokey than it came out. At the word *bastard,* Christine's eyes dragged his attention to their daughter, whose eyes and mouth were all zeros.

"Bad Dad," Michelle said.

Andy could feel his face reddening. Nothing he could do about it. He managed a weak laugh. "Yes, honey. So true. Daddy's a baddie."

CHAPTER 7

"It's a fine mess, Andrew."

Andy and his father-in-law were seated on the stone deck overlooking Whitney Hoyt's vast backyard. Off near the garden, some fifteen or so children gripping wicker baskets were scurrying about in search of eggs. Parents were positioned at certain key locations, like buoys in an open ocean, making exaggerated head fakes and little gestures whenever a child approached one of the hiding spots. The children—and for that matter, most of the parents as well—were dressed in Easter pastels. A lawn full of sugar-candy people.

Andy looked across the glass table at his father-in-law. "What mess is that, Whitney?"

The former governor and ambassador held the senator in a studied expression. "Well, let's see, Andrew." He ticked off the options on his fingers. "We've got the Yankees traveling all the way to bloody Japan to lose their season opener in a lopsided embarrassment. That's one mess. Or maybe you missed that one. Jennifer informs me that it is becoming harder and harder to locate a certain type of perfume that she prefers. That would be number two."

Andy held his tongue. Whitney liked to do things his way.

"Let's see, what else? Oh. Yes. How silly. The executive branch of our government is in the process of imploding. I knew there was another one. Three messes, Andrew. Any one you wish to discuss is fine with me."

Off next to the swinging love seat in the garden, one of the children had managed to shatter his own happiness. A sound like a toy siren carried up to the patio. Parents were swiftly converging.

"Chris has indicated to me that he can weather this thing," Andy said.

The former governor pulled the stalk of celery from his Bloody Mary. He let some of the liquid drip back into the glass, then with a flick of the wrist tossed the celery over the railing into the bushes below.

"The only *weather* is whether he leaves on his own or is pushed."

Andy smirked. "Cute."

"I'm glad you think so. But I'm dead serious. Your good friend did a service to nobody by making certain his skeletons remained locked away until after the election." Hoyt took a slow sip of his drink. The tip of his tongue darted snakelike along his lips. "For God's sake, John Hyland was always going to take the general in a landslide. Arnold the Pig could have been his running mate. Chris Wyeth was no do-or-die element to that ticket; everybody knew that going in. The man was handed the vice presidency with a kiss on the cheek and a pat on the ass, and now he has gone and crapped all over it in just two months."

Andy started to protest. "Whitney, I hardly think—"

Hoyt held up a hand. "Don't interrupt me, Andrew. I'm telling you right now, Chris is finished. This country is in too fragile a state. The whole reason John Hyland was elected was because this country is on life support. Mr. Hyland promised the cure. We can't afford for him to go lame this early. I'm serious, Andrew. At this point, the rest of the world will just shoot the patient if he shows signs of weakening."

"That sounds a little extreme to me."

"Do you know those old movies? You probably don't. No one's got time for old movies anymore. These were mainly the Westerns and the war movies. Two men running for their lives and one of them twists his ankle and drops to the ground. 'Go on without me.' That was the line you'd always hear. 'Save yourself. Go on without me.' All very noble."

Hoyt took another sip of his drink, studying the rim of the glass for a moment. Andy waited. He knew the routine. Hoyt finally continued.

"That's where we're headed, Andrew. If this country can't lead anymore, it's 'Go on without me' time. John Hyland can get away with twisting his ankle a little bit at this point. A little tiny twist. He's still in the honeymoon. But if he falls onto the dirt? It's not good. And if you come up with a self-serving vice president who is being outed by the press for past sins and you don't act swiftly on it, that's where you go. To the dirt. And the part they don't show you in those movies is when the vultures come down and start to work over the poor sap who's lying there. Before he's even a carcass."

Andy lifted his glass. "By the way, Whitney, happy Easter."

Hoyt barely heard him. "I'm quite serious. The plucking starts right away. I daresay it has started already. If Chris Wyeth is taking a nosedive this early in the game and the president doesn't act swiftly and skillfully on it . . ."

He allowed the rest of the thought to go unspoken. Over by the tennis court, Hoyt's wife, Jenny, and Christine were playing keep-away with Doc, tossing a tennis ball while the insistent animal lumbered back and forth between them, barking hoarsely. All of seven years older than Christine, Jenny had married Whitney just months after Hoyt's divorce from Lillian had come through. Jenny's own marriage—to a Greenwich real estate developer with a known drinking problem—had ended when her husband lost control of his car while scouting properties near Port Jervis. Whitney had known Jenny and Roger Mead socially. At first the age difference between the widow and the recently divorced former governor had raised some eyebrows. But by the time the two married in a small ceremony in Hoyt's backyard, the matter had lost its charge.

Spotting her husband looking in her direction from the deck, Jenny Hoyt waved over at him. Whitney Hoyt returned the wave and turned back to Andy.

"You're not being stupid about this, are you?"

"Stupid?"

"Our Mr. Hyland is going to need to find himself a new VP, Andrew. That's the endgame here. There'll be the usual denials and positionings and repositionings. It's the oldest dance in the book. I swear Arthur Murray himself taught everyone the steps. But Chris Wyeth is out, and Hyland is going to need a new man. Someone the country already knows and already feels comfortable with."

"Jeff LaMott looked like he was having a pretty good audition on the talk shows this morning."

Hoyt dismissed the notion with a wave of his hand. "Please. Jeff LaMott wants to please all the people all the time. Do you know what that qualifies him for? Kindergarten teacher. Don't be cute with me here. You know as well as I do how close you got to the ticket last year. It was Chris's time, of course. But you polled well, and everyone knows you did. And you did well by John Hyland in the general. His numbers here were outrageous. None of his people have a single thing to complain about when it comes to you."

"That's all well and good, Whitney, but I already have a job. Plus, if LaMott were to step up, that positions me for the head of Foreign Relations."

"I'm telling you, he won't. Hyland might make overtures, but he's not going to put that man next to the presidency. Besides, Foreign Relations? That's a fine thing, but is that where you're planning to park your car?"

Andy was not really in the mood for this conversation. Not with Whitney, at any rate. Attempting to lighten things up, he grimaced in mock agony. "Go on without me."

"Okay. I'll shut up now. I don't want to be the cause of your going stubborn." Whitney allowed himself a smile. "I know down deep you're a smart man, Andrew. For goodness' sake, you did a more than admirable job of choosing your father-in-law."

"Don't take offense, Whitney. But his sexy little daughter did figure into the equation. And by the way, I suppose you know Christine's views on all this?"

Hoyt scoffed. "John Hyland is not going to ask Christine to be his next vice president."

"You know what I mean."

"All I'm going to say is, she married you and she certainly didn't have to. You two seem to have done okay with your separate but equal lives."

"This would be different. The vice presidency. You know it would. So does she."

Hoyt again looked out over his backyard. Jenny and Christine were heading toward the house. He indicated the women.

"She's a strong kid," Hoyt said. "I raised her right. I wouldn't spend too much time worrying about her if I were you."

While the children were ushered to a long table set up on the grass, the adults took their meal on the upper patio. Lamb, cauliflower au gratin with capers and goat cheese, roasted red potatoes. Most of the guests were acquaintances of Whitney's and Jenny's from the Greenwich area—many of them from the club, others coming to them through Jenny's various charitable functions. A decidedly nonpolitical crowd, which was just fine with Andy.

He found himself seated next to a petite British-born woman named Hailey Jordan, who was the wife of Whitney Hoyt's long-standing personal secretary, Paul Jordan. They lived in nearby New Canaan. Andy had always found navigating a conversation with Hailey Jordan a tedious event. As he'd once commented to Christine, "There's prim, and then there's Hailey." There were times when Andy found himself fighting back a nearly irresistible urge to say something deliberately shocking to the woman, simply to observe her reaction.

Paul Jordan, on the other hand, was considerably less socially flat-footed than his tightly wound spouse. He possessed a wit only a dram less dry than the Sahara, but also the self-restraint to keep his arid barbs largely undelivered. Jordan had been with Hoyt for nearly fifteen years, beginning before the conclusion of Hoyt's ambassadorship. Andy knew from Christine that her mother had never found much to embrace in her spouse's secretary. The easy interplay between the two men had irked Lillian, and in fact had been one of the rare points of contention between Lillian and Whitney on which Christine had come down on the side of her mother. Neither much cared for Jordan, and both considered his wife to be a buttoned-up little snob. Andy's own feelings on the matter were much less charged. He simply found the couple tepid.

As he was pouring Hailey Jordan a glass of lemonade, Andy asked after her husband and was told that Paul was currently lying flat out on the floor in the family living room in New Canaan with a moist towel over his head. Andy passed up any number of wiseass remarks.

"Paul suffers horrible migraines," Hailey Jordan went on, her accent not flattened in the least by the years of being surrounded by vowel-chewing Yanks. "Although given Paul's agnostic bent, it's not implausible he only wanted to slither out of what he considers a patently absurd ritual."

Andy gave her a look of mock dismay. "Cute little children and colored eggs? Hailey! Your husband is one cold, cold customer."

The woman's explosive little laugh was like shrapnel to the eardrums. On Andy's private list of Hailey Jordan's "challenging" features, the hiccupy laugh ranked high. Andy made a mental note—again—to dial down the levity when he was in the woman's company.

The man who had been seated next to Christine at the table was an executive with Ogilvy & Mather, and he had worked hard throughout the meal to impress her with tales from the advertising jungle. Graciously, Christine had granted him the expressions he sought, though her private thoughts would have devastated him.

After the meal came the croquet, an amusing blend of the competitive and the could-care-less. The man from O & M proved to be one of the former, and he was managing to do his part in squelching the fun for the latter.

Andy sat out the croquet, logically asserting that the banging of wooden balls with wooden mallets was the precise sort of activity that the doctor who had stitched him up the other day had suggested he forgo for the immediate future. He parked himself in one of the children's chairs with a tumbler of scotch and watched the game from there. In truth, his head *was* throbbing. Alcohol was probably not the wisest medicine for someone in Andy's condition, but he had found himself edgy ever since arriving at the house and he could see no real harm in a little anesthesia.

Andy's mind wanted to drift back to Joy Resnick, but his heart resisted. Or possibly it was the other way around. Maybe it was his heart that felt the tug, but his mind was resisting. It was the kind of silly semantic distinction he and Christine enjoyed batting around with each other. They both were sticklers for precision in that way. Of course, Andy could not very well walk over to his wife and put the query to her. The details necessary to define the terms of the question would themselves... Well, it wasn't going to happen.

Andy sipped at his drink and traced the sweet liquor as it infiltrated his system. On the train coming up from D.C., Andy had briefly imagined coming clean with Christine about his involvement with Joy Resnick. Briefly. He had tried imagining Christine displaying astonishing grace and understanding of the affair as having come completely out of the blue. But that was nonsense. "Out of the blue" would have suggested that Andy's affair with Joy Resnick had represented a completely aberrant episode in his life with Christine, and this was simply not the case. Andy took grim solace in the thought that he could count on one hand the number of women he had slept with since being with Christine. The grim part being that with Joy Resnick, Andy had used up his last digit.

Two of the occasions had been completely anonymous, legs and mouths and shoulders with no names. The first had come prior to his and Christine's marriage, during a junket to Venezuela: a brisk bounce in a Caracas Hilton followed by a dark funk and raging hangover the next morning. The second nameless encounter—bizarre by any standard—had transpired many years later, in the back office of a Georgetown jewelry store where Andy had gone to buy his wife a bauble. Andy's heart could still get its beat screwed up at the memory of that one. The SORRY WE'RE CLOSED sign making an uncommon afternoon appearance on the store's glass door. The audacity of the tall, heavy-hipped woman's smirk as she insisted that Andy keep his eyes glued to her face the entire time. Her

painted talons kneading his thighs while the wall calendar ripped free behind her head. Andy had gone directly to the nearest bar afterward and
devoured a scotch, neat, almost fearful that the Amazon might march into
the bar any minute and lead him by the tie to the nearest cramped space
for round two. Andy's stomach still berated him every time Christine
lifted the necklace from her jewelry box.

Of particular bewilderment to Andy was an out-of-town encounter
with a friend of Jenny Hoyt's, no less. Extremely reckless, the incident had
occurred during a never-fully-investigated rough patch with Christine.
Happily for Andy, the woman's husband had taken a job in San Francisco,
a tidy continent away.

His only real affair prior to Joy Resnick had taken place during Andy's
first senatorial campaign, the same year that Christine's brother died and
that Whitney and Lillian had returned from London to see their floun-
dering marriage carom into the final wall. A bad year for the family. The
woman was a journalist with *The Washington Post,* and the genesis of the affair had been the sort of joshing and flattering attention that was common
in many of Andy's interactions with people. In the case of Rita Flores,
Andy would have characterized his attentions as "flirting without in-
tent"—that is, until the moment the candidate had found himself entan-
gled with the fiery reporter in the back of a limousine on the way to her
Arlington apartment. The fact that Andy had allowed his bantering
friendship with the journalist to develop into a full-blown affair had surprised him, and he had sworn to himself—and asserted to Rita Flores—
that his behavior with her represented no judgment whatsoever on the
state of his feelings toward his wife and his marriage. In fact, Andy felt—
but did *not* share with the journalist—that his tryst with her shined a bright
beacon of affirmation on his and Christine's relationship. Nifty trick, that
one. But both during and especially after every sexual encounter with Rita
Flores, Andy had found his mind (or was it his heart?) inundated with loving images of Christine, along with internal voices confirming that his sexual compatibility with his wife absolutely trumped the gymnastic session
just concluded with the aggressive Ms. Flores. His and Christine's pillow
talk was certainly far superior. Plus there was an edge to Rita Flores that
had never really agreed with Andy, a small hardness in the woman when it
came to considering the circumstances and conditions of others. Christine had none of that. Her heart was always on the side of the other. Andy
would drift off to sleep after every encounter with Rita Flores convinced

yet again that Christine was his one and only. A semantic minefield that Andy would forever have to wander alone.

Andy snapped out of his reverie. Christine was calling out to him from over by one of the wickets.

"And you *stay* in that chair until you're good and ready to apologize, do you hear me?"

She was standing next to the tedious ad exec who had been drooling all over her at lunch. A Greenwich action figure if ever there was one: the pale yellow slacks, sky blue Lacoste shirt, northbound hairline. In the instant of looking over at the two of them, the image of the ad exec climbing atop Christine in some hotel room flashed through Andy's mind. Jesus God, he thought, give the poor woman more credit than *that*.

Andy called back. "Whatever it was, I swear I won't do it again!"

Christine laughed. "If I can't forgive you on Easter, then when can I forgive you?"

Andy's glass was empty. He pushed himself out of the tiny chair and went inside for a freshener. Once there he decided against it. Instead, he went into the living room and dropped onto the green leather couch. He realized he was exhausted. The doctor had warned him about this, the possibility of sudden fatigue. Andy felt as if his bones and muscles had turned to water.

The Sunday *Times* was on the coffee table. The front page was dominated by the news—if that's what it could really be called—of Vice President Wyeth's growing difficulties. Andy had glanced at the paper that morning, primarily to see if his name had cropped up in any speculative sense concerning the crisis. It hadn't. From outside, the sounds of raised voices and agitation drifted into the room, but Andy's focus was elsewhere. His eyes ran across the newspaper like a pair of lasers. Over the three days since his stealth exit from Shelter Island, he had done his best to keep away from any coverage of the horrible bludgeoning death of the attractive thirty-four-year-old public relations executive at her family's beach house on Shelter Island. Andy knew this behavior was the same as poking his head into the sand. *If I don't see it or hear about it, it didn't happen.* Thankfully, the growing press interest in the vice president's situation had kept the story buried more deeply than it might have normally been.

But there it was, in the local section: Joy's face, alongside the article about her murder and its investigation. Tears rushed to his eyes when he read that Joy was to be buried the following day. He dabbed away the moisture and continued to scan the article. Now that he had lifted his head momentarily from the sand, there was a specific piece of information he was anxious to find out. In his heart, he already knew it. Unless the Suffolk County police had been trained at Ringling's Clown College, surely they would have figured this one out.

And yes, there it was.

. . . authorities are seeking at least two men in connection with the public relations executive's murder. Aside from the evidence of forced entry by way of the bedroom's rear door additional evidence suggests the presence in the bedroom with Ms. Resnick of a second individual. Police have collected blood and hair samples and are . . .

"Andy?"

Andy's head jerked up from the paper. Christine and Michelle were standing in the doorway. They both looked miserable. All the lift in Christine's face was gone; her eyes looked haunted. Michelle looked even worse. She was crying uncontrollably, her tears trailing down alongside her sniveling nose.

Andy's stomach clenched. *They know.*

He released the paper and rose dreamily to his feet. His knees didn't want to work properly. He felt as if the world outside the windows was spinning at blurring speed.

Michelle croaked, "Daddy."

Christine took a deep breath, closing her eyes for an instant. She looked as if tears were on her way, too. *Here it comes,* Andy thought. *The future is a complete void.*

"Doc is dead. He just collapsed."

Andy heard the words. But their meaning did not immediately register. Someone opened the sliding glass door in the kitchen and Andy became aware of the uptick in agitated noise from the backyard.

Michelle came running toward him. Andy released his breath, not even aware until that moment that he had been holding it. As he stepped forward and opened his arms to receive his bereft little girl, he felt a twinge in his stomach.

It was a most hateful twinge.

It was relief.

CHAPTER 8

Robert Smallwood knew a thing or two about angels.

As a child, he resembled an angel, or at least according to his mother he did. A large and doughy child, his wide, cornflower-blue eyes seemed to cover half his face. His slightly oversize head was perfectly round—like a pumpkin—and his hair remained fair and silky, soft ringlets that circled his scalp not unlike a halo.

By the time of his sixth birthday, Robbie Smallwood had amply accustomed himself to the winged creatures, having by then already visited New York City's veritable warehouse of angels—the Metropolitan Museum of Art—many dozens of times with his mother. For nearly a year leading up to that birthday, Robbie and his mother had engaged in a weekly ritual of visiting the museum every Wednesday afternoon. Tartly done up and with a smart little hat on her head, Vivien Smallwood would usher her son and his sketchbook to the museum's grand second-floor galleries and their scores of paintings that were crammed full with pink, dwarfish angels. Robbie was completely enthralled with the creatures. Their opaque, disconnected expressions. Their puckered limbs and pink-blushed skin. They hovered about on the canvases like little plump bumblebees.

Robbie's "special place" was the lacquered bench directly in front of Lorenzo Lotto's *Venus and Cupid*. Vivien Smallwood would park her son on the bench, give him a lingering kiss on the cheek, then disappear, flashing a smile at the ash-haired security guard who patrolled the galleries as she hurried off to the exit.

The painting was a complete wonder to the boy. *Venus and Cupid*. Each time he saw it, he was confounded anew. The angel in the painting was *peeing* on that naked lady. Actually peeing. A filament of liquid, clear as could be, arched from the cherub's pudgy little penis on its way to the lady's stomach. The lady herself—Venus—was also pink and quite fleshy, and thoroughly unashamed. More than that, she looked amused, reclining on the ground atop a gray blanket, one hand lightly brushing a swelling breast while this little winged urchin *urinated* on her belly! Robbie was enthralled by the look of coquettish mirth on the woman's face. Could she actually be enjoying this? Was she encouraging the imp to debase her in this way? Over the hour and a half of his mother's absence, Robbie sat on the wooden bench, scratching away feverishly in his sketchbook. Over the woman's head dangled a conch shell. Its pink, shellacked lip curved back in a fashion that Robbie instinctively found disturbing. Even more than the rest of the inscrutable painting, it was the spiral shell that burned itself onto Robbie's inner eye. His sketchbook was choked with his artless attempts to reproduce the incongruous mollusk. Each failed attempt— and there were hundreds of them—bore the concluding strokes of the boy's final frustration, the mean, jagged scratchings-over of his fat black pencil.

His mother's return was always punctual. Hearing the *click, click, click* of her heels on the parquet floor as she approached, Robbie would close his messy sketchbook and slide off the bench, bracing himself for the oversize hug.

"*My angel!*"

The security guard tended to regard Vivien Smallwood coolly as the two hurried from the gallery, though Robbie's mother never seemed to notice. Robbie noticed. He could read the man's expression. The guard was not impressed with his mother. Robbie could see that the old black man thought there was something distasteful about her.

And always the routine.

"I hope he was an angel."

"Oh yes ma'am, he was. I'm expecting those wings of his to start poppin' out any old day now."

She couldn't see it. The man was mocking her.

Robbie Smallwood had prayed like the devil for those wings to make their appearance. Straining as hard as he could, he used to imagine that he could actually feel them trying to break through the skin just below his shoulders. It was several weeks before his sixth birthday when his father caught him one morning standing stark naked on a chair in front of the bathroom mirror, twisting his body to get a better look at the reflection of his back. His father's abrupt entrance into the room took the boy by surprise, and he let out a cry as he half-leaped, half-fell from the stool. His father beat him. To Robbie's horror, his bladder released during the beating, some of the stream spraying onto his father's trousers. The anointing further enraged his father, and in due course a trickle of blood began running from one of Robbie's ears.

The day after Robbie's beating was a Wednesday. But there was no visit to see the angels. Instead, his mother remained in her bed all morning and into the afternoon, weeping copiously. Robbie slipped into the room silently and sat and watched. He was fascinated, though not especially moved. He had never really noticed before how his mother was also a little soft herself, in the same fashion as the Venus lady in the painting at the museum. He left the room once, to go fetch his sketchbook, then returned and sat in the chair working on his endless conch shells. Eventually, his mother's weeping subsided somewhat and she noticed her son seated across the room. She summoned him to the bed; dutifully he came to her. She wrapped the boy in her fleshy arms and told him in a soft cooing voice what a bad, bad man his father was. How mean. And how ugly. Robbie didn't disagree. His father *was* bad. But so was his mother. The both of them were ugly and foul. Robbie marveled that he could be the child of such people. He nestled in closer to his pathetic mother. She was as pliant as the pillows. Her milky skin was clammy. He felt as if he could sink deeply into it. *Vile.* Finally, his mother fell asleep, and soon after, so did Robbie. His dreams were black and bloody.

His dates with the angels had ended.

Robert Smallwood leaned down to plant a kiss on his aunt's cheek. The cheek was wet with the poor woman's tears. The light tang of salt transferred to Smallwood's lips.

"Oh, Robbie. Our *Joy.* I just don't understand the world we live in anymore. A beautiful young woman like that. My God, what in the world do you . . . ?"

If she even actually knew her question, she was unable to line up the words to complete it. Smallwood took his aunt's small hand in his own— the very hand that had delivered the necessary blows to Cousin Joy—and massaged her knuckles gently. What could he say to his aunt?

She deserved it.

The world is better off.

He remained mute. His aunt used her captured hand to lead Smallwood over to the pair of easels near the foot of the closed casket. The easels were covered with photographs depicting Joy Resnick on her thirty-four-year journey from birth to death. Smallwood released his aunt's moist hand while he gazed at the photographs. It was all there. Baby Joy. Little girl Joy. Elementary school Joy. Teen Joy. College Joy. First real job Joy.

Whore Joy.

Smallwood moved closer to the casket. He placed his fingers on the lid and let them travel lightly along the wood as he stepped toward the head of the box.

She was *there.* Mere inches below his hand. Sweet. Dead. Joy.

Later, Smallwood parked himself against the wall to observe Cousin Joy's former colleagues, who had turned out in full force. Joy's boss was among the mourners, an imposing bald man in an elegant smoke-colored suit. He was holding forth to a semicircle of sycophants, going on and on about Joy this and Joy that. The man was all praise and bullshit. But he was not the one who had been with Joy that night on Shelter Island. He was too tall. And the man with Joy had not been bald. He thought, *He fucked her, too. Smug, owl-headed hustler. Big bald cootch-sniffing prick.*

Smallwood inventoried Joy's other colleagues to see if any of the men showed signs of a recent wicked encounter with an iron pipe. None of them did. Smallwood knew for a fact that his blows would have required medical attention. Most likely there'd been stitches. None of these particular cretins appeared to have so much as a scratch on them.

As he stood looking over the gathering, Smallwood's eye snagged on a smallish woman who was standing off—seemingly by herself—near the rear of the room. She was somewhere in her mid- to upper twenties, with short bangs, thick dark eyebrows, and a quite complicated pair of eyeglasses, architecturally speaking. The eyewear seemed to be a statement, though Smallwood wasn't sure what the statement was. She was an odd duck. There was an anxious quality coming off her. Smallwood could practically smell it. Her small, pouty mouth was drenched in fire-engine-red lipstick, and behind her mad glasses her eyes seemed to be in continuous motion, deliberately surveying the other people in the room in much the way Smallwood was doing. Smallwood moved away from the wall and traveled slowly around the room, purposefully passing several times near the woman. Each time he sensed her roving eyes landing on him, he felt as if her gaze was crawling over him like worms.

Fascinating.

It was raining like mad. Despite the tarp affixed over the mound of earth next to Joy's grave, the pounding rain was having its way. Streams of chocolate-colored mud ran freely into the waiting grave.

A dozen folding chairs had been set up under a white canopy, sitting unevenly on the lumpy Astroturf carpet. Smallwood sat awkwardly in his chair, his legs overflowing the small plastic seat. He would have preferred to stand out in the rain, but Aunt Judy wanted him under the canopy, next to his grandmother. Doris Smallwood, in her early eighties and nearly as large as Robert, sat silent and sour through the entire service. If Smallwood felt like a giant in the wobbly chair, he suspected his grandmother did as well. The elderly woman lived alone upstate and didn't have much to do with the family these days. By all appearances, being forced to come down to attend her granddaughter's funeral hadn't done much to warm her heart up toward her kin.

At the conclusion of the service, Smallwood's aunt rose from her chair and was guided across the lumpy ground by her son, Jeffrey, who handed her the rose she was to place on Joy's casket. Smallwood's eyes had remained glued on Our Lady of the Funky Glasses, who was standing along the edge of the gathering, staring a hole through the casket. The rain running off her umbrella reminded Smallwood of a curtain of cheap plastic beads. As he sat watching, a man stepped up unnoticed behind the woman, ducking past the rain-bead curtain and joining her under the umbrella. He was of medium height and weight and was wearing a knee-length olive-green coat and a brown floppy-brimmed hat pulled down low on his head.

Smallwood's whiskers twitched.

The man had whispered something into the woman's ear. She went rigid. Even behind her cagey lenses, the fear that came into the woman's eyes was evident. The man continued to speak softly into her ear. Smallwood was certain the man must have told her not to turn around, but to remain facing forward. Was this *him*? Smallwood looked for signs of his handiwork on the man's skull, but the hat was pulled down too far. Whoever he was, he seemed to have a lot to say. Aunt Judy had completed her rose tribute and Jeffrey was guiding her back to her chair. Smallwood had to shift in his seat to maintain his view of the curious couple. The way the man was keeping his eyes trained on the side of the woman's face looked as if he wanted to see what her reaction was to his words. The woman nodded once. And then a second time. This seemed to be the desired response. He reached up with his hand and touched her lightly on the cheek, then backed away and disappeared into the light mist.

The heavens opened up even more. The crazy beating of the rain on the canopy was like machine-gun fire. So was Robert Smallwood's heartbeat.

The general movement toward the cars was swift. The priest came under the canopy and began his condolences to the family. Cousin Jeffrey had a hand on Smallwood's arm and was babbling something incoherent about Smallwood's parents, both of whom had been dead for years and were buried just several feet away, beneath a black marble angel. Smallwood was not even sure what he said to Jeffrey; he knew only that he freed his arm brusquely and trotted across the spongy grass toward the roadway. Miss Eyeglasses was just getting into a blue Mazda. Smallwood hurried over to her. The unknowing of what he was doing was exhilarating.

Reaching the car, he grabbed hold of the door frame just as the woman was about to pull the driver's side door closed. The rain was plastering Smallwood's thin hair to his head in silly bangs.

"Wait!" he yelled. His heart was still going crazy. He felt a surge of *power.* "What did that man want? I saw him. What did he want with you?"

The woman tugged at the door. "Let go!"

But Smallwood's strength was triple the woman's. She couldn't budge the door. "I'm Joy's cousin," Smallwood blurted. "I don't like some asshole bursting in on her funeral like that."

The woman pleaded. "I have to go. Please. I—"

Somehow she managed to jerk the door from Smallwood's grip, and it slammed shut. Smallwood watched through the window as she jabbed the key blindly at the ignition. It wasn't going in. Her hand was shaking too much, and her urgency was only lousing up her ability to hit the slot. She jabbed at the ignition several times and then, fully frustrated, threw the key at the dashboard and collapsed against the steering wheel, her arms crossing daintily to give her head a soft place to land.

Fascinating.

CHAPTER 9

On Tuesday, President Hyland faced reporters to talk about the European Union's new carbon emissions reduction timetable and a controversial inclusion in the program's legislation of a number of punitive actions proposed for E.U. industries whose tie-ins with noncomplying U.S.-owned entities would be taken into account in the overall carbon calculations.

Nobody in the press briefing room gave a rat's ass. Carbon emissions? Please. The vice president's head was nearing the chopping block; noxious gases could wait. The pencils were sharpened and the keyboards were ready to hum.

"Mr. President. Do you think it's wise at such an early stage in your presidency to risk losing the trust of the people who put you into office?"

The president answered, "Would it be wise? Of course it wouldn't be wise; it would be stupid." Hyland squinted briefly in the direction of the ceiling. "May I ask *you* a question, Jerry? Are you calling the president stupid?"

He got his laugh and moved on to the next question. It was a reworking of the previous one. Hyland was sufficiently skilled in offering many words to say practically nothing, and for the next thirty minutes of the press conference this is largely what he did. On the continually rebounding topic of Vice President Wyeth, Hyland voiced concerns about "the hearsay" and "the speculation" flying about. He declared, several times, that he had yet to be presented with any credible information that any of the allegations against his VP were true.

"If the American people want their president to start making major decisions about the running of the administration based on the prattling of blogs and rumors and, can we say, a little too much breathlessness in some corners of the media, I'm afraid they're going to be disappointed. But I don't happen to think this is what they want."

He continued, saying that he would maintain full support for any member of his staff and his administration until such time as that person was shown to have conducted himself in a manner inconsistent with either the law of the land or the ethical standards set by the president from day one in office. Hypothesizing, he said, was a waste of precious time.

"I am not being paid by the American people to spend my time playing *what if.* There is plenty of *must do* to be done."

A perfect exit line, as he and his chief of staff had determined prior to the press conference.

"Thank you."

The reporters barked questions at the president as he left the briefing room, but they remained unaddressed. As he headed back to the Oval Office, casting a rueful eye at a portrait along the hallway of Andrew Jackson's dainty little thug's face, Hyland said to his chief of staff, "I don't like this sort of holding maneuver, Ron. We advance nothing but the clock. They'll probably grant me that one, but we can't go playing Wiffle ball with them like that again. I want to know, damn it. When does Chris Wyeth stand naked before me? I need to speak with the man. The last thing I can afford to do is to start playing Wiffle ball with myself."

"No, sir. I agree. Wyeth has got to account for himself."

"Vice President Wyeth, Ron."

"Yes, sir."

The pair had reached the president's outer office. From her desk, Hyland's personal secretary gave him a *tsk-tsk. "De ceci, de cela, va une petite manière."*

Hyland paused, amused. "Meaning?"

"Meaning they won't be writing any songs about *that* press conference, sir."

Hyland entered the Oval Office and strode across the presidential seal. Casting his eye out the window, he swung neatly around the large desk and into his chair.

"Ron, tell the vice president we're having pecan pie tonight."

The chief of staff was still many steps behind his boss. "Sir?"

"Pecan pie. Chris Wyeth gets physically aroused in the presence of pecan pie. What's wrong, Ron, weren't you on the campaign?"

The chief of staff searched his boss's placid face. "Mr. President, am I missing something?"

Hyland smiled slyly. "I'd like to have a talk with Vice President Wyeth, Ron. Tonight. Face-to-face. Is he back yet from wherever the hell he's been hiding?"

"He is, sir. He returned to the capital this morning. I'll contact his office immediately."

The chief of staff took a step toward the door, then stopped. "Oh. Wait. The vice president plays tennis on Tuesday nights with Senator Foster. It's a standing date."

Hyland was shaking his head even before his aide had finished his sentence. "Andy Foster? No. Absolutely not. Break the date, Ron. I don't care if you have to get Roger Federer to stand in for him, one thing Chris Wyeth does *not* do is play tennis with Senator Foster tonight. You tell Foster's people, keep their man clean and keep him away from Chris Wyeth."

Hyland loosened his tie and leaned back in his chair. This was when he wished he still smoked. For certain it was too early in the day for a drink.

"If the vice president is toxic, I don't want him infecting anyone we may be wanting to call on."

"Senator Foster?"

Hyland stared off into the middle distance for a moment. When he snapped out of it, he held up a hand showing four fingers.

"LaMott, Harrison, Bainbridge, and Foster. Are they all vetted?"

"Marginally. Some more than others."

"Well, let's kick into high gear, then. You cancel the senator's love match and crank up the vetting on all four of them. Let's clear out those closets *now*, for God's sake. Obviously we want to do a better job this time."

"Sir, nothing of substance has been presented on the vice president."

"Ron, a bad scent *is* substance. Even if all this noise about Wyeth proves to be garbage, we should have picked up the fact that questions like this could even be raised. Arrange for the vice president to be in this office at eight o'clock tonight. Keep it quiet, of course. Keep it off my schedule."

"Yes, sir."

As the chief of staff neared the door, President Hyland added one more order.

"And Ron? If you're feeling brave, tell Mr. Wyeth that the president is not in the mood for Wiffle ball. That little press conference we just had makes me want to vomit."

CHAPTER 10

"**D**imitri, I look like . . . a monster!"

Irena Bulakov stood shivering at the bathroom sink. A transparent blue plastic smock held closed in front with large white snaps covered her bare shoulders. Dimitri was seated on the closed toilet lid. He ran his hands over his stubbled jaw as he considered his wife.

"You do not look like a monster. When you see a blond woman on the street do you call her a monster?"

"This is not blond, Dimitri. This is *white*."

Dimitri snorted. "Marilyn Monroe has this color hair."

Irena looked at herself again in the mirror. She could not believe the creature that was staring back at her. "Dimitri. I am not Marilyn Monroe. Look at me! I have a white animal on my head!"

"You are being hyster—"

"*I am not!* I want my old hair back!"

The tears were beginning. Dimitri ignored them. He rose unsteadily from the toilet. "Well, you cannot have it. This is what you look like now. Here. Wear these."

He pulled a pair of cherry-red sunglasses from his shirt pocket and handed them to his wife. Irena pouted as she took them from him and put them on. Dimitri gestured at her.

"See? Look and see."

Irena turned to the mirror. Okay, so it was a little better. With her eyes hidden, the bleached blonde in the mirror was not necessarily Irena Bulakov looking ridiculous, just some bad blonde in loud sunglasses. But she was still upset that Dimitri had made her do this.

"You want so no one will recognize me, but you make me so everyone will stare. That is stupid, Dimitri. It—"

The slap knocked the sunglasses off her face. They clattered on the tile floor.

"Who is *stupid*?" Dimitri raised both his hands in the air, but he did not strike her again. "I am making plans so you and me have one million dollars to our names, and who is stupid?"

Irena raised her face slowly. The pink sting of her husband's hand lit up her left cheek. Dimitri was glaring at her with his dull, unintelligent eyes.

"I am stupid," Irena said coldly. She bent down to retrieve the sunglasses and put them back on.

The man uncoiled.

"I don't mean to hurt you," Dimitri said thickly. "But you are not hearing me, Irena. This is a good idea, this disguise. Titov has many friends. You know this. But no one will recognize you now. Now you do not need to be locked up in here all day. You can take walks. You can bring back food for us."

Tears appeared from behind the cherry-red sunglasses. "I am not hungry. I don't want to eat. I want to go home."

Dimitri's last phone conversation with Titov had been the day before. Initially, Titov had played at consenting to Dimitri's scheme.

"Okay, Dimitri, I am listening," Titov had told him. "Here is what we will do. You will tell me who is this important man you have on your computer file. I read the papers, Dimitri. I know that this woman was killed. So you tell me who is this man and why you think he will give us so much money as you say. You want more money than the two thousand I was paying you? You want to renegotiate? Okay, Dimitri. You can have it. You will give me this file, and I will pay you more money. And if either my client or this man will do what you claim he will do to get it, if they will pay all this money, then you and I will split that. Just like you want."

Dimitri had balked. He wanted money up front from Titov. Without going face-to-face. "I will tell you nothing until I have fifty thousand dollars."

"Fifty thousand dollars?" Titov had sounded almost amused. "I will hand you a fat envelope. Will that make you happy?"

"No. You will mail the money to where I tell you to."

Aleksey Titov was not a man who took orders. He had tried to control the seething tone rising in his voice. Tried but failed.

"You are wrong," he said coldly. "I will not do this. I will put nails in my own father's eyes before I do something so *stupid,* Dimitri. What I . . . what

I will do is, I will find you and I will find your wife and I will be happy to split open both your skulls and serve your brains to my wife's cat! Do you understand, Dimitri? You are not smart enough to hide from me! I was doing you a favor when I gave you this job. I was helping you out because I pitied you, and you repay with the double cross? This means one thing only. This means you do not want to live. For that you are an idiot, Dimitri. You are a dead idiot."

That same night, vandals had trashed Paddles. The tables had been broken with axes. In the tavern, all of the liquor bottles lined up behind the bar had been smashed. Orange spray paint had gone wild all over the walls, the floor, and the ceiling. On the bulletin board in the cramped office that Dimitri shared with his brother and his part-time manager, a citrus knife from the bar had been used to pierce a photograph of Dimitri and Irena. The knife had been left behind, stuck into Dimitri's forehead.

Dimitri had learned all this in a phone call from his part-time manager, who was now his former part-time manager. After Dimitri had hung up, he had said to Irena, "Aleksey Titov is not so smart as he thinks. Now I need this money more than ever."

He had phoned Leonard, who was home now from the hospital, to tell his brother not to worry. The conversation had soured quickly, and Dimitri had ended it abruptly.

"Everyone is thinking small," he lamented. "I am outside this box now."

"**Y**ou look like a rock singer," Dimitri said to Irena after she had removed the plastic smock and pulled on a sweater. Irena had played around with her hair a little bit, pulling some of it back and tying it up with a rubber band, letting the rest drop like dog ears. She came over to where Dimitri was sitting on the edge of the bed, inserting his blue flash drive into the back of his computer. She sat down next to him and pushed the sunglasses up onto her head. Dimitri put a hand on her skinny leg and squeezed.

"Listen to me," he said. "If Aleksey does not want to hear me, this is his problem. We can become rich without him." He tapped the empty screen. "The man in here, he is going to make us rich. I am not going to show him to you, Irena. You are not to know, you understand? In this way, you are of no use to Titov or to anyone else. I am keeping you safe. This is smart. But I am telling you. This man? If we want his left ball and his big toe, we can have it. He will pay us for this file, Irena. Trust me. Anything we ask for, he will have to give it to us. I know this."

He squeezed her leg again.

"A man must pay for his mistakes, Irena. We are going to make this man pay. You will see how smart your husband is. Everyone will see."

And he squeezed again. A little higher.

CHAPTER 11

Ever since the beginning of the year, stopping off at the Boho Bakery on Bleecker Street on the way to Michelle's school in the morning had become a ritual. Spurred by the suggestion of her homeroom teacher that the students come up with a New Year's resolution, Michelle had declared her intention to eat one miniature cupcake a day for every school day, starting in January. Her goal, she had declared, was to eat a million cupcakes. A nice big round insane number. Christine was aware that in allowing her daughter this sugar indulgence she propelled herself instantly onto the list of Incredibly Irresponsible Parents, but she was willing to take the hit.

"I have my caffeine, the kid has her sugar. Fair's fair."

Over the past months, Christine and Michelle had become friendly with the bakery's employees. Occasionally, a new face would appear. A newbie, or as Michelle referred to them, a "New Bear." Michelle's most recent New Bear was a genial man in his late twenties. The seven-year-old had a not-so-secret crush on him. He was actor-handsome, with hazel eyes and thick black hair that curled out from beneath his baker's cap. Outside the bakery, in his real life, he was a sculptor. Large, muscular pieces. Mainly bronze and steel. Recently, his work had been included in a gallery showcase that Michelle had pleaded with her mother to take her to. Christine had considered it, but the time had slipped away. Once she learned what he did outside the bakery, Christine enjoyed observing the almost feminine delicacy with which the man employed his strong hands on the fragile pastries. For several weeks, a plan had been formulating in her head about doing a shoot of the sculptor slash bakery chef. In particular, a study of his hands at work on the pastries and then, in contrast, at his studio, contending with his far less pliable materials. The concept held potential, but she hadn't yet firmed up her thoughts enough to float the idea to him. He seemed the type who would be amenable.

The sculptor was waiting on a customer when Christine and Michelle came through the door on Wednesday morning. Michelle dawdled, waiting until her New Bear was free before stepping up to the counter. The sculptor threw Christine a knowing smile as he launched into full flirt mode with the little girl.

"Well, look who it is. Miss One-of-a-Million. Good morning, cupcake. How are you today?"

Michelle's face lit up like the rising sun. The man's charms brought out a rare bashfulness.

"So what will it be today?" he went on. "Let me guess."

"You know!" Michelle burst out.

The sculptor snared a paper tissue from the box on the counter. He looked again at Christine. "Do you have any idea how old we're going to be by the time this is finished?"

"Yeah. I think the dinosaurs will be back."

The sculptor laughed. "The dinosaurs, huh? What goes around comes around?"

Christine shrugged. "Beats the idea of complete and utter extinction."

"I guess we could say that's vaguely optimistic."

Christine considered the point. "It is if you're a dinosaur."

Michelle was poking her finger against the glass case. "That one!"

Mother and daughter made their way to the Little Red School House, where Christine kissed Michelle goodbye at the front door. She continued on to Carmine Street and Café Jamal for her morning cappuccino. Her own one-of-a-million. This time of year, the morning sun angled sharply through the café's window. Christine closed her eyes and drank in its comforting warmth. Now that Michelle was safely off to school, Christine could turn her attention to . . . herself. It seemed that this particular morning, there was a lot to go over.

Andy had phoned Christine from D.C. the night before to tell her that Chris Wyeth had canceled their standing tennis date. The reason for the cancellation was that Wyeth was meeting in the evening with President Hyland to discuss the flak concerning the vice president's conduct back in his state government days. The meeting was strictly hush-hush. Andy had gone on to tell her of Hyland's directive, channeled through Andy's aide-de-camp, Jim Fergus, about Andy keeping his distance from the embattled

VP, at least for the time being. On the face of it, the directive was completely absurd. Andy and Chris Wyeth had a long professional history together, as well as a long-running personal friendship. Wyeth had attended Andy and Christine's wedding, offering up the day's most eloquent and heartfelt toast. During his own stint in Albany—some ten-plus years after her own father's administration—Wyeth had been no small factor in assisting Andy in his bruising fight to hold on to the Senate seat he had inherited, as it happened, from Wyeth. Round and round it went. Andy and Chris Wyeth were inexorably linked. It seemed childish to order the two to keep away from each other.

Christine lost herself in the shimmering triangles of sunlight that played about her table. The nearby door opened and closed as customers passed in and out of the café. The occasional breeze caressed her skin. A ladybug appeared on Christine's spoon. It, too, seemed to be taking a long moment to do absolutely nothing. Christine picked up a slender red straw and poked at the froth of her cappuccino. She drew little designs in the foam. A couple sitting a few tables away were locked in a highly charged but whispered argument, and Christine settled onto the face of the young woman, trying to name to herself each of the woman's passing expressions. Eventually the couple paid their bill and left, and Christine finally called her focus back from its wanderings. It wasn't really her preference—she enjoyed these sorts of mental time-outs—but she knew she could only indulge in being nowhere for just so long.

She was troubled.

In their phone conversation, Christine and Andy had only nibbled around the very edges of the matter of the vice presidency. As absurd as it seemed, Christine did not know what Andy's innermost thoughts were should Chris Wyeth be forced to step down. Even when Andy's name had been floated as a possible second on John Hyland's ticket, he and Christine had not fully confronted the matter. Andy had great respect for Hyland, she knew this, and he had eventually played a strong part in helping to deliver votes to him, in particular the votes of the wary upstaters. But with Chris Wyeth being tapped to run for vice president, the question for Andy and Christine had remained abstract. On top of which, it had been anticipated that after the current governor of the state stepped down— now rumored to be at the conclusion of his current term—Andy would be throwing his hat into the ring for a trip to Albany. Christine already harbored great ambivalence about the déjà vu of a return to life in the governorship's fishbowl. So very *been there.* So very *done that.* It was also certainly not something she was anxious to wish on her own daughter. But as with many facets of her husband's career—too many—this was something Christine preferred not to think about if she didn't have to. So long as most of the matters remained abstractions—which up to now they had—there was actually nothing to think about.

Up to now.

Christine finished her cappuccino. As she headed toward the subway, her eye caught the cover of the *Post.* Someone had leaked the story of Vice President Wyeth's evening meeting with President Hyland. The front page of the tabloid showed a large photograph of Hyland looking irritated and one of the vice president in an uncommon expression of contriteness. The 72-point headline ran:

OKAY, LET'S HEAR IT

Christine dug two quarters from her purse and swapped them for the paper. She folded it lengthwise and continued on to the subway, beating the paper gently against her open palm as she went.

Heading down the steps at the Christopher Street station, Christine recognized a familiar tightness in her stomach. She had experienced a similar feeling—a low-level dread—the morning she had walked down the steps at her father's Greenwich house on the morning of her marriage to Andy. It wasn't Andy; she loved her husband deeply, and she had loved him well before they'd tied the knot. The spasm of dread on the morning of her wedding had come more from the full realization that in committing herself to this man, she was unwittingly following in her mother's footsteps: marrying the very possibly future governor of the state of New York. She had found herself assailed by the famous Santayana quotation about those who ignore history, and she had prayed she was doing the right thing. This was different, she'd told herself. Andy was not Whitney. *She* was not Lillian. Let irony have its day, and then move on.

As Christine descended into the station, the aroma of stale air rose to meet her. The rolled-up newspaper was beating harder now against her leg, like a steady drumbeat. Down, down, down she went.

———

She got off the subway at Columbus Circle and angled toward Central Park. The air was crisp, more like an autumn day than the middle of April, and the temperature dropped noticeably once she entered the park. Bicyclists were scattered along Park Drive, with their little ant-head helmets and their hard-pumping legs.

Christine crossed the drive at Tavern on the Green and headed east across Sheep Meadow. A handful of people dotted the vast green space. Some were reading; a few appeared to be meditating. There were some sleepers. The inevitable cell-phone yabberers.

When she reached the Promenade, Christine pulled out her camera. The wide walkway that ran north toward the Pond was one of her favorite parts of the park. There was something so stately and serene about the Promenade. Something timeless. The rows of black statues stationed on either side of the walkway. The high canopy of trees filtering out the sunshine. Christine always felt as if she were traveling a corridor that had been lifted in full from another era and very deliberately and subversively inserted into the park at these exact time and space coordinates. She had taken hundreds of photographs here. Her huge collage of the walkway in autumn greeted visitors and employees getting off the elevator at the fifth floor of the Ford Foundation headquarters, just a mile to the south. Another image of the Promenade she had captured, the trees and statues heavily frosted with silvery snow, had been blown up and mounted in an ice blue frame and hung in a place of honor in Placido Domingo's villa in Rialto, on the wall next to the tenor's gleaming Steinway grand piano. He had phoned Christine personally soon after the photograph's installation to tell her how "transporting" the image was.

Christine snapped away as she walked along the pathway. She could tell that her eye was a little off this morning. She wasn't transporting a damn thing. In the plaza, in front of the band shell, two teenage boys on midgety-looking bicycles were perfecting the stunt of heaving the rear of their bikes into the air and balancing both bike and rider on the stubby front tire. A lot of hop, hop, hop, fall. Christine shot a quick series. She thought maybe she might be able to do something with some of the shots of the boys as they bailed out. Bodies momentarily in flight. She'd have to see. The balancing part she just wasn't capturing.

The knot in her stomach had dissolved away. The park always did this for her. It leveled things off. Christine knew that the word *oasis* was always being dragged out whenever a person wanted to describe the key function of the park, but she had yet to locate a better one. It *was* an oasis, especially so during the week and the low tourist months. When she was fresh out of college, during the year in which Christine made her play to push back against the powerful gravitational pull of her relationship with Andy, she had entered into a brief and delicious affair with a dishy older man she had met at the Belvedere Castle. The man owned a Saint Bernard he'd named Frederick Law Olmsted, after one of the visionary designers of Central Park, and for a month and a half Christine had been convinced that the extremely sexy man and his heavenly beast of a dog were a fairy tale that she had tumbled into. Too good to be true. Which of course turned out to be the case. When the not-yet-ready-to-cut-the-cord ex-wife began leaving her scent here and there, the fairy-tale man had turned disappointingly real. Big-faced Frederick Law Olmsted had still maintained his charm, but there could be no splitting of the package. The bubble had burst, and Christine's rebel year concluded back in Andy's capable arms.

Christine came out of the park just south of the Metropolitan Museum and headed up the steps. A large blue and gold banner hanging over the entrance advertised the current van Eyck show.

In the Temple of Dendur, Christine walked a slow circle around the sandstone relic, then sat down on the low wall that rimmed the installation's large black pool. Dimes, nickels, quarters, pennies shimmered in the shallow water. In a too-rational world, people still toss coins into water. They still hold out for some magic. Christine loved that. She leaned sideways and let her fingers slip into the water. Mild ripples radiated out from her hand, disturbing the flat black surface. The clenching in her stomach had sneaked back up on her and she wanted to ignore it, but she couldn't. She knew it was going to remain until this thing with Andy resolved itself. The future was making a rush at her, and she was resisting. Futile, as they say. Christine wiggled her fingers, creating a small splash. Wishing for things to remain exactly as they were was folly. Christine's personal wishes for stasis were simply not under consideration. She could unload a thousand coins into the water, and it was not going to make a single bit of difference.

"Hey. You can't do that."

Christine jerked her head. A security guard was standing quite close, looming over her. A large man. The ceiling of the vast room floated several hundred feet above his head. Christine pulled her fingers from the water.

"Oh. I'm sorry."

The guard's face intrigued her. His head had the roundness of a perfect pumpkin, and he looked as if he had a light source buried within his skull, illuminating the cornflower-blue eyes from within. The expression on his face—not quite blank—was discomforting.

"Don't do that," he grunted again.

Before Christine could respond, the guard turned and started away. Strange bird. Christine grabbed her camera and fired off a few discreet shots of the receding figure as he headed off in the direction of the adjoining gallery. The image in her viewfinder sent chills through her. He moved like a man dragging a trail of heavy chains.

CHAPTER 12

Senator Andrew Foster (Democrat, New York) leaned into the microphone and pointed his finger across the moat of photographers to the witness seated at the long table. If the finger had been a pistol, the shot would have taken the witness at the bridge of his nose.

"Do you mean to tell me that you authorized a bonus of ten *thousand* dollars to be paid to Miss"—he stirred a few sheets of paper in front of him, then lowered the accusing finger to jab it forcefully against one of the sheets—"Miss Hammond? You paid this Miss Hammond, on top of her six-figure salary, a *bonus* for being the employee who, you will have to excuse my language, Mr. Sprague and Mr. Chairman, but I think in this case it is formidably accurate, who *screwed* more of your company's customers out of receiving necessary medical attention and treatment than any other employee? Is that what you are telling this committee?"

The witness glared back at the senator from behind his thick horn-rimmed glasses. His expression made him look as if he was sucking on an extremely tart lemon drop.

"Miss Hammond achieved a notable benchmark, Senator. We believe in—"

The senator cut him off. "Benchmark? Could you elaborate on that, Mr. Sprague? What we're talking about here is denial of benefits. Plain and simple, sir. Denial of *lifesaving benefits*. Did this Miss Hammond receive a bottle of champagne along with her ten grand? Perhaps a plaque?"

"Senator, it's not—"

"Is her picture up on the wall in the employees' lunchroom? Killer of the Year?"

The witness punched the table with his fist. "Senator, that is unfair!"

Senator Foster allowed the words to dissolve in their own sweet time. If he was a shade too theatrical in massaging the pause, so be it. Out of the corner of his eye he caught the knowing grin of the committee chairman.

"Mr. Sprague. I stand ready to apologize to the fortunate Miss Hammond for my characterization of her as a killer. I'm sure she is a lovely person, and she's just doing her job. It was a harsh thing to say." His eyes drifted to the gallery, then lowered again to the man at the table. "Perhaps, Mr. Sprague, you can show me how it's done."

The witness was confused. "I'm sorry, Senator. How what is done?"

"Apologizing, Mr. Sprague. Ross Foley's widow and two of her three children are seated in the front row of the gallery. If you turn around, you can see them. Go ahead, sir. Have a look. They're right there."

Sprague knew he had no choice. Reluctantly, he twisted in his chair and peered up into the gallery.

Andy pulled the microphone closer. "Mrs. Foley. I don't believe Mr. Sprague has any idea what you look like. Could you please help him out?"

A frail-looking black woman seated in the front of the gallery lifted her hand. She spoke some words, but they failed to travel down to the floor. A pair of preteens sat sullenly on either side of her.

Sprague turned back to the committee and waited for the senator from New York to complete the disemboweling. Andy Foster was only too happy to comply.

"If you'll apologize to Mrs. Foley and her children for the unnecessary death of the late Mr. Foley, I will beg the forgiveness of your . . . your Benchmark Achiever of the Year, Miss Hammond. Do we have a deal, Mr. Sprague?"

Back in his office, Andy hung up his jacket and loosened his tie. Jim Fergus, the senator's aide-de-camp, was already seated in his usual chair, fidgeting with a pencil. Grabbing a tissue from the box on his desk, Andy dabbed gingerly at the wound on his head. The stitches had come out that morning, and he had been warned of the possibility of slight oozing. The tissue came away dry.

Fergus asked, "Did you enjoy that? Beating up on the good Mr. Sprague?"

Andy moved behind his desk and dropped into his chair. "Did you?"

"If Frank Capra were alive, I'm sure *he* would have enjoyed it. Either that or started making plans to sue your ass."

Andy laughed. "The man is holding a one-way ticket to hell, Jim. He is literally in the business of killing sick people. Under the guise of providing *insurance.* It's seriously nuts. We're in the realm of outright lunacy now. Ass over teakettle or whatever the hell the phrase is. Our clueless Mr. Sprague and the rest of his kind are steering a perverse course for this planet."

Fergus gave a maybe-yes-maybe-no shrug. "Hey. Senator. The cameras are off. There's no need to convince me. I say give the man a pair of cement boots and let's move on."

The office door opened and a young woman wearing a blue blazer and pleated skirt entered carrying a cup of coffee and a file folder. She brought them both to the senator's desk, placing the cup down daintily. Andy cocked an eyebrow.

"What did you think, Lindsay? Did I beat up on poor Mr. Sprague too harshly?"

The intern blushed. "No, Senator. I mean, it's like you said. It's . . . To reward someone for refusing a person's medical benefits . . ." She trailed off. Her slight Buffalo accent remained in the air.

"Well it *is* Miss Hammond's job," Andy said, sliding the coffee mug closer to him. "Correct? She was doing precisely what she was paid to do."

The young woman looked uncertain. "But it's . . . No. I mean, it's not right."

"But my browbeating. That's what I'm asking. Was that right?"

Lindsay glanced at Jim Fergus, but he was no help. The intern attempted again to respond. "I don't think you . . . you had to be . . . I mean. What he's doing isn't right. You . . . I don't think *you* did anything wrong."

Fergus could not hold back his laughter. "Let her go, Andy. For Christ's sake, you're browbeating your own intern on the topic of browbeating."

Lindsay continued to blush. "I just finished, um, going over your Earth Day speech, Senator." She set the file folder down on the desk. "It's really something. It's very inspiring, sir."

"Thank you," Andy said. "We'll see how the greenies feel about it next week."

Fergus made a point of clearing his throat. "Ah . . . Lindsay? The senator and I need to talk."

"Oh. Of course. I'm sorry." The intern beat a hasty retreat.

"Cute," Fergus said as soon as the door had clicked closed.

Andy was wincing at the taste of the coffee. "Lindsay? Yes. Nice girl. I'm not really sure how much use she's actually going to be around here."

"She dresses the place up nicely."

"I was talking about the scared rabbit part."

"You're intimidating, Mr. Senator."

"Oh, come on. That girl could have landed in a lot more intimidating offices than this one."

"It's your animal charm."

"I'm moved."

"By the way, I heard she has the clap."

"What!" Andy nearly spilled his coffee.

Fergus was already laughing. "Good. That's the correct reaction. I just want to be certain those animal paws of yours stay where they belong."

Andy eyed him. "I think you're impugning my fine character, fine friend."

Fergus downshifted his levity. "Listen, it's unofficially official, Andy, but you're definitely on the short list. LaMott, Harrison, Bainbridge, and you. And I can tell you this, Harrison is not going to remain on the list for long." Fergus made a drinking motion.

Andy asked, "Is that official?"

Fergus shook his head. "Nah. The whispering of the mice. But you can take it to the bank. Harrison's out. That leaves three."

"So let me make sure I've got this straight. You're telling me to keep my hands off a nineteen-year-old child or else I won't even be considered for vice president."

Jim Fergus had known Andy long enough. "Don't waste your righteousness on me, Senator. You know what my job is."

"To be my mother?"

"If I didn't happen to know that you adore your mother, I would take that as an insult. Yes. Fine. Mother says. Hyland's people are going over all of you with an electron microscope. They blew it by not using one on Wyeth. They're not going to make the same mistake again."

"Chris might still be clean," Andy said. "It wouldn't be the first time a so-called scandal turned to dust."

"Do you think he's clean?"

Andy paused. The question had certainly been turning over and over in his mind ever since the faint whisperings had begun about Chris Wyeth's possible miscues. He didn't want to admit to the sense, however deeply planted, that the portrayal of young Chris Wyeth playing a little fast and loose was far too credible.

Jim Fergus did not care for his boss's pause. "Andy, if you actually know something, for God's sake . . . I don't even care if you skip the veep thing. But do *not* get caught up in this. You have to tell Momma right now. You and Wyeth go way back. Will your name be popping up in connection with any of these allegations?"

"What do your whispering mice tell you?"

"Screw them. What do *you* tell me?"

Andy took a slow sip of coffee. What he hated about himself at that very instant was the image that had popped into his head. It had nothing to do with the topic at hand. It was an image of Lindsay the intern. She was again crossing the office on her baby-deer legs and exiting through the doorway. But this time she was completely naked.

"I'm clean, Jim," Andy said to his aide. "When Chris Wyeth was AG, I was still chasing hillbilly girls down in old Virginny. I don't know what the man was up to, if anything. You have my word, Chris has not said a thing to me on this whole topic since the news broke."

"Fine. But I happen to know you haven't seen him since the news broke. No one has. Except Hyland last night. Apparently he was holed up at the estate all week."

"Well. True."

Fergus detected an evasion. He knew how to read Andy's face. "*Is* it true? This isn't your mother talking here now. It's Fergie. Of course there's no harm if you've talked to Wyeth over the phone in the last few days. But the man is radioactive right now. Loyalty takes a backseat in matters like this, at least until the air has cleared. Chris Wyeth has been, if I can coin the term, bunglingly out of D.C. until just the other day. It's very not good, his hiding out like that at his Hamptons manse and canceling his appearances. That bunker-mentality look is not one that too many pols wear well. Now, I know you two didn't have your tennis game Tuesday. And I know that you were in Miami until Friday, then you and Christine went up to Whitney's for Easter. And—"

Andy cut him off. "Jim. Should I submit to you my hour-by-hour diary?"

"Hey, I just want to know if you had any face-to-face with Wyeth. If you did, I wish you hadn't. It simply wouldn't look good right now. I just don't want to be blindsided. That's my job. To keep your handsome ass clean."

"I haven't seen Chris since last week."

Fergus took a beat to assess his boss's response. Normally, the senator was possessed of a pretty decent poker face, but not today. Fergus saw right through it. Something was wrong. He nodded grimly.

"That's good," he said. "Thank you."

CHAPTER 13

Andy sat at his desk with his chair spun toward the window. At the far end of the Mall, the Washington Monument softly pierced the darkening sky. The sun sat low on the horizon, just off to the right of the monument and some several billion miles away. Off to Andy's left, an airliner was beginning its descent into Reagan National. A sliver of mercury growing ever larger.

Andy did not want his thoughts to go back to the increasingly surreal memory of what had taken place on Shelter Island. But there was really no choice. One week. Was that possible? Joy Resnick was now buried. That dreary rainy Monday. God at his maudlin best.

As best as he could determine, the police on Long Island were nowhere near sorting out what had happened in the hillside house that Thursday night. Andy was still keeping disciplined about not seeking information on the Internet. God only knew what sort of cookie-crumb trails such searching could leave behind and who was sitting in some nondescript building in that very city at that very instant trolling about for any such crumbs. That's what the country was coming to.

Based on the various patterns of footprints in the wet grass outside the house where Joy Resnick had been murdered, the police were seeking two or three men. From what Andy did know, this much hadn't changed. The matter of whether all three men or only one had been involved in the murder was still a matter of speculation. The physical evidence had made it clear that Joy had been engaged in sexual activity at some point in the hours before she was murdered. Whether or not the authorities were leaning toward an assumption of rape was something Andy had not discerned.

Naturally, the police were speaking with anyone who might have had an intimate involvement with the late Ms. Resnick.

Andy sipped a scotch as he tracked another plane sliding through the sky. Figuratively speaking, any one person should be in possession of only one Achilles' heel, yet Andy seemed to have too many to even count. For one, his blood was on the scene. He'd done what he could before fleeing the house to mop up any of the blood that had oozed from his head wound, but he wasn't fooling himself. He'd left some behind; he had no doubts about it.

And there was the matter of his DNA. He might as well have left a note behind, signed Senator Andrew P. Foster. Should speculation ever turn to actual suspicion, law enforcement had him by the genes. The blood evidence would be kid stuff.

Andy set the glass down on the windowsill and bobbed the melting ice chip with his finger. Particularly disconcerting was the Thursday afternoon flight he had taken from Miami to New York. Not only was his name firmly implanted in the airline's computer system, but plenty of passengers had recognized him in both airports as well as on the flight itself. The pilot had even made a point of coming back to the cabin to introduce himself, and Andy had autographed a copy of his book for one of the other passengers.

What had he been thinking?

Andy plunged the ice chip down to the bottom of the glass and held it there. The most nagging thought, however, was the assailant himself. Joy's killer. Whoever he was, he had had ample opportunity to look at the face of the man who had attempted so vainly to ward off his brutal attack. Had he looked? Andy had no idea. He thought possibly not, but there was just no way he could be certain.

A very large and very nasty shoe could well be suspended up there somewhere above his head, just waiting to drop. This was the possibility that Joy had been murdered *because* of whom she was sleeping with. Because of Andy himself. Had someone somehow gotten wind of his and Joy's rendezvous and then targeted Joy for reasons that were yet to be revealed? Of the various thoughts that were plaguing Andy's mind, this was the most sickening. This was the question that had Andy jumpy when his phones rang, or when he logged on to get his emails. Was the mental hell of this past week a piddling prelude to what was about to unfold?

Andy stared down at the sliver of ice pinned beneath his finger. His mind was so many miles away that when a voice sounded suddenly, the jolt that went through Andy's body was enough to topple the glass.

"Senator?"

Andy could only imagine what the expression was on his face as he wheeled about, but whatever it was, it seemed nearly to make the new intern wet her panties.

"I'm . . . I'm sorry. I . . ."

Andy bent down and picked up the glass, grateful for the few seconds to pull himself together. Drinking by himself in his office. For Christ's sake, not terrifically SOP.

"No need to apologize," Andy murmured. "I was just . . ." He trailed off.

The intern's expression was not inquisitive in the slightest. She pushed her hair from her face.

"I'm sorry, I didn't mean to barge in like that. I just thought I should tell you. I've, um . . . I've gone through the day's phone messages. Greg and Linda both checked over my report. Maybe I . . . some people really do call in for funny things, don't they?"

Andy concurred. "They do."

The intern continued. "There is this one message. Actually, it's about five or six of them. I mean, they're all from the same person. Greg said to just erase them. It's some kook. But I haven't erased them yet. I didn't know if—if you wanted to hear them anyway? Just in case? Or is that just me being stupid?"

Andy slowly shook his head. "It's not stupid at all, Lindsay. Why don't we go give them a listen?"

He followed the intern to the outer office. Only one light remained lit, giving the room a snug feel. The two stood on either side of Lindsay's phone, which was at the edge of her small desk.

Lindsay pushed a key on the phone several times. "Here. This is the first one."

Andy allowed his eyes to settle on the intern's face as he awaited the message. She watched him as well, to read his expression. There was a soft *beep* in Andy's ear, followed by a man's voice. It was thick with an Eastern European accent. It could have been from any of a dozen countries.

"This message is for the coward. You know who you are, and I know who you are. That is what is important. I know you. You will want to talk to me, Mr. Big Man. You will want to be good to me. In a very big way."

The man interrupted himself to cough. A burbly smoker's cough. Lindsay's pert eyebrows rose, as if tugged from above by a pair of strings. The man continued.

"If I am your friend, you are free. No problems. But if you are a stupid coward, you will regret this. You want to be my friend. I will call back later, and I will want to talk to you. Make this happen."

The call clicked off. Andy marveled that the young woman couldn't hear his heart slamming in his chest.

"It's silly, right?" Lindsay said. "I should just erase it."

"The other ones?" Andy didn't recognize his own voice.

"They're pretty much the same. He seems to get a little angrier each time. Well, on the last one especially, he's pretty annoyed. Greg said he sounds drunk. I wonder if—"

She was interrupted by the sound of a commotion in the hallway. People were hurrying by the open door. A head appeared in the doorway. It was Senator Cutler from Colorado.

"Andy! Turn on your TV. Wyeth is about to make a statement!"

Cutler disappeared. Andy turned stiffly to the intern.

"Delete them," he said thickly. "Greg's right. He's a crank. I have no idea what he's talking about. Delete them all."

CHAPTER 14

No one at Masters and Weiss had quite decided what to do with Joy Resnick's administrative assistant. The simple fact was, nobody really wanted to absorb Marion Mann into their staff. Marion had always been considered competent as far as her work was concerned, but she was a divisive presence. Not a happy woman. Membership into the natural cliques and affiliations of the workplace had always eluded her, and as a result she tried too hard, pushing her way awkwardly into people's paths, making herself even more unwanted. On more than a few occasions Marion had allowed herself to be taken advantage of by men in the company. Most recently it had been the new jerk over in IT: a bumbling one-night stand in his messy gadget-filled apartment in Queens. Struggling through her hangover the following day, Marion had been mortified to overhear the jerk bragging to some of his buddies in the company lounge that he had "thrown Marion the Man a real bone last night."

The lukewarm feelings Joy Resnick had maintained concerning her assistant were known among the other account executives; everyone had gotten at least one earful over the past seven months. As Joy put it, the fit was just not fitting. In Marion's year-end review, Joy had couched her assistant's shortcomings as "a square-peg problem." Although Marion had been considered mildly quirky when she'd first started at Masters and Weiss—those kicky glasses she wore, along with what had initially passed for an inspired fashion anarchy—much of that quirkiness had failed to prove anywhere near as endearing as Joy had hoped.

Plus all the flirting. The sleeping around.

The end result of all this was that in the wake of her boss's murder, Marion Mann was now finding herself largely adrift at the office. A week after Joy's death, nearly all of her active accounts had been passed off to other account execs, and Marion had spent most of the week filling the other execs in on various nuances of their adopted projects—at least, those aspects that Joy had shared with Marion. But aside from those meetings, Marion had been pretty much free to sit at her desk and grow moss.

Only four days since Joy's funeral, the shock of her murder was still resonating throughout the office. People passing by Joy's office still paused to take a hushed look inside, as if they were peeking into a holy place. Except for the specific files that Marion had disseminated, Joy's office remained exactly as it had been the previous Friday when the pair of detectives from Suffolk County had arrived with their horrific news. Naturally, they had wanted to interview Marion. The interview had taken place in the company's hangar-sized conference room. Sitting at its comically huge table, Marion had felt like Alice in Wonderland in one of her shrinking episodes. The detectives had wanted to know if her boss had shared with Marion her plans for that past weekend. For example, had Joy spoken about anyone joining up with her at the place out on Shelter Island? Did Marion know if Joy Resnick had been seeing anyone? Any recent ex-boyfriends? Any enemies? Had Marion ever overheard her boss on the phone arguing with anyone? Had she seemed upset lately? Distracted? Anything?

Unfortunately for the detectives, Marion had been unable to shine any light on who of Joy Resnick's acquaintances could have possibly had anything to do with her murder. She did admit to the strained quality of her working relationship with her boss. Why bother trying to hide it? Any of a dozen or more other employees at Masters and Weiss would be telling them the same thing; the last thing Marion was going to do was put a false gloss on the matter. She told the detectives that her boss had been a perfectionist—which was true—and that as a result had not always been realistic in what she expected of other people. And not always so kind in the ways she demonstrated her disappointment when those unrealistic expectations went unmet.

"Would you say she had a temper?" one of the detectives had asked. The cute one. Detective Brown Eyes.

"You can write down the word *diva*," Marion had replied pertly. "It's shorter."

She explained to the detectives that there had been a lot expected of Joy at Masters and Weiss. Joy had been the company's golden girl, Mr. Masters's very own plunder some years back from one of the rival firms.

"This job can have plenty of stress, of course," Marion said sagely. "But that's still no reason to treat people the way she sometimes treated them."

Brown Eyes asked, "And this would include you? This sort of treatment you're talking about?"

"Oh, yes. Definitely me." Marion's laughter erupted nervously. "Probably me more than anyone else."

After the grilling, she had returned to her desk particularly proud of her interview. She had not hedged concerning her feelings about Joy. She'd spoken frankly, allowing the detectives to hear that there had been no love lost between her and her late boss. Certainly she had come off as a person with nothing to hide.

Which could not have been further from the truth.

Marion's hand was trembling as she hung up the phone. She paused, then lifted the receiver from its cradle and set it down on the desk. She didn't want it to ring again. She didn't want to hear that horrible syrupy southern voice again. Ever again. On the day after Joy's murder, the man must have phoned Marion half a dozen times at the office, and she had hung up on him each time without a word. All that weekend she had screened all her calls, refusing to pick up when she heard the snaky voice on her answering machine. It had been wishful thinking to assume that after Joy's murder the unnerving man would have simply evaporated from her life. It seemed that just the opposite was developing. He was not going away at all. Not in the slightest.

Marion removed her baroque eyeglasses and set them carefully down on the thick folder atop her desk. Her world went immediately blurry. As if she had descended underwater. Marion pulled a small plastic spray bottle from her top drawer, along with a blue chamois square, and methodically cleaned the lenses of her expensive glasses. Impressionistic blurs moved past her desk.

Looking down at the fuzzy telephone, her mind moved back three months to the night the unwelcome Dixie drawl first crept into her ear. For the umpteenth time that week, she wished with all her heart that she could undo the events that had followed that first phone call.

But of course it was too late for that. Her boss was dead.

And it was Marion's fault.

Late January, and Marion had been home in her apartment in Murray Hill, watching the results show of *Dancing with the Stars*. She'd voted twelve times the night before for the soap opera guy. So *cute,* she couldn't stand it.

The phone began to ring and she had dragged it onto her lap, her eyes still pinned to the screen.

"Marion Mann?"

Male. Southern accent. Strong. Almost a parody.

"Yes, this is Marion."

"I need to confirm here. The same Marion Mann employed at Masters and Weiss Consulting? Your immediate superior is a Ms. Joy Elizabeth Resnick?"

"That's right. Who is this?"

"I need to speak with you, Miss Mann. In person. It's quite important. This concerns Miss Resnick."

On the television, the soap opera guy was goofing around with his dance partner while awaiting the judge's scores. Marion wasn't so keen about that girl. Each week she seemed more naked than the week before. Marion switched the phone to her other ear.

"Who is this?"

"I assure you, it is in your personal interest that you meet with me. Will eight thirty work?"

"Eight . . . You mean tonight?

"There's a very pleasant Thai restaurant down at the end of your block. If I'm not mistaken, you are very fond of their pad thai?"

"How do you know that?"

"It's nice and public there, as you know. There are plenty of other diners. It's all perfectly safe."

"Perfectly safe for what? What the heck is this about? I'm not going—"

"I don't mean to frighten you, Miss Mann, but you most definitely want to meet with me. You'll understand once we've spoken. And please don't make any other calls after we hang up. I can tell you that if you attempt to, your call will be terminated immediately."

"Terminated? What are you talking about? This is some sort of joke, right? I'm hanging up. I'm not meeting anyone anywhere!"

"If you prefer, we can as easily meet in your apartment. I had simply assumed the restaurant would be more comfortable for you."

"My apartment? Oh, I don't think so. Whoever you are, you're not coming here, I can tell you that much."

"I can be there in five minutes."

"And what makes you think I'd let you in?"

"You wouldn't have to let me in, dear."

Marion's blood went cold. "What's that supposed to mean?"

He didn't answer right away. Marion thought for a second maybe he'd hung up. Just some strange crank call. But he hadn't hung up. The man gave a little chuckle.

"Miss Mann, I have a key."

Marion replaced her eyeglasses. She returned the phone to its cradle, and opened the thick folder she had pulled from Joy's files and began leafing through its contents. This was no longer one of the active projects; its termination date was the previous November. Joy had been a gigantic pain in the ass on the account. Marion had never seen such micromanaging from her boss before. Granted, it had been one of the highest-profile projects that Joy had commandeered in her four years with the firm. But even so, that was no reason to terrorize the hired help.

Marion continued flipping through the folder. The scripts, the thirty- and sixty-second spots, the print ads, insertion orders out the wazoo. Charts. Stats. The focus group analyses. Poll numbers. Joy's "inspired" theme packages. Her precious strategy wheels.

Marion's phone rang, and she nearly leaped out of her skin. It couldn't really be *him* again, could it? In the call she had just taken, he'd made the situation absolutely clear to her. What in the world could there be to add?

She hesitated, then picked up the phone. "Joy Res—" She cut herself off, glancing over at the half-open door across the hall. It was *not* Joy Resnick's office anymore.

"Hello. This is Marion Mann. How may I help you?"

"Hi. It's me. I just wanted to make sure we're still on."

Relief flooded her system. It was a voice she welcomed. "Oh, good, it's you. Sure, we're still on. Believe me, there's nothing chaining me to my desk. Is five still good for you?"

"Five. Yes."

"Great. Listen, I could use a drink *now*. I'm psyched. I'll see you soon."

Marion hung up the phone. This was more like it. Drinks after work. And not with any of the snotty clowns in the firm. She was through handing the goods over to that crowd.

Energized, Marion returned to the file folder, finally coming to the photograph she had been seeking. She had wondered if maybe Joy had already removed it from the file, but she hadn't. The photograph had been taken around a month before the closing date for the project. In it the client was dressed in a light blue dress shirt, with his tie pulled loose and his shirtsleeves folded back to his forearms, and he was standing in the wings of a high school auditorium stage. The picture itself didn't indicate the auditorium part, but Marion was familiar with the context. Fantastic news had just arrived. Truly a gift from the gods, and the photograph had caught the client at the precise moment of his reacting to the news. No smile could have been brighter or more joyful. A grease pencil square had been sketched around the client's head, cropping the photograph. That image of his beaming face would be the one dominating the final month of the project. It had been too compelling and appealing to pass up.

Cropped out of the image had been the upper torso of the client, his arms reaching forward to take in the person delivering the glorious news. Also cropped out was the beaming face of the deliverer herself: Joy Resnick. Joy's masterful strategy wheel had spun just as planned and had delivered the goods right on time.

Marion squared the photo on her desk and stared at it for nearly a minute. She happened to know that the evening the photograph was taken had also been the one when her boss and the charismatic client had first climbed into the sack together. Although Senator Andrew Foster's successful reelection was then still a little over thirty days away, the celebration had already begun. And Marion Mann—who had snapped the photograph—had sussed this out all on her own. She had a nose for these things.

Marion slipped the photograph into a large white envelope, which she put into her bag. The photograph had been on her mind ever since the Suffolk County detectives had brought up her boss's social life. By which, of course, they had really meant her private life. By which they meant, who was she sleeping with?

These are things that executive assistants know.

The photograph by itself proved nothing. Even so, Marion still could have fished it out of the file folder and handed it over to the two men without a word. A knowing look to Detective Brown Eyes would have cinched it.

But she hadn't. She hadn't dared to. The man she had been forced to meet with three months previous at the Thai place near her apartment had been blunt in letting her know what the consequences would be if she was ever to utter a word to anyone about Joy Resnick and the married senator. It was a point he had reiterated to Marion in his insidious low tone at Joy's funeral.

"Take a look at that grave, Marion. It doesn't look terribly comfortable, does it? You be smart, Marion. We'd hate to lose a little sweetheart like you at so young an age."

The entire time he had been whispering into her ear, the man's hand had been surreptitiously clenching and unclenching a portion of her rear end. If he was trying to demonstrate to her the tensile strength in his slender fingers, he'd achieved his objective.

Marion turned off her computer and her desk light. The receptionist said nothing to her as she was leaving. Marion was alone when she entered the elevator and was part of a small crowd by the time it reached the lobby.

The Madison Avenue sidewalk was alive with pedestrians. Marion walked the ten blocks north to the bar where she was to meet up with her date. She knew it was silly to get ahead of herself, but she couldn't help it. She needed to have some fun; it had been a rough week. She deserved someone who would treat her right and who appreciated her for all her best qualities. If it ended up getting cozy, what was wrong with that?

Marion picked up her pace. Her step was particularly light, and she covered the ground in no time, maneuvering through the crowded sidewalk with the precision of a slalom skier.

Robert Smallwood rose to meet her. Such a large man. And a gentleman. Smallwood had snared a booth, and he gave Marion a deep, sad-looking smile as she sat down opposite him. He really did seem to be a caring person. That had been Marion's impression at Joy's funeral, when he had sat with her in her car as she had tried to pull herself together. He hadn't pressed her any more about the man in the green coat. He'd been patient and gentle and very kind. Like a harmless bear.

The two sat down in the booth.

"It's good to see you," Smallwood said, placing his hand palm up on the table. The waiter stepped over. He nearly laughed out loud at the sappy expression on the face of the woman with the funky glasses as she delivered her little paw into the mitt of her large, odd-looking friend.

CHAPTER 15

Aleksey Titov's McMansion sat overlooking the green-gray waters of the Atlantic, at the end of Dover Street, in Manhattan Beach. The majority of the furniture was leather. Titov liked leather. White leather. Black leather. Brown leather. Leather the color of dollar bills. Titov liked its smell. He liked the feel of it and the look of it, and he liked the message it sent. An expensive message: the slaughter of cows for the sake of my comfort.

Titov was not much of a reader, but even so, soon after acquiring the house he had lined one entire wall of his ground-floor office with floor-to-ceiling bookshelves and paid a queer little man from Cobble Hill to fill the shelves with leather-bound volumes. There were complete collections of authors and writers Titov had never heard of. On a whim he'd taken a crack once at something by a guy called Trollope—*The Small House at Allington*—but found the experience tedious beyond words. On the rare occasion when Titov actually read anything for pleasure, he wanted *juice*. This Trollope character didn't have nearly enough juice. But the book cover was a nice copper leather with the title embossed in gold, so that was good.

Titov's living room was on the second level of the house, looking out onto the ocean. Chrome gooseneck lamps with helmet-shaped globes spouted from five different areas of the room. The leather sling chairs cost over two thousand dollars apiece. Twenty-five big ones for the L-shaped couch, which was white leather with black leather throw pillows. Dead cows everywhere. The fireplace was white brick. A black leather sling held the firewood.

Moo.

Directly above the living room was the master bedroom, also with a spectacular view of the ocean. Titov liked to tell people that his bed was the size of Rhode Island; he thought that was a clever line. Out of Titov's earshot, there were some who would add that his wife's hair was about that big. Gala Titov was a good nine inches taller than her husband, not including the hair. She was broad-hipped and big-boned, and possessed of an insatiable sexual appetite. The woman also enjoyed a little slapping now and then, which suited Titov just fine. Making love to his wife was like wrestling with a volatile bear. The rough stuff came a lot easier to him than all that cooing and gooing. That other crap just didn't work for the little thug.

Aleksey Titov never used his knuckles when he hit someone; instead it was always the balled part of his fist, the fleshy underside. He punched with the motion of a person wielding a knife. As a teenager in Moscow he had once received just such a beating, and it had made a lasting impression on him.

Now he was looking to make an impression of his own.

Leonard Bulakov was wheezing loudly. His lower lip was swollen to twice its normal size and split in two places. There was no white showing in his right eye, the one on which Aleksey Titov had been concentrating, only a lacework of red.

It was Leonard's nose that was causing the wheezing. The cartilage on the bridge had collapsed under Titov's relentless pounding, and both nostrils were flattened and clogged with blood, but Titov had not allowed the man to wipe any of it away. He had also warned Leonard that if any of that blood found its way onto any of his leather books or furniture, there would be additional hell to pay.

Titov had screwed up from the very first, and he knew it. Assigning a dullard such as Dimitri Bulakov to the job on Shelter Island had been a monumental lapse of judgment. The wrong bone to the wrong dog. Titov could not fathom why he had been so cavalier in sending Dimitri Bulakov out to do the job, but there was nothing to be done about that decision now. Titov's client was spitting nails. He wanted what he'd spent handsomely for, and Titov knew full well there would be real hell to pay if he did not deliver. Titov was under a microscope these days. Recently, his name had found its way into the newspapers in connection with certain activities that the U.S. government had a history of frowning on, and it had taken no small expenditure of effort on Titov's part to keep matters contained. Titov's client—a man he had never met directly—had presented himself as someone who knew a thing or two about such matters, and he had promised the mobster with regard to the "project" he was offering that he would advocate for Titov and help his problems disappear.

The project had seemed simple: a man, a woman, a hideaway out near the tip of Long Island. But now it wasn't simple. Upon hearing from Aleksey Titov about the complications brought on by Dimitri Bulakov, the client had been lethally precise in his explanation of how things were going to unfold for Titov if that video file fell into anyone else's hand but his. He was giving Titov until the end of the weekend to make matters right. Sunday, and no further. End of story.

Titov gave a signal, and the man keeping Leonard Bulakov from slipping to the floor dragged him to a chair that was covered with a large towel and dropped him into it. Leonard collapsed forward, his forehead hovering several inches above his knees.

Titov's man was named Anton Gregor. Gregor was hard-packed muscle in a modest-sized frame. Dirty blond hair and pale blue eyes. If it had been Gregor's nature to generate empathy, he might have done so for Leonard Bulakov and his ruined nose. Gregor's own nose was well on its way to hell. Flat on the bridge, torqued slightly to the left, and scarred like distressed leather. Gregor wore a sky-blue wide-collared shirt with the top three buttons undone, tight black jeans, and deeply scuffed cowboy boots. He lifted his foot and used the tip of one of those boots to nudge gently against Leonard Bulakov's ear. A quasi-human sound emerged from the man.

Titov spoke up.

"Leonard, I am only sorry that it is you we had to speak with like this and not your brother. Dimitri is giving me no choice. The message I need to send to him is that this is what will happen to the people he loves until he comes to his senses. I would prefer to tell this to him face-to-face, but he makes this impossible. So I have no choice but to ask you to deliver this message. I do not have the time for Dimitri to misunderstand me. What happened to you here—this happens to Dimitri unless he becomes smart and gives me what is mine. You will tell him this for me?"

Leonard Bulakov stirred. His head rose partway. Titov gave another signal, and Gregor produced a handkerchief and shoved it into Leonard's hand. Leonard brought it to his broken face.

"I don't . . . Dimitri is not saying to me where he is."

"Then you need to convince him, Leonard," Titov said. "He needs to come see me. Call him. Call his wife. I am putting Anton here in charge of locating Dimitri and returning to me what is mine. You will answer to him next time. With no offense, Anton is not a polite man. He is very less polite than me. But he is a loyal man, and his loyalty is to me and to what I want."

Gregor gave his boss a smirk and stepped over to an open closet.

Titov snapped. "Sit up, Leonard! Now!"

Leonard complied. His one good eye blinked plaintively. The handkerchief was turning red in his hand. Gregor reached into the closet. Leonard could not see what he was up to.

Titov crossed his arms on his small, puffed-up chest. "Remind me, Leonard. Are you left-handed or right-handed?"

Gregor stepped back over from the closet. Leonard twisted his head in order to find the man with his good eye. What he saw was that the hoodlum was holding a thick rubber mallet.

CHAPTER 16

Andy's promotional schedule called for the weekend to be spent in the Boston area. There had been some talk midweek about canceling the senator's appearances due to the injury to his head, but Andy had assured his publicist that he was fine and more than capable of making the trek.

Andy and Christine had decided to make it a getaway weekend for the two of them. On Friday morning, Christine packed an overnight bag for Michelle. Their daughter would be staying with Whitney and Jenny for the weekend. Michelle's best friend, Emily, was going with her. Paul Jordan was picking the girls up after classes at Little Red and driving them up to Greenwich in the Bentley. Christine felt a little uneasy with the plan—the privileged princesses scene was not one she enjoyed promoting—but she was simply too busy to run the girls up herself after school and still catch the shuttle in time to make the seven o'clock event in Boston.

Michelle got her fifty-seventh cupcake of the year at Boho, a little miffed when she learned that her secret boyfriend had called in sick. After her morning cappuccino, Christine swung by the framers on Hudson Street. At Easter her father had requested that Christine be sure to snap at least one photograph of each child so that he could present the photographs to the parents as mementos of the afternoon. A classic Whitney touch. Christine had chosen an array of brightly colored wooden frames for the pictures. The order was ready, but none of the frames had been wrapped for protection. Christine helped the clerk wrap the frames in brown paper and she left with them in a shopping bag. Retracing her steps, she dropped the bag off with the receptionist at Little Red, to give to Michelle to take up to Granddad.

Christine's appointment was in SoHo, at a place on Greene Street she'd been going to for five or six years. As she headed east on Prince Street she spotted a woman emerging from a residential building midblock. Christine grabbed her camera and fired off a series of shots as the woman crossed the street directly in front of her. The woman disappeared into a café, and Christine continued on to her appointment.

"Here," she said as she took her seat. She held up her camera, scrolling through the most recent images. "Do that."

Andy had flown up earlier in the day from D.C. to put in an appearance at an afternoon talk-news-entertainment program called *Your World,* which broadcast in the Boston area at noon. Despite his request that the issue of the vice president's current "situation" be left out of the discussion ("I'm here to push product," Andy had joked, waving his book in the air), the be-witching Lebanese-Australian co-host of the show had pressed him nonetheless.

"Seriously, Senator. If you're not aware that your name is being bandied about as a possible replacement for Vice President Wyeth, then you are seriously out of touch."

Andy's reply had been that if in fact he was so out of touch, then what sort of vice president did she really think he would make? The woman had flashed her chocolate eyes mischievously.

"Oh. A very handsome one. We already know that much."

Andy made a scheduled appearance that afternoon at Booksmith in Brookline, where he spoke briefly about his book to a sizable crowd, then settled in at a table to sign copies. Two local news outfits had sent crews to the store, but this time the publicist was able to act as a firewall and insist that the crews only take footage of the event; there would be no in-terviewing the senator. Of course, there was nothing to keep the cus-tomers who were lined up to get their books signed from expressing their thoughts to Andy about the current uncertainties within the Beltway. Andy fielded the comments with a practiced nonchalance, disarming jokes, declarations of his complete confidence in the system and the American people: his ready arsenal of nonresponse responses.

The evening's event was at a bookstore in Cambridge, and all of the chairs were filled by the time Andy and his publicist arrived. The standing-room-only crowd extended back from the events area all the way to the magazines section. The publicist was pleased.

Just before the senator was scheduled to begin his talk, a woman with tousled ginger-colored bangs and a terrifically appealing smile materialized in front of him and planted a kiss on his lips. A flash of confusion played over Andy's face, then he caught hold of the woman's arms.

"My God. Mrs. Miniver. Is that you?"

Christine poked her fingers into her hair. "Spur of the moment. You like it?"

"You look fantastic."

She gave him a playful scowl. "And how did I look before?"

Andy laughed. "I'm sorry, lady, but is the word *stupid* tattooed on my forehead? You could be wearing a gunnysack and be as bald as a cue ball and I'd still see my sweet, loving angel."

Christine's eyes rolled. "Oh my God, please. I flew all the way up here for a crock like that?"

Andy introduced Christine to the publicist, and the two chatted while Andy had a word with the bookstore's point person about his introduction. The publicist told Christine that he had reserved a chair for her in the front row, but Christine said she would prefer to stand.

"I'd like to take some pictures. Will that be a problem?"

She was assured that it wouldn't be. The bookstore rep introduced Andy to the crowd, and the senator launched into his spiel. The spiel was mainly canned, but Andy was good at making it sound fresh. His eyes traveled across the faces before him, connecting directly with as many as possible. Generally, they laughed where he wanted them to and were rapt where they should be rapt. Andy was a little annoyed when another TV news crew appeared halfway through his presentation and flicked on its glaring lights, but he did his best not to let on.

Considerably more distracting than the camera lights was his own wife. Andy was long accustomed to Christine's darting about with her camera, but tonight was different. Andy had not merely been playing spouse politics when he'd told Christine that her new hairstyle looked fantastic. It did. Not that she needed any years trimmed off, but the more casual style served that function anyway. On a whim, Andy decided to bypass the several excerpts he usually chose to read from and instead read from the section he had written about his first encounter with the daughter of then-ambassador Hoyt, back in their college days. Christine was standing off to the side of the crowd, some twenty or so rows back, and when she heard what her husband was reading, she stopped taking pictures and lowered her camera. As Andy recounted those golden days of their first getting to know each other, Christine was surprised to realize that tears were rising into her eyes. No less so than when Andy brought the section to a nifty close.

"To this day she has remained the source of light in my life."

He closed the book and gestured toward the woman with the glistening eyes and the camera slung around her neck.

"I ask you. Am I not right? Is she not absolutely radiant?"

Hours later, Andy and Christine made love for the first time in over a week. The hotel bed was huge and the couple hungrily explored its acreage. As his wife moved slickly beneath him, so perfectly calibrated with his own movements, Andy swore to himself yet again that his silly risky days were behind him. Why in the world would he unnecessarily put his perfect, perfect life in peril?

Was the word *stupid* tattooed on his forehead?

Andy was resolved. Christine was all the woman he ever needed. Ever. The visceral relief that surged through his system as this determination announced itself to him was palpable. Christine felt it. She squirmed beneath him, trying to accommodate this very evident infusion of energy that was inhabiting her husband.

"Jesus, Andy," she whispered into his rough cheek. "Jesus, Jesus, Jesus . . ."

CHAPTER 17

After a late breakfast, the Fosters rented a car and drove up to Marble-head for some beach time. A skittish wind forced them into purchasing a pair of heavy sweatshirts before they headed out onto the sand.

Christine made a point of keeping her camera in the car. She loved the rough ocean here and the massive black boulders scattered about the sand, and she could handily have taken dozens of pictures. But she didn't. For once, her instinct was to put the camera aside and enjoy the time with her husband unfiltered.

Christine and Andy had still barely broached the subject of the Chris Wyeth mess. Andy had flown back to D.C. first thing the Monday morning after Easter, and their several phone conversations over the week had drifted in other directions. Besides which, Christine told herself, Chris made his play to the nation on television the other night, professing his innocence of all alleged charges. He was going to fight this thing. The whole question could well be moot.

An elderly couple walking the opposite direction on the beach recognized Senator Andy. They were solid New England Yankees with lined, weathered faces and cotton-white hair, their worn and faded casual garb the slightly shabbier cousins of what nowadays fills the pages of the L.L.Bean and Lands' End catalogs. The man immediately engaged Andy on the subject of the vice presidency mess. The couple bookended Andy, giving him little space to escape. Christine was able to wander off without objection. She stepped down to the flat sand, bracing herself against the first rush of water as it rushed up to her ankles.

Gazing on the turbulent water, Christine allowed herself to admit how much anger had been crashing about within her of late. It seemed so plainly evident now that her husband had been moving in and out of a sort of fugue state over the past week. Or at least as fugue as someone such as Andy was likely to get. Naturally, the Chris Wyeth issue was weighing on his mind. Not only was there hanging in the air the surreal possibility of

Andy's being asked by President Hyland to consider stepping into the potential void, but for goodness' sake, Chris Wyeth was such an old acquaintance of Andy's! There was a lot of history there. It was only natural that Andy would be preoccupied with his friend's troubles. Those moments of drift that Christine could now identify in her husband over the past six or seven days were perfectly natural. In one way of looking at it, it was insensitive of Christine not to draw Andy out on the matter. At least to the point of finding out if he wanted to discuss it.

Andy stepped up behind her. The Yankee septuagenarians had finished with their grilling and were continuing down the coast. He wrapped his arms around Christine, and the two stood in a long silence, watching the waves of the ocean do what waves of the ocean do.

Christine bit down gently on her lip. *Not now,* she said to herself. *Not yet.*

They made love again back at the hotel, then fell into a pair of heavy naps. Christine rose more groggily from hers, and even after her shower she still felt a little as if she had been drugged. She towel-dried her hair and swept it into place with her fingers.

Nice.

Andy was to be interviewed that evening onstage at the JFK School of Government, in front of a paying audience. There would be a reception afterward, then a late dinner at the Beacon Hill home of Andy's Massachusetts counterpart in the Senate.

While the two were getting dressed, Jim Fergus called. Andy took the call in his black socks and boxers, his white oxford shirt halfway buttoned. The conversation was short, though still long enough to irritate him. Christine, over by the dresser putting on her earrings, watched him in the mirror.

"Well, Jim," Andy said testily. "How much nicer if you could just be up onstage and do all the damn talking for me. How about that? I'll just sit off to the side looking cute."

He flipped the phone closed and tossed it onto the bed. "I should have been a fucking Yorkshire sheep farmer," he muttered. The comment was a standing joke between Andy and Christine. Its intention was for levity, but Andy's mood seeped through completely.

"Yorkshire farmers have troubles, too," Christine said.

"They don't have Jim Fergus."

"Honey, you love Jim."

Andy didn't want to hear it. "Well, I guess if I pay the man to do my worrying for me, he's doing a bang-up job." He gestured at the phone on the bed. "In the event that *the topic* comes up tonight, which it will, he doesn't want me to say one single word in Chris's defense. He just used the phrase 'Don't align with a loser.' Isn't that sweet? Jim is positive that Chris is going down. He has these mice he listens to."

"Mice?"

Andy waved a hand. "Never mind. The point is, he feels it's time to start putting a clear distance between Chris and myself."

He reached for his pants and put them on. He tugged his belt tight. "Essentially, Jim wants me to moralize. I'm to talk about transparency and honesty and all that good stuff. All in the abstract, of course. For Christ's sake, I couldn't be specific about what Chris is supposed to have done if I wanted to. I'm totally in the dark about it."

Christine was running dark lines around her eyes. "Probably a good place to be."

"I suppose. Jim wants me to use the word *integrity*. At least four times, he said. He was serious. That's my word: *integrity*. Four times at a minimum. He's got this down to a science. He probably looked it up in the focus-group manual. Jim's been pulling strings with Mitch Cutler's and Barry Jefferson's people. They're both scheduled to hit the talk shows tomorrow. Would you care for a preview of what they're going to say?"

Christine paused with her lipstick and addressed her husband in the mirror. "Let me guess. 'Senator Andrew Foster is a fine man. A man of real integrity.' "

"Exactly. I'm now wearing the scarlet *I,* thank you very much."

"Well, it could be worse."

Andy stepped up behind his wife. His scowling face hovered over her shoulder. He started in on his tie, but he was all knuckles. Christine swiveled around and took over the job for him.

"Here. You're getting yourself all worked up. Hands off."

With those dark lines etched around them, her beautiful green eyes had an almost Egyptian quality. As Andy looked down at her deftly work-ing the tie, his sense of shame welled up. Shame and cowardice. His beau-tiful wife deserved better than he was giving. In all their years together, she had rarely complained about the bifurcation in their marriage brought on by his career, his workweek spent largely down in D.C. Theirs was already a relationship with unavoidable gaps; the last thing Christine deserved was to have her husband digging outright chasms. What she deserved was nothing less than complete honesty on Andy's part. The short weekend was going so nicely for the two of them; they were being reminded of their potential as a couple. Everything could be perfect.

But it wasn't. Andy watched his wife flipping the ends of his tie and his heart seized. Christine was loving a fraud. The man standing there was a facsimile of the husband she thought she had. *For Christ's sake,* Andy thought, *She doesn't even know who I am.*

He wanted to tell her. But that would be suicide. She would be justified in running the knot of his tie right up to his windpipe and squeezing it with all her might until the empty man toppled over dead. If *he* were in his right mind, he would welcome it.

Christine finished up the tie for him and patted him lightly on the chest.

"Time to buck up, Senator Big Shot. People aren't paying good money tonight to listen to an old sourpuss."

Christine stepped past him and over to the closet. Andy remained a moment, looking at his reflection in the mirror. He massaged his jaw and presented himself with the demeanor that was expected of him. She was right, of course. People were expecting certain things of him. But even as he practiced his winning smile, his heart dropped deep into the abyss.

Someone *did* know.

This message is for the coward. You know who you are, and I know who you are. That is what is important. I know you . . .

The interview went well. Andy's interlocutor was Scot Lehigh, the *Globe* columnist, and Lehigh opened the interview speaking of cracking open Andy's book first thing in the morning in his hammock up at his cottage in Maine and how he had missed an entire day of windsurfing as a result of his being unable to put the book down.

"You owe me, Senator," Lehigh joked.

Andy graced the anecdote. "Next time I'll write a dud, Scot. I promise."

For the bulk of the interview Lehigh held to matters relating to Andy's book. Only near the conclusion of the event did the columnist signal the shift of the discussion with both his body language and a palpable eagerness in his voice.

"Senator, I'd be tossed out of the fraternity if I weren't to ask you. You know what's coming. Chris Wyeth."

Andy leaned forward in his chair and leveled the columnist with a deadpan stare of intensity.

"Scot, could you maybe put that in the form of a question?"

The audience laughed, as did Lehigh. Andy continued on, speaking eloquently about the vice president. He did not distance himself from the embattled executive. At the same time, he certainly didn't take the man into any figurative bear hugs. Mainly Andy stuck with an appreciative recitation of Chris Wyeth's impressive résumé and his list of quantifiable achievements as a husband, a father, and a public servant. Christine noted, if no one else did, that "as a friend" did not make the cut.

Overall, the senator was affable and witty. He'd peppered the interview with several lengthy anecdotes. Before wrapping up, Andy spoke movingly on the role of public service and of his passion for seeking solutions for those who had little voice in matters that profoundly affect their own lives. In all, it was vintage Andy Foster. Even from her seat in the front row, Christine could sense that the crowd was eating out of her husband's hand. As she knew all too well, he was a hard person not to like.

And he had delivered the word *integrity* seven times.

Okay, Christine thought as she rose to join the standing ovation. *We've got that clear now.*

CHAPTER 18

Dimitri Bulakov spent most of the weekend drinking and smoking and watching television and yelling at his wife. The only times the television was not on were when Dimitri nodded off into a deep enough sleep that Irena could dare shut it off. Those infrequent periods of silence—Irena had long since trained herself to deafness with regard to Dimitri's raspy snoring—were blessings. Irena hated the television, and she hated the hours of her husband's life lost to the insipid garbage that Dimitri watched. Hours adding up to days, days adding up to months. It was such a waste, and it left her so lonely.

Dimitri was too nervous about being recognized by one of Aleksey Titov's goons to dare venture outside the room. Dimitri's brother had called him on his cell phone on Friday in a state of despair, telling Dimitri what Titov and his soulless employee had done to him. Dimitri had barely been able to recognize his own brother's voice.

"Dimitri. Whatever this is, you must stop. Our business is destroyed, Dimitri. I . . . I have been mutilated. Why is this, Dimitri? Whatever you are doing, you must stop. Aleksey will kill you, Dimitri. You and Irena both. This is a fact."

Dimitri had instructed his brother to leave Brighton Beach immediately. "Go away, Leonard. In a week, I promise, I will make Titov happy and I will make you happy. You must trust me. I will make everything good."

He also told his brother not to bother calling him again.

"This is for your safety, Leonard. I will call Titov and tell him myself. You will have no more contact with me. He has no reason to hurt you again. I will not be using this phone again. You see? His threats to you will be no use. It is now me who is calling all of the shots, Leonard. Trust me."

Dimitri had given Irena money to go out and purchase a disposable cell phone. Irena almost called Leonard while she was on the errand, but she had gotten scared that if she did so, she might inadvertently cause more trouble for her brother-in-law.

With her new blond hair and large sunglasses, Irena was the one who could move safely around the streets of Coney Island, though Dimitri insisted that she spend as little time as necessary away from the room. Mainly she fetched cigarettes and beer and food, mostly fried chicken and potatoes.

The room was taking on all the odors of the Bulakov diet: the sweet tang of beer, complimented by grease, infused with the stale smell of an overflowing ashtray. Dimitri had stopped shaving. His large jaw was looking increasingly smudged. His eyes were raw and tender, glazed from the beer and the hours of staring at the television. The first several nights at the hotel, Dimitri had insisted on climbing atop his wife and taking his pleasure. It certainly wasn't *her* pleasure, the hairy beer keg thrusting and grunting and exhaling his vapors on her. Irena always kept her eyes shut these days when she was making love with her husband. It was better this way; it gave her the fighting chance to reimagine Dimitri as the man she had fallen in love with. Dimitri usually reached his climaxes as Irena was only just beginning to sense her own faint stirrings, and he was always very rough at the end. His final belly flop rarely failed to knock most of the breath from Irena's lungs. Soon enough afterward he would slide off her, and she would be free to breathe and, if she wished, secretly take over where her husband had left off. Dimitri was always fast asleep, well into his sea-shanty snoring, by the time Irena's body clenched in its small tremor. Only then would she open her eyes to the familiar darkness. It was a darkness matched in too many ways by the deep hues within her heart.

The only other activity that occupied Dimitri's time were the sessions he spent in front of his laptop. Irena was forbidden to see what it was he was looking at. He would attach the blue flash drive to the computer, put on his headset, and back himself up to the flimsy headboard with the computer perched on a pillow on his lap. Irena could freely study her husband's face as he peered at the screen. His concentration sometimes was fierce. In a funny way, he almost looked intelligent peering the way he did at the images. Irena knew that whatever it was that was holding her husband so spellbound on his computer was the thing responsible for all that was taking place. It related to Aleksey Titov, of course, and certainly it was related to Dimitri's spasmodic pronouncements of "When we have our money . . ."

"What money?" Irena would implore. "When money? Why *our* money?"

Dimitri was no longer even acknowledging the questions.

Irena's only clue as to what was holding her and Dimitri hostage in this hotel room came that Sunday morning. She was arriving back at the room with a Styrofoam container of eggs and bacon and the Yankees baseball cap and sunglasses that Dimitri had told her to buy for him. She had paused at the door before knocking. Dimitri had given her two special knocks, one to let him know that she was by herself, the other to use in case anybody had identified her and forced her to lead them to him. Just as Irena was raising her fist to knock, she heard a sound like breaking glass coming from inside the room. The sound was followed several seconds later by a woman screaming. The television, Irena thought, and she knocked on the door. *Rap, rap.* Pause. *Rap.* The sounds ceased abruptly. The door opened, and a red-faced Dimitri grabbed Irena by the arm and pulled her forcibly into the room. The food spilled on the floor.

"What are you! *Spying?* You think now you are a spy?"

His fist was closed when he hit her. She fell sideways, catching her balance against the dresser. In the mirror she caught a reflection of the laptop, in its usual place atop the pillow. She could make out nothing on the screen except the movement of figures in a dark setting. Dimitri lurched over to the bed and flipped the computer shut.

"I am *protecting* you! Don't you see this! Do not be so stupid, Irena. You will trust me. Anything else and you will be *dead*! Are you understanding?"

The bruise came up within five minutes, just below the left eye. A lump the size of a mothball and the color of a ripe thundercloud.

Dimitri remained annoyed. "Do your sunglasses hide this?"

Normally he was kinder in the wake of hitting her. But now he simply cracked open another beer, showing more concern for the foam that spilled out onto his fingers.

The sunglasses did cover almost all of the black eye. Only a trace of purple halo peeked from beneath the dark lens.

"Good," Dimitri snorted.

Irena closed her eyes. She refused to cry. It had never helped in the past, and it was not going to help now. She wanted the old Dimitri back. She wanted the man she had married. She wanted to open her eyes and remove the sunglasses and be sharing with the old Dimitri a boundless field of yellow flowers.

CHAPTER 19

Robert Smallwood emerged from underground at Seventy-seventh Street and headed west toward Fifth Avenue. The day was uncommonly warm, and as Smallwood walked he felt his usual perspiration points activating, almost like timed explosions.

At the corner of Seventy-ninth and Fifth, Smallwood approached the iron-barred glass doors of the Cultural Services building of the French embassy and peered through the glass. In the middle of the circular lobby stood a modest-sized marble sculpture that had only several years back been authenticated as an early work of Michelangelo. All the years it had stood there, the sculpture had remained unidentified. An art professor from New York University had spied it one evening while attending a function at the consulate and, noting certain features of the sculpture, had shared his suspicions with his colleagues in the art world. After it was determined that the Marble Boy, as the work had unoriginally been dubbed, was indeed a work of the teenage Michelangelo, a skirmish had kicked up between the consulate and its nearby neighbor, the Metropolitan Museum of Art. There being—amazingly enough—no known Michelangelos in any museum in the United States, the Met had declared "the appropriateness" of trundling the sculpture up the street for enshrinement in the Great Treasure House. Of course, the French government rejected the argument as a preposterous and blatant attempt at cultural imperialism, and in the end the Marble Boy remained with the French.

Smallwood spent a minute gazing through the doors at the fragile figure, then crossed the street over to the museum. He picked up a pair of day badges from the membership desk, showing his employee ID to get them free of charge, then he parked himself next to the entrance to the gift shop to wait.

And wait.

Marion Mann was late. They had agreed to meet at eleven o'clock, and by eleven thirty she still had not shown. The large man's perspiration had long since had its way with him. Smallwood would have taken off the sports coat he had chosen, but this would have nullified the desired effect. Among the various lies that he had fed like chocolates to the gullible woman when they'd met at the bar the other day was the tall tale of his own employment. He'd told Marion that he held a position as a professor of art history at Columbia University, polishing the lie with the story of the discovery of the early Michelangelo at the French Cultural Services building, and further buffing up his own credentials by presenting himself as one of the experts who had been brought in to verify the Marble Boy's parentage. Marion had been duly impressed, exactly as Smallwood had intended her to be.

At 11:40, Smallwood began contending with the very real possibility that Marion Mann was not going to show. The notion depressed him nearly as much as it also pricked his anger. He'd been enormously solicitous to the woman, feeding her merlots and feigning interest in her thoroughly tedious-sounding life. Naturally, he had steered the conversation as often as possible onto the topic of his cousin, dipping his hook into the waters of Marion's knowledge of her late boss's activities in hopes of snaring the information that he was craving. He was dying to determine if the man who had approached Marion Mann at Cousin Joy's funeral and so clearly disturbed her was the same man whom Smallwood had dispatched with the iron pipe out at the house. Smallwood had gently broached the subject several times over their merlots, but each time Marion had evaded his questions. The evening had ended with no revelations as to the man's identity, and so Smallwood had proposed a rendezvous at the museum for Sunday morning, hoping he could devise the means by which to convince Marion Mann to open up. By that point in the evening, Smallwood had already endured the woman's wine-driven descent into clumsy flirtatiousness. He'd maintained his composure. Even when she pressed her taut body against his as they parted, Smallwood had gamely accepted the maneuver as his price to pay for pursuing his goals. When she had followed the clench by looking up at him in search of a good-night kiss, it had been all Smallwood could do to resist pressing his thumbs into the lenses of her screwball eyeglasses.

At 11:47, Marion Mann came hurrying through the museum entrance. She came into the vast museum lobby and stopped just shy of the information desk, swiveling her head left and right, putting her exotic eyewear to work. Smallwood spotted her before she spotted him. In his mind's eye, he etched a quick frame around her and hung her up on a wall. *Marion at the Museum.* She was wearing white Capri pants that were practically painted on, an equally tight-fitting flowery top—cut low—and a floppy straw hat ringed with a wide yellow ribbon. Fashion disaster. Smallwood decided that nobody threw together such an ensemble casually. This was something she had actually *aimed* for.

Making a show of unbuttoning his coat, Smallwood came forward. A smile leaped to Marion's anxious face.

"Oh. Hi! God, I'm so sorry I'm late."

There had to be touching. Smallwood grabbed hold of Marion's hands, the easier to sidestep the hug. Marion's beaming face tilted upward expectantly and Smallwood put a light kiss on its cheek, his eyes darting toward the information desk to see if there was anybody on duty who might recognize him. Marion's small hands squeezed his fingers tightly, then delayed in their release. Smallwood's unavoidable glimpse down the petite woman's low-cut collar disgusted him.

Marion wanted to see the van Eycks. Smallwood's eyes glazed over. He was so sick of the fucking van Eycks.

"Perfect," he said, showing his small teeth in a smile.

Marion stood in front of the Arnolfini Portrait as Smallwood rattled off factoids about the Flemish school in general and about Jan van Eyck in particular. He gave her the whole la la la about the painter's use of light and the painstaking re-creations of elaborate materials and fabrics. It was impossible to spend day after day in the galleries as Smallwood did and not pick up tidbits from the different docent talks. Smallwood had forgotten who the pregnant-looking woman in the painting was supposed to be in real life, so he just told Marion that it was van Eyck's younger sister. He indicated the figure's seemingly swollen belly.

"Local cleric. Huge scandal." Complete lie.

Marion was fascinated. He knew she would be. She was pathetic.

Smallwood guided his date through various other galleries, reciting snippets from the hundreds of talks he had heard over the years. He explained how Sargent had caused such a scandal with his original *Madame X,* placing the gilded shoulder strap of the haughty beauty's gown on her upper arm instead of up on her shoulder, and how he had been forced by Paris patronage society to rework the painting and put the strap aright or else face complete censure. Marion drank it up. This whole professor of art history thing—it was a snap.

The two had a light lunch in the trustees' dining room. Smallwood had lifted a pair of passes from the membership desk before leaving work the day before. Personally, he thought the trustees' dining room was a dreary dump. The public cafeteria was far and away the preferable place to go. But the venue allowed Smallwood to introduce a bottle of merlot onto the scene, and as he had witnessed during their previous meeting, Marion Mann was unabashed in her enjoyment of the medium-bodied grape. Over dry salmon and a limp salad, Smallwood forced himself yet again to feign interest in the minutiae of Marion's life and in her views on topics that were of zero interest to him. For the most part, he was able to convert her words to mere noise by the time they reached his brain. A nod here, the visual pretense of interest there; it took quite little on his part to appear engaged.

Thank God for small favors.

As the wine and Smallwood's parody of paying attention unloosed Marion's tongue, her chatter confirmed for Smallwood what he had previously concluded about the woman: Her life was completely void of meaning. She knew nothing about everything and everything about nothing; she was a space filler and very little else. The funny glasses, the sharp black bangs and the overly made-up lips, the drooping cut of her flouncy blouse—if he tried hard, Smallwood supposed he could find her amusing. As it was, the longer she prattled on in her nervous, inane way about nothing, what he really wanted to do was reach across the table and close his hands around her pale little birdlike neck. But he didn't. He allowed the woman her jabbering. He even allowed her to toy with his pinky, which by the time Smallwood ordered the second bottle of merlot the queer woman was doing obsessively. She might have been measuring the digit for a suit.

"Shall we go?"

Smallwood's apple tart sat partially eviscerated in front of him, bleeding vanilla ice cream onto the plate. The second bottle of wine had leveled off just beneath the label. Marion's eyes were brilliantly lit behind her lenses.

"Go?"

"Shall we go?" Smallwood said again, doing his best to bite back the note of sarcasm. He was only partly successful. "Leave? Vacate the premises?"

"Well. Okay. If you want."

Marion fetched her straw hat from the empty chair and placed it on her head. Her hand remained a moment on top of the hat, as if it were glued there. Her crooked arm looked to Smallwood like the handle of a teacup.

She asked, "Where should we go?"

Smallwood felt his furious heart slamming to free itself of its ribbed cage. He forced himself to remain calm. If he had to shake the damn woman like a rag doll until the information he wanted finally fell out, then that's the way it would have to go. His patience was about to expire.

"I was thinking about your place," Smallwood said.

Christine and Andy's driver coming in from La Guardia wanted to talk about the current political situation with his passengers, but Andy stopped him.

"My wife and I prefer silence," he snapped, one shade below testy. "If you don't mind."

The driver shut up. Andy and Christine gazed out separate windows the entire way into the city. Something unyielding had descended between them over the course of the weekend. Both were keenly aware of it; neither wished to discuss it.

They arrived at the apartment, and after dropping off their bags in the bedroom, Christine got on the phone with Michelle up in Greenwich. Andy went into his office and closed the door. Forty minutes later, Christine poked her head in. Andy was seated at his desk, a scotch and soda in his hand, gazing up toward the ceiling.

Christine waded in. "Andy. Is everything all right with us?"

With seeming reluctance, Andy came partway down out of the clouds. "We're fine," he said. "I've just got a ton on my mind right now."

Christine tried again. "Care to share any of it?"

Andy looked across the room at her. For a moment he looked as if he thought the idea might just have some merit. His eyes took in his wife for several long seconds.

"I'm sorry, sweetheart. No. I don't think so."

Marion came in from the kitchen pouting and dropped the white envelope on the coffee table. Smallwood was standing at a chrome and glass shelf unit, looking, uninterested, at Marion's collection of framed photographs.

"Are these your boyfriends?" he asked mockingly. His tone went undisguised. Ever since getting into the taxi at the museum, Smallwood's courtly facade had fallen away.

Marion was unhappy. Could things have really gone sour so soon?

"Those are my brothers."

"Stout lads," Smallwood said. He turned away from the photographs and settled into Marion's round swiveling red chair. Her prize possession. Marion sat down on the couch. She aimed a wounded look across the room.

"I shouldn't tell you anything."

All this man wanted to talk about was Joy. He was obsessed. The entire way downtown in the taxi he had pumped her for information about his deceased cousin. It was depressing.

Smallwood pivoted smartly in the chair. It looked like a giant cherry with a giant's bite taken out of it.

"You're wrong," he said snippily. "I think you should tell me everything. She was my cousin, after all. Family has a right to know everything."

Marion glanced down anxiously at the envelope on the table.

"I don't like being bullied."

Smallwood knew he was going to win. That much was obvious. How could a man with his brain not best a hurt little pup? Smallwood felt as if Marion Mann's brain was made of clear crystal and that the machinery was exposed for all to see. He could see the gears working. She was pouting, and she wanted his pity. This could be her only form of victory, the simple eliciting of Smallwood's sympathy. A pathetic victory. But okay, if you can't lead with your strength, lead with your weakness.

Smallwood locked his oversize eyes on the woman. "Who was my cousin screwing?"

Marion appeared ready to cry. "Why are you being so mean all of a sudden?"

"I'm not being mean at all," Smallwood said. "You're being coy."

"No, I'm not."

"What's in the envelope?"

"I shouldn't be telling you this," Marion said. "That was the whole point. That I keep my mouth shut."

"The whole point of what?"

"The man at Joy's funeral. If he knew I was talking to you, I'd be in big trouble."

"By talking to *me*?"

"By talking to anyone."

Haltingly, she told Smallwood the story about the man's phone call back in January and his insistence that the two meet that night to discuss a matter concerning Joy. Smallwood interrupted her as she told how he had given her no real choice but to agree to meet with him.

"How did he have a key to your place?"

Marion let her hands drop heavily to the couch. "How did he have a key to my *life*? I don't know! That was the thing. He *knew* things. It was just so creepy. He knew things about me and about my family. He knew that my relationship with Joy was strained. And then when I met with him, he told me that Joy was in some kind of trouble, but then he wouldn't elaborate and he said I didn't need to know the details. It was all a big lie. What he wanted was for me to spy on her."

"To spy on her?"

"Not follow her around or anything like that. But, you know, I kept her schedule. I knew her appointments. Heck, I knew who fed her stupid cats when she was traveling. All that stuff. He wanted me to do whatever I could to keep tabs on what she was doing outside the office. He . . ."

She trailed off. Smallwood remained silent as she did her best to drill a look into him.

"Robert, you have to promise me. Please. None of this goes anywhere else. It's completely crazy that I'm telling you at all."

"You can trust me."

"Joy was having an affair. I knew about it. As far as I'm aware, nobody else did. No one at the office, anyway."

"And how did you know about it?"

Marion gave him a wan smile. "Well, the truth? I'd already sort of been spying on her myself. In my position it was so easy. With our phone system at work it's a piece of cake to listen in on a call and not be detected. She and her boyfriend weren't exactly smart about it, either. They thought they were being all top secret and everything. He even used a code name whenever he called. Glen Watkins. It was a little joke between the two of them. It's Watkins Glen, New York, just switched around. That's where they first hooked up."

"You're a good spy," Smallwood said.

"Oh, I know I am. But so was this creep who called me. He already knew all about the affair. That's what he really wanted from me, to keep him informed about anything I found out about the two of them. That name, for instance. Glen Watkins. He loved that. He said he wanted everything I could get. Especially wherever they were getting together."

Smallwood swiveled giddily in his chair. He was feeling like a famous interviewer. "You told this man that Joy and her boyfriend were going out to Shelter Island."

"You've got to believe me. Never in a million years did I think that anything I was passing on to him was going to get Joy *killed*."

"But you just came right out and told him all this stuff."

Marion cringed. "He was paying me a thousand dollars a week. I swear I didn't know what he was up to. I know that's no excuse."

"Why haven't you just told all this to the police, anyway?"

"I *can't*. That's what I'm trying to tell you." She gave him an imploring look. "Would you come sit here?"

Smallwood unfolded himself from the round chair and stepped over to the couch. The moment he sat down, she took his hand and entwined her fingers in his.

"This is what he said to me at Joy's funeral. He left me a whole bunch of messages right after they found Joy, but I didn't listen to any of them. He's been harassing me ever since. He's telling me that if I want to keep my father safe, I'd better keep my mouth shut."

"Your father?"

"He lives in Bayshore. He hasn't been well."

"What's this guy going to keep him safe from?"

Marion swallowed hard. The tears were coming. "He didn't say. I guess he didn't really have to, did he?"

Smallwood wanted to leave. The shadows of the late afternoon sun, the crying woman—it was all weighing on him. Marion had broken down completely and was drinking wine again. She had lapsed back into her stubbornness, but this time Smallwood was able to bring her back along pretty quickly.

"So, do you think this guy from the funeral is the one who killed my cousin?"

Marion shook her head slowly. "I don't know. I don't know what to think. Honestly. The whole thing makes no sense to me. The police are saying there were two or three people out there that night. One of them certainly could have been this guy. I certainly wouldn't put it past him."

She leaned forward and picked up the envelope from the coffee table and deposited it onto Smallwood's lap.

Smallwood asked, "So, what's this?"

"It's someone else who might have killed Joy. Though . . . it's so hard to imagine."

Smallwood picked up the envelope. "Glen Watkins?"

"Oh God. I so wish that was his real name."

Smallwood unfastened the clasp on the envelope and pulled out an eight-by-ten photograph. Joy he recognized instantly, of course. Her beautiful face, her beautiful exuberant smile. The face of the man she was about to embrace was cordoned off by a grease-pencil square. Smallwood's eyes grew wide.

"*This* is who she was sleeping with?"

Marion slipped her arm through Smallwood's arm. She leaned over and pressed her cheek against his sleeve. She had managed to kick off her shoes, and she brought her feet up onto the couch and tucked them underneath her fanny. She nestled even closer to the large man.

But Smallwood was barely aware of her presence. His attention was gripped by the photograph in his lap. The handsome senator from New York beaming his marquee smile. A smile of a different sort—much less pretty—moved onto Smallwood's face.

CHAPTER 20

As the hearing broke for lunch, the senior senator from Colorado came up behind Andy and placed a hand on his shoulder.

"Andy, can you swing by my office in about ten minutes? There's something I'd like to talk to you about."

Mitchell Cutler's fingers weren't simply resting on Andy's shoulder, there was a bit of a grip going on. Andy got the message.

"Sure, Mitch. Ten minutes."

He was there in nine.

The outer office was empty, which Andy found peculiar. There was always at least one staffer manning the post. For a moment, the image of a surprise party entered Andy's mind. But it wasn't his birthday, and besides, why Mitchell Cutler's office? Andy and the Colorado senator were not particularly tight. Their one co-sponsored bill had been a disaster, from conception to the final failure of not even being brought to the floor, and the experience had left a slight residue of chill in the otherwise politically formal relationship between the two senators.

The door to Cutler's inner office was cracked open. Andy gave it a rap, and a voice called out from inside.

"Andy?"

The voice was not Mitchell Cutler's. Andy pushed the door open farther. Seated behind the large walnut desk was a man in his early sixties. He was leaning back in the chair, lightly tapping the stem of a pair of bifocals against his chin. For most of his career he'd had a stubborn thicket of what a Reuters reporter had once famously called "Huck Finn hair," but it had finally begun to lose some of its abundance over the past decade. It was now more of a sandy bristle, cropped short and punctuated with pale gray shoots. Although the face was seemingly serene, it was also showing definite signs of weariness.

Andy closed the door behind him. As he started into the room, the man at the desk tapped at his chin a few more times with the bifocals, then tossed them onto the desk.

"Have a seat, Andy."

Andy did.

The older man studied him a moment, as if the senator from New York were some sort of unusual plant specimen. "I see the head is healing nicely."

Andy ignored the comment. "I take it Mitchell is not a part of the meeting?"

"Cutler?" The man frowned. "God, no. I just wanted some privacy for the two of us. You understand." He picked up the bifocals again, this time putting them on. As he reached into the inside pocket of his jacket, he said, "I hear you're the main attraction at the Earth Day rally tomorrow."

"I wouldn't say 'main.' They're shuttling me on and back off pretty early into it. All the sexy stuff comes later."

The man produced a rectangle of newsprint from his pocket, which he unfolded daintily. His eyes skimmed the tops of his bifocals, remaining on Andy.

"I want you to know, Andy, that I do appreciate your having kept me in the dark on this thing. If I'm ever asked what you did and didn't tell me, I won't have to lie. If it ever comes to that. Which of course we both pray it won't. But that was shrewd of you. In fact, the word is *politic*."

Andy said nothing. He had already guessed in general terms what was being unfolded, and when the man at the desk laid the paper out on the blotter, smoothing it with his thick fingers, Andy saw that he was correct.

"You don't need to confirm this for me. In fact, please don't. I need to remain officially in the dark. But obviously I guessed it as soon as I heard the news the next day."

Andy knew there was a point to all this, and he knew that nothing he might say was going to hasten its arrival. The man lowered the specs on his nose and looked down at the clipping.

"Masters and Weiss. She worked on your campaign?"

"That's right," Andy said. He found he was focusing inordinately on the man's tie. Tiny blue clovers seeming to hover above bright mint green.

"Closely?"

"She ran it."

The man winced. "Ouch. Not so good."

Andy waited. An irrational image presented itself to him. A hand grenade emerging from his coat pocket. His pulling the pin, placing the grenade on top of the desk. Smiling grimly. Waving bye-bye.

The man at the desk referred to the newspaper article: "It says three men."

"I know it does. Myself and the man who killed Joy. I have no idea who else they could be talking about."

"You only saw one man?"

"That's right. Just before he turned my lights out."

The man folded the article back up as daintily as he had unfolded it. He returned it to his inside pocket, clicked the stems of his bifocals together, then poked the glasses into his breast pocket.

"Two questions, Andy. And for the life of me, I can't imagine why you would choose to lie to me."

"I didn't kill her," Andy said. It felt good simply to say it out loud.

"Good. As I'd assumed, of course. But you do understand, an SOS call in the middle of the night to have me come pluck you off Shelter Island, and then you arrive looking the way you did? A person has to wonder."

"You saved my ass. For Christ's sake. You know my gratitude is through the roof on this. I promise I won't drag you any further into it."

"You're just lucky I was at the house."

Andy gave the man a grim look. "I'm sure you understand it's kind of a tricky night for me to assign anything like *good* luck to. But you're right. It could have gone much worse." He added, "For me, anyway."

A small chuckle escaped the man. "Good Lord. You crawled onto the boat like a goddamned castaway. So, my second question. I'm sorry, it's two more questions, not one. First, do you know this other man? The one who murdered Miss Resnick."

"Absolutely not."

"Good. That's very good. So you have no idea why he murdered your friend."

"He just came crashing in like King Kong."

"King Kong loved the lady, remember? He was tender."

"Fine. You know what I'm saying."

"Of course I do. So . . . I guess this is the sixty-four-thousand-dollar question. Did *he* recognize *you*?"

Andy hesitated. Of course he had examined that question already, countless times. On the face of it, he hadn't thought the assailant had recognized him. It had been sufficiently dark in the bedroom. His only real exposure to the assailant had been brief, just as the iron pipe was coming down on him.

So he'd thought not. At least until just before the weekend, when the awkward intern from Buffalo had handed him her headset and played back his messages for him.

"I don't know," Andy said. "I think maybe he did."

From the expression that came to the man's face, it didn't appear he'd been anticipating this response. He took a few seconds to let the information settle in, running his hand over his bristly hair. Petting a porcupine.

"Well, fuck," he said at last. "If that doesn't stink up the stew, I don't know what does."

"I'm keeping you out of the loop, though. I'm not telling you why I think he might know who I am."

The man was frowning. "Have you been contacted?"

"I'm not telling you a thing. Your ship's in rocky enough water as it is. If mine goes down, we don't want you anywhere near it. You know zero about this. We've got to be pragmatic."

The older man passed a sympathetic look across the desk, accompanied by a large sigh. He picked up the phone receiver and dialed a three-digit number. "All ready."

He hung up the phone.

"Can't talk anymore, Andy. I've got to go kiss the queen of Denmark."

"It's a bitter job," Andy said.

"Could be my last queen."

Andy sagged. "For Christ's sake, Chris. What do I say to that?"

Both men stood. Chris Wyeth ran a hand down his ugly tie. Behind Andy, the door to the outer office opened an inch. "Do you think you're ready to start kissing the queens, Andy?" Wyeth immediately held up a hand to silence the senator. "You know what? Don't answer that. But you and I do have to talk, my friend."

"What was this?"

"This?" Wyeth glanced about the office. "This never happened. I'm at Blair House as we speak, getting my kisser warmed up. I haven't seen you in over a week, buddy boy."

"Longer, Chris."

Wyeth came around from behind the desk. "Right. Longer. Long time no see. Give Christine my love, will you?"

"That would mean you and I have talked."

"Well, Andy. If we can't trust our wives to keep a secret, who can we trust?"

He didn't wait for an answer. The office door opened a few more inches as he approached, and then a few more as the vice president of the United States passed silently through it.

CHAPTER 21

The last thing Christine needed was her mother's opinion.

Christine had the cordless phone clipped to the pocket of her jeans and was wearing the headset so that she could remain mobile. She was kneeling on the floor of the sunporch amid an angular semicircle of newspaper pages. Her absurdly hearty spider plant, removed from its large pot, lay on its side on the newspapers. The dense cluster of packed soil and entwining crisscross roots looked menacing, the turgid roots having grown bound up and restrained in the pot and been forced to perform under such unnatural imposition.

Christine performed this surgery on the plant only every several years, and each time she did, she was convinced that her intervention was finally going to prove fatal to the plant. Discovering her mother at the other end of the line in the midst of the operation did not qualify as a reprieve from the task at hand. If anything, it felt more like a harbinger.

"You need to put your foot down, darling," Lillian was saying. "Men are not the mind readers we'd like them to be. You have to spell it out for them, otherwise they'll just assume that what they want is what you want. Think of your father, sweetie. Ambitious men are bullies. That just comes with the territory. Now, I know Andrew has his very sweet side; I'm not saying he doesn't. Though of course you know my real opinion of that. Maybe the less said the better."

Yes, Christine thought, squeezing the shears open and closed against nothing. *Maybe the less said.*

Lillian's pause for breath was brief.

"You don't have to live in that awful fishbowl. I know full well you don't want to. I certainly don't want my granddaughter playing hopscotch with her little Secret Service friends. Good Christ, what a horror. This is not a *life* we're talking about here, Chrissie, it's a freak show. Don't take this the wrong way, but you don't have the temperament. You know I'm not attacking you when I say this. As far as I'm concerned, being unfit to be a politician's wife is a sign of superb mental health."

"Thank you for the diagnosis."

Lillian continued. "You're just not cut out for this. And frankly, your husband is blithely overlooking this fact. I'd say, *conveniently* overlooking it. This is what they do, Chrissie. Trust me."

"You seem to be awfully good at mind reading."

If Lillian was hearing the edginess in her daughter's voice, she was ignoring it. "Well, yes I am, thank you. I do have an intuitive sense about these matters, Chrissie. That's nothing to poke fun at. Even your father had to admit I was good at reading people."

Eventually, Christine got Lillian off the phone. She pulled off the headset and tossed the phone onto the coffee table. She went at the huge fist of soil with her shears for several minutes, hacking off some half dozen or so roots, shaking loose dirt like black dandruff onto the newspapers. Finally she let the shears drop to the floor. She stared grimly over at the phone.

The most depressing aspect of their chat was that this time around Christine felt her mother had been pretty much on target. Being in agreement with her mother was always troubling to Christine, if only on principle. On this particular topic, it was all the more disconcerting. Integrating her own life and career with that of her husband's had been a formidable challenge from the very outset. Michelle's well-being and "normal childhood" had served these past seven and a half years as their shared focal point, the place to go whenever they felt the need to check up on themselves. Even so, Andy's career carried a profound gravitational force, one that neither Christine's parenting nor her photography counterbalanced. For the most part, Christine had come to terms with this. The bottom line was that Michelle was not a neurotic, spoiled, confused gorgon of a child. Not yet, anyway.

Senator Harrison's drinking issue had reached the point of public dialogue over the weekend, so his potential as a replacement vice president was essentially kaput. According to all Christine was hearing, this left Michigan senator Jeff LaMott, former secretary of state John Bainbridge, and seven-year-old Michelle Foster's daddy. Lillian was right on the money. Entering into this arena of politics would be a point of no return for Christine and Michelle. Secret Service shadows at every turn, the heightened press scrutiny, a husband infinitely more absorbed in matters he either could not or would not discuss with his wife. Less sharing. Less family time. All of the cautions, in fact, that had presented themselves to Christine back when Andy had proposed marriage to her. She wondered gloomily if perhaps she was doomed to continue approaching her life with her eyes wide shut. Not at all a heartening thought.

Christine picked up the shears and positioned them at the base of one of the prime roots of the spider plant. Taking a two-handed grip on the gummy red handles, she bore down with all her strength, compressing her back teeth. The root did not want to give. It was thick and stubborn. The effort called out the thin squiggly vein that ran vertically up Christine's forehead, and she groaned ever so slightly as she bore down on the shears.

Snap!

It sounded like a gunshot.

After Christine finished the repotting project, she picked up the newspapers and loose soil and deposited them all in the trash chute in the hallway. She washed up, then phoned Shelley Tanner to confirm the afternoon shoot. Shelley was Christine's business manager slash agent slash favorite outrageous acquaintance, the latter category being the one Christine prized the most. A fire-haired woman from Tasmania, of all places. When Christine needed a break from so-called real life, Shelley was her ticket.

Christine was scheduled to shoot toothpick-thin Judy Starling, the quivering-voiced alt-rock chanteuse who was currently riding atop her largest career wave yet, along with her enfant terrible boyfriend from the group Cody. Or perhaps the boyfriend's name was Cody. Christine wasn't really tuned in. Shelley had organized the whole thing, Judy Starling was ready for photo documentation of her fabulous twenty-three-year-old life, and according to Shelley, Starling was "super eager" to add her waiflike form to Christine's modest portfolio of celebrity images.

Shelley confirmed the shoot for two o'clock at Judy Starling's Tribeca apartment.

"I hope you're not allergic to parrots," Shelley said, her fantastic Tasmanian accent attacking every word. "I've heard rumors of twenty or more."

"I can't wait."

"Just so you know, the boyfriend is going to be wanting to highlight his tattoos. I have to admit, they're an impressive collection."

"Oh yippee."

Christine hung up the phone. An hour and a half later she had her equipment packed and was waiting for the buzz from the lobby to tell her that her car was there. She paused in front of the Mexican mirror in the hallway and poked at her new hair. She was wearing tight jeans and a simple V-necked sweater. On a whim, she ducked into the hallway bathroom and emerged with a green scarf knotted into her hair and trailing down her neck.

The intercom buzzed.

"Car's here, Mrs. Foster."

"Thank you, Jimmy."

As she hoisted her bag onto her shoulder, the phone began to ring. It was already nearly a quarter to two. Christine leaned into the kitchen to check the caller ID.

Metropolitan Museum of Art

They want money, she thought. *You'd think five thousand dollars a year might buy me some peace.* She let the phone ring and headed out the door.

As the door closed behind her, the answering machine in the kitchen picked up. The recorded voice of Michelle Foster was tinny, accompanied by bits of static.

"Hello. You have reached the home of Michelle and her parents. We are unable to come to the phone. Please leave a message after the beep."

The long tone sounded. It was followed by a second or two of silence, then a man's voice.

"Hello, Michelle. I was just calling to let you and your mother know that your father is an evil man. Right up to his stinking white perfect teeth. Okay? You should know this, Michelle. You sound like a nice little girl, but even nice little girls can sink like a stone in this world. So you be careful, okay? That's what I want to tell you. You be very careful. I'll talk to you later. Bye-bye."

The answering machine clicked and went silent. A second later, its small yellow light began to blink.

CHAPTER 22

The first thing Dimitri Bulakov did Monday morning was fire up the laptop and review the three images he had chosen the night before. Each image brought a larger smile to his face than the previous image. He was happy with his choices, and he copied the three files onto his flash drive, which he then unplugged from the computer and slipped into his pocket.

"You do not move," Dimitri said to his wife, who was watching him from the bed. "Today it is me who will get some fresh air. I will bring home food."

Before leaving, he pulled the Yankees cap down low on his head and grabbed his sunglasses. At a local FedEx, Dimitri spent ten minutes at a computer and printer and came away with a paper copy of each of his three images. The quality was not great, but the important thing was that it was clear what was happening in each of the pictures. It was amazing to consider that the different activities captured had taken place mere minutes from one another. How quickly everything can change. If the only activity Dimitri had captured had been the first one, Dimitri would have collected his two thousand dollars from Aleksey Titov a week ago, put some of it against his and Leonard's debts, blown the rest, and that would have been that.

Dimitri put the three printed pages into an overnight envelope, addressed it, kissed it, and handed it to the clerk.

"Tomorrow?" Dimitri said. "You promise?"

The clerk checked the address. "D.C. Yes, sir. By noon tomorrow. Guaranteed."

Four blocks away he found a bar that was open. Two of the three patrons looked as if they had been glued to their stools for years. The third was a thirtysomething woman who looked closer to sixty. She was holding down the far end of the bar, using a glass of whiskey as her anchor.

Dimitri ordered a beer. The woman muttered something Dimitri couldn't make out except that it was clearly not complimentary. He drank the first beer fast and ordered another. When the front door opened, bringing an unwelcome flash of sunlight into the dark den, Dimitri's heart skipped a beat. Of course it was illogical to fear that Aleksey Titov himself was the short silhouetted form coming into the bar. *Don't be stupid,* Dimitri told himself. *Don't be paranoid.*

It wasn't Titov. It was a small old man with a gray mustache and a limp. He took a stool near the door, pulled a pair of glasses from his shirt pocket, and spread a newspaper out on the counter.

Dimitri picked up his half-empty beer bottle and headed for the bathroom. He had to pass the unsavory woman to get there. She gave him an uninterested look as he passed. It was only as he was pushing open the cheap wooden bathroom door that Dimitri realized the woman had slipped off her barstool and followed him.

The door was partway open, and the bathroom's sweet and sour fumes rolled out like an invisible wave.

"Twenty," the hardened woman said. She looked as if she was about to spit on Dimitri. When he said nothing, her look turned even more sour. She held up her right hand, languidly pumping her fist. "Ten."

Dimitri sputtered, "I am going to the bathroom."

On anyone else, what she did with her face might have been a smile. "Well, we're real proud of you, Boris. Let's try not to insult the toilet, too, while you're at it."

She held her look for a moment then turned back toward the bar.

Dimitri locked himself into the single toilet stall. He didn't need to use the toilet; he simply needed privacy.

He pulled out the disposable cell phone. Before dialing the number he had already phoned a half dozen times on Friday, Dimitri downed the second half of his beer in a long unbroken swig.

He dialed the number. He knew the routine now, and he pressed the numbers to cut directly to the answering service. As the long tone sounded, Dimitri let out a matching belch.

"Mr. Coward. The games are over now. You will know this when your FedEx arrives. Is tomorrow. We will deal now, I hope. You are not so stupid. I am giving you a phone number. Call it tomorrow night at seven o'clock. You will—"

The door to the stall swung open.

"Shit!"

The phone dropped to the floor as Dimitri leaped to his feet. His foot kicked over the empty beer bottle.

It was the woman from the bar.

"What're you doing, Boris? You shitting with your pants still on? Girl's got to do everything. Christ sake."

As she moved forward, reaching for his belt, Dimitri shoved her. His hands landed on her bony shoulders and she rocketed backward, tripping on her own feet and falling hard against the bathroom wall. The sound her head made as it hit the wood was like the perfect crack of a whip. She collapsed to the floor.

Dimitri started for the door, then remembered the cell phone and scooped it off the floor. He knelt down to see if the skinny woman was breathing. He grabbed her chin and shook it, and a low groan emerged from her lips.

As he left the bathroom and hurried out of the bar, the bartender called after him, but Dimitri kept moving. The old man near the door never looked up from his newspaper.

Irena was seated at the window when Dimitri returned to the room. He was ranting even as he came through the door.

"Alexsey Titov is a coward! He is an idiot! Is he taking any of the risks? No! That is all me! I'm not sharing my money with this man! The great Alexsey Titov is a phony! He is the stupid one, not me! Titov is a nobody anymore! Do you hear me? Alexsey Titov is a *phony!*"

Dimitri's Greatest Hits.

Irena remained motionless while her husband continued on in this fashion. She offered no reply to his outbursts. She was tired. She also noticed that her husband had failed to return with any breakfast.

The ranting lasted nearly five minutes before Dimitri finally stormed off to take a shower. "I smell like shit," he snarled, as if somehow this was *her* fault.

During his rant, he repeated Aleksey Titov's name a dozen times at least, maybe more.

The disposable cell phone was on the dresser, where Dimitri had tossed it when he came into the room.

It was still on.

Still connected to the number Dimitri had dialed from the toilet stall.

Still broadcasting.

CHAPTER 23

It turned out his name was not Cody. It was Butcher. At least that was his name now. Christine had no clue what his parents had called him when he was a pink little baby.

The grown-up Butcher wanted nothing else but for Christine Foster to photograph him emerging naked from a bathtub filled with milk. He had done the research already.

"See? You get all slathered up with olive oil first. Then you sprinkle salt all over your body so when you're coming out of the milk, it flows in all those really cool patterns. It's a pisser of an effect. You'll love it."

Butcher was in red cargo shorts and no shirt when she arrived at Judy Starling's apartment for the photo shoot. The young man was all muscle. And all visible muscles were saturated with a dizzying swirl of tattooed images. Given the totality of the tattoos already on display, it did occur to Christine that perhaps a naked Butcher would not look too terrifically different from the nearly naked Butcher. Even so, she wasn't going to encourage the boy.

Judy Starling looked like she might have *been* one of her boyfriend's tattoos. Somewhere between gamine and anorexic, the British singer had the large brown eyes of a Disney animated deer. Her mouth was practically a red pinprick, and her filament-thin gold-colored hair fell down straight to her nonexistent fanny.

She was lovely and strange, and Christine would have been happy to see Butcher drown in his ridiculous milk bath so that she could focus her camera exclusively on the ethereal creature. But this was to be the Butcher and Judy show; the reed-thin singer made this clear.

"Celebrity valentine," Christine muttered to Shelley Tanner as she was unpacking her equipment. "Remind me to fire you."

"I'll fire myself, sweetie," Shelley said. "That's what you pay me for."

Christine let the tripod's telescoping legs fall to their full length. "If M. C. Escher spoke, I'm sure he'd say things like that."

"Sweetie, I'm sure the man spoke."

"You know what I mean."

Judy Starling proved as flexible as a pipe cleaner, and Christine moved her all around the apartment. The singer perched high up on her floor-to-ceiling bookshelf. She seemed to hover in space at her Celtic harp. Inspired by the young woman's supreme willowiness, Christine and Shelley cleared the refrigerator of its organic this and vegan that, removed metal racks, and folded Judy Starling into the cleared-out space as if it had been built specifically for her. The doe eyes looked out from the refrigerator with a plaintive yet knowing beauty. Christine fully suspected that one of these shots would emerge from the session as the real keeper of the day.

Then there was Butcher. Physically, the two did make an interesting couple, but any hope of juxtaposing Butcher's highly inked muscles against his girlfriend's milky simplicity remained that: a hope. He was too big, too physically distracting, a buffalo beside a moth. Christine earned her nickel with a series of shots in which half a dozen of Judy Starling's pet parrots perched about their mistress as if she were a clothes rack, while Butcher in his own parrotlike plumage flexed his beefy biceps next to, behind, and at the feet of his fair lovely.

And in the end, Christine indulged the bad boy in his bathtub-of-milk fantasy. Butcher stripped naked without a second thought. Shelley let out a gasp.

"Oh my God," she murmured to Christine. "Use your zoom. Do not deny me a print of *that*."

Christine felt ever so light-headed as she clicked off the shots. Judy Starling's pet parrots seemed agitated as well. Slashes of blue and red and green shot about the room as Christine aimed and clicked, aimed and clicked. Judy Starling stood close behind Christine while she worked, and the little noises the woman made as Butcher arose again and again from the milky bath gave Christine a mild case of the willies. Packing up her equipment at the conclusion of the shoot, Christine sensed that there were more dairy doings awaiting the wispy singer and her tattooed hunk.

Shelley turned to Christine as the two emerged onto Reade Street. "I need a drink."

Christine pulled tight the zipper on her equipment bag. "I don't know what I need."

Shelley's response was cut short by the ringing of Christine's phone. Christine checked the caller ID. "It's home," she said, putting the phone to her ear. "Hello?"

"Mommy!"

Blood drained from Christine's face. "Michelle? What's wrong, honey?"

But the child only screamed.

Lindsay sat at her desk, pressing the earphone tight to her ear. At Linda's desk across from her, Jim Fergus was wearing a pair of earphones. A YouTube video of the Who flickered on the computer screen in front of him, and his right arm circled in miniature pinwheels as he air-guitared along with the muted performance. His mumbled singing was not quite as under his breath as he might have thought.

Lindsay checked her watch. She was timing the latest phone message. She wasn't quite sure why, but she felt she might be asked for it. So far it was thirteen minutes.

Fourteen.

Fifteen.

Fergus concluded his side of the video with a flourish. He pawed the earphones off his head and tossed them onto the desk. His face was ever so slightly flushed. "Damn. I think I've just discovered the perfect substitute for caffeine." He rose from his chair, eyeing the intern. "Hey, what's rocking over there in Lindsay land?"

Lindsay's gaze fell nowhere in the room. "It's nothing."

Fergus shrugged. "Okay, spy girl, have it your way." He grabbed his coat and left the office.

Lindsay checked her watch.

Sixteen.

The man on the message had just started into his flip-out. Lindsay pulled her keyboard closer and began transcribing. The man was in the middle of the flip-out when Senator Foster came into the office.

"If Aleksey Titov knows what is good for him, he will know I mean business! This son of a bitch!"

Lindsay checked her watch again and made a note of the time. Andy was just disappearing into his office.

"Senator?"

Andy paused at the door. "Yes?"

There was a curtness to his manner that was unfamiliar to the intern. "I don't mean to bother you, Senator. But there's something really strange on the messages that I think you should hear."

"What do you mean, strange?"

"It's . . . peculiar."

Andy frowned. "Has Greg or Linda heard it?"

"Well, no, sir. They haven't. I kind of think it's something maybe *you* want to listen to first?"

Andy hesitated before replying. He could not read the intern's face. But the little questioning tone . . . She was trying to say something to him.

"It's him again, Senator. It's the Russian."

"I see." Andy turned back into the room. "Perhaps you should just erase it, Lindsay."

But the intern was already shaking her head. "No, Senator. I don't think that's a good idea. I know you're busy and everything. But I really think you need to listen to it."

"Is that right?"

She removed the headset and held it out for him. The silver pendant on the chain around her neck caught a light somewhere and sent off a spark.

"I'm positive. You do."

"I am so sorry, Mrs. Foster."

Michelle's nanny, Rosa, folded her hands over her cup of tea. It was one of the woman's ritual habits. Along with the forlorn expression on her face, the gesture completed a portrait of profound repentance.

"You have nothing to apologize for, Rosa. Michelle always checks the messages as soon as she gets home. You know that."

The distant sounds of *Tomb Raider* were audible in the kitchen. Michelle was parked in front of the television in the front room, eating ice cream and watching videos. Funny way to calm a kid down, sugar and stimulation.

Christine asked, "How bad is it?"

Rosa slipped her hands down around the teacup and lifted it. "I only heard the very end. I was in the living room and Michelle called out my name. I heard the man say, 'I'll talk with you later.' "

"He said *that*?"

"Yes, ma'am."

Christine muttered, "Jesus H. Christ." When Rosa blanched, Christine added, "I'm sorry, Rosa. Okay. Let's hear this thing."

She glanced in the direction of the front room and adjusted the volume on the answering machine.

"Hello, Michelle. I was just calling to let you and your mother know that your father is an evil man. Right up to his stinking white perfect teeth . . ."

Christine listened to the entire message. By the time the *beep* came, Rosa looked ready to cry.

"Who would say that about Mr. Foster?"

Christine was shaken. "Sadly, there are plenty of people out there who would say that, Rosa. And much worse. That's not what I'm worried about. It's the fact that he's directing himself to Michelle. That's no good."

She gazed down at the answering machine. The sounds of explosions

drifted in from the front room. *That's* not scary. Explosions. Animated car-
nage. But *this?*

Christine took a breath, held it, and hit the replay button. The message
chilled her even more the second time.

"I'll talk to you later. Bye-bye."

Christine turned to her nanny. "Could you go sit with Michelle? I'm
going to get Mr. Foster on the phone."

Senator Foster's gaze came back from middle distance. His intern sat on
the edge of Greg's desk with an impassive expression, watching the senator.

"Can you pause this?" Andy asked.

"Yes." Lindsay dropped to the floor, stepped over to where Andy was
seated, and hit a combination of numbers on the phone keypad. She returned to Greg's desk and leaned up against it.

Andy asked, "How long does this go on?"

"I'm not sure. I was timing the whole thing when you came in. His
ranting goes on like that for at least another couple of minutes."

Andy's throat and mouth were dry. There was only one person this
Russian could be. He had to be the man who had smashed his way into Joy
Resnick's beach house and murdered her. Andy was aware he was general-
izing about the man being Russian. The accent could have been from any
of a dozen Eastern European countries. Russian was just the most conve-
nient. It was Lindsay who had said it first.

Lindsay. Nineteen years old. A naive little witness to this horror show.

Andy cleared his throat. "How would you characterize the rest of this?"

In his mind he saw the young woman shrugging. *Well, Senator, there's this
whole part in there about, like, you having sex with this woman right before she was killed?
You mean, like, how would I characterize that?*

Lindsay replied, "You've gotten to the part where he is yelling and
screaming?"

"That just ended." Andy could not believe this was happening. *So* many
things were wrong with this picture.

"There's not much more after that," Lindsay said. "The man and the
woman talk about some stuff. Food, I think. Then the television comes on,
it's hard to hear much after that."

"How does it end?" Andy was able to summon a grim internal laugh. *Yes. How does it all end? Please. Tell me.*

"He says 'Shit.' "

Andy raised an eyebrow. "Shit?"

"Yes. It sounds like he must have finally noticed that the phone was still on. His voice suddenly gets louder. Like he's approaching the phone or something. He says 'Shit,' and then it goes dead."

Andy looked down at the pad of paper on the desk. He'd written the words ALEKSEY TITOV in block letters, going over them several times as he'd listened to the message machine. The outlines of the letters were now thick and black. Andy made a steeple of his fingers and lowered his chin onto it.

"Lindsay, I need you to do something for me."

"Yes, Senator. Of course."

Andy slapped the story together in his mind. A quick patch here, a patch there. No time for finesse.

"First, I need you to remain quiet about this." He emphasized his point with a no-nonsense look. "You're to mention this to no one."

"Not even to Greg and Linda?"

"No. To no one. It—" He took a sharp breath. "I'm afraid this involves Greg."

Lindsay's eyes widened. "Greg? What do you mean?"

"You'll understand if I don't go into any details with you. The point is, this has to remain between you and me. It's absolutely vital."

"But what's it about? Is Greg in some sort of trouble? Oh Jesus."

Andy was a little taken aback by how swiftly the hook had been sunk. He fell into his best conspiratorial voice. "Here's the other thing I need you to do, Lindsay. You heard this man. Something is coming tomorrow by FedEx. You have to contact them."

"Contact who?"

"FedEx. We need to head it off. We do not want that package arriving here at the office. Greg cannot see it. Linda can't. Nobody can. Call FedEx and arrange for this package to be held at one of the FedEx places in the city. I'll get you all the identification you need. I want you to pick this thing up and deliver it to me personally." He paused. "But not at the office. That's very important. You're getting all this?"

She nodded. "I'm to keep the FedEx from coming here. I'll pick it up at one of their offices, and I'll deliver it to you."

"Outside the office. Exactly."

"But—"

"But what?"

The words came out harsher than he'd intended. Suddenly he was feeling as old as the hills. What he couldn't afford to do was lose this young woman's confidence. Lindsay was leaning up against Greg's desk, looking increasingly scared and uncertain. The feeling in the air was not a good one. She was gathering doubt. Andy could see it. He endeavored to loosen his tone.

"Listen, Lindsay. Greg has gotten himself in a little jam. It's nowhere near as big as I'm making it sound. He's done nothing wrong, it's just the nature of the business we're in. Greg still has my complete confidence. In the end, everything comes down to trust, doesn't it? I know you care abut Greg. I'm trusting you to do him this favor. I'm terrifically grateful for the work you've been doing for us here. I know it's not always so glamorous. And neither is this. But what I need is your silence on this. This is just how the world operates. Can I count on you, Lindsay?"

Andy would have paid a small fortune to know what was going on inside the young woman's head, as her face was revealing nothing. Her expression was like a white wall.

Andy had a cocktail reception to attend at six. He had planned to walk to it, but the threatening phone message and his talk with his intern had scuttled those plans. Christine had called, but he hadn't bothered retrieving the message. He phoned her from the back of his taxi. He lowered the window, allowing the cool early-evening air to bathe his face.

Christine was enraged. "Where the hell have you been?" she snapped. "Didn't you get my messages?"

"I . . . no. I didn't play them back. I've been in—"

"I need you to talk to Michelle. Right away!"

She was shrill. Christine was never shrill.

"Of course," Andy said. "Put her on. What seems to be the problem?"

"What seems to be the problem is that some nutcase called here and left a message for Michelle about *you*."

Andy's heart slammed up against his ribs. "Me?"

"Yes, you. A crank call. I don't know how he got our number. But thank you very much, our daughter was nicely traumatized. Oh, I do so love life in the public fucking eye."

The taxi was passing the Washington Monument; the blinking red lights at the very top looked like dragon eyes. Andy braced himself. "Settle down. What exactly did this crank caller say?"

"Oh, just garbage. You're an evil man. Crap like that."

Andy waited, but Christine had finished. He wanted desperately to ask if the man had some sort of an accent.

"Was that it?"

The White House came briefly into view then vanished again. Sometimes it appeared more like a hologram than an actual place. Especially at night.

"No, that wasn't it. He scared your daughter half to death! He told her to *be careful,* whatever that means. Oh. And he said you had perfect teeth."

"I *what?*"

"I'm not having this, Andy. I am not having our daughter terrorized by wackos who have some sort of problem with you. She's seven years old. This is completely unacceptable."

"Look, put Michelle on. I'm sure I can convince her I'm not evil."

"You're missing my point, Andy."

"I'm sorry, Christine. *What is* your point?"

There was a pause on the other end of the line. "Nice," Christine said at last. "Snap at your family. Why the hell not?"

"I didn't mean that," Andy said.

"My point is, since you asked . . . It's . . . My point is, something's not good. It's this whole thing with Chris Wyeth, and it's not this whole thing with Chris Wyeth. Jesus Christ, Andy, you might be the next goddamned vice president of the United States, and we haven't even *talked* about it! I'm sorry, but I don't think your family has wrapped its head around this yet. I guess I'm as much to blame as you. But still."

"Look, that's all still very much up in the air. I don't really—"

Christine cut him off. "It doesn't matter! People are calling here and telling our daughter that nice little girls sink like stones and that her daddy is evil. I won't have it, Andy. Something is in the air. And I'm just telling you, for the record, I'm creeped out. I don't like it."

Andy heard a sound in the background. It sounded like a cat mewing. Christine's voice went faint.

"It's Daddy, sweetheart. He wants to talk with you." She came back fully on the line. "Andy? Michelle would like to speak with you. Convince her that everything is all right." Her voice lowered to a whisper. "Lie if you have to."

Andy nodded his head, as if his wife was sitting right in front of him.

That's exactly what I'm going to have to do, he thought. *Lie through my perfect teeth.*

CHAPTER 25

By eight thirty a.m., the Mall was throbbing with Earth Day energy. People. Blankets, Frisbees, banners. Oversize green and blue balloons. Painted faces. Dozens of wooden stalls hosting environmental action groups and coalitions from all over the country. Over by the National Museum of the American Indian, a green-bearded Uncle Sam on ten-foot stilts marched about stiffly, chanting through a megaphone, "Washington hot air feeds global warming!" Nearby, a small fleet of solar-powered wheelchairs bumped silently over the grass, their riders passing out pamphlets made from recycled hemp. A flatbed truck had pulled up before sunrise in the area behind the Air and Space Museum, bearing a massive ice sculpture of the earth. The ice was now in the process of melting, the runoff collecting via aluminum troughs into cups and handed out to passersby.

The main stage had been set up near the Smithsonian Castle, on the south side of the Mall. A pair of towers situated on either side of the stage held gigantic video screens that made the onstage activities visible from nearly every part of the north end of the Mall. After an invocation from a Native American elder opened the day's proceedings on a somber note, speakers and comedians and musicians began their rotation on the stage.

By ten thirty, the lineup was already behind schedule. During a longer-than-intended break to prep for a short set by Tori Amos, the green Uncle Sam had somehow made his way to the front of the crowd, where his tottering presence was blocking the clear view of the center of the stage and was, in any case, a complete distraction. A rumbling chant developed. "Down with Sam! Down with Sam!" As the tall green figure continued bellowing and ignoring exhortations to move out of the way, a contingent from the crowd finally took the matter into their own hands. Taking hold of the stilts, they brought the green man down to earth, sideways and slowly, and the crowd cheered. A few minutes later Tori Amos appeared onstage, looking like a green bumblebee, and offered up nine and a half minutes of anguish. The crowd cheered her, too.

Andy had been scheduled to follow Ms. Amos at eleven o'clock and to speak for roughly ten minutes. He was standing backstage, waiting his turn, obsessively checking his watch. At eleven thirty, the diminutive singer hit her final chord on the piano. The emcee approached the microphone, and Andy glanced down at his notes. The senator wasn't turning any new ground here; this was a sermon to the choir. Applause lines guaranteed. Andy folded his notes and stuck them into his pocket.

The crowd looked good. Easily ten thousand already. The stage manager was standing several feet away, listening through his headset to the emcee. He looked over at Andy, holding one finger up in the air.

The senator's cell phone sounded. Andy pounced on it. It was Lindsay.

"Senator, I have the package."

"Good! Just hang tight. I'm about to go speak. Just wait where you are and I'll call you."

The stage manager dropped his arm. "Go! Go! You're on!"

Andy flipped his phone shut. The adrenaline surged through his system as he headed to the front of the stage. The general din of applause and cheering came into focus for Andy only as he reached the microphone and raised his arms to acknowledge the spirited greeting. In his mind's eye, he imagined his intern from Buffalo standing on a street corner several miles away, clutching in her arms a FedEx package. Bringing his focus back to the crowd, his ears finally caught not just the simple cadence of the chant that had erupted. They caught the two letters.

"Vee Pee! Vee Pee! Vee Pee!"

Senator Foster took several minutes with reporters after his address to the crowd. He had to insist—forcibly, in one case—that the focus remain strictly on matters of the environment and on his carbon credit bill, which was currently working its way through the committee. A reporter with *The Washington Post* was pushing him to comment on the Earth Day crowd's wishes that Andy declare his feelings about the vice presidency.

"Senator, with all due respect, your views on the environment are not exactly news at this point. But don't you think that should you become the vice president, you would be in a position to make some real progress on those issues? Especially in a global sense?"

Andy replied glibly, "I don't spend my energies on ifs."

The reporter was not impressed. "If you were offered the position, wouldn't you be able to push your agenda more aggressively?"

"Not nearly as aggressively as you're pushing yours."

"Is that a no?"

"That's a nothing."

The woman cocked her head slightly, tapping her pencil against her chin. "Rita Flores warned me about you."

Andy jumped in immediately. "I'm very glad to hear that. I'm all for warnings. That's precisely why these people have gathered here today. If we don't turn warnings into policy, then we have produced nothing but hot air. And in our case, we will have failed our children's generation and the generations after theirs."

"That's cute," the reporter said. "Rita warned me that you're one of the most evasive men she has ever covered."

Andy cued up his smile. "Anything that is not an outright condemnation I'll take as a compliment."

After several more questions, Andy finally extracted himself from the press trailer. He was thanked profusely by several of the event's organizers; then he walked over to Independence Avenue and hailed a cab. From the backseat he dialed Lindsay's number.

"Have you got it?"

"Yes, it's right here. I'm at Starbucks."

"Okay, I'm on my way. Sorry that took so long. Seventeenth and Massachusetts, in about ten minutes. Northeast corner. I'm in a Gem Cab."

He disconnected the call and fell back in the seat. He checked his watch. It was twelve thirty-five. As far as Andy was concerned, time officially stopped at seven that evening, when he was supposed to be on the phone with the goddamned Russian. Brought down on Earth Day. He couldn't exactly pinpoint the irony, but he suspected it was there.

Lindsay left the Starbucks as soon as Senator Foster called. Her mind was elsewhere, a million miles away. She vaguely registered the *click click click* of her shoes as she moved along the sidewalk. The FedEx envelope was tucked firmly under her arm. Mere mortal hands could not have pried it loose.

At the next block she began looking for the senator's cab. A red pedicab was tooling slowly up the street, some twenty or thirty yards back. Up at the end of the block Lindsay saw a Gem Cab pulling over, but as she stepped off the curb, she saw the rear door of the cab opening and an elderly woman getting out. Not the senator. What she didn't see was a gleaming black motorcycle that was weaving precariously at just that instant past the pedicab. The motorcycle was pitched at such a severe angle that the driver could have practically reached out his hand and touched the road surface. He was losing control of the machine.

The roar from the motorcycle caught up to Lindsay a split second in advance of the vehicle's rear tire swerving sideways into her leg. Its brakes locked, and the six-hundred-pound machine immediately fishtailed, whipping in a complete circle. Lindsay was clipped a second time, just below her left hip.

The nineteen-year-old rocketed into the air.

She landed on the road surface some fifteen feet away, tumbling helplessly until she bumped up against the curb. The motorcycle, meanwhile, had lost its driver. The machine continued riderless down the street in a ruckus of blue smoke and orange sparks, skidding to a stop at the crosswalk, just as the light hanging over the intersection turned from yellow to red.

Then came the screaming. The shouting. Onlookers rushing to the two downed people. Fingers punching 911 into scores of phones.

All the while, blood flowed from Lindsay's mouth.

CHAPTER 26

The cab driver slammed his hands down on the steering wheel in exasperation. "Forget freedom of speech! How about a little freedom of *driving*?"

Andy leaned forward to peer out the windshield. "What's going on?"

The driver gestured out the windshield. "Look at this. Those bozos care so much about the environment? I'm wasting perfectly good gasoline waiting on these clowns. You think these people think?"

Andy was dialing Lindsay's number. A parade of eco-protesters was making its way slowly along Fifteenth Street, backing up traffic in both directions. Somewhere there seemed to be a kettle drum. There was chanting, though from this distance the words were indistinguishable. Andy peered through the windshield of the immobile cab at a large puppet figure of a polar bear floating into the intersection. The bear was accompanied by dozens of small penguins on sticks.

Lindsay's voicemail picked up. Andy waited impatiently for the beep.

"Lindsay, it's me. Look, I'm being held up in traffic here. You just hang tight, okay? I should be there in . . . I don't know. Not long. But you just stay put."

The polar bear puppet had stopped in the middle of the intersection. The little penguins were racing around it in circles.

"This isn't happening," Andy muttered.

Car horns began honking, first a few, then dozens. In no time the air went thick with blaring horns. The penguins continued dancing.

I'm in hell, Andy thought. *My little stupid hell. All mine.*

The motorcycle cop removed his sunglasses.

"I know you," he said.

Andy didn't even look at the man. He was still seated in the back of the cab. Several fire trucks, an ambulance, and three police cars filled half the block of Massachusetts. "What happened here?"

"Accident, Senator Foster," the cop said. "Nutcase on a Harley."

Andy saw the black motorcycle lying on its side in the middle of the intersection.

"What happened?" he asked again.

"Witnesses said the biker was barreling through like a bat out of hell. He lost control. Slammed right into a woman who was crossing the street."

Andy knew. It was clear to the senator that Lindsay would have been waiting on that corner even if the final bombs had started falling. She was nowhere to be seen.

Andy put every ounce of effort into appearing to be only casually interested in all this. The last thing he needed was a police officer shooting off at the mouth about the senator who was all flipped out about this accident.

"Would you happen to know which hospital the woman was taken to?"

The policeman knew. He told him.

Andy thanked him and rolled up the window.

"Did you get that?" he asked the driver.

"Georgetown University Hospital."

"I'm not going to ask you to run any red lights," Andy said. "But—"

"It's okay, Senator." The driver checked the side-view mirror, already having turned the wheel. "Just buckle up."

CHAPTER 27

Christine had to admit it: Butcher covered head to foot with milk and tattoos made one hell of a photograph. She projected the image with her enlarger, blown up as big as it could go without losing definition. The rocker's torso was dominated by a two-headed dragon that was shooting orange and red flames from engorged nostrils onto Butcher's shoulders. The dragon's ornately inked body dominated Butcher's chest and abdomen, the spiky tail slithering on down in a lazy S toward his crotch. The image Christine had chosen to print showed Butcher posing like Botticelli's Venus. His left hand was draped casually over his crotch area, and his expression showed a demure but still quite masculine deadpan. The veil of milk running down the rainbow body gave the image an opaque ghostliness.

It was a good shot.

Christine made a print of the image and mounted it in a cherrywood frame. She removed her Magritte print from the wall and hung the Butcher photograph in its place and stepped back for a look. She liked it. Gothic and kitschy, to be sure, but it was also oddly poignant—the disarming nature of Butcher's pose and expression was riveting. And unquestionably sensuous. The blue-green dragon snaking down Butcher's milky stomach paralleled his tattooed arm, the two converging dead center on the pelvis, where the rocker's broad hand failed to obscure completely the goings-on beneath it.

Christine was still admiring the image when the phone rang.

It was Miss Brandstetter, Michelle's homeroom teacher. Christine glanced at the clock: one fifteen.

"What's wrong?"

"There's nothing to worry about, Mrs. Foster," the teacher said. "But Michelle seems to be quite upset. We were in the middle of an urban archaeology game in Social Studies when suddenly she just started crying. It was quite violent at first. She was shaking all over."

"Oh Lord. Where is she now?"

"We're in the infirmary. Michelle's much better now, but she says she wants to come home. I think—"

"I'll be right there."

Michelle remained silent while her mother spoke briefly with Miss Brandstetter. She stood by, sniffling and looking forlorn. Christine thanked the teacher, and she and Michelle exited the building. Out on the sidewalk, the child took her mother's hand. Her voice was barely audible.

"Did he call again?"

It was what Christine had suspected. Michelle had posed the exact same question at the breakfast table first thing in the morning.

They crossed Sixth Avenue and started for home. "No, honey, he didn't. Like I told you this morning, I'm sure it was just some sad, silly man. I'm sure he wasn't calling us specifically. He heard your voice on the answering machine and just started talking that way. I'm sure we're not going to hear from him again. Sweetie, there's nothing to worry about."

"But Daddy—"

"Daddy's fine. He gave his speech this morning down in Washington. When we get home we can see if anyone has put it up on YouTube."

Michelle brightened a little. "Can we call him?"

"Of course we can. But you know Daddy doesn't always answer. He's very busy."

Michelle implored. "But we'll call him?"

Christine squeezed the girl's hand. "Of course we will."

"Daddy's not a bad man, Mommy."

The light at Grove changed, and the two stepped off the curb to cross. The afternoon sun hung over the distant river, almost colorless, and uncommonly blinding.

"No, honey," Christine said. "Of course he's not. Your daddy is one of the finest men alive."

Andy dropped a handful of bills onto the front seat.

"Thanks."

But if the driver responded, it fell on an empty backseat. Andy sprinted past a pair of ambulances parked in the emergency-room bay and pushed through the automatic doors. It was as he approached the nearest admitting window that he realized *he didn't know her last name.*

A stout African American woman looked blankly at him from behind the glass.

"Can I help you?"

Andy took a beat to catch his breath. "A young woman. She was just brought in. She was hit by a motorcycle. It was on Seventeenth Street. Massachusetts and Seventeenth."

The woman's poker face remained intact. "And who are you?" she said—polite, not exactly friendly.

"I'm . . . her boss." Andy was glad that the woman didn't seem to recognize him, but glancing around at the other people waiting in the ER, he knew it was doubtful he would remain so lucky for long.

"Have a seat over there." She indicated a row of molded plastic chairs, half of which were occupied.

"Um, if there—I'd really like to find out about the young woman's condition. Please. Her name is Lindsay."

"Uh-huh. I know who you're talking about. They're working on her now, sir. As soon as somebody knows anything, we'll let you know. You want to give me a name?"

Andy was confused. "Lindsay. I just told you. I don't know her last name."

The comment earned him a look. "I mean *your* name. So we can let you know how your em-ploy-ee is."

Two red dots rose on the senator's cheeks. "Andy."

"Good. Okay. Have a seat, Andy, and we'll let you know as soon as we can."

Andy started away from the window, then stopped. The woman seemed to have anticipated that he would.

"Yes?"

"I was just wondering. Lindsay's personal effects. I mean, her purse. Things she had with her when she was brought in. Where would items like that be kept?"

An eyebrow rose. "You want her purse?"

"I told you, she works for me. She was carrying some important papers."

"We'll let you know. There's nothing back here. You'll have to talk to a doctor. I can't tell you what I don't know. Just have a seat. Please."

He opted to stand.

As Christine and Michelle approached Eleventh Street, Christine asked her daughter if she wanted a cupcake. Michelle shook her head vehemently.

"That's the morning," she murmured.

"Well, I know. But you can still have one now if you'd like. A treat."

They had paused in front of the bakery. Michelle looked in the shop-window. "Would it still count?"

"You mean toward your million? That's completely up to you."

"What if it's cheating?"

"Cheating who? Goodness, you're not competing against anyone. You're simply keeping count. It's a game."

As Michelle was wrestling with the dilemma, the door to the bakery opened and the sculptor emerged. Instead of his customary paper bakery hat he was wearing a green baseball cap pushed far back on his head. He smiled broadly as he recognized the pair on the sidewalk.

"Well, look who it is! Little Miss Cupcake herself. What are you up to? Trying to slip in an extra one?"

Michelle spun on her mother. "See? It *is* cheating. I told you."

The man looked quizzically to Christine. "What? Did I just misspeak?"

"No, no. Don't worry. We were just trying to figure out the wiggle room on this whole cupcake thing. It's quite complex, you know."

The man nodded sagely. "Oh, I'm sure it is. It'd be such a drag if the poor thing had to start all over."

Michelle protested. "I'm not a poor thing! I have ten dollars."

A look passed between the adults. The sculptor bounced down to a crouch to address the girl. "Well. Ten dollars. That's a whole different kettle of wax. I had no idea I was dealing with a Rockefeller."

Michelle looked to her mother for clarification.

"I believe your friend is withdrawing his charge of poverty, honey. He's decided that you're filthy rich."

"I'm not filthy!"

Christine laughed. "Welcome to the Land of the Literal."

The sculptor pulled off his cap. He ran his hands over his hair and squinted against the low sun at Christine.

"Listen, I'm glad I ran into you two. I wanted to let you know that I've just concluded my bakery career."

"Really?" Christine said. "You've quit?"

"Yeah. The thing is, I am not a morning person. But with this bakery thing, I'm up to my elbows in dough before the sun has even come up." He turned to Michelle. "That's *flour* dough, hotshot. Don't go laying that Rockefeller thing onto *me*."

"That's too bad," Christine said.

The man shrugged. "Well, yeah. There's definitely something to be said about being forced out of the studio. You do get to see people."

Christine laughed. "You make it sound like you'd been a monk."

"Hey, listen. There are days, believe me."

Michelle had fallen noticeably silent. The shadow that had been accompanying her since her mother had picked her up from school was moving back in. Christine moved closer to the sculptor, lowering her voice.

"It's not exactly been the best day for Miss Cupcake."

"I'm sorry. Is she all right?"

"She'll live. She's been rattled, that's all. But now . . . I just hope you're prepared for the death of your fan club."

"Ouch. That's harsh."

"Just saying it like it is. You go breaking little hearts like that, you've got to weather the consequences."

The door to the bakery opened and two young women exited onto the sidewalk. They had NYU *student* written all over them. The more attractive of the two waved at the sculptor as they disappeared around the corner.

"Okay, then," Christine said, laughing. "Midsize hearts, too."

"Hey, it's not as if I'm vanishing from the city. I mean, my studio's right up on Fifteenth."

"This would be your studio or your monk's cave? I'm getting those confused."

He reached into his pocket and produced a business card, holding it out to Michelle. "Here you go, kiddo. Take this. This is where I hang out. You and your mother can come by anytime and visit me."

Michelle's eyes widened. "Really?"

"Absolutely. Open invitation." Michelle accepted the card and the sculptor turned back to Christine. "Seriously, I'd love it if you came by and took a look at what I do." He pulled out a second card. "Here."

"Oh. One's fine," Christine said.

"No. Take it. You know, in case Miss Cupcake is off at school or something and you decide you want to swing by. She's got her card, you've got yours."

Christine paused. A touch of mirth tugged at the corners of the man's mouth. The sunlight was picking up flecks of gold from his eyes.

"Take it. It's just a card. It won't bite."

Christine felt the moment edging toward awkwardness. She took the card, tucking it into her back pocket without looking at it. She reached down and took hold of her daughter's hand. "Let's go, honey."

Michelle was holding the sculptor's card up to her face. "Your name is Michael!"

He made a small bow. "At your service."

"My name's Michelle. It's almost the same name!"

"You're right, it is." He looked over at Christine. "And what do they call you? Besides 'Mommy,' I mean."

She was blushing. There wasn't a thing she could do about it.

"I'm Christine."

"Good. I guess we're all old friends now."

He put his cap back on his head and reached down to muss Michelle's hair. "So, Cupcake, tell me. What do *you* think about your mommy's new haircut?"

Michelle was giggling uncontrollably. The sculptor aimed his smile over at Christine. "Yeah. I agree. It's a good look."

CHAPTER 28

Jim Fergus was apoplectic.

"You are sitting in a goddamned emergency room?"

"I told you," Andy said into his phone. "I got the doctor to squirrel me away in an examining room."

"Big deal! You're at a *hospital,* and you're playing nursemaid to your intern! Andy, is it me? You can tell me. Is it something I said? Sweet Jesus, man. Pull a hat down over that pretty face of yours and amscray right now! This *is* your mother speaking."

"Listen, Jim—"

But Fergus was on a roll. "No. You listen. Senator rushes to cute intern's bedside. No, sir. Not on my watch. If you want to commit political hari-kari, give old Jimbo the heads-up first so he can watch the train wreck from the safety of the unemployment line, okay?"

"Don't you think you're being just a little bit dramatic?"

Fergus ignored the question. "Look, you're not a doctor. Your being there is zero help to that girl. I'll send someone over. Let me get Linda over there. Girl to girl. In the meantime, you find yourself a back door and get the hell out of there. This is no time to start losing your instincts."

The door to the examining room opened, and a doctor in surgical scrubs stepped in.

"I've got to go, Jim," Andy said into the phone. "Fox News just showed up and they want an exclusive."

He disconnected the call and fielded an odd look from the doctor.

"Private joke," he explained. "So, where are we?"

He remained seated. The doctor allowed the door to *shoosh* closed behind him.

"It was pretty much like I thought, Senator. The lung was definitely punctured. I'm seeing five ribs injured. Three broken outright, the other two severely fractured. That'll hurt, but that'll be fine. The internal hemorrhaging was bad, but of course we're fortunate that we got her here so quickly."

This was essentially the information Andy had received in his first briefing with the ER doctor. He knew he had to be patient. Some doctors prefer the checklist approach. Andy also knew that they saved the worst for last. He felt a trickle of perspiration moving in starts and stops down the very middle of his back.

"I'm afraid it's the leg, Senator—the leg and the hip."

"What about the leg? Christ's sake, just tell me if she's going to lose it."

The doctor assured him, "We can rule that out. But there's going to be scarring. Even with cosmetic work. But it's the hip I'm more concerned about."

"Oh, God."

The doctor continued, "We've got a triple fracture. The pelvic plate is a horror. We have to go in immediately and pin this whole mess back together. The last thing we need is bone breaking free."

"It sounds awful."

"Pretty it ain't. There's really no choice. Damage like this, if we don't get to it right away she could very possibly never walk normally on that leg again."

"Jesus." Andy lowered his head. Nineteen-year-old Lindsay No Name, on a secret mission to retrieve something Andy could only assume was very, very, very damaging. And now she was about to be surgically put back together.

Andy glanced at his watch. "Um. About the other matter?" The doctor looked confused. Andy added, "There was a FedEx package?"

"Oh. I see. You mean the patient's possessions?"

"I'd like the FedEx, please."

"Well. Technically, patients' possessions are not released until—"

"My name is on the package," Andy said, holding on to his temper. "It was in the patient's possession, but it is *my* property." He stood up. "Look, I have to be going. My press secretary is on her way. She'll take care of things with Miss . . . with Lindsay. You've been very helpful, Doctor. I appreciate your sensitivity. If you could arrange for me to get my package now, I would be grateful."

"Of course, Senator. You can come with me. We'll take care of that."

The doctor pulled open the door, and Andy followed him into the corridor. The doctor paused, turning to Andy. "Oh, I almost forgot. Would you like to see her? She's groggy, but—"

"I'm sorry. I can't. I'm just . . ." He trailed off. He felt completely ashamed.

The doctor took a beat. "Okay, then. Just thought I'd check."

Andy called for a car service and had the driver deliver him to his apartment. He went immediately into the kitchen and poured himself a drink, which he took out to the living room.

He dropped onto the couch.

On the wall next to him was a photograph Andy had taken of Christine during a vacation in Martha's Vineyard several years before, cuddled in a hammock, asleep. It was one of his favorite photographs of his wife. In it he had managed to capture the beatific serenity gracing Christine's face. The image never failed to move him, even if only a little. As he took a long sip of his drink and set the FedEx envelope on his lap, the image moved him a great deal. It made him feel like dirt.

He checked the time. A few hours still until he was supposed to call the man he was now thinking of as the Mad Russian. Andy took a long sip of his drink then worked open the stiff FedEx envelope. There was a piece of paper with a note on it. Andy set it on the coffee table, facedown and unread. He was more concerned with the rest of the envelope's contents.

Andy felt as if all the hair follicles on his body were tingling. He realized he was a little light-headed, experiencing a slight sense of vertigo. He set the three photographs facedown on his lap and placed his hands on them. He would have preferred their images to simply transmit through his palms directly to his brain. He didn't want his eyes involved. For nearly a full minute he remained still, studying the photograph on the wall next to him. Christine asleep in the hammock. He recalled the vacation, the particular day, the moment he picked up his wife's camera and snapped her picture. He ached for those days.

What have I done?

Finally, he lifted his hands from the photographs on his lap and looked at each of them. His first pass was eerily cool and dispassionate. He merely gathered in the information represented in each of the three shots, only a vague curiosity rising as to who in the world took these pictures, and how and why. Of course, he knew the basic content. This first look was primarily to confront the shock. It was real now. It was actually happening.

Andy took a sip of his drink and closed his eyes for a moment.

It was during the second pass through the photographs that the raw muscle of Andy's heart turned to light steel, crumpling like a flimsy can.

CHAPTER 29

Irena Bulakov knotted the white cotton scarf at her chin as she made her way down Neptune Avenue. There was only a slight mist in the air, not even actual rain. An urgent tune had lodged itself in her head as she'd left the hotel, and she was helpless against it. Her feet moved in time with the tune, somewhat faster than she would have normally walked. The storefronts passed in flashes.

She was scared.

Irena crossed the street at Thirty-third. The ocean was now behind her, the setting sun a dead gold coin in the colorless sky. A bell over the door of the Treasure Café jangled as she entered. Irena clawed the sunglasses off her face.

Leonard Bulakov was already there. He was seated as far from the window as possible, and Irena gasped when she saw him. She might not even have recognized him, except for a particular quality in his bearing. Irena had always felt that her brother-in-law was an elegant man; Leonard was naturally soft-spoken, the very opposite of his brother, and, also unlike Dimitri, he was thoroughly gentle.

The bandaged creature slowly rising up from the chair radiated the same gentle purposefulness of Leonard. And so, Irena concluded, it must be him.

She made her way over to him, then broke into tears.

"Leonard."

One half of his face was swollen, and his left eye was hidden behind a purple balloon. The white bandage over his nose and spreading out over his eyebrows looked to Irena like a crude crucifix. Most troubling to Irena, though, was her brother-in-law's one good eye: It held such a sadness. It had witnessed the unspeakable evil of what had been done to him, and what Irena saw in that single unhappy eye pierced her own heart directly. She felt her own faith in the power of goodness evaporating. *Surely,* she thought, *it has already evaporated for Leonard.*

Leonard lifted a hand that was wrapped in a mound of gauze, and he gestured for Irena to have a seat. He waited until she had landed in her chair before retaking his. He gave her his best effort at a smile.

"I am not recognizing this beautiful Hollywood star," he said softly. "Is my brother now married to a sexy symbol?"

Irena's tears flowed even harder. Leonard reached across the table with his good hand, and she took it, squeezing it as hard as she could.

"You cry," Leonard said. "Is okay. Out comes the poisons. You feel better."

Irena brought the tears under control and withdrew her hand to dab at them with her napkin. Leonard had already ordered a pot of tea, and he poured Irena a cup. Irena untied her scarf and pulled it from her head.

"How can Dimitri do this to you?" she said.

"Aleksey Titov did this to me."

"You know what I am saying. This is the result of Dimitri."

"My brother does not know we are meeting," Leonard said. "Is this still correct?" He lifted his teacup to his lips. The mere process of taking a sip was terrible to witness.

Irena said, "Dimitri would kill me if he knew I called you. But I had to, Leonard. He is more and more crazy. I do not know what to do. I tell you, Dimitri is talking as a madman. He says he can crush Aleksey Titov. Dimitri? But look at what Titov has done to you. And you are much smarter than Dimitri."

Leonard managed a small laugh. "The brain is not always the best muscle to defend the body, Irena. Now listen, you must tell me. What is it exactly that my brother is doing?"

"He will not tell me. He says I am safer not to know. It is something on his computer. I know this. Dimitri is obsessed. He has the little stick he is attaching to it? It goes into the back of the computer. He will hold up this blue stick and say to me, 'This is our future. There is more money in here than you or I have ever seen.' He is scaring me."

Leonard was frowning. "This stick. This is the driver for holding files outside the computer?"

"Yes, I think so. I don't know. I am not the computer person."

"What is Dimitri doing right now, Irena? How did you know you could meet me tonight?"

"Dimitri tells me yesterday I must be out of the room tonight at seven o'clock. He does not say why, only that it is important and that I cannot be there. I told him I was going to see a movie."

Leonard smiled again. "You are seeing a monster movie, Irena. Is that not so?"

Irena missed her brother-in-law's joke. "I am so worried, Leonard. Dimitri is going to die. It is something I cannot stop feeling. Especially now. Now that I see you." She took a sip of her tea, then set her teacup down. It rattled gently as it settled into the saucer.

"It is true," she said, nearly whispering. "He is dead."

Dimitri hung up the disposable cell phone and cracked open a beer. He was proud of himself. Even Aleksey Titov himself could not have been a better businessman, Dimitri thought.

Dimitri had decided. Five hundred thousand dollars now as the first payment. Serious money, to show that he was a serious man. This was what he had just told Mr. Coward. The senator. Dimitri would give seventy-five thousand of this money to Titov. Who would not be happy and impressed with seventy-five thousand dollars? After this first payment, Dimitri was demanding five thousand dollars a month for him to keep his video file private. Dimitri thought that this lifetime income was a fair amount to ask. This man in the video could afford it. His wife, everyone knew, came from a wealthy family. And Senator Coward could not afford not to pay to keep this video unseen by the world.

Dimitri paced back and forth in the hotel room as he drank his beer. This was Tuesday. He would have his money on Monday, less than a week. This was the result of his discussion on the phone. Even a rich person needs some time to pull together such cash so that nobody notices. Dimitri was not an idiot. He had spoken to the man as a business partner. He had been very polite with him, very professional. He almost wished he had not sent Irena away, so that she could have heard what a polite and smart businessman her husband could be.

Dimitri was looking forward to escaping this hotel room. He was looking forward to giving Aleksey Titov so much money that everything between them would be equal and respectful from now on. He was looking forward to buying Irena a big house and buying her driving lessons and then buying her a red Cadillac.

Good. To. Go.

What Dimitri Bulakov was not looking forward to was being killed. But this was the intention of Anton Gregor, who slid off the bus-stop bench across the street as Irena Bulakov exited the café and began making her way back to the hotel. Irena again knotted the white scarf over her head as she walked, which meant it was all that much easier for the man to follow her through the ashy night.

Who knows, Gregor said to himself as he fell in behind Irena. If it turned out that he had to kill them both—Mr. Titov had told him this might be the case—maybe he could have a little fun with Mrs. Bulakov before running his brand-new knife across her throat.

Just a thought.

CHAPTER 30

Nothing good was going to come from getting drunk. But then again, nothing about Andy's current situation was going to look any better through sober eyes. So why not?

The Mad Russian had spoken: half a million dollars up front, then five thousand a month from now until the sun turned cold. By the Russian's terms, this hell was to be with Andy until the end of his days. There was something almost comical about it. *Me and my Russian, till death do us part.* Andy imagined their meeting up once a month, year in and year out. Old comrades.

How're the wife and kids, Vladimir? Did little Sacha do all right on her geometry test? What about Mikail? Has he made you a grandfather yet?

The Russian wanted the five hundred thousand by Monday. He'd originally said Sunday but Andy had convinced him that he would need more time than that. It had not been too difficult to convince him. The entire negotiation had felt absurd. Surreal. Andy had been tempted to drop the name Aleksey Titov into the conversation—the name he'd picked up from the Mad Russian's open cell phone—but had decided against it. The name Titov was not wholly unfamiliar to Andy. It had rung a faint bell when he'd heard the Russian throwing it around over and over again on the answering machine. A few minutes online and Andy had been able to refresh his memory. There were scores of people out there with the name Aleksey Titov, but he was fairly certain that the Aleksey Titov who popped up at the top of his search was the one he had somehow fallen in with. This Titov had been in the news over the past winter in connection with federal probes into Russian money laundering, and various green card and Social Security card forgery schemes. Andy had no idea how, or for that matter *why*, this Aleksey Titov would in any way have been involved in the shakedown that the Mad Russian was orchestrating. He couldn't piece together a logic there. Andy had no direct role in any of the Senate investigatory bodies that might have been looking into Titov's business matters. Organized crime was not his arena. None of this was making any sense.

By eight fifteen Andy had murdered nearly a third of the bottle. He had also exhausted all the people even remotely qualified to share the blame for his dilemma. The only person who even came close to truly sharing the responsibility would have been Joy Resnick, but Andy knew perfectly well how pathetic it would be to foist blame onto the dead woman. And how perfectly pointless. Andy finally stopped his childish finger-pointing (President Hyland, Chris Wyeth, Jim Fergus, Rita Flores, Whitney Hoyt . . .) the moment it veered absurdly in the direction of Christine. Of all his imagined targets, that was the worst. Andy was disgusted with himself that he would even entertain the notion of blaming his infidelity—let alone its nightmarish fallout—on his wife. Especially because he knew what the real culprit was: his own hubris. It didn't take a rocket scientist to come up with that one. The fault lay in his own vanity.

Sometime after nine a call came in. It wasn't from Christine, thank God. It was Linda. She was calling from the hospital to tell the senator that Lindsay's surgery had gone well.

Andy's tongue was barely functioning. "Good."

"We've issued a statement. Your prayers are with Lindsay and her family. Lindsay has been a dedicated worker and extremely helpful in the day-to-day operation of the office, blah blah blah."

"Good," Andy said again. His gaze fell on the photograph of him straddling Joy Resnick on the large white bed. He spoke robotically. "Did the statement say I spoke with the family? Shouldn't I do that?"

"That's up to you, Senator. I think it's a good idea. They're here now, if you'd like me to put them on."

No!

"Sure," he said. "Put them on."

The conversation with the mother went by in a blur. Andy got up and stood at the living-room window, looking out at the passing traffic as Lindsay's mother wept over the phone. She was followed by her husband, who had some harsh things to say about the entire intern program, politicians in general, and Washington, D.C., in particular. Apparently there would be "hell to pay" if his daughter came away from all this unable to walk perfectly.

"I have a daughter, too," Andy heard himself saying. "I know how you feel. If someone hurt her . . ." The thought went unfinished. Andy had no idea what he would actually do if Michelle was ever seriously harmed or injured. "We'll do everything we can for Lindsay. Anything you need. You tell that to Linda. Tell her I said so. I'm terribly sorry, Mr. . . ."

Jesus. He still didn't know his intern's last name.

The man on the other end of the phone let out a sound of disgust. "It's Packard, Senator. I'm Tom Packard. My wife is Ruth. The little girl who has been volunteering her time for you is Lindsay Packard. You might want to write that down somewhere."

Andy winced as the man hung up on him. An ambulance raced by on the street, silent but with its lights flashing urgently. A silent police car followed tight on its tail.

Andy returned to the couch and dropped into it. The three ugly photographs were laid out on the coffee table, in sequence. Despite himself, Andy stared down at them.

Here's the end of my world.

He picked up the first photo. A man and a woman making love on a large bed. The woman was diagonal on the mattress. The man was on his knees, vertical, his face turned partway to the left, in perfect profile for the camera.

A sob erupted from Andy. He imagined his daughter gaining access to this picture. That's how things happened nowadays. He didn't care about the rest of the world—they could have it—but not Michelle. Not Little Wizard. Daughter of the most loathsome daddy on the planet.

Irena sensed trouble the instant the dirty-blond man entered the elevator with her. She hadn't noticed him until she'd been halfway across the small lobby of the hotel. She paused before hitting the button for the fourth floor; the man made no move. Irena hit four and then the man leaned past her and hit the same button. He smiled into her face.

"Hello, neighbor."

At the fourth floor the man waited until Irena got off the elevator, then remained several steps behind her as she moved down the hallway toward the room. As Irena reached the door she could hear the television set blaring inside. Her mind was racing to remember the code Dimitri had given her. She remembered the "all's safe" knock, but not the other one. It had vanished from her head.

The man had stepped up behind her. Warm fingers rested on Irena's neck.

"Do not be a fool, Mrs. Bulakov. Just open the door."

Irena stammered. "I—I don't have the key."

"Well then, tell your husband to let you in. Or were you planning to just stand out here all night?"

There was a movement next to Irena's right eye. A large knife blade came into view for a moment, then disappeared.

"Tell him to let you in."

Irena knocked. It wasn't the danger code, but it certainly wasn't the "all's safe" one, either. She rapped half a dozen times. The volume lowered on the television.

Irena spoke in a loud whisper. "Dimitri! It's me. Let me in."

For a few seconds, nothing. Then the sound of the door being unlocked. The door opened only a crack, and immediately the man shoved Irena through the doorway. As she stumbled into the room, she glimpsed Dimitri in his undershirt and boxers standing on a chair that he had pulled up next to the door. She fell forward onto the floor.

Dimitri was holding an empty beer bottle over his head. As the man pushed into the room Dimitri swung the bottle at him, but his aim was off and the bottle bounced ineffectually off the intruder's shoulder. The blond man spun to his right. He whipped his arm in an arc, and a slice appeared across Dimitri's undershirt. In a flash, the hoodlum brought the knife back, and this time it sank into Dimitri's ribs, all the way to the handle. Irena let out a scream. A look of dumb confusion came to her husband's face as his shirt began to redden. Using the embedded knife as a lever, Dimitri's assailant pumped his arm forcefully and brought Dimitri down off the chair and crashing to the floor.

Irena screamed and scrambled up onto the bed.

The blond man jerked the knife free, and as Dimitri struggled to rise to all fours, the hoodlum launched a hard kick into his side. The two had cleared the doorway enough that he could reach over Dimitri and swing the door closed. Irena scooted farther back on the bed, her knees crunching right over Dimitri's laptop.

Dimitri was trying to stand, but the blond man put a foot on his shoulder and toppled him easily. In an instant he was hunched over Dimitri, plunging the knife into his chest two, three, four times. His arm pumped as though it were a machine; the blood was spreading across Dimitri's undershirt.

"Stop! Stop it!"

Irena's screams ripped at her lungs. But the man was not stopping. He was grunting with his efforts. Dimitri, too, was making grunting sounds. But his were smaller. Weaker.

Oh, Dimitri.

Irena grabbed hold of the laptop. In a single bounce she was at the foot of the bed. As she raised the laptop, she noticed the blue flash drive poking from its side, and she snatched it from the machine. She lifted the laptop over her head. Red bubbles were foaming from Dimitri's mouth. His eyes met hers. At least, Irena thought they did. She had never before seen such sadness in them.

Irena brought the laptop down with all her might, hooking it at the last instant like a batter swinging for the fence. It caught the hoodlum full force against his face. Irena saw something the size of an aspirin propel to the floor as the man sprawled sideways on top of Dimitri.

Irena slipped off the bed. With the firmer footing, she brought the laptop down again, hard hits against the back of the man's head. Two. Three. Four. The final swing of the laptop caught him on the side of his head, and Irena saw his eyelids flicker as he tumbled sideways onto the floor. She took one last look at her husband.

Stupid, stupid man.

Irena jerked open the door. Her feet moved with a rodent's swiftness, silent on the carpeted hallway. They steered away from the elevator and found the stairs. They brought her round and round and round, down to the ground floor, then carried her swiftly across the hotel lobby. They did not slow down for the man at the front desk, who was calling something out to her.

Clutching Dimitri's computer to her chest, Irena hit the sidewalk at full speed. The sound of her own footsteps spurred her to run faster. She was undaunted by the light rain and the random puddles and by the fact that she had no idea whatsoever where in the huge, scary, lonely world she was going.

CHAPTER 31

After a set of early morning tennis, Whitney Hoyt and his wife showered separately then shared breakfast in their bathrobes out on the stone patio. Eggs Florentine. Tomato juice. Caffe latte.

While their plates were being cleared, a deer made an appearance at the edge of the trees. The deer grazed on the grass, then raised its head in alarm and stood stock-still for some twenty seconds before bounding back into the trees. Jenny went inside to change, and Whitney spent the next forty minutes with the *Times* and the *Journal* and *The Washington Post.* The world—no surprise—was still a mess.

At ten o'clock, Whitney dressed. Jenny was off to a meeting of the Greenwich Flower Festival, of which she had volunteered to be co-chair. Whitney was in his study when she popped in to say goodbye.

"This is really happening, isn't it?" she asked.

Whitney slid his glasses up onto his forehead. "Anything is possible. But yes. I'm beginning to feel a sense of inevitability."

Jenny paused, her hand resting lightly on the doorjamb. "What do you suppose this is going to mean to Christine?"

"Christine understands. Whatever fuss she makes, it will remain private. You'll help her with that. You're a good sounding board for her."

Jenny took off. Twenty minutes later Paul Jordan poked his head into the room.

"Whitney? The shoes are coming."

Hoyt was flipping through some papers. A play of amusement crossed his face. He looked up.

"You're certainly Mr. Cloak-and-Dagger these days, aren't you?"

Shoes was a term for federal agents that Jordan had picked up from the movies. Jordan and his wife were unabashed movie junkies, particularly American gangster films. For nearly a dozen years, the love of their life had been their Scottish terrier, which Hailey Jordan had named Baby Face.

Jordan adopted a tone of mock solemnity.

"The president, sir, and two of his men."

Hoyt waved a hand. "Show them in."

Jordan stepped back from the door, and two Secret Service agents appeared. The agents glanced impassively around the room, then took up positions on either side of the door. Paul Jordan bowed his head slightly as President John Hyland entered the room. Hoyt stood and started around his desk, but the president covered the distance in four long strides.

"Governor. It's good to see you again."

"Likewise, Mr. President. Sorry to disturb your morning."

The two men shook hands. Hoyt directed the president to have a seat in the mahogany red leather chair in front of his desk, while he took the rocker opposite.

"It's not a problem," Hyland said. "I was able to cancel a very boring breakfast." He glanced at his watch. "I'm afraid we don't have much time, however. The boring lunch is a little harder to nix."

Hoyt nodded. "I understand that."

Hyland gave a signal, and his shoes left the room. Paul Jordan surveyed the room intensely for several seconds, giving a terse nod to Hoyt, then joined them. The door clicked closed behind him.

The president leaned forward in the chair, grasping his hands together. If he looked like a man wearing handcuffs, the impression was not wholly inaccurate.

"Okay, Whitney. I gather from your message that you have a few things to tell me about Chris Wyeth. Not as if I haven't been hearing more than enough the last couple of days."

"True enough," Hoyt said.

"Nothing good, I assume."

"Chris certainly wouldn't think so."

Hyland studied the man in front of him. The relationship between the new president and the former governor had always been cordial and primarily superficial. Hyland was well aware that even in his role as private citizen, Whitney Hoyt still commanded respect and loyalty in certain political circles. He was far from being a person without influence.

Hyland asked, "Is it even worth my asking why you didn't come forward with your information last year while we were vetting him?"

"Not worth asking, John."

"I see." Hyland waited, but it was apparent that Hoyt had no more to say. "Okay, Governor," Hyland went on at last. "This is all in your court. I'm begging, you're giving. How are we going to run this?"

Hoyt rocked his chair slightly. "We don't have to be so arch here, Mr. President. It's simple horse trading. The good old-fashioned style."

"Wyeth is finished," Hyland said. "I get that. That seems to be established. I take it you're holding the nails to the coffin."

"I doubt you'll really need them. But yes, I am." Hoyt leaned sideways and lifted a manila folder from the edge of his desk.

"It's always been a real love-hate matter with you and Chris, hasn't it?" the president said.

Hoyt brought the folder onto his lap, considering the president before responding. "It's neither love nor hate, Mr. President. Either of those would suggest that the man holds a special enough place in my heart. That's simply not the case here. It's my country I have in mind, not Chris Wyeth's specific failings. Granted, Chris is smart and he's capable and he's shrewd. It's impressive how he's maneuvered all these years. One really does have to respect a man who is good at his game. You, for example. I've enjoyed watching you, Mr. President. You're immensely skilled. You've got the common touch down cold. People relate to you. They trust that you're going to deliver. Hell, you're the Joe DiMaggio of politics."

Hyland scoffed. "I hope that isn't to say I'll end my days selling coffeemakers."

Hoyt smiled blandly at him. "I hope not, too. And take this from one who knows. It's definitely the final act that's the trickiest. They take away all your toys, but you're still expected to be having fun."

"You're doing okay for yourself, Governor."

"Well, yes. I've got a good wife and fond memories and loyal friends. For the most part, I'm a happy man."

Hyland eyed the folder in Hoyt's lap. "But clearly something has made you unhappy."

Hoyt cleared his throat. "I'm afraid you simply didn't pick the best man for the job, John. I love my country. I want to see it thrive. For all his smarts and his obvious successes, Chris Wyeth sitting in the Oval Office does not say *thrive* to me."

Hyland smiled. "Last time I looked, I was the one sitting there."

"Of course you are. Let's just say that Chris Wyeth is too close for my tastes. It's not always a healthy thing for a man to get everything he wants."

"And you think Wyeth wants my job?"

Hoyt waved his hand. "Christ, man, of course he does. Don't play silly with me. Chris Wyeth has been aching for that job since he was in diapers. This is no secret. You took on an eager beaver, Mr. President."

"Do you mind my asking you something, Governor?" Hyland said.

"Please."

Hyland shifted in the chair. "You looked like a pretty eager beaver yourself at one point in your career. There are a lot of people who never understood your not taking a crack at the office."

Hoyt continued rocking slowly in his chair. "That's a statement. You said you wanted to ask me a question."

"The question is, why didn't you ever run for president when you were so clearly positioned for it?"

Hoyt's eyes twinkled. "Oh, can't we just say I wanted to spend more time with my family?"

"If it means anything, Whitney, I feel you would have made a superb chief executive."

"Well, thank you, Mr. President. That's very kind of you. Not that I be-lieve that's how you really feel." Hoyt gave his guest a measured smile. "And I hope you enjoy your time at the top. With the world the way it is now, I don't know if I envy you or pity the living hell out of you."

"If those are my choices, I'll take the latter." The president glanced down at his watch. "I'd love to spend the morning kissing each other's tails, Whitney. But I really don't have much time. We should move on to the business at hand."

"Of course. You do have a country to run. My apologies." Hoyt lifted the folder from his lap. "So. Our man Wyeth."

"Horse trading."

"Yes, sir."

The president eyed the folder. "I take it Andy Foster is the other horse?"

"Best in the stable."

"Better than John Bainbridge?"

Whitney Hoyt gave an overtly theatrical blink. "Bainbridge. Oh. Wait a minute." He dropped the folder back onto his lap and reached over to the desk and picked up a second manila folder. "I'm sorry, John. It's this one. *This* is the sad, silly story of your vice president. I'm so sorry. My mis-take."

He leaned forward in the rocker and handed the second folder to the president. "Chris was always a little *too* eager for his own good. Too eager to remember to cover his tracks. One of those fatal flaws, I'm afraid."

Hyland despised this man. This was precisely the sort of politics that had been degrading the people's regard for the governing process for decades. It was Hyland's fervent hope that political dinosaurs like Whitney Hoyt would complete their damn extinction already and stop spawning new little dinosaurs. It was dispiriting.

"Okay, Governor. I have to say, *your* eagerness is not terrifically becoming. So what's in the other folder?"

Hoyt was unmoved. "John Bainbridge would be a foolish choice, Mr. President. Read it and weep." He picked the folder up off his lap and handed it to the president. Hyland immediately tossed it up onto the desk.

"I'm not even going to look at this."

"Have it your way, Mr. President."

"And my way is Andy Foster?"

Hoyt rocked backward in his chair. "That strikes me as a very inspired choice."

Hyland held a steady gaze on his host, then stood up from his chair.

"Inspired."

He put as much disgust into the word as he could. It was not nearly enough to faze his host.

CHAPTER 32

"There's *Daddy!*"

Michelle dropped her half-eaten toast and practically leaped at the small television on the kitchen counter. Christine was scraping her spatula along the bottom of the pan; she gave the scrambled eggs one last stir and flipped off the flame.

Good Morning America was showing a clip from Andy's Earth Day speech the day before. Christine set down the spatula and turned to the television. "Oh, look at those sunglasses. Your daddy is such a dude sometimes."

Michelle's nose moved to within inches of the screen. *"Shhh. Listen!"*

The little girl's father was exhorting the Earth Day crowd: "Renew your sense of compassion and your kindness and your caring! Renew your respect and appreciation for this precious planet and for all the living beings on it! *We* are the renewable energy that can save our earth. *We* are the ones who can fix what we've broken. So let's get together and renew!"

The picture cut to the chanting crowd—*"Vee! Pee! Vee! Pee!"*—then switched back to the studio and the unabashedly smitten expression worn by the morning show's political reporter as she turned to the show's cohost.

"It's pretty clear they like him. They really, *really* like him."

The story continued with footage of Andy signing books in a bookstore somewhere, the line of customers snaking off out of sight, and then several seconds of a campaign appearance Andy had made with Chris Wyeth in Cooperstown during the fall campaign. The voice-over put particular emphasis on Senator Foster's ability "to really connect with the people." The piece concluded with the studio reporter assuring the cohost that "the country could do much worse than to welcome Andy Foster as its next vice president should circumstances open such a door."

"Turn that down, please," Christine told Michelle as she divvied up the eggs onto two plates.

"Is Daddy going to be the next nice president?"

Christine eyed the girl warily. "Okay, are we just being cute here?"

"Is he?"

Christine decided that the malapropism was genuine; she'd have to re-member to share it with Andy. "Nobody really knows that right now, honey," Christine said. "A lot of things would have to come together in a certain way. I think the smartest thing right now is to focus on your break-fast."

"Miss Brandstetter asked me yesterday if we were going to move to Washington."

Christine wasn't thrilled to hear that. "Tell you what. If anyone else asks you any questions like that, do what I do."

"What's that?"

Christine set her fork down and pressed her hands over her ears. "La, la, la, la, la, la, la, la . . ."

Michelle's face lit up. She clamped her hands on her own ears. "La, la, la, la, la, la, la, la . . ."

Well, that's fine, Christine thought as she and her daughter made moony faces at each other. *La, la, la, la . . .*

But how long is this really going to work?

Andy had his game face on.

There was no avoiding the scrum of reporters and cameras waiting to ambush him as he arrived at the Capitol building. He recalled his father-in-law's advice: Give them everything and give them nothing.

Senator Foster gave them his attention, even suggesting with an amused smirk that he respected the badgering their job required them to do. A windup clown doll could have just as well tottered along the side-walk and recited the nonsense that Andy offered, though the clown doll would have lacked the charm that Andy brought to the task. The senator even allowed a modicum of eagerness to bleed into his presentation. He winked and grinned and expressed authentic uncertainty about what was happening in the executive branch right now.

"You know, it's just too early in the morning. Let me get my first cup of joe and I'll get back to you on that."

A handful of reporters stuck with him as he made his way inside the building and along the corridor toward his office, a Pied Piper scene played out time and time and time again in those fabled halls. The door to his offices beckoned, and it opened just as he and his gaggle reached them. An amused Jim Fergus stood there to welcome his boss.

Andy turned to the reporters and demurred in earnest. "Honestly, at this point I'm as much in the dark as all of you are. So right now, I'm just going to get on with the work of the people. That's what I'm being paid for. Everything else, we'll see what we see when we see it."

And with that, his aide-de-camp ushered him into the office and closed the door.

"You know, there's an easier way of saying that," Fergus remarked.

"Let's hear it."

" 'Surely I shit you. I shit you not.' "

Shortly after 11:30, Senator Foster excused himself from a tedious meeting of the Senate Ethics Oversight Committee and made his way by foot to the J. Edgar Hoover Building. Within several minutes of his arrival, Andy was shown into the office of William Pierce, the director of the Federal Bureau of Investigation. The two greeted each other and Pierce steered the senator to an anteroom just off his office.

Andy joked, "Is the lighting better in here for the hidden cameras?"

"You tell me what you consider your best side, Senator. We like our customers happy."

The jesting notwithstanding, as Andy took his seat in one of the comfortable chairs, he took in the lamps and wall switches and various accoutrements in the room. Something in the room was recording the scene. Only a fool would think otherwise. Pierce launched right in.

"Your friend Chris is certainly pissing blood these days, isn't he?"

Andy knew from experience that the director liked to swing heavy hammers. He floated a disarming smile across the room. "Why, I was saying just the same thing to the little lady the other day."

Pierce did not return the smile. A shade over six feet, with a head full of thick hair now gone the color of steel and the sort of powerful features that could well have been carved from the granite mined in his native New Hampshire, William Pierce's tenure as director of the Bureau now spanned three administrations. He was known to be fully at peace with the nickname that had been attached to him for most of his career: Iron Man. At sixty-seven, he remained in impressive physical condition, still working out strenuously on a daily basis and still keeping up with competitive rowing, a passion developed in his college days in New Haven. Andy had found occasion several times over the years to join the director for a round of golf. Pierce couldn't putt to save his life. But his tee shot was a wonder to observe.

Pierce settled a hard look on his visitor. "In case you're wondering, you're good to go. At least from where I sit."

"Good to go?"

"The veep job, Andy. Let's not sit here pretending you don't know you're being vetted up the ass to replace Wyeth."

"That's not why I'm here."

Pierce didn't seem to have heard him. "Also, just so you know. Screwing Spanish girls is not going to disqualify you for the office." He paused, looking for a reaction. Andy gave him none. That is, unless one of the hidden instruments in the room was monitoring the pace of his heartbeats. Pierce continued. "Hell, we've all screwed a Spanish girl at some point. In a manner of speaking."

"Rita Flores."

"Here's the thing. If you were actually running for the office and needed real votes, it'd be over. Married man? Nice pretty wife like you've got? But this is an appointment by the president. John Q. is not going to get to weigh in."

Andy shifted in his chair. "Is it worth my asking how you know about that?"

"It is not."

"Does Hyland know?"

"You'll let me worry about that," Pierce said flatly. "Like I said, nobody is squeaky-clean, Andy. So don't *you* worry. You're every bit as qualified as the president's other choices."

The FBI director was an old crony of Andy's father-in-law. The two had come up together, both politically and socially. Andy recalled how Bill Pierce in particular had bolstered Whitney during the ugly months following his and Lillian's return from London; he'd been fiercely loyal to his friend and cohort. Andy's own relations with Pierce had always been cordial, if not exactly cuddly. The director brought out the natural wariness in a person. At least, if the person had any common sense.

"I need to ask you something," Andy said. "Different topic. Though, thank you for that ringing endorsement."

"Don't mention it." Pierce took a beat. "In fact, *don't* mention it. So what is it you want to know?"

"First, I'd like to ask that there be no strings attached."

"Strings?"

"I want you to promise me that you don't open a file the moment I walk out of here. This is really nothing more than a fishing expedition on my part. It wouldn't be good for this conversation to get around. Clearly I'm not going through channels. Those would be the AG's office. I just don't happen to have as open a listener over at Justice as I do here."

"Okay. That's the suck-up part," Pierce said.

"Exactly." Andy paused. He wanted to make sure he had his white lie in order. Especially if it was being recorded. "I've got a constituent, Bill. Up in the city. You'd know him if I named him, and I'm not going to name him. He's got his fingers in pretty deeply with some import and export entities. All on the up and up. I've checked. Believe me, I wouldn't be wasting either of our time if it were otherwise."

"That's a very wise disclaimer, Andy," Pierce said.

The director didn't sound as if he was wholly swallowing Andy's tale, but Andy pressed on.

"The problem here is that it seems there have been some whisperings of late linking this individual with a man by the name of Aleksey Titov. You know about this Titov, don't you, Bill?"

Pierce maintained his poker face. On his right ring finger he wore a large gold signet ring inset with a light blue stone. He had hold of the ring with his index finger and thumb and was rotating it in half-circles on his finger.

"Go on."

Andy cleared his throat. "Ostensibly, this Titov runs his own import business. Actually, I shouldn't say ostensibly. He does. He's a businessman. He's registered. But I'm sure you remember the dust that was kicking up around Christmastime about this? I wasn't really paying it much attention myself, except that this Mr. Titov lives in New York and he seems to throw a lot of money around. So anything that might develop around a character like that is something my office would want to keep an eye on."

He paused for Pierce to pass comment, but the director maintained a stony silence. The expression on his face gave Andy nothing to read. The room was cold, and Andy could feel the Freon chilling the perspiration that had formed on his neck and at his hairline. It was too late to second-guess his plan; he plunged ahead.

"I guess that's what I'm after, Bill. There was that little flare-up of interest over the winter. As I recall, it looked at the time as if Titov was being given an extremely close look by the Feds. I guess I'm just sort of wondering what the status is there. I know the guy's a mobster. He's organized dirt."

Pierce nodded almost imperceptibly. Andy paused again. Pierce still gave no indication of being ready—or willing—to weigh in on what he was hearing. Andy plunged forward.

"I'm strictly fishing here, Bill. I'm just looking to see if there's anything interesting that might not yet be in the public record that might be something I can pass along to my friend. Like I said, my guy is just trying to make a buck the old-fashioned way. It's pathetic that someone like Titov can steal the food off his plate. For that matter, it wouldn't do me any harm to know what's going on in my backyard either, would it? Call me curious. I'm just wondering if this Titov has got anyone in particular in his pocket that we know about. Is he considered a big player? Or maybe angling to become one? Basically, I'm trying to find out his status."

Pierce allowed his head to tip slightly to the side. "His status?"

"Sure. Or the status of any investigation that might be going on with regard to him. For example, I'd love to be able to tell my friend if this Titov was about to explode. I'm just looking to get more of his story."

Andy wasn't sensing an especially receptive vibe from the director. Now that he was actually airing his vague inquiry, the story wasn't sounding terrifically convincing. He needed to be more blunt; William Pierce had too good a nose for the decorative bullshit. Andy skidded forward in his chair.

"Bottom line, Bill. How big a target is Aleksey Titov? On the scum factor. High? Low?"

"This is for your friend?"

"That's right."

"And what's good for your friend is good for you?"

Andy didn't care for the implication of Pierce's question, but then again he wasn't in a position to quibble. Andy straightened in his chair. He had to pull the plug on this thing.

"Forget it, Bill. I'm being vague, and you're right to call me on it. Next thing you know, I'll be seeing Russian mobsters under every pillow. Forget it."

"I'll look into it," Pierce said.

"No, honestly. No need. I was really more curious to see if there was anything off the top of your head. You stick with the big fish. And feel free to come waste my time whenever you wish."

Pierce gave a shrug. The two men chatted for several more minutes. Andy had the distinct feeling that the FBI director was gently batting him around, the way a cat does with a smaller creature in advance of snuffing it out. When Andy rose to leave, Pierce clamped a hand on his shoulder and walked him to the door.

"You know I'm apolitical, Andy," Pierce said as they paused at the door. "My personal feelings have no place in my job. But—"

Andy jumped in. "Thank you for your time, Bill. Seriously. All this noise going around about Chris and the rest of it. I guess I'm just trying to distract myself."

A trace of a smile appeared on Pierce's face. "Give my regards to your lovely wife, will you?"

"Sure thing."

Andy passed through Pierce's outer office and made his way back to the street. He knew that the FBI director's window looked out in the direction of the Mall and that even if Pierce had wanted to stand at the window watching his visitor's departure he wouldn't have been able to. Regardless, knowing this did not keep Andy from the feeling that he was not walking down the street unobserved.

Oh good, he said to himself as he reached the corner of Pennsylvania and Ninth avenues. *Paranoia. I'd been wondering where the heck you've been.*

CHAPTER 33

Andy caught the three forty-five out of Reagan National. He attempted to occupy himself during the short flight with the latest Richard Russo book. To a large degree, Russo wrote the same book over and over, but that didn't really matter to Andy, nor apparently to thousands of other readers. Each version of the story generally improved on the previous rendering. Deeper poignancy. Richer humor. Harder heartbreak. All the good stuff.

Andy couldn't concentrate.

By the time his tray table was locked in its upright position and the swirling grid of single-family dwellings adjacent to LaGuardia filled the window by his elbow, Andy hadn't turned three pages of the book. The flight landed, and Andy put his smile on autopilot as he navigated his way to the arrivals area, where a car was waiting for him. He felt both relief and suffocation as the door closed behind him, entombing him in the rear seat of the car.

Traffic was already slowing as the car made its way along the Grand Central Parkway toward the Midtown Tunnel. Andy's gaze was aimed out the tinted window at the Manhattan skyline, but the calliope of skyscrapers was not registering in his mind. Abruptly, he lurched forward in his seat.

"Brighton Beach. How long would it take us to get down there?"

The driver caught his eye in the rearview mirror. "No longer than it'll take us to get through the tunnel."

"Do it. Head down there."

The driver hit his turn signal and slid into the left lane. "Do you have an address, sir?"

Andy was already lost again in thought. "I . . . No. No address. We're not really going anywhere."

"Sir?"

"Just go! It doesn't matter. I just want to see the goddamned place."

———

The director of the museum's Costume Institute was off in Greece for two weeks, a tidbit of information that Smallwood had stumbled onto the day before.

The director's office was small and cramped, and Smallwood felt like a lumbering giant in it. He was standing at the photocopier. Although it wasn't necessary to close the lid in order to produce workable copies, Smallwood did have to press down hard on the original in order to ensure the clearest copy, so he couldn't simply let the machine do its work without him.

As the copier's light scanned horizontally back and forth beneath the glass, its emerald glow illuminated two naked mannequins that were standing off to one side of the machine, lending them a sense of animation. The emerald light was bathing his face as well. Every time it crossed his face, Smallwood lowered his eyelids, enjoying the wash of green. In addition to the low hum emitted by the photocopier, there was a rhythmic series of clicking sounds as well, sounds that Smallwood fell into duplicating, clicking his tongue along with them.

Smallwood was making five hundred copies. A good round number. More than he really needed, but that was all right. At first he had feared the original might not reproduce so nicely. But the copies were looking good enough. The photocopier engaged a series of plastic racks where the copies exited the machine, and after each rack collected fifty copies, it automatically shifted up a notch to the next empty rack. Smallwood appreciated the machine's efficiency of design. He found the whirs and clicks and pulsating green light extraordinarily soothing. He also appreciated the dungeonlike quality of the ill-lit office, and the two naked mannequins bathing in the rhythmic swipes of light. Smallwood felt he could have remained down in the office for days on end.

The plastic rack clicked up its final notch. Smallwood's eyes remained open for the final copies. The pages slid out onto the rack, one every second, accompanied by the photocopier's rhythmic *click . . . click . . . click . . .* They arrived faceup, momentarily suspended before dropping down softly onto the previous copy.

The cute little girl and her evil father.

As Smallwood watched the final fifty copies coming from the machine, it seemed that the father was becoming more and more evil with every passing sheet of paper. It really wasn't right that the little girl was saddled with such an evil creature for a father. Not right at all. And apparently this man held a lot of power. His influence could be felt by millions.

Smallwood plucked the next copy as it came out of the machine and studied the handsome face. It was unacceptable, this person wielding such power. Something had to be done about it. If for nothing else, Smallwood thought, at the very least for the cute little girl who was whispering into her daddy's ear.

Christine had been pleasantly surprised when Andy phoned to say that he had been called to New York for a meeting and that he'd be able to be home for dinner.

"Sweet of you to drop in on your constituents."

She thought that the family could do with a special dinner. She headed over to the market to pick up the ingredients for one of Andy's favorite dishes, Dublin fish stew. She decided to keep Andy's night at home a surprise for Michelle. Rosa was picking up Michelle and her friend Emily at school, and the three of them were planning to head over to Hudson River Park. Christine added some artichokes and a bag of forbidden rice to her shopping basket. At the pastry counter she nabbed a strawberry cheesecake. Her husband would *drool.*

Christine was oddly keyed up when Andy arrived home, but she immediately sensed that his energy was much more subdued than hers. He looked drawn. When she asked him what business had brought him up to the city, he brusquely waved the question aside.

"Nothing. Just stupid stuff."

Andy changed into his jogging clothes and went out for a run. Christine's joy over choreographing the special dinner was gone. As she cut the haddock into chunks and washed the irritatingly dirty spinach, she realized just how angry she was with Andy. A part of her knew it was unfair of her, but she was furious that no matter what, it always came down to being all about *him.* His campaign. His decisions. His speeches. His career. The long-ago echoes of her mother's tangles with her own self-involved husband didn't help to pacify Christine in the slightest. Christine measured out the rice and lined up the spices. She ran cold water over the hard-boiled eggs and peeled them in the sink, then took a knife to the eggs, slicing them swiftly with a practiced precision.

As she whittled the eyes out of the potatoes with a paring knife, Christine replayed in her mind the weekend she and Andy had spent together in Boston. She marveled at how swiftly they had fallen into sync and right back out again. The past three days seemed only to have deepened the sense of estrangement she was feeling.

When Andy returned from his run, he had Michelle in tow. He had come across her and Rosa in the park. So much for Christine's enjoying her surprise. But Michelle's delight over having her daddy home in the middle of the week served to shove Christine's irritation to a static part of her brain. Andy announced he was going to take a quick shower before dinner.

Except for the slightly overdone artichokes, the meal was delicious. Andy uncorked one of the bottles of the Benziger Reserve Chardonnay they had picked up during last spring's visit to Sonoma Valley and entertained Christine and Michelle with tales of the Earth Day event. His mood seemed to have lifted since his return. He thought his story of meeting Tori Amos would get a rise out of Michelle, but the child could not have looked more bored.

"Sweetie, your cluelessness is showing," Christine said to her husband. "Our daughter isn't even eight years old. Tori Amos is a dinosaur."

Midway through the meal, Andy started in on a story about his intern and an accident she had been in the day before involving a motorcycle. The story seemed to have come out of the blue. It sounded horrible. The young woman's left hip was essentially shattered. Christine sat speechless as her husband shared the gory details. It was bad enough that he was telling the story in front of Michelle in the first place. But even worse was the oddly casual gloss he was putting on the tale, as if he were doing nothing more than sharing with his family a mildly interesting little snippet of information. It was clear from Michelle's face that Andy's story was upsetting her. Christine intervened.

"Andy? I think this can keep until later."

Andy seemed confused. "I just thought . . . Well, I figured you should know, that's all."

"Fine. So I know. And so does our daughter. Thank you for sharing."

Andy's reply was interrupted by the phone ringing. Michelle hurried out of her chair.

"I'll get it!"

As Michelle sped into the kitchen, Christine felt the blood rushing into her face.

"What the hell are you *doing*? Your daughter is still freaked out about that phone message and now you come waltzing in with some goddamn story about a girl who might not walk again?"

"She's going to be able to—"

"That's not the point! The point is, I don't want to hear about this at the dinner table! For God's sake, Andy, I was just trying to have a—"

"*Daddy!*" Michelle was calling out from the kitchen.

Andy's chair was already pushing back from the table as Michelle came back into the room. "Who is it, sweetie?"

"It's Grandpa. He called me a poodle."

Andy mussed his daughter's hair. "Well, you are a poodle."

He disappeared into the kitchen. Christine reached for the wine bottle and topped up her glass. The call was brief. Andy came back in from the kitchen and retook his seat without a word.

"Well? What was it?" Christine asked. "What did he want?"

Andy took hold of his wineglass and lifted it. He was offering a toast, though from the expression on his face it looked more as if he were about to announce the nuclear obliteration of a dozen small countries.

"Chris Wyeth is announcing his resignation tomorrow. Effective Monday."

Christine froze. "We're *toasting* that?"

"Hyland wants me for VP."

Christine felt as though light were passing swiftly back and forth through her body. Too swiftly. Her chair skidded back from the table.

The table swam sickeningly in front of her.

"Great news, Andy. It's wonderful. And so good of you to pop in and fucking share!"

"*Mommy!*"

Christine fled into her workroom. She stood in the middle of the floor, trembling with rage. Andy arrived seconds later, stepping over to her and wrapping his arms around her from behind. He brought his mouth close to her ear.

"Honey. Shhh. It's okay. Everything's going to be—"

He stopped abruptly. His attention had been hijacked by a large photograph on the far wall showing a naked man standing in a bathtub. The man was rippling with muscles and covered from head to foot with tat-toos. Some sort of slick white liquid ran down his body.

"What the hell is *that?*"

Christine wormed her way free from his arms and spun around to face him. Her eyes were as red as the devil's.

"It's a naked man covered with milk, what do you think it is? That's the kind of crap I get up to while you're off saving the fucking world!"

CHAPTER 34

Rob Smallwood went up on his toes to run out the last bit of Scotch tape, then came down from the chair and returned it to his small kitchen. The remains of his dinner were still on the table. He'd been too excited to finish it.

Tomorrow would be two weeks since his benevolent execution of Cousin Joy. Smallwood still carried a sadness that her removal had proved necessary. But he also knew that sadness was not an excuse for not taking action.

How different everything might have been if Cousin Joy had remained pure. If she had taken the time to listen to him as he grew older and wiser, instead of shutting him out and avoiding him the way she had, she might still be here. She might have understood what he was telling her, and she might have respected him. They could have had fun together, like they had when they were both young.

Smallwood kept his head down as he returned to his bedroom, keeping his eyes trained on the floor as he undressed. He was humming a tune, but if anyone had asked, he would not have been able to identify it.

Of course, there was no one to ask him. Eleven years in this apartment and there had not been a single human sound made here that Smallwood had not made himself.

But maybe that was about to change.

His eyes still lowered, Smallwood got into his single bed and pulled the sheet and the thin blanket up to his chin. He reached down to the floor and picked up a flashlight and turned it on. Turning off the bedside light, he trained the flashlight beam onto the wall at the foot of the bed. Only then did he allow himself to raise his eyes.

It had required far fewer than a third of the five hundred copies he had made, but that was okay. Smallwood moved the cone of light from copy to copy. The cute little girl whispering into the ear of her evil father. Except that Smallwood had removed the father from the copies and made it look as if the little girl was whispering to her other self, who was in turn whispering to her other self, who was in turn whispering to her other self, and so on. Everywhere the flashlight landed, there she was.

Smallwood flicked the flashlight over to the other wall, the one with the window that looked out onto nothing. He ran the beam around in swift circles then stilled it. One hundred twenty-seven copies of Cousin Joy, aged nine, leaping from the front porch of the house on Shelter Island. Frozen in midair. Her little skirt lifting, and that wonderful look on her face. It didn't make a difference where the flashlight beam landed, it always landed on Cousin Joy. And now she had a new friend.

CHAPTER 35

Vice President Christopher Wyeth went before the cameras at eleven thirty on Thursday morning to announce his pending resignation. His demeanor was remarkably loose, all things considered. As he entered the White House briefing room, he joked with a number of the assembled journalists.

"If anyone here needs a second for tennis anytime in the near future, I believe I'm going to be extremely available."

Wyeth's wife, Laura, and their two grown sons had been positioned in front of the American flag behind the podium. As Wyeth fussed with his notes, he glanced up into the glare of the television camera lights and lowered his reading glasses to the tip of his nose.

"Does anyone here by any chance happen to have a dagger? These occasions often seem to call for one."

The laughter was understandably nervous. Laura Wyeth looked as if she were ready to break into little pieces. The two sons maintained respectable poker faces.

The vice president cleared his throat.

"I'd like to begin by asking anyone here who has never made a poor judgment in their life to please identify yourself and leave the room." He paused, arching an eyebrow as he swept the room with his eyes. "Right. I just wanted to confirm that we're all human. So, let's get down to it."

Once more he cleared his throat and fiddled with his reading glasses. He half-turned to give a bucking-up smile to his wife, then faced forward again and proceeded.

"From the perspective of absolute truth, which is often a far cry from the reality of how we actually conduct our business here on the planet, the act of governing should be a humbling endeavor. Choosing to shoulder the responsibility of looking after the welfare of one's fellow citizens is *not* a noble choice. Or perhaps I should say it ought not be considered a noble choice by the one who takes it on. In a perfect world . . ."

Wyeth paused, allowing his gaze to meander about the room.

"In a perfect world, there would be no place for a sense of loftiness or entitlement in those who steer their lives in the direction of public service. But maybe you've noticed we don't live in a perfect world. Even so, I want to take this opportunity to tell you that over the course of my thirty-seven years as a public servant, I have never felt entitled to the various positions I have held in government. I hope I have never been made to feel lofty by the powers I have acquired along the way."

The vice president paused again, allowing himself once more to swim through the sea of faces. When he resumed, his eyes were fixed on the bank of TV cameras in the rear of the room. He rose slightly on his toes, pitching ever so slightly forward on the podium.

"Today I am announcing that, due to forces that I can only characterize as pathetically petty, you are losing an imperfect but nonetheless devoted public servant."

A general murmur rose up in the briefing room. An army of Black-Berries were already at work. Behind the vice president, Laura Wyeth lowered her head. The son nearest her sought her hand and gave it a squeeze. The face that rose was damp with tears.

But Chris Wyeth had the look of a man who was just getting started. He adjusted his glasses and glanced down at his notes.

"Of course I'm bitter. Let's not be silly about it. I stand before you delivering my political eulogy. I made some classic poor judgments in my early career, and here they are, decades later, extinguishing my flames. There's no deflecting here. It's my turn to pay a dear price for a few foolish acts of hubris committed in my younger, hungrier political days. I know as well as anyone else, that's how the game is played. I assure you that nothing I may have done in the past in any way compromised my service to the people who had entrusted me with my responsibilities, and I assure you that nothing in my past stood any chance of harming my abilities to serve my president and my fellow citizens as vice president of this great country. But individuals come and go. I am sure that the world will keep spinning and that this country will keep doing what it does best with or without the participation of the man who stands before you."

He paused, allowing his gaze to travel the room.

"But here is what I want you to consider. *You* were the ones who voted me into this office, but *you* are not the ones who are voting me out. Let it be clear, I am not blaming President Hyland. John Hyland is a good man. An honorable public servant who has earned your trust and who will do his very best to re-earn that trust every day he is in office. He is still your president. Score one for you."

From the corner of his eye, Wyeth saw his press secretary engaged in a heated argument of whispers with a member of the president's executive inner circle. Wyeth had not cautioned his press secretary concerning the scope of his remarks, and the president's man was furious.

Wyeth continued.

"But even John Hyland is also only as human as you and I. And although you will hear from many quarters over the coming days and weeks that the system worked, I would counsel the citizens of this country to ask precisely who did it best work for? If you are truly concerned about the state of your republic, then alleged decades-old kickbacks and arm-twistings by a resigning vice president should be the least of your worries. They're certainly the least of mine. As I prepare to join you as a private citizen, I advise you: Upgrade your worries, people. Thank you."

Wyeth collected the pages of his statement and squared them off with a few taps against the podium.

"And good luck."

Whitney Hoyt threw the remote across the room, but it fell short of the television screen.

"That double-talking low-life bastard!"

Paul Jordan rose from the couch and retrieved the remote. "I take it you're going to pass on the commentaries?"

Hoyt was red in the face. "That son of a bitch. Have you ever heard such a load of crap in your life?"

Jordan tried again. "Do you want to—"

"Hell, no! Turn the damn thing off. If there is even half a God, that's the last time I'll ever have to see that son-of-a-bitch double-talker. Fine public servant my ass, trying to rile up the country like that on your way out. What the hell are people supposed to make of that nonsense? Doesn't the man have the simple decency to resign with dignity instead of shooting his fool mouth off?"

Jordan turned the television off. He shared a look with Jenny Hoyt, who had watched Wyeth's speech while seated on an ottoman. Jenny pivoted toward her husband.

"Whitney, I'm going to say something that might upset you."

Hoyt snapped. "It couldn't be any worse than the crap we just heard!"

Jordan took a step toward his boss. "Perhaps you should listen to your wife."

Hoyt eyed his personal secretary with a withering disdain. "Thank you for that advice, Paul. I'm so fortunate to have a voice of reason on my payroll."

After fifteen years as Hoyt's assistant, Jordan knew well the boundaries of his employer's tolerance. He knew there was an inch or so yet remaining.

"Your reaction to this is not especially startling," Jordan said plainly. "Speaking from my side, I'd like to hear Jenny's take."

Sulking, Hoyt turned to his wife. "Go ahead, Jen. Mr. James Bond is fascinated to hear what you have to say."

"You're simply too close to the situation," Jenny said. "There's too much history between you and Chris. Everyone knows that."

"Everyone knows it, so what is the point in your repeating it?"

"I'm sorry, dear," Jenny continued, "but in my opinion, what Chris just said was one of the most courageous political speeches I have ever heard."

Hoyt scrambled to his feet. He skirted the coffee table, moving quickly over to where his wife was seated.

Jordan started forward. "Whitney!"

Jenny rose up calmly from the ottoman. Hoyt moved forward, getting his chin to within an inch of his wife's. His watery eyes were livid.

"I don't *ever* want to hear you say something like that again. Is that clear?"

Jenny Hoyt held her ground. There had never been any issue of physical violence in her nine years of marriage to Whitney. Still, she had rarely seen her husband so enraged. She responded to Hoyt in a cool tone. "For goodness' sake, this is what you wanted. Chris Wyeth is gone. His career is over, Whitney."

The flames remained in Hoyt's eyes. He was so angry his body was trembling.

Jordan came closer. "Whitney, she's right. Let the man have his final hurrah. What were you expecting? Tears?"

Jenny took her husband's freckled hand in hers and squeezed it lightly.

"You did this, sweetheart. You pulled the levers. Whit, you did this to be happy. Can't you be happy?"

Generally speaking, for a man his age Whitney Hoyt was terrifically fit. But at certain times in their life together, it would hit Jenny Hoyt just how old her husband actually was. After all, the years did have the man by the throat, and sometimes their grip showed itself.

CHAPTER 36

President Hyland's meeting with Senator Andrew Foster in the Oval Office was not on the schedule that was made available daily to members of the press. Officially, Hyland was in the White House gym, looking after the little pair of love handles that had attached themselves to him since his inauguration in January.

The two men were at the seating area, drinking tea. The teapot was a Royal Patrician Antique Rose Chintz six-cup teapot, exceedingly delicate and feminine-looking and, according to Hyland, the very pot from which Franklin Delano Roosevelt had taken his tea for most of his three-plus terms in office.

"Nothing to fear but fear itself," Hyland remarked after giving Senator Foster the provenance of the teapot. "That man delivered some killer lines. I just love that one." He recited the phrase again. "It's so true. There *is* no fear except when you cop to it. It's brilliant. If any of my speechwriters ever delivers a gem like that one to me, I'll fall to my knees."

Andy wasn't exactly sure how to respond to the president. He wondered if perhaps Hyland had spotted something in his eyes. Fear was Andy's constant companion these days; it was piggybacking everywhere he went. It had risen with him that morning in New York when he'd slipped out of bed before sunrise, and it had stayed with him on the early shuttle down to the capital. It had managed to slip past the elaborate White House security with the ease of light. Hyland's delight in the phrase eluded him. *I have much to fear,* Andy thought, and he imagined sliding the three photographs of himself and Joy Resnick onto the president's desk and asking the chief executive, How about these? Pretty fucking frightening, wouldn't you say?

Hyland held his Royal Patrician teacup in both hands, as if he was warming them. Andy was somewhat unnerved by his gaze; the man looked as if he hadn't a care in the world.

"I'd like to clear away the Whitney issue first thing, if I may," Hyland said.

Andy shifted in his chair. "Whitney?"

"In truth, there's very little to discuss," Hyland said. "Except that I do want to make it clear to you, Andy, that you are here because *I* want you here. Whitney Hoyt did not choose you to replace Chris Wyeth. I did. Of course, we both know that the governor is delighted with the choice."

Andy agreed. "I imagine it won't make him unhappy."

"I'm assuming Whitney told you about our meeting?"

"No," Andy said. "He didn't say anything to me."

"Well, we met." A small laugh escaped Hyland. "Whitney summoned me, is more like it. Grand Caesar that he thinks he is. The bastard had the goods on Wyeth. This whole kickback garbage. He'd had that information tucked in his pocket all along, I'm positive. Stupid and completely foolish stuff, of course. Chris basically said as much in his statement this morning. Simple greed and stupidity. How many eons do you suppose it is going to take before the best and the brightest finally stop also being the stupidest? For some ungodly reason, we keep thinking, '*I'm* the one who's going to get away with it. I'm the special one.' "

Andy felt ill. How dare he be sitting here with the president of the United States discussing his own imminent ascension?

Hyland continued. "I assume you saw what else Chris did this morning? His little twist of the knife?"

"I guess you could say he told America to watch out for the Whitney Hoyts of this world."

"Exactly! Beware the pissing contests."

Andy looked across the coffee table at John Hyland. Even though Andy's own political position in a Chris Wyeth presidency would have been superb, privately he had been glad when Hyland had prevailed in the primaries. He liked the man. He thought Hyland was the right man for the job at the right time in history. The fact that Andy was sitting in the Oval Office sipping tea with the president and discussing the strategies for presenting himself to the country as Hyland's new vice president was astounding. He wanted this job. History seemed to be flinging a lot of horseshoes helter-skelter right now, and Andy was watching his own spinning through the air in achingly slow motion, right toward the golden pole. If he could somehow manage over the next few days to turn his nightmare to dust, it was completely possible that his horseshoe could come down with a resounding *clang*. A classic ringer. He wanted this opportunity. He wanted to contribute palpably to the new president's vision. He'd wanted to discuss this with Christine the night before, after receiving the official invitation, but their discussion had devolved swiftly. Andy could never have imagined the severity with which his and Christine's visions diverged. It was as if the two were inhabiting completely separate worlds.

President Hyland set his teacup aside and leaned forward in his chair. "I'd like to ask you something, Andy. You're under no obligation to answer, but it's something that has always perplexed me. It has perplexed a lot of people."

Andy nodded tersely. "Shoot."

"Precisely how many blind babies did Wyeth have to rape in order to become such a pariah in your father-in-law's eyes? I just find it fascinating. For so many years those two were of such a piece."

"I can't honestly tell you the whole history behind Whitney's antipathy toward Chris," Andy said. "I've never had any real discussions with either of them about it, and frankly, that's worked for me. Old story. The politics got ugly and the friendship curdled. After Whitney resigned from the governorship he was counting on Chris's support for his run for the presidency, and Chris essentially stabbed him in the back. I hated to see things between them degrade the way they did, but you know as well as I do, this is a rough business."

Hyland allowed a trace of a smile onto his face. "So I'm hearing." The president straightened in his chair. Andy could practically hear the shift of gears. "So, then. What say we get on to you."

Andy gestured with his cup. "No time like the present."

"Here's where we are, Andy. The most important thing for the nation right now is that we handle this change in the administration in a way that reassures everybody. Chris Wyeth has been a popular political figure for a long time. Nobody is arguing that Chris didn't have superb qualities that more than justified his spot on the ticket. And that valedictory he gave this morning is certainly not going to hurt his brand equity one bit. There are plenty of people out there who don't want to see him step down. But that decision's been made. Our great fortune in having you in particular available to step into the job is the continuity it brings. You and Chris are already associated in people's minds. In good ways, I mean. Your politics,

your social connections. Your careers have been something of a comple-
ment to each other, so we're going to be emphasizing this continuity. This
is as close to not rocking the boat as we can get."

"I think I see where you're coming from, Mr. President."

"Of course, what we don't want is the continuity of scandal. I've been
assured that you're as clean as a Boy Scout."

Andy considered the details of his little sit-down with William Pierce
the day before. Either the FBI director was keeping a few of his cards from
the president, or Hyland was running a little bluff here to sound out Andy.

Andy raised three fingers pressed together. "I'm prepared."

"Good. So as you know, we're looking at Monday morning to make the
announcement. That means by Sunday, of course, the word is out. We've
already been in touch with your office about the Sunday shows. You're not
to do any of them. We're quite firm on that. In fact, it might be best if you
and your family were to be away for the weekend. Out of media range altogether, if that's even possible anymore. Maybe you want to take that
lovely wife of yours away for a little getaway. It's likely to be your last crack
at normalcy for quite a while."

Andy's thoughts raced again to the night before and the look of be-
trayal that had settled onto his wife's face. The number of ways it broke his
heart was too great to tally.

"I'll think about that, Mr. President."

CHAPTER 37

The wind was whipping hard, creating tiny whitecaps on the water. Metal umbrellas out on the pier trembled vigorously, the slicing wind setting off a low moaning sound. It was also stealing the stinging tears from Christine Foster's cheeks, blasting them away the instant they appeared.

Christine gazed across the river. The New Jersey skyline had nothing of note to offer. Christine felt like such a snob. Weehawken. Hoboken. Jersey City. She had lived on the river for what seemed like forever and had never bothered to get clear what was what across the river.

Somewhere over there, Alexander Hamilton and Aaron Burr had fought their infamous duel. It was her brother who had first told her the story. Thomas Jefferson's vice president and his unrelenting political nemesis had risen early in the morning and each ferried across the hard-running river in rowboats to play out the asinine ritual on the cliffs of Weehawken. Vice President Burr had killed Hamilton with a shot that had purportedly been outside the confines of the rules of the duel. Whatever in the world that meant. Killing is killing; where precisely *rules* found their way into the barbarity was something that escaped Christine's way of thinking.

Christine was seated on one of the green metal benches lining the waterfront. The heels of her feet were wedged up on the lip of the bench, her arms looped tightly around her knees. She'd left the apartment and come out to the riverfront walk an hour ago. At the moment, she could not conceive of ever getting up from the bench and going anywhere else. It wasn't so much that the river or the modest New Jersey skyline was particularly jazzing; it was that Christine simply could muster no enthusiasm for taking any of the various next steps that life was presenting. If anything, she wanted to take steps that led backward.

Christine tried to recall Peter relating to her the story of the Burr-Hamilton duel. She could not remember if Burr had finished out his term after the incident. Back in the day, did they allow for the victor in a so-called gentleman's settlement to continue in office? Had history recorded a known murderer working in the White House? Christine's gaze traveled the landscape across the river. She tried to imagine two little puffs of smoke. One distant body falling to the ground.

She missed her brother. Sometimes thirteen years felt more like thirteen seconds, and this was one of those times. Christine recalled the exact feeling of hearing the news that Peter was dead. She and Andy had just returned from a weekend with friends out in the Hamptons; the message had been waiting for her on the answering machine. Her father had left it.

"Your brother's slow-motion suicide has finally ended, Chrissie. Your mother's a mess. Give me a call when you get in."

Peter's body had been discovered by his girlfriend on the bed in his cramped Hell's Kitchen apartment. By the time his system had seized, the combination of vodka and barbiturate cocktails had long become the only steady ingredient in Peter Hoyt's diet, rendering his bloodstream essentially useless. Whitney Hoyt's bland pronouncement of slow-motion suicide, cold as it sounded over Christine and Andy's answering machine, had been essentially accurate. Christine's unfortunate brother had not so much gone off track during his short life as he had never really found his way onto the rails in the first place. Certainly this had been Whitney's verdict on the boy, and this was one thing Christine would never understand: why her father had felt that he had to be so hard on Peter. Right out of the gate, the standards that Whitney had set for Peter seemed to have been specifically designed to be unattainable. From early on in his life, Peter had felt that his father was purposefully sabotaging his chances of ever achieving a satisfactory level of . . . anything.

"If the son of a bitch wants me to fail so badly," he'd once said to his sister, "I'll show him just what a real fuckup can achieve. Maybe that'll make the bastard happy."

Of course it hadn't. It hadn't made anyone happy, least of all Peter. After dropping out of college midway through his senior year, Peter had never gained traction on any path except those that led swiftly to dead ends. Peter had shared his mother's exquisite bone structure, and before his purposeful defeats finally began to register on his appearance, his physical beauty had been nearly unsettling. Peter had readily used his extraordinary looks to his advantage—he was rarely without a delicious-looking female at his side. So many doors had been open to him. To the envious observer, Peter Hoyt should have managed just fine. There seemed no reason why his feet would have even needed to touch the cruel ground.

But tell it to the boy. Peter had suffered.

Not finding sufficient release from the suffering of his place in the world, Christine's brother had sought to redo the chemical mix within himself and see if maybe any of those concoctions could minimize the pain. Sometimes they had, but only temporarily. And ultimately, the various means of temporary release lost their capacity to lift Peter from his personal tortures. They turned on him, as he knew they someday would. When Christine heard the message about Peter's death, she had experienced the heartbreaking strain between shock and gratitude—a sad thankfulness that her brother's anguished life was blessedly over.

Christine still missed him horribly. Lonely Peter. The person who had understood her best. Better, she often feared, than even Andy could.

As Christine's eyes rested, half-seeing, on the choppy Hudson, it dawned on her by degrees that what she might be fearing most about the seemingly inevitable plunge her husband was taking was that she was also going to lose *him*—Andy—in ways she just wasn't certain she could accept. She was sick of the disappearing men. If Andy took on this job, to a much deeper degree than was already happening he was going to become phantom family. It wasn't just the logistics of the two-city living; those she could navigate. It was the devouring nature of political power itself that Christine feared. She missed talking with Andy the way they used to in their early years together. Already, something fundamental had been quietly corroding. And she was finding no joy whatsoever now in confronting the abject certainty that she was about to lose even more of what she already had so little of.

A black silhouette cut in front of Christine. She paid it no attention. Her eyes had ceased collecting data. A moment later, the thin black arc of a bicycle tire moved into Christine's peripheral vision. Vaguely, she sensed it.

"I thought that was you."

Christine looked up. At first she didn't recognize the bicyclist. Not until he removed his helmet, releasing the coal-black curls.

"Are you okay?"

It was the sculptor. Michael. Formerly known as New Bear.

"Hi. No. I'm fine," Christine said.

Straddling his bike saddle, the sculptor moved his bicycle closer to her. "No offense, but you don't look fine."

A retort rose to Christine's lips, but she let it die there. The young man moved the bike closer still. Christine closed her eyes. The sobs began.

"You're right. I'm not."

CHAPTER 38

Christine hated Andy.

She hated her father.

She hated her mother.

She also hated her brother. Right now, him most of all. She hated Peter for the simple fact of his being dead and not here to help her anymore.

The sculptor had moved up directly behind her as she stood at the metal sink, mindlessly rolling a ceramic mug around in the rush of hot water from the spigot. His arms looped easily around her, and he gently took the mug from her fingers, leaning in closer. She felt his breath on the back of her neck.

He placed the mug down in the sink and his hands disappeared, landing lightly on her shoulders. Strong hands. Of course they were. His thumbs circled slowly on the taut cord of muscle running down her neck.

Christine's chin lifted and she found herself face-to-face with a round mirror that hung above the sink. The artist's studio filled the circle of glass: curved metal sheets, massive bronze pillars throwing back sharp copper light, giant-size lightning bolts slashing wildly at one another. The effect of so many ambitious twists of metal vying for space created an ethereal landscape. The floor was a film of rust-colored particles.

Christine had fallen into a seriously dreamlike state—if not already out by the river where the young man had taken her gently by the elbow, then certainly in the catacomb of a building that held his showcase of alien structures. The sense of moving through fog had intensified as the two rode the cagelike freight elevator up the fourteen floors to the stranger's studio, a disturbing *clack* sound echoing from the darkness with each passing floor. The elevator door was not so much a door as a mesh gate that opened north-to-south from the middle, reminding Christine of a large square mouth. When the two portions had clattered apart, she'd been un-clear whether she was stepping out of the mouth or into it.

Now she knew.

The young man shifted his weight. He drew her away from the sink and began to maneuver her in a slow pirouette, until he had rotated her a full hundred and eighty degrees. Christine dared to look up into his face. From elsewhere off in the building, the clacking sounds she'd first heard while on the freight elevator continued to echo.

Christine gasped, and he responded, sliding both his hands down along her hips and pulling her forward to him. He was lifting her as if she weighed nothing at all. She gave herself over. The toe of one of her shoes traced a trail on the floor's reddish powder.

They reached the white brick wall, and Christine lost her breath as her shoulders pressed against the bricks. She clutched at his back and he shifted his grip, bringing his face to her neck. Christine became aware of her thin skirt bunching at her hips, and a pair of assured fingers working their way past the elastic of her panties. From deep within her came a low moan. Her eyes fell on the battered teakettle that her host had set on the portable burner to boil water for tea. The kettle was burbling and spitting mutely, its whistle long since dead. She moaned again. This one was longer and more sonorous.

And scary.

"No!"

Christine grabbed at his arms. With a tremendous effort, she pulled free from where she'd been headed and extricated herself from the hand-some young sculptor's grip. Tears rushed to her eyes as she batted at her skirt, getting it back into place. Her cheeks were on fire.

"I'm . . . I'm sorry. I just—"

Her body began to tremble. A wooden stool stood along the wall, and he helped her onto it. The tears continued down her face, and he soothed her. His touch—now—could not have been more light.

"Shhhh, it's okay. Everything's fine. Not to worry, okay?"

Christine's head remained lowered. She would not look up at him. The rust-colored floor swam in her eyes. It was *not* all right. Her chest ached in a way she could barely recall it ever aching before. It *hurt*. It hurt horribly.

———

Every person on the street knew exactly where she was coming from and exactly what she had almost done. Christine found her ability to put one foot smoothly and naturally in front of the other was pathetically impaired. The ball wanted to land before the heel. Every movement of her body seemed eager to betray her. Passing a large blacked-out window on Hudson Street, she paused and raked her hand through her hair. She wanted to address the image in the window, but all she could do was stare—horrified—at the stranger staring back at her.

Christine did not register the presence of two police cars in front of her building. When Jimmy at the front door gave her a dark, troubled look, she felt certain that he knew already about what had almost transpired in the sculptor's studio. Mysterious footage must have instantly made its way out into the world, and the doorman would never look at her the same way again. He used to think highly of the senator's wife. Nice lady. That sweet little kid of hers. Now she was just some flat back flouncing home from her afternoon romp with sculptor boy.

Christine rode the elevator with old Mrs. Ames and her Yorkie. The Yorkie knew. The disparaging look in his half-hidden eyes could not have been more evident.

The elevator stopped at her floor, and she got off and saw the two policemen at her front door. *They're going to* arrest *me?*

One of the cops was black. He spoke first. "Mrs. Foster?"

Christine moved down the hallway on undependable feet.

"What is it?"

The door was open. From inside the apartment she could hear Rosa's voice, going at top speed.

"Can you step inside, ma'am?"

Her blood turned to ice. "What is it?"

"Miss Christine!"

Rosa was running down the apartment hallway toward the front door with her hands waving over her head, as if her hair were on fire. Christine's hands flew to her mouth.

"Andy?"

The cop answered. "It's your daughter, ma'am."

Rosa reached the front door. She fell into Christine, pouring tears onto her blouse.

"I'm sorry, I'm sorry, I'm so sorry . . ."

Christine was tumbling. Back into her nightmare. Was there to be no waking up? The worst words imaginable assaulted her mind, rebounding dreadfully inside her skull.

God hates me. My daughter has been killed.

PART TWO

CHAPTER 39

At approximately 3:45 in the afternoon in New York Criminal Court Part Four, NYPD detective Megan Lamb raised her right hand and promised to tell the truth, the whole truth, and nothing but the truth.

At 3:47, leveling her finger at the well-dressed man seated at the defense table, she told it.

"That man is an arrogant, abusive rapist *and* a murderer! He knew exactly how to exploit the vulnerability of—"

The lead defense attorney leaped to his feet. "Objection, Your Honor!"

Rolling her shoulders, Megan thundered right back, "Oh, I bet you object!"

As a chorus of rumblings—and one "Right on!"—erupted from the onlookers, the judge's gavel did a superb impression of gunshots.

"That's enough!"

It took several more cracks of the gavel to silence the room. The defense attorney remained standing, red faced and sputtering, his words momentarily backed up in his brain. With a final look of warning to the witness, the judge sustained the objection. She waved her hand dismissively at the lawyer.

"Counselor, please sit down."

As the lawyer retook his seat, the judge addressed the jury.

"You are to disregard the witness's outburst. This was not testimony; it was mere opinion. I'm instructing the court reporter to strike it from the record and you to strike it from your memories."

She shifted in her seat to more squarely face the witness.

"And I'm instructing you to do your job, Detective Lamb. You're not new to any of this. Give these people the facts as you know them. Your own personal conclusions are of no interest to anyone in this courtroom except yourself."

Megan Lamb scowled at the judge. Off on the periphery of her vision, the smugness of the defendant showed itself in the overlarge recrossing of his arms. If the dapper man was attempting to hide the smirk on his face, he was failing. Megan turned back to the courtroom and leaned forward in her seat, her gaze leveled on the defendant.

"My conclusions *are* the facts," she said.

And the whole cacophony erupted once more.

Megan was positioning her computer on her desk. Again. After leaving it for a day and a half on the right side of the desk, she was thinking maybe the left side was preferable after all. She slid the phone closer to the center of the desk—again—next to the photograph of Helen. *This is stupid,* she said to herself. Simply resetting things on the desk precisely as they'd been when she was uptown at the 21st Precinct was . . . yes, it was stupid.

Be here now.

She repositioned her coffee mug next to the computer monitor. Somewhere in the move from uptown the mug had received a chip on the rim. When she'd first discovered the nick, Megan had nearly hurled the mug against the nearest wall.

She slid the photograph a little to the right.

Stupid.

"I hear you got a little testy just now in court."

Megan wheeled around. She hadn't heard anyone approaching.

Malcolm Bell was standing behind her, his arms crossed, a mirthless expression on his mocha face. Bell was Megan's superior, the captain at the 6th, though not much more veteran there than Megan. Two new kids on the block.

Megan swiveled her chair to more directly face her boss.

"There was nothing *testy* about it," she said. "I blew my stack."

"That's the word I'm hearing. The assistant DA gave me a jingle."

Megan did a double take. "Rogers? He *called* you?"

"We had a number of matters to discuss. He was of the opinion—"

"Bullshit! Larry Rogers is blowing this case right in front of everybody's eyes."

"You were an inch away from contempt," Bell said.

Megan wasn't having any of it. "Oh no, Captain, there was no inch left. I was *there*. That so-called doctor had this woman on so many drugs she could have thought it was the man in the moon climbing on top of her.

This is her *doctor*! The man she went to for help! Instead he systematically abused that poor woman to the point—"

Bell was trying to put the snakes back into the box. "Okay, okay, I know all—"

"She *killed* herself, Captain! That smug bastard is responsible for that poor woman's death. And in the meantime, the upstanding Larry Rogers's bungling is going to let the son of a bitch go free!"

"When my detectives are on the stand I'd like them to display a little more gravitas."

The face Megan made was not a pleasant one.

Bell's voice darkened. "If you don't care for the word, Detective, we'll just settle for the word *professionalism*. I trust I am being clear."

Megan murmured, "Gravitas. I hear you."

Bell took a deep breath and held it momentarily.

"What are you working on right now?"

"Right now?" Megan pulled a pair of pencils from her desk drawer and dropped them into the coffee mug. "Right now I'm putting my house in order. Why do you ask?"

Bell's hand waved vaguely at his detective's desk. "That's going to wait. I want you at Andrew Foster's apartment as quickly as possible."

"Andrew Foster as in Senator Andrew Foster?"

"That's right. Romano and Collins are there with the senator's wife. So far no media. That won't last long."

Megan asked, "What's the problem?"

Bell's cell phone went off, and he pulled it from his belt and checked the readout. He didn't appear to like what he saw.

"Out of the chair, Detective. The senator's house is in a lot worse order than yours right now. You'll have time to play with your pencils later. Let's move it."

Megan wondered how much longer the woman was going to remain standing at the window looking out toward the river. Compared with the postage-stamp-sized view of the Hudson in her own apartment, the Fosters' picture window was practically CinemaScope. Christine Foster stood dead center at the window, arms wrapped tightly around herself, confronting the distant disk of the sun as it scorched the low bank of clouds spread over New Jersey.

Megan looked over at the two patrolmen, Romano and Collins, who were standing uncomfortably in front of the open kitchen counter. The nanny, Rosa, stood several feet behind her employer, also hugging herself. The poor thing was trembling like an autumn leaf.

Megan caught Romano's eye. "Officer, could you get Mrs. Rodriguez a glass of water?" Romano fetched the water. As he approached the nanny with it, Megan added, "You can take Mrs. Rodriguez into the den, please."

She signaled Collins to follow them. As the trio disappeared down the hallway, Megan addressed the distraught mother.

"You're blaming the wrong person, Mrs. Foster."

Christine murmured, "You have no idea who it is I'm blaming."

Megan rapped her fingers against her notebook, where she had just taken down the nanny's statement.

"The element of surprise. I can't imagine anyone reacting any differently."

Christine brushed irritably at her bangs. "You're not hearing me, Detective. I'm not blaming Rosa for this. I'm blaming myself. And I'm blaming my husband. We're the parents."

Megan knew better than to get into a parsing match. "I'm going to need to speak with your husband, of course."

"Andy's on his way from Washington."

"It's my guess that the FBI is going to get here a lot quicker than your husband."

Christine blinked dumbly. "FBI?"

"They just can't help themselves," Megan said. "This is clearly the jurisdiction of the NYPD, but you can count on it. A man like your husband? You'll get the federal treatment, Mrs. Foster. But please don't worry. We'll cooperate and coordinate with them. It'll be fine."

"It's going to be a media circus, isn't it?"

Megan nodded. "I'm afraid so. Clowns and all."

Rosa Rodriguez had picked up Michelle Foster from the Little Red School House at three o'clock, as scheduled. Michelle had been waiting just outside the school, still on school property, with several of her classmates. Her homeroom teacher, Miss Brandstetter, was keeping an eye on the children while they waited to be picked up. The nanny and Michelle had headed off in the direction of Hudson River Park. Proceeding west on Perry Street, Rosa Rodriguez noticed a man standing midway down the block. She would describe him later as large, possibly six-three or six-four. Male, Caucasian, and wearing a Panama-style hat and a green windbreaker.

A white van with no markings was parked at the curb, next to where the man was standing. Rosa contended that it was possible that the van had passed the two of them as they had started down the block and had pulled over to the curb some twenty or so feet in front of them. She simply could not be sure. Maybe.

As she and Michelle approached, the man hailed them. He was holding a map, and he asked Rosa if she could help him with directions. As Rosa leaned her face into the map, the man let the paper slide away to reveal a small pistol in his hand. The pistol was angled downward, aimed at Michelle. The man calmly told Rosa to get into the van and to instruct Michelle to get into the van as well. Rosa had hesitated, and when she did, the man took hold of her arm with his free hand and forced the nanny to her knees. Then he kneeled down along with her, so that they were both face-to-face with Michelle. He instructed Rosa a second time, and this time the nanny urged Michelle to do what the man said.

The side door of the van was already open, and the three piled into the vehicle, the large man sliding the door shut. Several strips of duct tape were hanging from the roof of the van. Holding the gun to Rosa Rodriguez's temple, the man instructed the nanny to place one of the strips over Michelle's mouth. After she did that, she was told to bind Michelle's hands behind her back with a longer piece of tape and then to bind her ankles together. The next thing the nanny knew, the door was sliding open and she was falling backward out of the van. She landed hard on the sidewalk, skinning her elbow and suffering a tear in her skirt.

A blast of blue smoke belched from the rear of the van as it lurched forward, rounded the corner, and disappeared.

Megan concluded her phone conversation with Malcolm Bell. She flipped the phone closed and stepped in from the hallway.

Rosa was back in the living room, drinking a cup of black coffee and waiting for her husband to show up. The final blast of predusk sunlight was radiating in the apartment, saturating the living room in a brassy assault. Collins and Romano were gone.

Christine remained seated. A moment earlier, one of the purpling clouds had brought to her mind the abstract sculptures in a certain studio in a building some blocks north of where she was sitting. Christine knew that the events that had transpired in the sculptor's studio had no connection to her daughter's abduction. Of course they didn't. Even if Christine hadn't accepted the young man's invitation to come to his studio, Michelle would still be missing. The two events were not related. Even so, Christine was finding it extremely difficult to separate them. One way or another, the day had demanded that the family be violated, and Christine felt enormous shame. As she watched an airplane slice across the sky, she wondered if Andy was feeling shame as well. As much as Christine didn't want to admit it—it was nothing but spite—she hoped that he was.

Megan Lamb stepped over to where Christine was sitting.

"I'm going to have to ask you for a picture of Michelle."

Christine responded as if she had read the detective's mind. She reached over to the nearby lamp table and picked up a copy of her husband's book.

"Here. This is a great one. Everyone loves it."

CHAPTER 40

The food containers from Mama Buddha remained largely untouched on the kitchen counter. The container of ginger chicken—Michelle's favorite—had not even been opened. Christine couldn't imagine what had been going through her head when she ordered it. Magical thinking? A pathetic symbol of hope? The thought was so ridiculous she didn't want to cop to it.

Christine kicked herself for having deleted the crank call that had come in at the beginning of the week. Megan Lamb had endeavored to assure her that the authorities would likely have picked up nothing worth acting on even if they'd had a chance to review the message. The detective had urged her to consider that there was no guarantee that the call had even come from Michelle's abductor.

But Christine knew. Megan Lamb didn't have any children. She couldn't be clued into this one. Christine *knew*.

The kitchen phone was now an object of aversion. As was Christine's laptop. The story of the abduction of Senator Foster's daughter had broken soon after six o'clock, with special bulletins interrupting the non-news programs while the all-news channels had launched immediately into breathless wall-to-wall coverage. By seven, Christine's email inbox had collected seventy-two messages and counting, nearly all of them from complete strangers. The majority were short messages of support, with not a few of those urging the senator and his wife to trust in God to deliver their daughter safely back to them. The remaining messages were divided into those from people using the opportunity to excoriate the senator for his politics, those claiming to have spotted Michelle, and those claiming to be from Michelle's kidnapper. Messages in this last category were blunt and crude and vicious. The answering machine was also collecting some calls from strangers, though only a handful of these in the hate category. Neither the Fosters' home number nor Christine's email address were supposed to be in general circulation, but apparently those were securities that were easily breached.

As predicted by Detective Lamb, a team of FBI officials had arrived at the apartment, and when Andy got in from the airport soon afterward, he had immediately fallen into battle with them over their plan to route all of Christine's emails to their own surveillance account as well as to maintain an open tap on their phone. Christine had joined the battle, but on the side of the federal agents' recommendations, and so her and Andy's first face-to-face exchange concerning the crisis with their daughter had been one of rancor. A bad start.

In the absence of any fresh developments concerning Michelle's abduction itself, the news channels were essentially airing any footage they could scrape up that included either Michelle or Christine. They were running loops about Christine's childhood as the daughter of Governor Hoyt, her marriage to then-congressman Foster, her career as a photographer (the print Christine had sold to Placido Domingo was clearly slated for some massive overexposure), and, of course, Michelle's "Little Wizard" moment.

"This is like my very own designer hell," Christine remarked after the fourth or fifth viewing of footage showing her aiming a pair of thumbs-up as she emerged from a voting booth. "Who are the *freaks* who are watching this crap?" The voting booth clip was replaced by a clip of Andy address- ing the Earth Day rally. Christine rose from the couch.

"*Stop looking at us!* For Christ's sake. Get your own goddamned life!"

Andy clicked to a new channel. Michelle was riding atop her daddy's shoulders. Christine's mouth dropped open.

"Where the hell did they get *that*?"

Andy studied the screen. "Isn't that Whitney's seventieth?"

Christine was already fumbling with her cell phone. "That son of a bitch! I can't believe he—"

"Don't call your father!" Andy set down the remote. "Chrissie, seri- ously. I'm sure he didn't—"

Christine's arm jerked and she threw her phone across the room, miss- ing the television by several inches. It hit the bookshelf behind the televi- sion and clattered to the carpet.

"*Michelle!* Please, God. Where *is* she?"

Andy caught his wife before she collapsed to the floor. Her warm tears flooded onto his neck, and he guided her to the small leather couch next to his desk and lowered her onto it. Tears choked in his own throat as he held his sobbing wife. Over the twenty minutes the two sat clinging to each other on the small couch, Christine emerged twice from the voting booth, Michelle appeared three times as a newborn in her proud father's arms, and Andy's face flashed across the muted screen too many times to count.

Christine offered only the smallest resistance when Andy came into the bedroom rattling the bottle of Tylenol PM. She was dressed for bed, backed up against the pillows. Andy handed Christine a glass of water and shook two tablets into her hand.

"I regret everything," Christine said, her voice slightly hoarse from her crying.

"Shhhhh. That doesn't make any sense."

"I do."

"Sweetie, you're exhausted. You're beat. We're both beat."

Christine's red-rimmed eyes implored him. "Can't we talk, Andy? We have to talk."

He touched a finger to the middle of her brow. "It's late. Neither of us is going to be articulate right now." He urged her to swallow the mild sedative. Christine popped the tablets into her mouth, washed them down with water, and handed her husband the half-empty glass.

"Why is this happening?"

"Shhhh," he said again. "This isn't the time."

He stripped down to his boxers and climbed into bed next to his wife. She folded her body against his and laid her cheek on his chest.

Twenty minutes later Andy slipped delicately out of the bed. Christine's breathing was gentle and deep. In his den, Andy sat at his desk, staring at the slip of paper on which he'd written the phone number of the Mad Russian. They had only spoken that one time, three nights ago, when the blackmailer had laid out his staggering demands. Four days remained until Andy was supposed to be at the ready with half a million dollars. Andy's thumb remained poised above his cell. The Russian *must* be involved in Michelle's abduction. He had to be. Andy was convinced that his daughter was being used by the blackmailer to seal the deal. Andy himself might have been willing to accept his sordid behavior becoming public knowledge and his career immolating in a nanosecond, but there was no chance he would allow his very own daughter to suffer as a result of his pathetic indiscretions. Not a chance. The Russian would presume this. Or Aleksey Titov would. Or who-the-hell-ever.

Andy punched the number. It rang and rang and rang. He gave it a full two minutes before cutting off the signal. He sat at his desk another ten minutes, staring a hole into his future. It never became large enough for him to crawl into. At any rate, even if it had, Andy suspected it could only have been a very cold and very lonely and very unforgiving place.

CHAPTER 41

The ringing of the phone pierced Megan's dream. Sweeping out with her arm, she pawed the instrument off the bedside table.

"What."

The red digits on her bedside clock showed 3:52. Otherwise, blackness draped the room.

"Detective Lamb? It's Sergeant Friedlander. I'm sorry to wake you."

Megan croaked, "Who says you woke me?"

"I . . . It's four o'clock. I just assumed."

"What is it, Sergeant?"

"I knew you'd want to know. We've got a positive on the vehicle you're looking for."

Megan was in a sitting position before she knew it. She pulled the phone onto her lap. "The van?"

"White step van. The one used in the Foster abduction."

"Hold on." Leaning sideways, she turned on the bedside lamp. She tugged open the bedside drawer and pulled out a pen and paper. She thumbed the detonator on the pen. "Okay. What do you have?"

"It's in a parking garage," Friedlander said.

"Address?" She scribbled down the address the sergeant gave her. She underlined it violently. "Shit. You've got to be kidding me."

"I just got off the phone with the attendant. The van's up on the roof. The attendant was moving it out from under one of those bunk-bed slots to get to the car on top and he saw something in the back of the van."

He paused. Megan stared up toward a corner of her ceiling. "Are you going to tell me what he saw, Sergeant?"

"It's a body. Female. The throat's been slashed."

"Shit. Is it the girl?"

"There's no ID yet. It's all still sketchy. The call just came in."

"No one's on the scene?"

"Just the attendant. A unit's on the way."

"So am I."

Megan disconnected the call with her finger. The phone remained on her lap. Her eyes traveled again to her ceiling. The image coming to her mind was all too keen and all too unwelcome. A solitary figure, as white as a snowflake, rising up through a pitch-black sky. Megan was sick to death of ascending angels. Truly sick of them.

She lifted her finger and began poking out a number. With each digit she pressed she felt like she was setting off little bombs.

A pair of early morning jetliners were crossing overhead, reflecting the softly bruised sky so completely as to be nearly indistinguishable from it. Detective Megan Lamb stood at the barrier wall of the rooftop lot, watching the planes and also the windows of the buildings along the New Jersey side of the Hudson igniting with golden light.

She felt like a dope.

The APB from the day before had alerted law enforcement officers in all five boroughs, as well as the states of New York, New Jersey, Connecticut, and Pennsylvania, to keep their eyes peeled for the nondescript unmarked white van used in the abduction of Senator Andrew Foster's daughter. Of course, Megan would have been a *real* dope if she hadn't put out the call immediately. This wasn't the problem.

The problem was that while she had envisioned the van streaking away from the city as fast as it could, she had failed to consider that Michelle Foster's kidnapper would have driven all of four and a half blocks from the spot where he snatched the little girl and tucked the van into a parking garage. Since yesterday afternoon, the van had been sitting right here on the roof of the garage.

Megan turned her back on the sky and looked over at the van. A person stumbling onto the scene might have thought that a commercial was being shot, or a movie. Two pairs of strong spotlights had been set up, bathing the vehicle in an unreal semblance of noonday brilliance. The morning was light enough now that the illumination was no longer necessary for the technicians to do their work, but nobody had bothered yet to flip the switches.

The van was being thoroughly dusted and fluoroscoped; if so much as a common housefly had landed anywhere on its surface—exterior or interior—its teensy footprints would be noted. Those were Megan's orders.

The coroner and the photographer had already finished their preliminary work with the body. The blood-soaked mover's quilts in which it had been wrapped were secured and on their way to the lab. The van's tires were being scraped for traces of any materials that might suggest where the vehicle's recent travels had been. In general terms, Megan already knew the story the tires would tell. She had almost told the technicians not to bother. Ninth Avenue and Thirty-second, where the van had been rented. Traces of the West Side Highway. Hudson Street. Perry Street. Possibly—probably—some greased grime from the asphalt of the parking garage. Not a terrifically illuminating story.

The small body remained on a gurney, tucked away in the parking spot previously occupied by the van. It remained covered with a gray blanket. Two men emerged from the stairwell. One was in a suit. The other—the older of the two—wore an open-collared shirt, dark slacks, and a navy blue sports coat. FBI.

"Polly wolly doodle all the day," Megan muttered to herself, and she crossed the roof and met the two in front of the van. The older agent spoke first. Megan knew that he would.

"Do we need those lamps?"

"We did," Megan replied. "We were here before the crack of dawn."

"I would have liked to have been here before the crack of dawn." The senior agent's irritation was on full display.

"We were a little busy," Megan said evenly. "You can probably imagine."

The agent's name was Taylor. He didn't reply immediately. He decided he had made his point. His partner, Brian Armstrong, was practicing his smart-ass smug face. Already, Megan didn't care for him.

"You might attract a traffic copter with those lights," Taylor said. Megan shrugged. Who cared about a silly traffic copter? Taylor indicated the van. "So, it was here all along?"

"Appears so. He drove it over here right after he grabbed the girl. It was clocked in here at three twenty-seven. Quick and easy off the street."

"Sweet," Taylor said, though there was nothing dulcet about the way he said it.

Megan shook her head. "He boned us." The word earned a spark of life from the younger agent. Megan wanted it clear between her and the federal agents that she wasn't a whiner or an excuse maker. She also wanted the word *us* in there. Share the love, share the blame.

She went on, "Of course we all thought he would get the hell out of Dodge. Ninety percent of the time that's what they do. They scram. We know that. It doesn't mean he's smarter than us. He had the luxury of planning. We had to leap."

We, we, us, we. That should do it.

Taylor appeared willing to concede the point. "Do you want to show us the vic?"

The three moved over to the gurney. Brian Armstrong glanced overhead at the empty parking rack above them, and Megan explained to the agents the parking choreography.

"Guy came in from the clubs around three. His car was up there, so they had to move the van to get it. That's when they found her." She added, "Good thing they moved things around. We might not have caught this for days."

Taylor frowned. "We need to keep thinking in terms of hours on this, Detective."

"I'm just saying."

He indicated the gurney. "Let's see it."

As Megan reached for the blanket, the spotlights over by the van clicked off. The effect was something like the opposite of a camera's flash, everything plunging into a thick darkness for the several seconds it took until the eyes adjusted. Megan took hold of the blanket and pulled it down past the victim's neck. The neck was where the damage had been done. A deep black slice. There were also several small cuts around the eyes.

Taylor asked, "Any prints anywhere?"

"There's a pair of eyeglasses. It's too early to tell for certain. But there looks to be a pretty sizable thumbprint on one of the lenses."

"A thumb would be nice."

Megan looked down at the stilled face. "They're pretty strange-looking glasses. I mean, style-wise. Nothing you'd catch me wearing."

Armstrong spoke up for the first time. His smile revealed baby-sized teeth.

"Wouldn't be caught dead, huh?"

CHAPTER 42

The siege outside Andy and Christine's apartment building had thickened overnight. The police had been forced to bring in metal barrier gates in order to keep the sidewalk in front of the building clear. Anyone entering or exiting the building was ripe for interviewing by the scrum of media that swarmed the block. Across the street, onlookers gathered on the sidewalk, numbers of them pointing up toward the top floor of the building. Some of the gawkers looked authentically forlorn, though the vast majority of the faces were lit with the adrenaline of anticipation. The mood was faintly festive; something was *happening*.

Andy stood in his kitchen watching the small television on the counter as the orange-haired woman from 3E pretended that she and the Fosters were fast friends. Nothing could have been further from the truth. To Andy, the woman was a certified harridan: She had petitioned the building to have Doc banned from the elevators simply because she didn't like the way the dog had looked at her once. Andy sipped his coffee and listened as the woman spun a compelling fiction to the reporter about her devotion to Michelle Foster and some of the "lovely times" the two had allegedly spent together going up and down the elevator.

Andy poured himself a second cup of coffee and went in search of Christine. He found her in Michelle's bedroom, at the window. Her cheek was pressed against the glass.

"Hey, sweetie."

Christine turned from the window.

"We can't stay, Andy. I'll kill you. You'll kill me." She indicated the window. "I won't be able to kill *them,* which is what I want to do the most. Either way, we can't stay. At least I can't. I don't know about you."

The mad dash to the waiting limo felt like a trip through one of Alice's less savory wonderlands. The klieg lights. The towering satellite poles. The buzz of gnashing voices, like a white noise of grasshoppers.

"Any word on Michelle . . . ?"

"Senator, do you think that Michelle . . . ?"

"Have Michelle's kidnappers . . . ?"

A Secret Service man had materialized in the lobby, a silent broad-chested specimen direct from central casting. He shadowed the Fosters as they made their way to the waiting limo. Christine caught a glimpse of his weapon as his suit jacket flapped open.

She and Andy settled into the plush leather seat. Cameras and faces descended on the car's blackened windows. From the front seat, a second Secret Service agent was twisting around to face them. He drew Andy's attention to a black phone mounted just above the armrest on Andy's side, where a small red light was blinking.

"The president would like a word with you, sir."

The car pulled away from the curb—slowly, so as not to crush anybody. Andy seemed momentarily stunned. He had not made a move for the phone.

"Better get that," Christine said sourly. "Maybe he wants to invite us down for dinner."

Christine could not abide the thought of reclaiming her childhood bedroom. Instead she and Andy settled into Peter's old room. All traces of her brother were long gone. Christine draped a light sweater over her shoulders and stepped to the window, which looked out on the tennis court and the small gazebo just beyond it. She did so less to take in the view than to make it clear to Andy that she was not in the mood to talk. She watched absently as a sparrow flitted from perch to perch, too agitated—it seemed—to settle on one spot for more than a second. A second bird darted in from around the corner of the house and took up pursuit of the sparrow. For a brief instant the pair tangled and plummeted partway to the ground together, then they separated again and zoomed out of sight.

Christine felt her cheeks reddening. For the past eighteen hours or so, the events surrounding Michelle's abduction had handily shoved Christine's encounter with the sculptor off to a dormant corner of her brain. But now, images of the heated scene were beginning to make a play for her attention, and Christine was startled anew as she considered just how close she had come to allowing herself to give in to the man's—and her own body's—urgings. Had that really been *her* in that studio? Couldn't she just blame all this on a Christine doppelganger? There was scant solace in the fact that she had ultimately resisted the sculptor's advances. The bottom line was that at nearly the precise moment her daughter was being snatched off the street, not ten blocks away, Christine had allowed herself to be led to the brink of adultery by an eager and handsome young stranger. She had almost allowed the door to swing wide open. And it had been astonishingly easy.

Behind her, the springs squeaked as Andy sat down on the edge of the bed. Christine's fury spiked. She refused to shoulder all the blame for what was happening. Not for Michelle's disappearance and not for whatever was transpiring in her own heart. The fault was equally Andy's. *He* had failed to make everything right. *He* had failed to keep his family safe. This was his job, too—his responsibility—and he had failed at it completely. The memory of the sculptor's strong hands rose back up in her mind, and it took all her will to keep from putting her fist through the glass in front of her.

"I'm going for a walk," Christine announced. She yanked the sweater off her shoulders and turned to face her husband. Andy was watching her closely from the bed.

"Would you like me to go with you?"

Christine pulled the sweater on over her head, tugging it tightly.

"That's the last thing in the world I need."

Her father's personal secretary was coming up the stairs. Paul Jordan and Christine reached the landing simultaneously and paused. Jordan looked earnestly into Christine's eyes.

"I want you to know that Hailey and I have you and Michelle in our prayers. And the senator, of course. If there is anything you need from either of us, you're not to hesitate to ask. Anything. Hailey wanted me to tell you that you're to feel free to seek her out."

Christine mumbled her thanks.

The secretary went on. "Your father is devastated by what's happened. But you know how he is; he's going to show you a brave front. That's just the governor."

"Thank you," Christine murmured again.

Christine stayed in place as Jordan continued up the steps. He disappeared around the curved banister. As she listened to the man's light footsteps receding down the hallway, the thought came to her that everyone else in the world was still going about the regular business of conducting their regular lives. It wasn't the planet's nature to screech to a halt every time disaster struck one of its inhabitants. Maybe to the being experiencing the disaster it felt that this was what *should* happen, but this belief was only the perversity of self-importance. The planet kept spinning; it's what planets do. And the countless Christines of the world simply had to rig together whatever coping mechanisms they could manage.

Long after the sound of Paul Jordan's footfalls had faded, Christine remained where she was standing, suspended in the precise middle of the staircase.

No up.

No down.

CHAPTER 43

It was Jim Fergus who phoned Andy with the news that the van that had been used in Michelle's abduction had been located at a parking garage right there in the Village. Andy had assigned his aide-de-camp as his point person, providing Fergus's number to the police rather than his own. Fergus told him that there was no sign of Michelle, then added, "They did find something, Andy. It's not good."

Andy had been in the kitchen speaking with Jenny when the call came in. He told Fergus to hold on and retreated to his and Christine's bedroom to conduct it in private. He perched on the edge of the bed.

"Go on."

Fergus told him of the body that had been discovered in the back of the van, rolled up in a greasy mover's blanket. The woman had been identified as Marion Patricia Mann. The ID had come through the rental company on Thirty-second Street where Ms. Mann had picked up the van early Thursday morning.

"They want to know if that name means anything to you," Fergus said. "The detective would like you to give her a call."

Andy tried out the name. "Marion Mann."

"She could go by Patricia. Or Pat. I guess even Mary."

Andy conducted the roll call. Marion Mann. Patricia Mann. Patty Mann. Mary Mann. Familiar? Not wholly *un*familiar. But they were all fairly normal-sounding names, the sort one hears all the time.

"It's not ringing a bell, Jim," Andy said. Even as he was saying this, however, the name Marion was circling back on him. Andy felt he was hearing the name being said aloud. It was more the attitude of the speaker that was teasing his memory, not so much the name itself.

Marion . . . Marion . . .

Andy asked, "What are the police saying? There were no signs of Michelle at all?"

"None. Like I said. At least nothing they shared with me. The lady cop prefers to speak with you directly. I tried to explain that you've got a lot going on right now, and you'd prefer I run interference for you. She doesn't appear to be the type who's too easy to impress."

"I guess in its way that's refreshing."

"I think we need to be realistic about this, Andy. Whoever it was who snatched Michelle most likely murdered this Marion woman. That's not good."

"Certainly not good for her."

"That's not what I'm saying."

"I know what you're saying, Jim."

Andy caught sight of his drawn face in the mirror above the dresser. Next to zero sleep the night before was showing.

Where the hell was his *daughter?*

"Jesus Christ, Jim. This is fucking madness. What in the world would anyone gain by killing a—"

The bedroom door had opened. Christine stood in the doorway. She had heard her husband's truncated question.

"Hold on," Andy said into the phone. Christine's knuckles were white on the doorknob. Andy lowered the phone to his lap. "They found the van, Chrissie. No trace of Michelle yet."

"You said *killing.*"

Andy felt the blood rising to his face. "There was . . . they found a body in the van. A woman."

"Oh my God!"

"It doesn't mean anything. It's—"

Christine exploded. "It doesn't *mean* anything? Are you out of your mind?"

Andy returned the phone to his ear. "Let me call you right back, Jim."

Christine shrieked. "No! *Talk* to him! Don't call him fucking back. Maybe *he* thinks it means something!"

She vanished from the doorway. Seconds later Andy heard the sound of her feet pounding down the stairs. He squeezed his eyes closed. Even as his wife's footsteps receded, a voice was floating up into his memory. A female voice.

"My God, Andy, what the hell was I thinking when I hired that girl? I swear some days I could throttle her. I mean, seriously. I don't know how long I can take it. Little Maid Marion is going to drive me mad."

Andy's eyes popped open.

Joy's assistant.

Dear God.

Andy watched impassively as the man in the mirror brought the phone to his ear. "Keep me posted," he murmured; then he tossed the phone onto the bed.

CHAPTER 44

The president was swimming laps in the White House pool. Although the chief executive's butterfly days were long over, his breaststroke was still aggressive, and as he powered down the lane the displaced water lapped over the sides of the pool, slapped against the very near walls, then reversed direction to pour right back into the pool. The taste of chlorine filled the narrow catacomb, and wobbly reflections of the churning water bounced about the curved ceiling.

The British prime minister was across town speaking at the National Press Club. She was due to arrive at the White House in a half hour for a belated getting-to-know-you meeting with the new president, followed by a Rose Garden press conference. Hyland had eagerly taken advantage of the rare gap in his schedule to don his goggles and log his thirty laps.

Generally speaking, Hyland's ritual laps served to clear his head, allowing him to forget, at least temporarily, the full burden of his responsibilities. On this particular afternoon, the president's mind was not achieving the temporary amnesia that was his custom. Far from it. The wound that had been inflicted on his fledgling presidency by the forced resignation of his vice president was threatening to worsen. Serious wounds need to be tended to quickly or else infection sets in, which was precisely the worry that Hyland had taken with him down to the chlorine-drenched room. And it was precisely the worry that was not washing away as he powered through the water.

His choice to replace his newly resigned vice president was in the midst of one of the worst personal crises imaginable. His daughter was missing. Snatched right off the street. Hyland could not imagine how he would respond if such an event happened to him. His heart was at Andy and Christine's full disposal. He had made that clear to the senator earlier in the morning by phone.

The official leaking of Hyland's choice of Senator Foster to replace Chris Wyeth had not yet begun, but Hyland knew full well that the unofficial leaking was under way, even before Wyeth's televised resignation. Even if the White House were to seal itself up as tight as a steel drum, those who didn't know that Hyland had tapped Andy Foster to be the next vice president would know soon enough.

And now the senator's child was missing. If Michelle Foster's abduction was not directly related to her father's newly minted status as vice president in waiting, then Hyland would go out and buy a hat and eat it. A great big one. A big straw sombrero. This was, in two words: Fucking. Awful.

Hyland reached the far end of the lane and performed a perfect flip turn, kicked off, and glided for several feet just below the surface. Over the final five laps he powered down to the standard crawl, an easy metronomic stroke. For the first time since he'd entered the water he could feel the exhilarating burn across his shoulders and in his thighs from the breast-stroke regime. He felt a modicum of tranquillity settling in during his final laps. The move from power to grace tipped the scales for him, and he glided back and forth in a no-zone zone, largely mindless. Strictly physical. Briefly a fish once more.

The night before, within hours after the news broke about Michelle Foster's abduction, Whitney Hoyt had contacted the president to counsel him not to even consider withdrawing his invitation to Senator Foster to become his new vice president.

"Whoever it is that's taken my granddaughter, that's what they want," the former governor told him. "It's bullshit, and somebody is going to pay dearly for this. But Andy is still in. We're clear on that. The timetable is probably shot, and your people will obviously have to look into that. But don't let this thing throw you off, John. If you panic, you're screwed. You must know that. This can screw up your entire term, right here. Withdrawing the offer to Andy on humanitarian grounds is not an option. I don't know what the answer is at the moment, but for Christ's sake, don't you dare let the country see its president pissing in his pants. Andy stays."

Hyland was out of the pool and toweling off when Ron Abbey appeared, his shiny shoes clicking in echo from tile to ceiling.

"Tell me that the prime minister ate some bad fish and that we're scrubbing the afternoon, Ron," Hyland said. "Please."

"No, sir. I'm afraid she's due in ten minutes."

Hyland shrugged his shoulders. "Jolly good, then."

The president's chief of staff cleared his throat. "Um, it's something else, Mr. President."

Hyland slung the towel over his shoulders. "It's always something else. I'm thinking of having that printed up for the front of my desk. What is it, Ron? Is it about the Foster girl?"

"Yes and no, sir."

"Don't do that to me, Ron. Not right now."

"They haven't located the girl," Abbey said. "Though they did locate the vehicle that was used to kidnap her. I've just been on the phone with the FBI. The director told me not to disturb your swim."

Hyland blanched. His chief of staff saw immediately that he'd made a gaffe.

"Ron, when I'm unscheduled don't ever tell the director a word about what I'm up to. They're FBI. If they want to know things, they can damn well dig for it."

"Yes, sir. I'm sorry."

Hyland waved it off. "So what did our dear director have to say?"

"The body of a woman was found in the vehicle. Murdered."

Hyland's eyes traveled up to the low ceiling. "Great mother of hell."

"It gets complicated, sir."

The president lowered his gaze to his chief of staff. "Oh, does it, now? How novel."

"The woman worked for Masters and Weiss. One of their top executives was murdered on Long Island a few weeks ago. Joy Resnick. That's kind of where the complication comes in, sir."

"Ron, the prime minister is going to be sitting up there watching my tea grow cold. What is it precisely?"

"Sir. The woman they found today. She worked directly for Joy Resnick."

"I see."

"No, sir. That's not all. Resnick was the chief executive at Masters and Weiss in charge of last year's reelection campaign for Senator Foster."

"Hold on here. Keep me straight on this, Ron. Joyce Resnick—"

"Joy."

"Joy. Murdered a couple of weeks ago."

"Yes, sir."

"Have any arrests been made on that?"

"No, sir."

"And now *her* assistant has been murdered? That's correct?"

"Yes, sir."

"Link this up for me, Ron."

"Sir, Resnick's assistant has been found in the vehicle that was used to abduct Senator Foster's little girl."

Hyland draped the towel over his neck and took a hard grip on both ends. "So, whoever kidnapped Michelle Foster and killed this woman—does she have a name?"

"Marion Mann."

"Somebody kidnapped Michelle Foster and murdered this Mann woman." He grimaced at the unintentional word combo. "And a few weeks ago, somebody murdered Miss Mann's boss?"

"Who worked full-time last year for Senator Foster's reelection."

The president gazed into the water. "I'm not liking this."

"Like I said, it's complicated. I only just now got all this from Director Pierce."

The president said nothing more. His chief of staff was correct: It *was* complicated. It could mean something, it could mean nothing, or it could land someplace in between. The only thing Hyland knew with any certainty was that he wanted nothing else right now but to get back into the water.

Finally he spoke. "Prime minister in five minutes?"

"Yes, sir."

"Stall her. I'll need ten."

CHAPTER 45

She had moved beyond exhaustion. Each day brought with it a numbing fatigue. Leaden feet. Delayed response time.

Amazing what scant sleep can do.

Her first night, she had crawled under one of the overturned rental rowboats in Prospect Park and passed a fitful night dreaming of the cold blue eyes of the man who had murdered her husband.

The following morning, after sinking the battered laptop in the lake, she had made the trip over the great cathedral bridge, inching with reluctance toward the city, and that night she had made her bed beneath the wall of the Museum of Jewish Heritage, tucked unseen between the outside wall and the low row of box bushes bordering the building. An automatic sprinkler system had roused her early in the morning, and she had emerged back onto the streets, soggy and exhausted.

Later that day she had spent precious dollars to have her hair cut short and spiky, after which she had made use of a public bathroom at a library downtown to trade in its bleachy white for something dull and cinnamon.

She was hungry.

It wasn't so much her minuscule funds she was concerned about as the fact that eating itself felt like a supremely optimistic act. As she stood in a doorway staring down at her feet, a bald woman in red robes placed a tangerine in her hand. She tried to say "thank you," but her throat was too dry, and no words came out. That evening she lay down in the small courtyard of a church near a busy street, but sleep never came. The following day—somehow she had identified it as Friday—the notion made its way into her head:

This is how people become lost.

This is how they disappear.

She was fine with this. She wanted to disappear. She was toxic. It was why she had to vanish. She had led her own husband's murderer directly to his door, and she had watched as he'd begun to bleed to death on the hotel room floor. And she still held in her pocket the reason he had been killed. The little blue piece of aluminum. Her husband had praised it as the key to their future. More than once over the past week he had held up the little stick to her and declared that it contained inside it an entire house. A fancy car. A trip around the world. Clothes. Food. Anything she wanted.

But it had also contained his death. He'd forgotten to mention that, hadn't he? The little stick was like one of those golden stones in a fable. She recalled those stories from when she was a child. It was a source of fortune, and at the same time it was a source of ruin. Good luck and bad luck, all rolled into one. Like life itself.

She was exhausted.

She made her way uptown to the park behind the huge library and saved precious pennies by fishing a half-eaten sandwich out of a trash can. She sneaked onto a subway and rode it up to the end and back again. Twice. Time stretching in two directions.

The exhaustion had moved into her bones. It had made her body light and her head seemed like a helium balloon, dragging the rest of her along like a string. She came up out of the subway station with the hot breath of the tunnel trailing her to the street. The helium was beginning to leak away. The energy to keep her feet moving was disappearing. The sidewalk was threatening to rise up and claim her.

A bed.

The very thought of an actual bed brought an ache to her chest. She could not sleep on the ground for a fourth night. She just couldn't. She simply wasn't vanishing quickly enough.

Her small hand slid into her pocket and her fingers closed around the golden stone. It was time to confront it. So many questions she needed to ask it. Why was her husband dead? Why hadn't the new life he had promised her appeared? What had the stupid, stupid man gone and done? He'd been mean to her sometimes, yes. But she knew it was because he'd been scared and frustrated. His abilities had been so much smaller than his fantasies. *Maybe he has gone to a better place. Maybe he learned something valuable from his many mistakes, and maybe now—at last—he will have a chance to shine.*

She walked into a copy center near Grand Central. Ignoring the peculiar look the clerk was giving her, she placed the golden stone on the counter.

"I want to look at this."

The clerk directed her to a computer cubicle and showed her how to bring up the files.

"If there's audio, you might want to use a headset."

She waited until the clerk was back behind the counter. She put on the headset. For a full minute she sat motionless in front of the blank screen. When she felt ready, she tapped the key that the clerk had indicated. A bluish image burned onto the screen. An empty bed appeared, seen from above. Then a vertical line split the screen door down the middle. The empty bed was now visible on the right side of the screen. On the left side was a large, lumpish white rock. No. It was a *pillow.* It looked so inviting. She sat staring at the screen for another two minutes before anything began to take place. It was a person, passing in front of the bed. A woman. She was pulling her dress over her head.

If a single muscle in Irena's body moved over the next forty minutes, it did so without her permission.

CHAPTER 46

It was deemed quicker for Special Agents Taylor and Armstrong to take a chopper out to Brookhaven on Long Island and go over the Suffolk County Homicide Department's materials on the murder of Joy Resnick there on-site.

Agent Taylor had done the deeming. This was one of the precise areas where the Feds flexed their muscle. Megan hadn't even put up an argument, something for which Malcolm Bell, for one, was relieved. Detective Lamb was well known for putting up arguments.

The lead investigating officer from the Suffolk County squad had been called in from the field to synopsize his work for Taylor and Armstrong and to answer any of the agents' questions. Detective Frank Cotton was a taut figure with a gingery mustache and a wind-torn complexion. It was easy to imagine the man jerking a marlin from the deep blue while his buddies crowded around, ready to hand him a Bud. In the two weeks since Joy Resnick's murder, Cotton and his deputy had interviewed over forty persons. Family, friends, work colleagues of the victim, neighbors in her Park Slope neighborhood, as well as those persons with homes in the proximity of the Shelter Island house where the murder had taken place. The captain of the ferry who was on duty the night of the murder had been questioned, as well as the two-person crew.

There were several boxes of physical evidence. The bloodied sheets. The pillows and pillowcases. Joy Resnick's dress, her underwear, her shoes. The murder weapon had not been located, but it was presumed to have been an iron pole from the horseshoe set located in the side yard. One of the two poles was missing, and the coroner's work with the remaining one had led him to an eighty percent certainty that it was identical to the weapon used to bludgeon Joy Resnick to death. The other pole had been bagged and was included along with the other physical evidence.

Fingerprint evidence had proved disappointing. The house had been used by members of the victim's family, as well as being rented out several times over the year. The place was awash with whorls, but none that could be isolated as having particular significance in the case of the murder. Parts of the house—the bedroom, the kitchen—showed signs of having been wiped down. Joy Resnick's prints were abundant, but no one really needed fingerprints to prove that Joy Resnick had been in the house. That part everyone knew.

The captain of the ferry reported shuttling the victim over from Greenport early in the evening. He reported to the police that she had remained in her car for the ten-minute crossing, and that he had not noticed whether there were any passengers in the car. Likewise, the two crew members could not say with certainty whether Joy Resnick had been accompanied. One of them thought she'd been alone; the other knew only that he was not certain.

Possibly the most comprehensive story was coming from the sets of footprints on the grass and dirt around the house, though the interpretation of the story was not as clean as the investigators would have liked. Cotton's forensics consultant had settled on a total of four different sets of footprints, one of the sets being those of the victim. The other three sets of footprints showed movement in the driveway, around the side of the house, and in the back as well. One set appeared to head off in the direction of the trees that bordered the property at the rear. The woods had been scoured, the search yielding a faded orange Frisbee and a deteriorated life vest, also once orange.

Agent Taylor wanted to hear the investigator's thoughts on the entrance onto and presumed egress from the island of the murderer or murderers. "It's an island. Have we got three men arriving together on the ferry and three men leaving?"

Cotton answered, "Not to anyone's memory."

"How about just two men?"

"Who notices a couple of guys getting on a ferry?"

"So that's a no," Taylor said.

"Correct."

"There'd been sex," Armstrong said.

Cotton gave him a cool look. "That's right."

"Multiple?"

"The ME sees a single act."

"Pretty woman," Armstrong said, waving the picture. "Why does only one of our boys get lucky?"

Taylor frowned at his partner, as did Cotton, who replied to the question. "Maybe they drew straws, Mr. Armstrong, I honestly don't know."

Agent Taylor was trying hard to work it all out. "Okay, we might have her in bed with someone she's intending to be in bed with, and then two goons break in. That's one of our possibles. And if she did go over on the ferry alone, then she met up with her bed partner on the island. He was already there."

Armstrong spoke up. "Or he hid in the car going over."

Cotton asked, "Why in the world would he do that?"

"I don't know. Because he was planning to join his buddies in a little pile-on and didn't want to be seen in advance with the victim?"

Cotton turned to Agent Taylor. "Is this what I missed by not getting my training at Quantico?"

Armstrong balked. "Look, we're just trying to lay out all the possibilities, Detective. Two weeks into this thing and I'm not seeing a hell of a lot of progress here in Mayberry. We've got to step it up. The clock is ticking on Michelle Foster."

Taylor snapped at his partner. "Brian!"

The younger agent held his ground. "We don't have the luxury of time, Tom."

Cotton didn't appear to be affected by the agent's attitude. "That's fine, Agent Armstrong. I'm with you. Let's run it down. One. Miss Resnick either went over with her lover in the car or she went over alone and her lover was already on the island. Two. There was no lover at all, just a nasty bunch of gangbangers, and for whatever reason only one of them got the prize. Three. They were already on the island when she got there, went over together or separately, either on the same ferry run or earlier that day or some other day. Or, for that matter, in their own boat. I think that covers it, right? Though since we'd be smart to lay out *all* the possibilities, I suppose they could have come swinging out of the sky. Except we've gotten no reports of any helicopter sightings or anyone hearing all that racket they'd make, but hey, you know, it's possible Uncle Sam has developed himself some sort of stealth helicopter that we rubes here in Mayberry know nothing about." He held up a hand to stop Armstrong's protest. "In which case we'll dispatch some hound dogs to go check out the secret hangars where y'all keep these hellies. That is, if we can get the government to cooperate and let us have a look-see." He gave the young agent a broad smile. "I suppose this is where you could come in extra handy, friend."

Armstrong glowered.

Cotton indicated the photograph that was still in the agent's hand. He also dropped the hayseed accent.

"I've got a teenage daughter, Mr. Armstrong. Whoever did all this, I want to see them skinned alive. Okay? You can trust me on that. I'm doing my job, sir."

The lawmen got back on track. The Feds were especially interested in the interviews that had been conducted with Joy Resnick's circle. The portrayal was of a capable, dynamic woman. Single, with a seemingly healthy dating life. Nothing kinky. No known risk-taking tendencies. There was nothing in her personal history to raise a red flag. As best anyone knew, she had not been seeing anyone on a regular basis for several months at least. There were no indications that she had been either distracted or worried or moody in the days leading up to her trip out to the island.

"Unless this really is just an unfortunate case of some good old boys getting some serious rocks off, we're looking for a single assailant with a supersize grudge," Armstrong said. "Ninety percent of the time, victims know their killers. Someone had it in bad for this lady."

Cotton appeared on the verge of taking on the agent's comment, but he let it slide. Taylor declared that he wanted to see the murder site first-hand. He instructed Armstrong to take the list of people interviewed back in Manhattan and to revisit select ones, starting with Joy Resnick's colleagues at Masters and Weiss. Clearly Armstrong's questions were to now include the matter of Marion Mann.

"Two of their own have now been murdered. That should be stirring them up more than a little. See if anyone is afraid that they might be next, or has any theories about who a third could be. Look for professional jealousy, anything like that. Detective Lamb is doubtless pumping these people as we speak, so you'll get some resistance. Focus on anyone who had any part to play at all on the Dracula account, even if it was peripheral."

Dracula was the code name the agents had chosen for Senator Foster. The name had popped into Agent Taylor's head.

Taylor concluded, "I'll go walk the scene with the detective here. You go find out why someone has got their pants in a twist about this PR agency. We'll rendezvous in the city at nine."

———

Agent Taylor and Detective Cotton drove the forty miles east to Greenport and took the ferry over to Shelter Island. It being a Friday afternoon, the ferry's small deck took its maximum number of vehicles. Maybe a dozen foot passengers from the train also made the short crossing.

The road from the ferry drop rose up into the island's main village then angled to the east, climbing a narrow serpentine route that bordered the water.

"Pipes Cove," Cotton said, indicating the blue beneath them. "Technically, Peconic Bay. You like oysters?"

"I've had them," Taylor said. "I can't say I'll die if I never have any more."

"Time was, oysters practically oozed out of the waters down there. Clams, too. And especially scallops. These parts were known for our scallops. The hurricane in thirty-eight wiped out a good third of all the harvests. You never heard of Widow's Hole?"

The veteran FBI agent laughed. "I'm not touching a line like that."

"Yeah. Sounds kind of queer at that, doesn't it? It's a brand of oyster from these parts. Big and plumpy. All your big restaurants in the city are serving Widow's Holes."

"You strike me as a fishing type, Detective," Taylor said.

Cotton looked over at him. "Is that fancy FBI profiling, or do I just reek of fish?"

"Profiling," Taylor said. "Though I wouldn't necessarily call it fancy."

The winding road ended in a gentle descent down toward a wide inlet. Cotton jerked his thumb out the window next to his head. "The house is up on the very top of that hill. We pretty much switchback to get up there."

He turned left off the main road. Off to the right, Taylor noted a motel adjacent to the beach. It looked like an okay place to leave the world behind for a few days.

The car moved up the hill along a zigzagging wooded road that ended at the foot of a steep pebble driveway. They moved up the driveway. As the house came into view, Cotton frowned.

"Someone's here."

A faded blue Fairlane was parked in front of the house. The landau roof's years of exposure to the sun were evident in the peeling fabric.

"Looks like someone took a wrong turn in 1969 and ended up here," Cotton said, pulling up next to the car.

"The scene's not still secured, is it?" Taylor asked.

"Two weeks in? God, no."

Taylor remarked, "Nice-looking old place."

"Yeah, it is, isn't it? The way I've got it, the family has been here for quite a while. The victim's grandparents bought the place back in the fifties. Half the time it's rented out. You'll get a nice nickel, location like this."

The two got out of the car.

"Stays decent cool up here, even in the summer," Cotton remarked as they approached the porch. "Your breeze comes right up from the cove, plus you've got all this shade. It's prime turf, to be sure."

Taylor concurred. "I'd take it."

The pair went up onto the porch and the detective knocked on the front door. Agent Taylor jammed his hands into his rear pockets and twisted around to survey the view from the porch. Behind him, the front door lock clicked. Cotton began to speak.

"Hello. I'd like—"

As Taylor started back around a second *click* sounded, simultaneous with an explosion. A piece of the back of Detective Cotton's skull lifted up toward the trees, and the man dropped.

Taylor's face was slapped with a red mist. A howl formed instantly deep within him. It never even cleared his chest. His hands never left his rear pockets. A second shot was fired point-blank, and Taylor collapsed like a puppet cut free. His body folded indecorously across that of the fallen Suffolk County lawman.

CHAPTER 47

Paul Jordan frowned as he responded to the doorbell. The reason he was frowning was that there should have been no doorbell. The iron gate at the foot of the driveway was secured, and no one had buzzed up to the house requesting entrance. The others were lingering over their desserts at the table, a tableau of normalcy upon which Whitney Hoyt had insisted.

A woman in a black pantsuit stood on the front step. An abundance of silver-streaked hair was piled and clipped atop her head and a knowing smile was planted on her bright red lips. A green suitcase stood at her side.

"My goodness, if it's not my dear ghostly past. Hello, Paul."

Jordan recovered quickly from the surprise. "How did you get past the gate?"

Lillian Turner demurred. "Well, it is a delight to see you, too."

"How did you get in?"

"Twelve years and you can't even be bothered to change the silly code. I'm surprised. You never know when the loopy old ex might come calling one night, do you?"

Jordan conceded. "I guess one doesn't."

"So, are you going to invite me into the home I once occupied, Paul? Or have we already arrived at an Alamo moment?"

There was a movement behind Jordan. Lillian looked past her ex-husband's secretary to see Jenny Hoyt coming in from the dining room. Jenny stopped in her tracks when she saw who was standing in the open door.

"Good Lord."

Lillian grabbed hold of her roller bag and bumped it through the entrance. From farther back in the house Whitney's voice sounded. "Who is it, dear?"

Lillian answered first. "No one in particular, Whit! Just a bad old memory!" She turned her false smile to Jenny. "I must say, you look good enough to eat, dear."

Swift footsteps were sounding on the marble floor, then Whitney Hoyt rounded the corner. "Oh, shit."

Lillian tsk-tsked her ex-husband. "Whitney. Not in front of the help."

Jenny summoned Whitney into the kitchen.

"How much do I have to say, Whitney?"

"Very little, Jen."

"Well, I have to say *some* of it. That woman has got the balls of a bull! I know, I know, it's her granddaughter, too. Of course. I'm not evil."

"Nobody said—"

"Has she ever heard of a hotel?"

"Of course she has. But you remember how she is. Miss Lillian needs her audience. A woman like that would go berserk all alone in a hotel."

"This is my house. I'm not anyone's audience in my own home! Besides, she *is* nuts. Are we really going to let her just walk all over us like this? How about *I* get a hotel room? Maybe I'm the odd man out here. Michelle's not my blood relative, after all. What if—"

"No. Jen. Please. Don't you be dramatic now."

"What!" She lowered her voice. "We've got Sarah goddamned Bernhardt sitting in there, and you're accusing me of being dramatic?"

"Oh God. This is exactly what she does: divide and conquer."

"I know, Whitney. I've seen her in action before, remember?"

"It'd be a bum's rush to hustle her out of here at this hour. She's just flown halfway across the country. Her granddaughter has gone missing. You can't blame her for wanting to be close."

"Well, there's close, and there's close. But don't you see how she operates? She comes waltzing in here with her suitcase and her oh-I've-been-in-an-airplane-all-day routine, and now if I make so much as a peep of protest, *I'm* the bad guy here. I'm the one who is rude. Look, let me talk to her in the morning. I really do think at this point we give her tonight. It will only start things off on a bad foot if we tangle right now. It's late. Everyone's wiped out."

"Fine. Sure. Should we grant her the master bedroom? I don't think that outsize persona of hers is going to fit in any of our lesser rooms."

"We can shove her in the attic if you'd like," Hoyt said gently. "This is still our household."

Jenny raised her hands and let them drop. "Oh, hell. It doesn't matter.

She's not my ex-wife, she's yours. I'm not going to kick the woman out onto the street. I'll just put on my armor. I can handle her. She got the first blow in, that's all. Why would I expect her to be on her best behavior?"

Whitney leaned forward and kissed his wife on the forehead. "Lillian has no best behavior. Once you stop hoping for it to appear, it gets a little easier."

The faded blue Fairlane bumped over the yellow connector ramp onto the ferry. Up ahead, a local teen wearing an orange reflecting vest motioned the driver to keep coming forward. The car advanced slowly, its headlights bathing the deckhand in its crossed cones of light. The teen made a slicing move across his neck, and the driver touched the brakes.

"That's good!"

The driver remained behind the wheel, watching through his side and rearview mirrors as four other cars bumped over the ramp and packed in around him. A thin thumbnail of moon hung in the black sky, just visible at the top of the Fairlane's windshield. Six or seven people emerged from the other cars and moved off toward the ferry's railings.

A low baying call sounded from the ferry's horn, and the vessel began drifting off-angle from the dock. With a hard growl, the boat's engine sprang to life and a mass of churning water began chasing the vessel away from the dock. Robert Smallwood watched as the scattered lights of the silhouetted island receded. His heart was heavy for the families of the two men he had been forced to eliminate. But there had really been no choice. As the two men had arrived at the front door, the little girl had popped a small blood vessel in her left eye, trying to make her scream heard through the layers of duct tape. He felt bad for that, too. Such a mess all the way around. He'd been forced to act so swiftly. The banging on the door. Men with sidearms. Such a monumental pain in the ass.

As the small ferry powered forward, Smallwood's eyes swept across the black water. He'd considered sinking the two men in the inlet. With all the house construction sites on the island these days, he could have fetched as many cinder blocks as he would have needed and used those to anchor them. He could have taken them out into the bay in a rowboat and quietly slipped them overboard. But in the end, he hadn't taken the time. He had no way of knowing how quickly the men would be missed or how soon someone might come looking for them. Instead, he had dragged the dead weights into the house and let them remain there in the front hallway, one piled atop the other.

The ride to the mainland took less than ten minutes. In Greenport, the ferry sidled up close to the dock, reversed its engines, then cut them altogether. The deckhand and his counterparts on the dock exchanged heavy ropes and secured the vessel. After affixing the ramp in place, one of the deckhands stepped onto the ferry and came over to the Fairlane.

"Hey, anytime you want to sell that car, man, let me know, okay? It is *so* cool."

Robert Smallwood said nothing. The other deckhand removed the chain gate from the front of the ferry, and the Fairlane made its way slowly onto the ramp and back to terra firma. Within seconds it had dissolved into the night.

Irena Bulakov watched as a fat juicy June bug crossed along just beneath the lip of the countertop, out of sight of the black man who was manning the front desk. The man was pointing out directions on a map to a young German couple who spoke no English whatsoever. His voice seemed to be growing louder in direct relation to the couple's decreasing volume.

"You want to take the *B train* down to *Columbus Circle*! You got that? *Downtown!*"

The June bug covered the length of the counter and then came up onto the counter itself, though it remained behind the silver desk bell, still hidden from the black man's sight. The German couple folded their map politely and left through the front door. As Irena stepped forward, the black man disappeared into a small office. A lanky blond boy wearing a gigantic backpack came through the front door, stepped brusquely past Irena, and brought his hand down over and over on the silver bell.

The June bug scooted swiftly down the wall in a panic.

The man emerged from the office and immediately began yelling at the boy. The boy yelled right back. Irena couldn't follow their sentences enough to know what their problems were.

She looked down at the tabloid newspaper she had picked up after leaving the copy shop. If she had stared once at the photograph of Senator Andrew Foster and his wife and daughter posing in front of the Statue of Liberty, she had stared at it a hundred times. It was *him*. This same man from Dimitri's little movie. It was this United States senator from New

York. Here in the newspaper. He was a horrible man. She knew this. She had seen him with the woman who was now dead. The woman who was not his wife.

And now somebody had kidnapped his child.

Irena had wanted children, but her body had forbidden it. Three times her body had let her down. She had never shared this with Dimitri, but she had wanted twins. A little boy and a little girl. Irena had thought about it so often over the years that she could bring the fantasy children's images to her mind whenever she chose. In Irena's mind, they were nearly seven already, both in school. *He* was very, very good with his numbers, possibly a future engineer. One day he might build impressive buildings and bridges. *She* showed creative talent. She could draw, and she was also a beautiful little ballerina. Both of them were popular with their fellow students and with their teachers. The teachers called them "shining examples." The imagined term itself could bring actual tears to Irena's eyes. Shining examples.

Irena's imaginary children were the same age as the girl in the newspaper, the senator's daughter. In a world where anything can happen, they might have been friends.

The black man and the lanky blond boy concluded their argument, and Irena stepped forward. The sign on the wall told her how much was needed to rent a room. Irena placed the exact amount on the counter and asked for a room.

Five minutes later she was testing the mattress with her hands. The springs made a little bit of noise, but this didn't matter. It was a bed. She was not going to be sleeping on the ground. This was her current definition of heaven.

There was a shower down at the end of the hall. Even though she had no clean clothes to change into, Irena took a shower. She also had no towel, and since the man at the front desk had said to her that none were provided, she used the bed's thin bedcover. There was a slender chip of soap on the floor of the shower, and Irena ran it over her body until it disappeared altogether. The water pressure was not very strong. But the water was hot. As hot as she could stand. And this was good. The hotter the better. She closed her eyes and pretended that the searing water was dissolving her skin all the way down to her bones. This was also good. The old skin was the old Irena. It was all that remained, and now it, too, could be made to vanish. At the end of the shower, she could step out and begin to let the new Irena blossom. Maybe this one would have better luck. Maybe this one could have real children. Maybe this one could marry a man who devoured her with love, could be less nervous, could be more happy.

Back in her small room, Irena dabbed herself dry with the bedcover, then got naked into the bed. She had the tabloid newspaper with her. She also had the blue stick from Dimitri's computer in her hand. She scrunched up against the thin pillow and set the newspaper and the blue stick on her lap. She was ready.

CHAPTER 48

The last thing Christine wanted to do was cry in front of her mother, but once she had gotten it out of the way she felt somewhat better.

The two women were seated together in the squeaking wooden love seat out in Jenny's garden. Far above them, the three-quarter moon was playing hide-and-seek with an endless stream of curling clouds; the way its dim light wobbled off and on reminded Christine of an errant bulb loose in its socket.

The two were each wrapped in thin shawls against the brisk bite of the late evening. Each also cradled a wineglass in her lap. As the others had headed off to bed, Lillian had snared a bottle of Sancerre from her ex-husband's wine cellar and cajoled her daughter into staying up with her for a nightcap. The decision to move it outdoors had been Christine's. To whatever degree the semidarkness might ameliorate Lillian's hawklike scrutiny, all the better.

"The hair is cute, by the way," Lillian said to Christine after a few minutes of uncustomary silence.

Christine wiped away the last of her tears. "Thank you." She poked at her hair. "It feels like a thousand years ago."

Lillian's wineglass floated near her chin. "Listen, darling. I hope you don't take this the wrong way, but I have to say it. Andrew seemed awfully dead tonight."

The words that rose to Christine's tongue were precisely the ones she knew better than to use in response to her mother. She forced herself to take a beat. But even then, she couldn't keep from at least nibbling at the bait. "That's a hell of a thing to say. You know, you might want to remember that Andy's under a lot of pressure right now."

Lillian dismissed the remark. "Oh, the pressure. Yes, I remember that one. You seem to forget I was married to one of those men myself for over thirty years. I always thought it must be nice to have a big important wall like that to hide behind."

"Andy is not hiding behind any wall. His daughter has just been kid-napped."

Lillian was unimpressed. The shifting moonlight slid across her face as she sipped her wine. Even in the dimness, the terrible beauty of her eyes prevailed. She trained them on her daughter.

"I believe *your* daughter is missing, too. But I don't see you all cloaked in your own thoughts."

"I'm plenty cloaked, Mother. It's just that you can't see it."

Lillian dipped a finger into her glass, then brought it to her lips. "All I can say is that something's up with the two of you. I know it is, Chrissie. My radar's too good."

"There's nothing 'up' with us," Christine said, more tersely than she'd intended. "I know it disappoints you to see that one of these marriages can actually work, but I guess you're just going to have to live with that."

Lillian was unmoved. "Oh, please. I cut my teeth on men like your hus-band. All I'm trying to do is protect you from being hurt."

"I'm not you."

Lillian floated her glass up near her daughter's face. "What I'm talking about is you keeping your eyes clear, young lady. You're telling me that An-drew is different from your father. That's fine. I'd like to see him show it, that's all. My whiskers are twitching, Chrissie. Your little girl is out there somewhere, and none of us knows where she is or why she has been taken away, and I'm sorry, but that handsome husband of yours should have you tight in his arms, end of story. I don't know where that man is, but I'm telling you where he's *not*. He is not altogether here, he's off somewhere by himself. A tragedy of this proportion should be drawing people so close together they can barely breathe. And that's just not happening."

Christine's chest tightened. "Is that what happened between you and Daddy when Peter died? You drew close? I'm sorry, but you'll have to re-fresh my memory. I seem to recall the two of you acting like complete and utter jerks."

Even in the semidarkness, Christine could tell that she had scored.

"That was different," Lillian said curtly. "That marriage was already on fumes by the time your father and I got back from overseas. Of course, that's easy for you to forget. You weren't around to see just how much things had degenerated between Whitney and me. You were over here busy helping your man get to the Senate. What Peter's death did to my marriage was hasten the inevitable. So don't go lumping all tragedies together like that, Chrissie. Besides which, there was a lot more going on. You don't even know the half of it."

"The half I saw was more than enough, thank you."

Christine knew she was pressing her mother unfairly, but she was feeling too helpless in her own fear to back off. Lillian was correct. The months surrounding Peter's anguishing death had been an uncommonly volatile time for everyone. Chris Wyeth's decision to leave the Senate in order to run for Whitney's old job in Albany had been the precise opening that Andy had been waiting for, and so he had launched full throttle into what proved to be a contentious campaign to capture Wyeth's vacated seat. Nearly simultaneous to this, Christine's father had resigned his ambassadorial post and returned stateside—a move that was largely, and correctly, regarded as evidence of the former governor's intention to make his much-delayed run for the presidency. In the middle of all these raging political hormones, Peter Hoyt had expired on a thin mattress in his joyless Hell's Kitchen apartment, and his mother had subsequently fallen completely apart. The buildup to Hoyt's announcement of his presidential candidacy began to veer off course. Intimations of the long-standing estrangement that had existed between Whitney Hoyt and his son started to surface, along with a whispering campaign concerning Hoyt's insensitivity toward his grieving spouse. Hoyt's ambitions to mount a national campaign to capture the White House in the face of his family's tragedies began to appear distasteful to a growing number of people. In the end he had been forced to pull the plug for a second—and final—time on his presidential aspirations. The divorce came through five months later. Lillian had contested nothing. She fled.

Christine could sense her mother's eyes resting heavily on her. She regretted snapping at her. She knew this must be especially difficult for Lillian, returning as a visitor to the house where she once ruled.

"I don't know what the problem is," Christine said quietly. "You're not completely wrong. About Andy." She looked down at her wineglass. The tiny reflection of the moon skittered in the dark liquid like a spark.

"They want Andy to be the new vice president."

Christine couldn't believe she had just said this. She raised her eyes to see if by some miracle maybe she hadn't actually said it out loud. Lillian appeared unimpressed with the news.

"Surely you don't want that," she said blithely.

"It's complicated," Christine muttered. *Complicated:* one of her mother's favorite words.

"What's so complicated about it? I think it's pretty simple. Can you imagine what your life would have been like if your father had gone ahead and actually run for that damn office? If he'd won? Don't kid yourself. I know that a lot of people feel sorry for your father. But as far as I'm concerned, the best thing in the world for all involved was that man's dreams being thwarted."

"Andy is not Daddy."

"No, he's not. I've already conceded that point. But he *is* of the same species. You can't just dismiss that fact. Type is important. We've all got our own tribal rhythms, darling, and you can predict quite a lot based on types. If Andy—"

Christine cut her off. "Stop! Don't do this. I'm serious. Please do *not* sit there and dissect and dehumanize my husband. It is such a bullshit thing to do."

The shared seat was trembling with Christine's agitation. She didn't dare look at her mother. A moment later, Lillian slipped off the swing.

"My train wreck is behind me, Chrissie. It's been dragged out of the tunnel and cleared away." She paused, pulling her shawl tighter around her. "I love you, whether you like it or not. I don't want to see you hurt. I'm only suggesting you keep an eye out for that tunnel. You make sure you've got your lights on nice and bright before you go plunging in."

She adjusted the shawl again.

"Good night, darling. You should go get some sleep. You really aren't looking your best."

CHAPTER 49

The rookie cop was stationed behind the industrial-size trash bin, with a clear view of the fire escape of the five-story apartment building. The smell coming off the metal container was sweet and rank. A low-volume burst of static sounded from the officer's shoulder radio.

"Unit One. In place?"

The cop peeked his head around the side of the trash bin. As he locked his eyes on the third-floor window, he caught a movement out of the corner of his eye. He turned his head and watched a hunchbacked rat galloping across the alley. It practically collided with the officer's shoes on its way to squiggling beneath the trash bin.

The cop twisted his chin and muttered into his shoulder. "One. Roger."

Atop the building, the rookie's partner waved his arm overhead. "Back off, dude," he muttered to himself, the sentiment aimed at the rookie down below whose head was clearly visible behind the metal trash container.

"Unit Two?"

The cop twisted the shoulder radio as close to his face as he could. "All set."

Some half a mile to the west, a police chopper hung suspended over the East River, the glass cockpit pitched slightly forward. The cop's radio crackled again.

"Big Bird, you read?"

The words were followed by a barely discernible voice competing with the roar of the helicopter's engine.

Megan Lamb glanced sideways at FBI agent Armstrong. The man's features were set on "grim." Megan didn't like his vibe one bit.

The two were standing in the stairwell of the five-story building, between floors two and three. The dimly lit wall was the color of a grocery bag, spackled in spots with blotches of green paint.

"We're knocking," Megan said in a low voice, her tone halfway between an instruction and a reminder.

Armstrong's response was terse. "Fuck that."

"No. Fuck *that*."

Armstrong snapped, "You want to give this ape the heads-up? Fine. That's two more men dropped at the door."

Megan ignored the gender point. "I told you. We flank. I kneel, and you're at five off the door, head shot ready. If he comes out with a weapon, he's neutralized."

"Goddamned Taylor didn't neutralize him."

"We're not goddamned Taylor," Megan said. "*We're* ready."

Megan knew that the agent was sick at heart and furious. When word had come in from the Shelter Island police about the two bodies found just inside the door of the house where Joy Resnick had been murdered, Armstrong had destroyed a gooseneck lamp in the 6th Precinct headquarters. Several hours later, with confirmation of Joy Resnick's cousin, Robert Smallwood, having arrived on the island Thursday evening and exited again on the late night ferry on Friday, Armstrong would have gladly jammed a shrapnel grenade down Smallwood's throat, he'd been so enraged. For her part, Megan was not at all happy having a rabid federal pit bull for a partner on the operation to bring Robert Smallwood into custody for questioning. But her power to sideline the seething agent had proved nonexistent.

Megan had a key to apartment 3B. The landlord of the building lived off-site, and he had been rousted from his bed just after four in the morning to cough it up. Megan had no illusions that Armstrong was going to stand by quietly while she fiddled with a key, assuming that their knocking brought no result.

"We need to talk to this guy," Megan reminded the agent as the two prepared to mount the remaining steps. "That means he remains alive. The girl might not be in there. We need him to tell us where she is. Let's not make a mess of this, okay?"

Armstrong's grunt did little to communicate agreement.

The two unholstered their weapons as they climbed the stairs and stepped soundlessly down the hallway, their muzzles next to their ears and trained at the flaking ceiling. Armstrong continued past the door and assumed a three-quarter shooting stance, bringing his weapon to an approximation of where he figured the head of a six-foot-four individual would be when the door opened. It was Megan who rapped on the door. *"NYPD! Open up!"*

She fell to one knee, training her gun at the door. The two could make out the distant sound of the police chopper closing in fast from the river. The agreed-upon count was ten, but Megan was not surprised when Armstrong moved on eight.

"Move back." He stepped in front of the door, raising his left foot waist-high and crashing it forward against the door's flimsy lock.

"Go!"

Megan hit the door low with her shoulder and tumbled into the apartment. Her weapon came up, swinging left, right, straight ahead.

Nothing.

Armstrong was charging in behind her.

"Kitchen!" He ran down the short hallway and straight-armed the door at the end. Megan came out of her crouch and leaped into the small kitchen.

"Clean!"

She stepped back into the hallway and kicked open a closet door directly in front of her. Empty.

"Bathroom clean!" Armstrong yelled, charging back up the hallway. *"Bedroom! Bedroom! Bedroom!"*

As Megan angled for the room, Armstrong swung around the corner. The sound of the chopper was now ten times louder. Megan pushed open the door to the bedroom and stepped inside, weapon at the ready. She froze. Armstrong came racing in behind her.

"Holy shit."

Lowering her weapon, Megan stepped over to the far wall of the small room. Her radio crackled, but she didn't even hear who was saying what. She was too fixated on the sight of what looked like several hundred photocopies of Michelle Foster's face. Armstrong appeared behind her, his eyes scanning the wall display.

Finally, Megan twisted her chin toward her shoulder. "Stand down," she said into her radio. She took a step closer to the wall, her eyes darting from image to image to image.

In a voice no one heard but herself, she added, "But not too fucking far."

CHAPTER 50

This time the news came in directly to Christine. She was up early, grinding fresh beans for coffee, and almost didn't hear the sprightly notes of "Anything Goes" coming from her cell phone, which was sitting on the counter. In her haste to get the call she tipped the lid of the grinder. Freshly ground coffee carpeted the counter.

The caller was Detective Lamb, and her information was, for the most part, not good. Christine tilted back against the counter as the police detective explained how a link between the woman found dead in the van used to abduct Michelle and a recently unsolved murder on Shelter Island had led a pair of investigators out to Shelter Island the day before, and how the two had been brutally murdered as they had approached the scene. Christine had to ask the detective to repeat the last part. The words had failed to register as a reality.

"Agent Taylor," Megan said flatly. "And a detective from the Suffolk County Police. They were both shot at close range."

Christine's free hand had landed in the loose coffee. "Michelle?"

"No sign of your daughter."

The detective went on to explain that the identity of Michelle's kidnapper had now been established. Minimizing the details, she informed Christine of the early morning raid on Robert Smallwood's apartment in Queens and encouraged Christine not to lose hope.

"Every law enforcement agent in the country has the man's picture. His car is distinctive; it's not going to be difficult to spot. He's been flushed out not only from his home but from the house on Shelter Island, where he was most likely holding Michelle. This means he's on the run. Whatever his plan was, it's falling apart. Smart money says he'll just drop Michelle off somewhere and try to make a run for it. I just want you and your husband to hang tough, okay? Things are falling our way, Mrs. Foster, not his."

Jenny had come into the kitchen as the detective delivered her assessments to Christine. She froze as she heard Christine say, "But he's killing all these *people*."

Megan conceded. "The victim on Shelter Island. That is, the first victim. She's been identified as Smallwood's cousin."

"Oh my God."

"It's fresh information for us. We're trying to piece it all together. This man, Robert Smallwood. Does the name mean anything to you? He works as a security guard at the Metropolitan Museum. We don't really have much else on him yet."

Christine was shaking her head. "I don't . . . None of that's ringing any bells."

"How about Mr. Foster? Is he there with you?"

"No. Andy's . . . I don't think he's gotten up yet."

There was a pause on the line. Christine smiled wanly at Jenny and shook her head slightly. No Michelle.

"Mrs. Foster," Megan said. "I'm going to ask you to have your husband give me a call as soon as he's up."

"Would you like me to go get him now?"

"There's no need for that. I've got plenty to occupy myself here. But . . . well, when he does get up, you can ask him if he has any knowledge of this man Smallwood. And something else. Both Smallwood's cousin and the woman we found in the van, they worked together here in the city. They worked for an organization called Masters and Weiss. Public relations work. Are you familiar with this company, Mrs. Foster?"

"Well, yes. They handled much of my husband's campaign last year. You're saying both these women worked for *them*?"

"I'm just trying to piece things together, Mrs. Foster."

Christine moved away from the counter and dropped into the chair opposite Jenny.

"Tell me more, Detective."

Irena Bulakov waited on the corner of 110th Street and Lenox Avenue, on the northern end of Central Park. She stiffened as a mounted policeman on a chocolate-brown horse passed behind her on the gravel path just inside the park, then glanced furtively around as the animal continued by. The helmeted policeman turned his head in her direction, but his eyes were hidden by a pair of aviator sunglasses. Irena could not swear he was not looking at her.

Ten minutes later a blue Toyota pulled over to the curb. Irena pushed aside an open map as she got into the passenger's seat. Her first thought was that the policeman on the horse would circle back and see this mummy at the wheel of the car and gallop over to investigate.

"Drive!" she gasped, pulling the door closed.

Leonard Bulakov offered his sister-in-law a smile. "And today, a red-head. I cannot keep up with you, Irena."

He checked the mirror and pulled out into traffic. His bandaged right hand participated minimally with the steering. He gestured with his elbow, indicating the map.

"I have put a circle around Greenwich. You must help me to get out of the city. I think this is the hardest part."

Irena clawed the map onto her lap. She repeated to Leonard what she had said to him on the phone earlier that morning.

"I have to do this, Leonard."

Leonard spoke soothingly, switching lanes to move past a stopped taxi. "I know, I know. You do not have to feel bad."

"They have stolen the daughter of this woman. She is a little seven-year-old girl. I want this woman to have her daughter back home. I have to do this for her, Leonard. I must."

"Yes, yes." Leonard's hand crossed the seat and landed on the map. "It's good. You are a good woman. We will do this."

Irena was gripping the blue flash drive in both her hands, so tightly that her palms were moist with heat. The golden stone. Was the golden stone going to bring the little girl home to her mother? Irena would be so happy. This would be today's definition of heaven.

A small circular island appeared. In the middle was a statue of a man standing next to a piano. Leonard frowned, then found the lane that guided him partway around the circle. He cut back to the outside lane and veered off onto the street to his right just in the nick of time.

Behind the Toyota, two car lengths back, the driver of the black Explorer muttered as well, jerking the wheel to make the sudden turn.

"Shit."

A crackling voice sounded over the speakerphone under the dash-board. "What's going on?"

Anton Gregor wished his boss would just leave him to do his job. But the man was anxious.

"Nothing," Gregor said.

The phone crackled again. "Where are they going?"

Even two car lengths back was too many. Especially in the city. They weren't going to notice him on their tail.

"I don't know yet," Gregor said, tipping the wheel to the left. There was so much horsepower at his command he felt he could bring his vehicle to pounce right on top of the little blue car if he wanted to. Who knew? Depending on the destination the two Bulakovs had in mind, maybe this is exactly what he would do.

"They are going nowhere, Mr. Titov," Gregor said. "I promise you this."

Andy was not in bed. Christine glared at the indentation left by his head on the pillow. She fought back an almost overwhelming impulse to attack the pillow.

As Christine emerged from the bedroom she nearly ran into her mother, who was coming down the hallway from Christine's old room. Lillian was wearing a green silk robe that rode tightly on her hips.

"Well if it—"

Christine silenced her with a look. "Not now."

She found him out in the gazebo, seated up on the railing. He was talking on his cell phone, but he disconnected the call as she approached.

"Fergus," he said, by way of explanation.

Christine stopped at the lip of the gazebo. One thing Andy Foster never looked was frail. He exercised. He was smart about what he ate. His varsity quarterback good looks were always robust. But right now he looked bad. His pallor was not all that far from the pale gray of his sweatshirt. His eyes were red-rimmed from lack of sleep and as puffy as Christine had ever seen them. The sight brought a pause to Christine. But only long enough for her fury to gather force.

"I don't care who you're talking to! What are you doing, hiding out here?"

"I was just calling Jim. I thought it better if I conduct business away from the house."

"Business." Christine injected bile into both syllables.

"This isn't easy, Chris. I'm . . . I'm trying to do all the right things."

Christine stepped up into the gazebo. "What aren't you telling me?"

Andy parroted the question. "What am I not telling you?"

Christine was struggling to keep herself under control. "About Michelle. About her kidnapping. You know more about this than you're telling. I demand to know what it is!"

"What do you think I know?"

She wanted to hurt him. She wanted to throw herself at him and dig her fingernails into his skin. She took a breath. "I just got off the phone with Detective Lamb. They know who took Michelle."

Andy slid off the railing. "Who is it? Who has her?"

"He has ties to Masters and Weiss," Christine said. "He has murdered two people who worked there. One of them was his cousin."

"His *what*?"

"It was Joy Resnick, Andy."

She watched her husband closely for his reaction to the name. Christine had met Joy Resnick on any number of occasions during the course of the campaign. The two had even embraced on election night. Andy's gaze remained vacant.

Christine continued. "The police are saying it was Joy's own cousin who murdered her. It was something like a week or so ago. Out on the island. The woman they found in the van yesterday was her assistant."

"Joy Resnick's *cousin* murdered her?"

"Did you know about that? That Joy Resnick had been murdered?"

Andy hesitated, which was answer enough for Christine.

"This man killed two more people last night," she said flatly. "Two men, Andy, including one of those FBI men who were at our apartment. Damn it, this is about *you*, Andy. This is—"

Andy started forward. "We've always known—"

"No! If you take another step, I'll kill you, I swear."

"Chrissie—"

Christine's foot stamped down hard against the wood floor.

"Don't say anything, Andy! You're going to lie, I can tell. I don't want to hear it. There's something bad here. Really bad. Lillian picked up on it right away."

"Chrissie, please. Your mother?"

"Don't go bad-mouthing her, Andy! It's time out on Lillian bashing.

We're not playing that game. Though frankly, I don't know what game we *are* playing."

Andy took another step forward. As he did, Christine moved backward. She held up a warning finger to her husband, and he froze where he was.

"If you touch me right now, Andy, I promise, I will hurt you. Our daughter is in the hands of a killer. Okay? Is that getting through to you? This man is *killing* people, Andy, and he's got Michelle. Nothing else matters. I don't matter and you don't matter. It's our daughter. Nothing else. Detective Lamb says that now that they know who they're looking for, she thinks they'll locate him quickly. All I'm saying to you is that if you know *anything* that can help them find her . . ."

She let the sentence go unfinished. She turned abruptly and left the gazebo. Andy watched her as she made her way across the grass. Halfway to the house she broke into a run. Even from where he stood, Andy could hear her sobbing. By the time she had disappeared through the sliding glass doors, he was on his phone.

Jim Fergus answered on half a ring.

"Andy. What's going on?"

The senator spoke tersely. "Call Hyland's people. I'm not taking the job."

He disconnected the call before Fergus could reply. The phone was already vibrating by the time he slipped it into his pocket. He ignored it.

CHAPTER 51

Irena was musing again about her two nonexistent children. The twins. There really wasn't any reason why they wouldn't be able to be friends with the little girl she and Leonard were going to help rescue. Was there? They were smart as whips, the both of them, and attractive, so why not? The little girl's mother would be so grateful to Irena.

Of course, not everything was going to be good. The golden stone was going to help the girl come back home, but it was also going to present a very big problem for the girl's mother and father. The father was not a good man. But things were going to happen to him. Probably he would have to go away. Irena stared out the windshield at the passing buildings and imagined the bad man going far away, hopefully with an idea to make himself better. She thought of Dimitri. Maybe Dimitri was also far away somewhere trying to become a better person again.

Maybe.

Irena continued to clutch the flash drive in her hands. They should have been out of Harlem by now, but Leonard was already lost. He told her he must have missed the road that led to the bridge out of the city.

"We can find the highway another way," he assured he. "At least we are still going north. We are fine."

The map was open on Irena's lap. The city of Greenwich was in a circle of red Magic Marker.

The twins would like to live in this Greenwich, Irena thought. It is safe there and very rich. It must be very pretty. She imagined the bad father going away and his wife inviting Irena and the twins to stay with her. The newspaper said that she was waiting in her father's mansion for her daughter to come home safely.

Mansion.

Dimitri would have been so happy for Irena to be living in a mansion. The twins would enjoy living in one. Irena closed her eyes. She saw a beautiful oblong swimming pool, surrounded by Greek columns. She saw herself on a telephone next to the pool, talking with a handsome movie star who was insisting on coming over.

"But I am married."

"No, you're not. Your husband is gone."

"But all those beautiful women."

"Bah. They have no brains. You are a beautiful woman, Irena. You have beautiful eyes."

"I have to make dinner for the twins."

"No, you don't. I will fly the twins to Paris on my airplane. I am friends with a famous chef there. It will be an adventure for them."

"Well . . ."

"And we can be alone, Irena."

"Well . . ."

"We can make each other happy."

Irena opened her eyes. Harlem was so ugly compared to her new life. She decided this was her last time ever in the city. Maybe she could arrange for a cozy cottage near the mansion, for Leonard, who had been so dear and so kind.

The light at the next intersection turned from yellow to red, and Leonard pulled to a stop. Irena shifted toward him and placed a hand lightly on his arm. She was about to speak when she noticed the black car behind them had pulled up very close and put its hazard lights on. A man was getting out of the car and coming over to Leonard's side. Instinctively, Irena squeezed the golden stone even tighter. The moment had arrived. Her life was changing.

The man pulled open the door behind Leonard and got into the car. He had a hard but handsome face. It was a familiar face. He gave Irena a sexy smile.

He placed the barrel of a gun against the back of Leonard's head.

"Turn here."

The light went green, and Leonard did what he was told. He took a right turn onto a narrow street.

"Pull over," the sexy man said. "There."

Leonard pulled over next to a wooden fence that fronted a vacant lot.

"Turn off the car."

Leonard did. The man ran the tip of his tongue over his lips. He leaned back as far as he could and squeezed the trigger of his gun. The sound of the gunshot was much softer than Irena would have thought. A simple *pop*.

A spray of red splashed across the windshield, and Leonard fell forward onto the steering wheel.

Irena was back in her dream. The twins were already on their way to Paris. In a fancy jet plane. They were many miles above the ocean. They were safe.

The man in the backseat spoke.

"You have something for me."

Irena raised her closed fist and then relaxed her fingers. As the man reached over the seat and took the golden stone from her, she turned to face him. She noted that his eyes were the same cold blue as the water in her fancy swimming pool.

"We are alone," she said. She was surprised and delighted by her own husky whisper.

The man smiled at her again. He placed the barrel of his gun against Irena's temple.

"You're cute."

CHAPTER 52

The FBI director was out of the car before it had even stopped moving. William Pierce chucked the White House security guard on the shoulder as he strode past the small gatehouse, his black briefcase swinging high in his other hand.

"Everything good?" Pierce asked.

"Yes sir, Mr. Director."

"Good."

Pierce entered the White House at a clip and was met just inside the door by the president's chief of staff. Ron Abbey fell in beside the director.

"The president appreciates your rearranging your schedule on such short notice."

"He's the boss," Pierce replied brusquely.

Pierce barely broke stride. His gait was powerful and self-aware. As the two rounded the corner at the end of the hallway, Pierce remarked, "I hope you've all enjoyed your honeymoon. That's clearly over."

"We're fine," Abbey said. "Nobody's naive about any of this, least of all the president. We're staying out ahead of matters."

The two approached the president's outer office and Abbey reached for the door. Pierce stopped him, placing a hand against his chest.

"I think that will be all, Ron."

Abbey balked. "I'm in this meeting. We all need to go over—"

The director stopped him, patting his hand reassuringly against the chief of staff's chest. "Don't you worry. Your boss and I will sort all this out. Why don't you run off and go see your little friend over at Commerce?"

Abbey was taken aback. "My—?"

"It's Gleason, if I recall. Janet?"

"How do you . . . ?"

The chief of staff broke off his question. The director's smile could not have been more unctuous. He tapped Abbey again on the chest. More firmly.

"Your boss and I have a lot to discuss, Ron. You go on. We'll be fine."

The custom of the handshake originated as a mutually accepted means for two persons who were meeting to determine if either of them was carrying a weapon—most often a knife—attached to his forearm, hidden by his loose sleeve. Thus the handshake's original form, the clasping of hands accompanied by a second hand-grabbing hold farther up the arm. A little trust went only a little way.

As President Hyland came around from behind his large desk to greet his FBI director, this factoid darted through his mind. The president's eyes followed the director's briefcase as it came up and landed heavily on the desk. In this town, *that* was where the weapons were usually hidden.

Pierce took a seat as Hyland returned to his chair. "I'm going to be blunt with you, Mr. President."

"By all means, Bill. Speak freely."

"I don't mean to come off like a diva," the FBI director continued. "But it's a little disconcerting to be ordered to run what is essentially an errand." He indicated the briefcase. "There is nothing here that your people haven't already pored over this past week."

Hyland balled his hands together and leaned back in his chair. "Well, there sure as hell ought to be."

Pierce frowned. "What is that supposed to mean?"

"It means that when I authorize the FBI to provide my staff with a full and factual report on someone, what I expect is a full and factual report."

"You'll have to excuse me, Mr. President, but I don't know what you're talking about."

"I'm talking about my being summoned to Whitney Hoyt's home three days ago to be told that there's too much dirty laundry hanging on John Bainbridge's line for him to be my next vice president. I'm talking about why such information would be in a file folder in Governor Hoyt's hand and not in one in *my* hand, placed there by *your* office."

Pierce allowed the question to settle before replying. "I'm supposed to respond to that?"

"Damn right you are." Hyland came forward in his chair. "I'm going to appreciate it if you don't take me for a fool, Bill. New kid on the block doesn't mean stupid kid on the block. You're so good at what you do and you've got so much support out there, I couldn't dump you even if I wanted to. And I don't want to. I'm not going to ask you to convince me that Whitney Hoyt can get his hands on information that your office can't. I'd be asking you to convince me that you don't know how to run the show, and that's patently ridiculous. You've got the show down pat."

Silence is a powerful magnet for information, as Pierce well knew. So he said nothing, offered his most placid, patient expression, and waited.

Hyland went on. "If Bainbridge is mortally wounded for the job, the only reason I can think you wouldn't volunteer the information to us is that Whitney Hoyt requested the privilege of blindsiding the new president this past Wednesday morning. He certainly did seem to enjoy the role."

"I suppose you'd have to ask Hoyt about that," Pierce said.

"I happen to be asking you."

"I'm sorry, Mr. President. I'm going to have to ask you to give me a clear question. I'm just not sure what you're trying to get at."

"Gladly. Did your office withhold from the president information on former secretary Bainbridge that was then shared with a private citizen?"

"Don't be absurd."

"That's a no?"

"Correct."

"And if I find out that you have just lied to me, do I have your word that your letter of resignation will be on my desk?"

"If I just lied to you, Mr. President, I don't suppose my word stands for much."

Hyland abruptly slammed his hands down hard on his desk. "Damn it! I need a vice president! I'd like to know what the hell is going on here."

Director Pierce recovered quickly from the president's outburst. "Mr. President, my personal involvement in this whole process has been peripheral. I couldn't even pretend to be interested in whatever the politics are that are going on with your VP situation. Frankly, I'm a better director for that particular ignorance. If I've learned nothing else over the years, I've learned that much. But I'm not completely deaf. Nor am I stupid. You have Andy Foster in the bag for your veep. I know this whole mess with his daughter is a royal nightmare right now, but the man is vetted, qualified, and ready. I'm missing the problem here."

Hyland's eyebrows rose. "You know he's ready?"

"I know how to analyze rumors," Pierce said plainly.

"What you know is that Whitney Hoyt is hell-bent to land his son-in-law in the copilot seat. Isn't that right?"

"I wouldn't say that news would surprise me."

"You and the governor go way back, Bill. I'm sure very little about Whitney would surprise you."

"Don't be too certain about that, Mr. President. Whitney is a crafty fellow." Pierce gave a shrug. "But sure. My job is to be as informed as I can be."

"Your job is to see that *I* am just as informed as you."

"Mr. President, I do my best."

"Let me ask you something, Director," Hyland said. "Would it surprise you to hear that Senator Foster's office contacted me less than an hour ago to express the senator's wish that his name be withdrawn from consideration?"

Hyland didn't need to hear Pierce's answer. He saw it in the man's expression. He had less than a second to see it, but that was all he needed. He followed his question with another. "Do you suppose Whitney Hoyt knows of this decision?"

"I can't speak for Governor Hoyt."

The president's intercom buzzed. Hyland hit the flashing button on the phone.

"Sir? Governor Hoyt is on the line."

Hyland was fully aware how obnoxious the expression was that he aimed at his FBI director. And he was fine with that. As far as the president was concerned, there was already more than enough obnoxiousness in the room. "Well, how about that? Why don't we just see what the good man himself has to say on the topic?"

President Hyland lifted the receiver and pushed a second button on the phone. He leaned back in his chair, loose as a goose.

"Governor? John Hyland here. What can I do for you today?"

CHAPTER 53

Whitney Hoyt chose Schubert. Sonata in E-flat Major, performed by Marta Deyanova. He waited for the first notes to sound, then stepped over to the sideboard.

"I don't give a damn what hour it is, will you join me, Andrew?"

Andy was standing by the window on the far side of the room, gazing out in the direction of the garden. It wasn't exactly calmness he was experiencing, though it could have been mistaken for it. He was numb. Since being confronted by Christine in the gazebo, Andy suspected he had slipped into a mild state of shock. He turned from the window.

"Sure. I'll join you. If it will make you happy."

Hoyt's smile suggested that it would. "Thank you, Andrew. Bourbon?"

"Fine."

Hoyt picked up a small silver hammer to tap free some ice from the frozen mound in the ice bucket. "My mother was a pianist," Hoyt said. "I'm sure you've heard all this. Quite the phenom when she was young. She was performing extensively by the time she was twenty. She gave it all up to marry my father. The touring, I mean. The career. To hear her tell it, it was a blessing. That kind of life is truly grueling. The all-day practicing. The paranoia about the hands. Not to mention the pressures of performing. She said she used to get violently ill before most of her recitals."

He cocked his head, listening intently to the music. "I always prayed that Christine would take a real interest in the piano."

"You're saying you wished that sort of hell on your own daughter?"

"Don't be ridiculous. That's not what I'm saying. My mother didn't give up the instrument, only the performing in public. We always had this sort of music wafting through the house. I find it so soothing. I admit, with Christine it was just a case of foisting my own wishes on my daughter. I guess I'm a sentimentalist and controlling bastard all at once."

Jenny had arrived in the garden, wielding a trowel. Andy turned from the window.

"Gosh, Whit. I never thought you were a sentimentalist."

"Aren't you the funny one." Hoyt crossed the room and handed Andy his drink. " 'Cheers' doesn't seem appropriate under the circumstances."

Andy took a sip of his drink. The bourbon bit his tongue and sent a liquid warmth into his bloodstream. He knew it was utterly foolish to be drinking at all, let alone so early in the day. "What are you planning to do about Lillian? I don't think poor Jenny's got enough weeds out there to keep herself busy all day and night."

Hoyt looked out the window. His wife was down on her knees, digging the trowel in the soft dirt. He tapped his glass against Andy's. "I'm leaving Lillian in your and Christine's hands, Andrew. If Chrissie wants her mother here, that's fine. It's a large house."

He moved back over to the couch where he remained standing. "Jenny will roll with whatever is needed. That's the kind of person she is. She's pliable. I mean that in a good way, of course."

Andy smirked. "That must be nice."

Hoyt looked sharply over at his son-in-law. "Let me tell you something. Until you've lived with someone like Lillian you have no idea what *unpliable* is. You and Christine have conducted yourselves admirably, in my opinion."

"I agree." Andy stepped to the armchair and dropped into it. "All told we've been pretty fortunate. But this VP thing, Whit. Even before this whole nightmare with Michelle, it was shaping up to be a major problem."

"But not an insurmountable one."

Andy shrugged. "I guess that doesn't really matter now."

Hoyt lowered himself onto the couch. "Well, in fact it does."

Andy froze. "What's that supposed to mean?"

"I've spoken with the president," Hoyt said.

Warily, Andy set the glass down on the coffee table and inched forward in his chair. "What do you mean?"

"I called him. I told him he might not want to be too quick in accepting your decision to turn down his offer. Certainly not in publicizing it. Obviously he knows the pressure you're under with this whole situation with Michelle. I told him to expect a call from you to—"

"*What?*"

"I said—"

"I fucking heard what you said, Whitney! What I want to hear is why you said it!"

Controlling bastard. His very own words. Andy was struck with a nearly unstoppable urge to fish out an ice cube from his glass and whip it at the old man's head.

Hoyt remained placid. "I said it, Andy, because I believe it's a rash decision on your part. To say you are currently under a lot of pressure is the understatement of all understatements. This is not the time to be making sweeping decisions, certainly not on something of this magnitude. I told Hyland just to sit on things for now. It's Saturday. Nobody expects any news from the White House on a Saturday. I told him I would be having a discussion with you."

"And you are," Andy said hotly. "A little Schubert, a little bourbon. Nice lubrications, Whitney. But if it's all the same to you, I'd prefer to make my own decisions."

Hoyt's fist came down so swiftly against the coffee table it seemed to catch both men by surprise. "You are making *shit* decisions, young man!"

Andy attempted to respond but was waved off. Hoyt's words came on like a slashing saber.

"For Christ's sake, do you think an opportunity like this just comes along every year like the goddamn flu? It doesn't! Trust me. For most people who have even an *inkling* of desire for the presidency, an inkling is as close as they will ever come to the real thing. You're in the catbird seat, my friend. Life has been such a cakewalk for you, you're not even aware of how rare this opportunity is. This is a once-in-a-lifetime moment, son. And this whole casual oh-what-the-hell stance of yours is unacceptable! Jesus H. Christ, you are being *handed* the reins of the mightiest country on earth! Do you even understand that?"

"The vice presidency is not the reins—"

"Stop it!" Hoyt's eyes shone with a silver gleam. "Stop it. You're sounding like an idiot. Listen to me. For all your smarts, you apparently have no idea how swiftly a political career can descend. You're a young handsome stud on a fantastic winning streak. But let me tell you, that does not last forever. Shit happens. You know that phrase. Shit happens. It sure as hell happened to me in my day, and whether you believe it or not, it can happen to you."

"Oh, I believe that, Whitney. Don't worry on that count."

"Good! Believe it! Count on it. *Act* on it. You think you've got the rest of your life to do what pleases you, but in this game you do not. There are too many other people trying to do what pleases them as well, my friend, and there just aren't enough goodies to go around. That makes for a very few winners and many, many losers. It's time you started understanding that a little better."

"Would you stop calling me your 'friend' like that? It sounds ridiculous."

"I *am* your friend! Jesus Christ, Andrew, if I didn't look out for you, I don't know who would! Certainly not my daughter. I love Chrissie to pieces, but that woman's dreams are not the ones we need to focus on right now."

"And whose dreams do *we* need to focus on?" Andy asked.

"Yours! If you could get your head out of your ass and recognize them!"

Andy leaped to his feet. His body was trembling. Hoyt remained seated, his chin tilted slightly, almost as if he was daring his son-in-law to take a clear swipe at it. When Andy finally spoke, the shakiness in his voice betrayed his fury.

"I have a daughter . . . who has been missing . . . for two days. I don't know why she was taken. But you can bet it has everything to do with my being in the public eye."

Hoyt began to speak, but Andy cut him off.

"Hold on. Let me finish. Michelle is missing, okay? Not a single thing on this planet means anything to me right now except getting her back home safely. Second on that list, I would like to keep my marriage. I love my wife. Pliable, unpliable, I don't care. I love her, and if truth be told, I haven't always treated her as well as I should have. I want the chance to do that. If turning down the VP job is one way of doing that, that's fine with me. I don't care. Grabbing the reins of the country was *your* dream, Whitney. I'm sorry it didn't work out. But what *I* want right now is my life back. You know that cliché? I want my life back? That means my wife and my daughter. That's my life, Whitney. Not all this other crap."

Andy finished off his drink. He was convinced that with almost no extra effort he could have crushed the glass with his bare hand.

Whitney took his time getting to his feet. He looked directly at Andy as he rounded the couch. He stepped over to the rolltop desk near the front window, where he pulled open one of the top drawers and extracted from it a piece of gray paper. He returned to the couch and read a name from the paper.

"Pamela Hunt."

Andy flinched. Pam Hunt was a former friend of Jenny Hoyt's. Briefly, a particular acquaintance of Andy's as well. Very briefly. Years ago.

"What about her?"

Hoyt consulted the paper again. "Rita Flores. *Washington Post.* Good writer, as I recall. A little strident, but so many are these days."

"What's this all about?"

The older man snapped the paper in Andy's face. "It's about a man who says he wants to maintain the marriage to the woman he says he loves. It's also about a man who has been pretty damn reckless going about it. Not to mention foolishly reckless if he ever really did hope to make it to the Oval Office someday."

He consulted the paper again. "Rachel Bittman."

"Who is that?"

Hoyt allowed himself a small smile. "Perhaps you don't collect the names of all your trophies, Andy."

Andy exploded. "But *you* do? Where the hell did you get these names from? What the . . . do you have *spies* following me around?"

"I don't know *spies,* Andy," Hoyt said calmly. "Spies are CIA. I've never really been comfy with that crowd."

Andy's knees were not doing their job. He lowered himself back into the chair.

"Andy. This does not need to be a problem between us. I want you to understand that. The last thing in the world I want to do is show these names to Christine."

"They're just names," Andy said thickly. "Why would she believe they meant anything?" But even before the words were out of his mouth, his heart sank. "You have evidence."

"Audio. And only Miss Flores. Not Jenny's friend. And certainly not your busty jewelry-store girl. That's the Bittman woman, in case you're curious. Though she was quite willing to provide an affidavit if we wished. Not for cheap, mind you. That's one hard-bargaining lady you tangled with there."

"You're a bastard," Andy said.

Hoyt shot right back. "You, my friend, are reckless."

"That's my own business."

Hoyt shook his head sadly. "Not so. You're married to my daughter. That makes it partly my business. But more to the point, you are so perfectly positioned to make it to the White House, Andrew. For sweet Jesus' sake, I simply cannot stand by and watch you screw up that opportunity."

"And so . . . what? You had me *spied* on? What's the game here, Whitney?"

"The *game* here, son, is that I'm not accepting your giving up on the vice presidency."

Andy was dumbfounded. "Excuse me? *You're* not giving up on it?"

"I'm sorry to break this to you, Andrew, but there's nothing original about you. I've seen many versions of you through the years. I know your game. You enjoy the thrill of simply not getting caught. It really is the damnedest thing. Life hands you good looks, a good brain, charm by the bucketful, and it kicks open every single door you'd like to see kicked open. Yet that's still not enough. It's all too easy for you. You're out there walking on water with no effort whatsoever, and the only real hardships are the ones you come up with on your own. Though it's not really hardship, is it? It's just a challenge of your own creation. And the challenge isn't getting women to sleep with you. Golden boys don't have that problem. The challenge is in not getting caught."

He gestured with the gray paper. His face was florid.

"Except you've *been* caught, son. I've had you pegged since before you married my daughter. I'm not being a prude, Andrew. And I'm not even questioning your feelings toward Chrissie. You and I both know you can love your wife wholeheartedly while you're running around playing barnyard rooster. But if you think there's never going to be a price to pay for your behavior, you are just dead flat wrong."

He handed Andy the paper. Andy could barely bring himself to look down at the names typed on it. There would be plenty of time later to process all that Whitney had just said. But right now, Andy's mind was sprinting as fast as it could in order to stay ahead of all this. The only important point—he felt sick even acknowledging this to himself—was whether or not the name Joy Resnick was on the sheet of paper.

It wasn't. Andy cleared his head as best he could.

"What exactly is this about, Whitney?" he asked again. "If you've had this dirt on me all along, why are you showing it to me now?"

"Fair question," Hoyt said. "There are several reasons. The first, I want it to stop. You've had your adventures. You've screwed your last jewelry-store salesgirl. Enough is enough."

"Fine. What else?"

"The other reason is that I would like to know that the next vice president would have the wisdom to accept the wise counsel of certain senior statesmen from time to time."

Andy's eyes narrowed. "Is this for real, Whitney? You want to know if I would listen to your *opinion* if I were to be in the White House? You're going to blackmail me so that I will *talk* to you?"

"So that you will listen to me."

"And you're thinking you'd control me with this garbage?"

Andy went ahead and fished an ice cube out of his glass. Pressing into its natural indentations, he could feel the frozen water giving way to the heat of his fingers.

"Please," Hoyt said. "That is way too dramatic, Andrew. Let's give me some credit here. I don't happen to care for the direction this country is taking. John Hyland is a smart fellow, and clearly popular. But he's naive. People seem to like that these days. But naivete and fairy-tale thinking will sink this country and sink it fast. I don't want that. And I don't think you want that, either. We need to pull this country back. We need to pull this government back. I want influence, Andrew. I do know a thing or two about what's best for this country, and I want to contribute."

"You want influence."

"I want guaranteed influence."

"I'm sorry, but I seem to be missing the part where you were *elected* to do this. By the people."

Hoyt looked as if he couldn't decide whether to laugh or shriek. "Don't you pretend to be so naive. You know full well how many people actually pull the strings in Washington, and the *people* have no goddamned clue who they are. If you accept Hyland's offer, Andrew, you won't be there by the invitation of the people, either."

"But isn't this all moot, Whitney? I told you, I've turned down Hyland's offer. I've pulled my name from consideration."

"And you're going to pick up this phone right now and put it back in! Or you're going to see the sort of rollout of public disclosures of private behavior that you've never seen before. It will be very ugly, Andrew. Devastating. That's a guarantee. And as for your wife and your daughter . . ."

Andy's voice trembled. Only part of it was anger. "I might not even have a daughter."

Hoyt was unmoved. "You have a wife. I happen to feel you still love her deeply. Do you want this for her? Do you really want to spit in that lovely girl's face like this? You have to ask yourself. What has she done to deserve this?"

Hoyt stepped back over to his desk. He picked up the phone and offered it to Andy.

"I know the number by heart," he said. "I can dial it for you if you'd like."

Feeling like a man wearing a dozen lead suits, Andy got himself out of the chair and stepped over to the desk and took the phone from Hoyt's hand. For the briefest of moments he entertained the urge to pound the phone deep into the older man's skull.

CHAPTER 54

Aleksey Titov bounced a pair of kisses off Anton Gregor's cheeks and took the thug into an embrace.

"I knew I could count on you, Anton."

Gregor had showered and changed out of his bloody shirt. His hair was wet-combed straight back on his head. False modesty floated in his eyes as his ebullient boss fussed over him.

"I am sorry to take so long," Gregor murmured.

Titov waved off the apology. "Not important. This is all good now. Did you have any trouble convincing Mrs. Bulakov to return what is mine?"

There was a barely audible sound from the area of the stairway, and Titov's wife appeared. Her long bronze legs seemed to enter the room well in advance of the rest of her. She paused, noting that Titov was not aware of her presence but that his henchman certainly was. She was wearing cuffed white shorts and a mint-colored button-up shirt pulled into a knot at her abdomen. Her bee-stung lips were thick with freshly applied red lipstick and her eyes were dopey with sleep. The eyes landed on Anton Gregor and seemed perfectly content to remain there.

"Some women are easier to convince than others," Gregor said, glancing past his boss. "I had no problem with this one, Mr. Titov."

Titov nodded tersely. "Good. I will only ask you this. Will we be hearing from Mrs. Bulakov again, Anton?"

Behind him, Titov's wife cocked her head. Her eyebrows rose as if tugged by strings.

Gregor answered, "The woman has no more to say."

Titov's wife made a throat-clearing sound, and Titov spun around. "Gala."

"I want to have a party," the woman announced to her husband. "We're getting boring. I want to have a party tonight."

"Tonight?"

"Tonight. Tomorrow. I don't care. Soon. Not next week. We could all be dead next week."

"We could all be dead today," Gregor observed.

Titov's wife considered the man. "That's true. Maybe we should have a party every night, just in case."

Titov spoke sharply. "Go upstairs. We can have your party tonight. We can buy you a new dress."

Gala Titov showed the men her toothy smile. "Lucky me." She turned and left the room like a woman walking on stilts.

Titov phoned his client.

"I have it."

The two had already agreed on the new price. When the client asked about the others who had been in possession of "the materials" over the past several weeks, Titov replied, "All this has been taken care of. You have nothing to worry about on this."

"That's good."

They set the time for the handoff. Four o'clock. They didn't need to go over the details on the phone. The client fully suspected that Titov's phone was not clean, and for his part, Titov had no reason to think otherwise. The details for the handoff had been covered weeks ago.

Aleksey Titov explained the arrangement to Gregor. He concluded, "You don't see him, he doesn't see you. Except maybe your back."

Gregor understood.

Titov fished a cigarette from a silver box on the glass coffee table. "Please don't *you* get silly ideas, Anton. The client will call me as soon as he has the materials. If his call is not what I expect, please believe me, you will not make it back into the city with your eyes open. You understand this?"

Gregor understood. He pulled his car keys from his pocket. "Thank you, Mr. Titov. Everything will be fine."

Gregor left the house and Aleksey Titov climbed the stairs to his bedroom. His wife was already in bed, a travel magazine propped on her bare breasts.

"I don't like that man," she lied.

Titov snuffed out his cigarette in the ashtray on his side of the bed and began to unfasten his belt.

The magazine slid to the floor.

"Let me."

The woman's torso twisted beneath the sheets. Her long arms came toward her husband like a pair of eels.

Andy was giving her images.

Christine didn't want them, but she had no choice in the matter.

They were tawdry. They were images of a man she thought she knew . . . and of women whose faces Christine did not want to imagine. But he was making her do just that. He was making her look at them all.

In its way, it was practically a joke. A whisker away from a big cosmic put-on. Sitting there, unable to move, Christine could have been one of her own cameras. That was the joke. A broken camera, with its shutter jammed open, forcing her to collect image after image. An assault of images. Had she known how, she would have slapped on a lens cover. Or sabotaged the exposure. Or blurred the focus to the point where none of the wretched things that her husband was showing her could be seen.

But she couldn't. The images poured out of her husband and completely filled her mind. He gave her names, he recounted dates on the calendar, he rattled off locations. He gathered unconscionable scenes and foisted them onto her and she was helpless against the assault. The worst of them, he saved for last. He filled Christine's mind with the image of a bedroom, a shattering glass door, a swift and brutal attack.

And Andy was a part of each image. Her husband's beautiful face bobbed to the surface of every single picture he was showing her.

She simply wanted to shriek.

Clouds were moving in as Anton Gregor took the left exit off the Palisades Parkway and pulled into the defunct gas station. The pumps had been removed more than a decade ago, their rectangular footprints now the home for weeds and cracked pavement. Faded white lines on the north side of the absent pumps delineated parking spaces for about a dozen cars. A green Dodge compact was parked there. So was a Mercedes: cream-colored, with thoroughly tinted windows.

Gregor pulled in next to the Mercedes and cut his engine. He removed a small gift-wrapped box from the glove compartment and set it on the passenger seat. Gregor thought that the gift-wrapping was a pretty stupid touch. But that was Titov's touch. Gregor wouldn't have handled things this way, but he supposed the man could go ahead and be cute if he wanted.

The former gas station building had been converted into what was advertised as a bookstore. A peculiar location for a bookstore, until one discovered that the inventory was strictly guidebooks of the local area—maps, books about flowers and birds, trail guides. A man and woman who looked so similar to each other that they were either brother and sister or a long-married couple were leafing through several of the slim volumes when Gregor went inside. Gregor picked up the first book his fingers reached, and he leafed through the pages, paying absolutely no attention to the contents. He was listening for the sounds of car doors. He heard one closing, and then some twenty seconds later the same sound again, though this one was decidedly more elegant.

The brother-sister/husband-wife duo left the ersatz bookstore, and Gregor had the place to himself. There was a wooden box mounted on the wall where people could leave money for any of the materials they took with them. An honor system. Only twenty-five miles outside the big bad city. Gregor considered smashing the box and taking whatever money was in it, if only to keep people from developing too much false hope in mankind.

But he didn't.

The green Dodge was pulling back onto the parkway. A light rain had begun to fall. Gregor left the little building with his head lowered and got back into his car. The gift-wrapped box was gone. In its place was a bulging green daypack. Gregor zipped it open just enough to confirm its contents. He started up the car and reversed out of his parking spot, pausing to flip on his windshield wipers. He could see from the Mercedes' tailpipe that the car was idling. The windows were as black as ink. It could have been anyone from Santa Claus to the Easter Bunny sitting in there watching him—he *knew* he was being watched. Gregor flashed his headlights at the car, twice. Maybe Santa Claus would think there was some sort of code he was supposed to have been told. Mess with him a little.

Gregor swung the wheel to the right and pulled onto the parkway ramp. He glanced in his side-view mirror. The rain was falling more heavily, steel pellets lacing straight down. The Mercedes had not budged. Maybe the Easter Bunny was busy oohing and aahing over his little gift.

———

Christine had the sense to come in out of the rain.

The trees at the edge of her father's property had stood by in silence as she sobbed. They had known her as a baby and a young girl and an adolescent, but nothing in that history approached the enormity of sorrow that spilled from the woman.

Raindrops began hitting against the high leaves of the trees. With the water chasing her, Christine ran across the lawn back toward her father's house and all the uncertainties that awaited her. She crossed along the side of the house and entered through the front door, to find Jenny emerging from the hallway bathroom.

Christine asked, "Where's Andy?"

"I don't know. I was just in the kitchen making up a stew. Are you in the mood for cutting vegetables?"

"I don't think you want me handling sharp objects right now."

Christine headed up the stairs, peeled off her clothes, and took a shower. The water assaulted her skin. Hot enough was not hot enough. Mist curled over the frosted glass confines and brought the small room to a state of near invisibility. Before she was done, her chest heaved violently and a whole new set of tears spilled out, mixing with the water circling down the drain.

When she was dressed, she walked into Peter's old bedroom. Lillian was sitting on the bed, up against the headboard, leafing through a photo album. She closed it gently.

"I have to get out of here," Christine said.

"Here?"

"This house. My skin. I'm going to kill someone. I'm going to break something." She ran a hand through her wet hair. "I'm going to explode."

Lillian set the photo album aside and swung her feet to the floor. She was studying her daughter closely. "I know the feeling. Come on. I'm sure there's a car around here we can steal."

She slid off the bed and slipped her feet into a pair of moccasins.

"This is good. There are a few things I've been needing to tell you."

CHAPTER 55

As far as Megan was concerned, Brian Armstrong should have been pulled from the field the moment word came in of his fellow agent's murder.

Megan knew only too well the mind-sets that kicked in as the result of a colleague losing his life in the line of duty. The Three Rs: Regret. Revenge. Recklessness. She didn't want any of those mind-sets anywhere near the Robert Smallwood manhunt. There was a child involved. The price was too high.

"Unacceptable," she said flatly to Malcolm Bell. "I can read this guy, Captain, and I'm telling you, it's not good. He was barely keeping his cool before Taylor caught it. I don't want to be taking part in a damn blood hunt."

The conversation was taking place in Bell's office.

"Nobody wants a blood hunt," Bell assured the detective. "I was on the phone with Armstrong's boss just an hour ago, and he's gotten it straight from the director himself. And now it's coming from him to me to you, Detective. The world's watching. We want precision here, not a pool of blood."

"Tell that to Armstrong."

"Armstrong's not mine. You are. So trust me, if William Pierce is weighing in on this from D.C., local FBI is sure as hell listening."

"Easy to say."

Bell allowed the comment to hang in the air a few seconds. "There are some people who might find that a little belligerent, Detective."

Megan responded immediately. "I'm sure there are. There's not much I can do about that. I'm only trying to do my job. I've got concerns, and I don't think you'd be happy if you only heard them after the fact."

"Thank you," Bell said. "I've heard them. And you've heard my response. We don't know what Smallwood wants with this girl, but we do know he's killed at least three times in the past twenty-four hours to get it."

"Plus Joy Resnick."

"Plus Joy Resnick. Though how that connects with all the rest of this is something we don't know yet." Bell consulted a pad of yellow paper on his desk, tapping the service end of a pencil against it. "Here's where we are. Suffolk County is out of it at the moment. They've been told to stand down. They're sitting on their thumbs, and you can be damn sure they're not happy about it. They've got three murders in their backyard, including one of their own. We only have the Mann murder. But the prime suspect lives and works in *our* backyard, and this little girl he has taken lives in our backyard, so we're leading the investigation. One turf war down. And if you've got a hard-on about the FBI, just remember, it's Washington that bumped Suffolk County out of the picture. We've got a U.S. senator in play here. They're not past lowering the boom on us as well, trust me."

Megan saw no need to conceal her smile. "So, that's what a hard-on feels like. I do believe I've learned something here today, Chief."

Bell ignored the crack. "Well, learn this, Detective. We need the turf war kept to an absolute minimum. Here's what I've arranged with our federal brethren. Armstrong and his team are taking Smallwood's work colleagues, his friends, acquaintances, neighbors, drinking buddies, favorite hookers, whatever they find outside his bloodline. You've got the family."

Megan began to balk, but Bell cut her off. "I didn't say you *want* the family. I told you that's what you've got. If you want to spend ten minutes arguing with me, that's ten minutes you're wasting that you could be spending looking for this creep. Nothing's going to change the situation. You don't need to like it, Detective, you just need to do it. I think that's pretty clear?"

Megan rose from her chair.

"One more thing," Bell said. "Any move on the suspect himself is to be coordinated between us and the FBI. That works both ways. Armstrong doesn't make a move without you, and you don't make one without him. Naturally, extreme circumstances are extreme circumstances. Otherwise, you two go after the perp holding each other's hands. Is that understood?"

Megan hesitated a moment. "Understood."

"Fine," Bell said. "Go find this creep."

———

Jeffrey Resnick had a one-word assessment of his cousin Robert.

"Freak."

Resnick delivered this verdict to Detective Megan Lamb in a brightly lit waiting room filled with several dozen young girls between the ages of twelve and fifteen, most of them accompanied by their mothers. All of the girls were impeccably perfect—to Megan's mind, unnaturally so. A perfection of hair, a perfection of makeup, a perfection of calculated poise. With her own unkempt hair and complete lack of cosmetic enhancement, Megan felt like a separate gender altogether.

"Are we looking for the new Nancy Drew here?"

Resnick answered, "In fact, we're looking for Annette Bening's daughter."

"I see."

"Or possibly Julianne Moore's, we're not sure yet. For that matter, I've been hearing Holly Hunter's name thrown around as well. That's the nature of the biz."

Megan asked, "Could we talk somewhere in private?"

Jeffrey Resnick gestured at the little beauties. "We're already way behind schedule."

"The nature of *my* business is to locate your cousin as quickly as I can. I'm sorry if you're running behind schedule, but your girls are going to have to cool their pretty little feet for a few minutes longer. There's a child out there we need to find pronto. Let's get to it."

Resnick showed the detective into a room where a camera and tripods were set up in front of a pair of card tables. The camera was aimed at a bentwood rocker on which sat several pages of a script. Megan picked up the pages and took a seat. Resnick told his assistant, who was seated at one of the card tables, to leave the two of them alone for several minutes. Jeffrey Resnick pointed at the camera.

"Do you want to record this?"

Megan ignored the question. She was leafing through the pages. "Is this a comedy?"

"That'll depend on if anybody laughs."

Megan cocked an eyebrow, setting the pages aside. "I'm sorry about your sister."

Resnick had flipped a folding chair backward and lowered himself into it. He was a foot-tapper. Nerves. Caffeine. A generally high-octane system. His shoes were doing a real number on the wooden floor.

"It sucks, doesn't it?"

"Were you two close?"

Resnick shrugged. "I'd say moderately close. We didn't hang out together or anything like that. We're both . . . we *were* both busy people."

"What were your thoughts when you heard your sister had been murdered?"

"You mean, did it cross my mind that Robbie might have done it?"

"Did it cross your mind?"

Resnick's shoes shared an exchange. Megan studied the man's face. From the photographs she had seen of Joy Resnick—when she was alive—she could see the family resemblance. Soft brown eyes. Narrow nose. Resnick scratched hard at a spot on his head.

"I don't think about Robbie all that much. If Joy and I hardly hung out together much, I can tell you Robbie and I never did."

"Did you have a theory about the murder?"

Resnick shrugged again. "My theory was that Joy must have pissed off the wrong man. There are a lot of wrong men out there. I'm sure in your business you know all about that."

"I've run across a couple," Megan said. She shifted in her chair. "So, let's talk about your cousin."

From the transcripts of the interviews with the Suffolk County police, Megan had the vague outlines of Jeffrey Resnick's cousin.

Megan asked, "What can you tell me about the death of Robert's parents?"

Resnick answered, "I was fourteen when that happened."

"How old was Robert?"

"Same age. Robbie and I were born the same year. He's the older by three months."

"Go on."

"It was ugly. Uncle Ray shot Aunt Vivien while she was taking a bath. I mean, can you imagine?"

"And then your uncle shot himself?"

Resnick held a finger pistol up to his temple. "Correct."

"What kind of man was your uncle?"

Resnick gave her a confused look. "What difference does that make?"

"A father resorts to murder, his son resorts to murder. Catches my interest."

"He was pretty distant. I mean, he wasn't exactly one of your piggyback-ride-giving uncles. Uncle Ray never seemed particularly happy."

"And your aunt?"

"Sexy." Resnick's shoes tapped a snappy beat.

"Do you want to elaborate on that for me?"

"We're off the record here, right?"

"I'm not a reporter, Mr. Resnick."

"I know. Just kidding." His feet finally stopped moving. "To put it bluntly, Aunt Vivien was a fox. I'd be lying to you if I didn't tell you I had a crush on her. Maybe not a crush, but I know I was always jazzed whenever I saw her. You remember when you were fourteen, Detective? A sexy adult can be pretty powerful stuff at that age. Aunt Vivien was a number."

"I understand that your uncle killed his wife because he thought she was having an affair."

"That's the word on the street."

"And what about your cousin? How did Robert respond to losing both his parents in that way?"

Resnick paused a moment before answering. "I guess I'd say that he went inward. Except the thing is, Robbie was always inward. So . . . more inward."

"Prior to their deaths, what would you say was your cousin's relationship with his parents?"

"Easy. Closer to Aunt Viv than to his dad."

"And after his parents' death, Robert moved in with your family."

"That's right."

"Is there anything you can tell me about that?"

"Not really. Except that I was snotty about it at first. The idea was that I would share my room with Robbie, but I refused. So we redid the TV room, and that's where Robbie stayed. The TV went into the basement. That always kind of pissed me off."

"You *were* snotty."

"Guilty. What can I say? Having Robbie move in with us was definitely not a bonus. But if you're asking if he caused trouble or anything, the answer is not really. He read a lot. He didn't really interfere with me. Frankly, Joy was a lot friendlier to him than I was."

"That's how you'd characterize the relationship? Friendly?"

"Sure. Joy had more patience than I did. She'd also been pretty tight with Aunt Viv."

"Did Robert have any friends?"

"A few."

"Any friends in particular that you remember?"

"I'd say his closest friend was this guy named Jonathan Cole. He's the one I remember who'd actually come over to our house to hang out with Robbie. An okay kid. Kind of a suck-up. A lot more talkative than Robbie. But then, so is that chair you're sitting in."

Megan jotted down the name. "Do you have any idea if the two maintained the friendship?"

"I guess it's possible. I seem to recall that Cole became, like, a chiropractor, I think. Or a dentist. Something."

"Any idea where he lives now?"

"Jonathan Cole? Not a clue."

Megan questioned Resnick a little longer. Resnick answered her as best he could, but the fact was that as soon as he went off to college he pretty much severed ongoing contact with his cousin.

"Joy saw him now and then, I think. She felt sorry for him. Robbie took that job at the museum, and we all just figured he'd stay there forever. Not much of a life, if you ask me."

Megan had one final question.

"Do you have any idea why Robert might have taken the Foster girl? Any idea at all?"

The feet came back into the act. Resnick tugged thoughtfully on his chin. "Maybe he's looking for a friend."

The little wannabe starlets all looked up as Megan and Jeffrey Resnick emerged from the audition room. Megan produced her card and handed it to the casting agent. "Anything at all comes to you, don't hesitate. Call me."

Resnick tucked the card into his shirt pocket. "I understand that Robbie got a raw deal in life, but that's no reason to take it out on others. Especially not Joy. Do me a favor, Detective. When you find him, I'd like the first crack at strangling him."

CHAPTER 56

Three days after nineteen-year-old Lillian Burkett arrived in New York City from South Carolina she was date-raped by a sailor from Moscow, Idaho, who was in town for the annual Fleet Week festivities. Memorial Day weekend. The two had met on the Staten Island ferry, when the sailor hit her up for a cigarette. He carried a gold-plated lighter and showed off a fancy move of flipping open the lid using the palm of his hand and striking the flint all in the same maneuver. Fast. Like a seasoned gunslinger. He told her his name was Carl.

The two had some drinks at the Bridge Café, tucked beneath the Manhattan side of the Brooklyn Bridge, before venturing into Chinatown to find something unusual to eat. Lillian insisted that unless a steamed pig was hanging in the window she would not consider the place unusual enough. One of her girlfriends back home in Blacksburg had tucked this bit of wisdom into the gregarious brunette's head. They found a place on Pell Street (no pig, but a wire draped with leathery red ducks) where no English was spoken, not even on the menu. The only English word in the entire place was *Coke,* and Lillian and the sailor ordered some of that to go along with the bottle of Bacardi that Carl had picked up at a liquor store on Pearl Street.

Lillian Burkett was a broad-shouldered skinny Minnie in those days, tall and seemingly weightless, except maybe for her thick nest of chestnut hair. Her face was nothing less than stunning. Pale as a pearl, sharp-lined nosed, and large dishy eyes the color of violets. She had moved to the city, she told Carl, to meet interesting people.

Carl would not turn out to be one of them.

After dinner, they went to the top of the Empire State Building, where Lillian screamed like a child at all the lights on display so far below her. In her flamboyance she accidentally knocked a quarter out of the hand of a man who was about to feed the coin into one of the viewing telescopes, and the man and Carl nearly got into a fight about it.

Carl took her to Roseland, where he turned out to be not a half-bad dancer. Lillian had to admit to herself that her date was not exactly the most loquacious log in the pile. But so what if he was a little moody? Plus, he was only a few degrees shy of handsome, and she knew from their slow dancing that he was as strong as a cannon. How nice, she thought, that a chance cigarette had opened the door to a fun little evening.

Then it all went awry.

Carl had been keeping Lillian's glass filled. Eventually the dance floor began to spin. The sailor took her outside for some air, and the next thing Lillian knew she was sitting at a table in a brick-walled club listening to a trumpet player and a hulking black man who was practically draped over his weathered stand-up bass. She and Carl had switched to wine, thick and red and too sweet for Lillian's taste. The music was disorienting. By the time Lillian told the sailor she wanted to leave, the walls of the small club seemed to be listing sideways.

They left, and for some reason Lillian allowed the sailor to accompany her to her room, which was a weekly rental near the river. While he was off in the bathroom, Lillian tried to raise the stubborn window so that she could maybe get some air into the place. Carl emerged from the bathroom, and that's when he attacked her. At first she thought he was just playing some not-so-funny joke, but he wasn't. Not the way those mean hands were working. He had way too many muscles for Lillian to combat him, and her sputtering *Please don't do this* had only seemed to urge him on.

"Say it in Southern," he grunted at her. "Come on. Let's hear it."

He was rough. And when he finally finished, he hitched up his pants and said to her, "Listen up, girl. For the record. It ain't Carl, and it ain't Moscow." Then he left.

The experience didn't throw Lillian Burkett off for long. She was not about to distrust all of humanity on the basis of one lout. Soon enough, she found her interesting people. Writers. Painters. She found a nice-looking lawyer who worked in the district attorney's office downtown and who had family money and no problem figuring out ways to spend it. He appreciated Lillian's vivacity, and she found him refreshingly clever and outspoken.

After their first night together, Lillian was thrilled. It would be a month and nearly a dozen more sleepovers before Lillian would discover that her lover was engaged to be married. Lillian was more furious than she was heartbroken.

To the surprise of no one who was close to the situation, the lawyer's engagement fell apart, and after a period of resistance, Lillian accepted the rascal back into her bed. But she had wised up.

"You and I are strictly recreational," she informed him. "Fun's fun, but I am looking for Mr. Right and now I know you're not him."

For months the arrangement worked well enough for the both of them. Lillian truly enjoyed the man's company but never entertained any second thoughts concerning his ultimate viability. He was not for her. The two tore up the sheets with gusto every now and again and then happily pillow-talked away into the wee hours. But that was the extent of it. Both were in agreement.

During this same period, Lillian had enjoyed several chaste dates with a new prospect, a lithe and handsome colleague of her lover's. This one seemed much more grounded than her randy lawyer, and more of what Lillian considered an "authentic" gentleman. Not to mention insanely well-off. Within months of their meeting she accepted his offer of marriage. Her fiancé promised Lillian that if she stuck with him she would one day find herself in the White House.

"As sure as you are the most beautiful woman I have ever come across," Whitney Hoyt said to the ravishing twenty-year-old, "I'm going to be president one day. It's my destiny, and there's not a single person who is going to stop it from happening."

Whitney promised her that the wedding would be huge. The guest list would include the mayor and the current governor, as well as a number of noted national politicians. Hoyt saw to it that there was a smattering of celebrities included, as well as some of the usual suspects from Manhattan's A-list. "Diamonds and dragons," in Lillian's vernacular.

Lillian and Whitney had not yet slept together. Hoyt had surprisingly old-fashioned notions in that regard. It was just under a month before the wedding when Whitney Hoyt began chastising his fiancée behind closed doors for the "overexuberance" of her behavior at the most recent set of social outings. A social columnist for the *Times* had recently written that Miss Burkett "could charm the paint off a wall," while in another publication she had been referred to as "Dixie dynamite." The specific occasion of Whitney Hoyt's complaint to his fiancée was a reception held for the Italian ambassador to the United Nations in the Rainbow Room, atop Rockefeller Center. Too many martinis had loosened Lillian's tongue, and she had embarrassed her fiancé by launching into battle with the ambassador's attaché, a man with whom Lillian had been gregariously flirting earlier in the evening. The finer points of Lillian's disagreement with the Italian had been lost in the sheer physicality of her explosion, which had concluded with her removing her shoes and aiming them at the astonished attaché.

Whitney had read her the riot act in the taxi afterward.

"We're not in some movie here! I'm telling you right now, it's not going to work, you running around spouting every fool thing that pops into your head! You threw your *shoes* at that man! We're not going to have that, is that clear? I'm not saying you can't be the life of the party, but what you cannot be is its jester! I won't allow it."

Lillian was furious, and she ordered the driver to reroute the cab to her apartment, where she leaped out and slammed the door shut with all the melodrama she could muster. Her roommate was away for the weekend, so Lillian unloaded her fury to the silent walls. "We're not going to *have* that? You're not going to *allow* it?" Her fiancé had treated her like a child, and she was livid.

Lillian opened a bottle of wine and drank it down well past its label. She was not able to recall later if it had been during one of the spells of self-pity or fire-spitting anger that she had picked up the phone and called her lawyer friend. She knew only that she called him and that he showed up and that for the next thirty-six hours the two of them slipped coolly into an alternate reality. Or not so coolly. Her demands on her friend were outsize—even by the standards of their history together—but he endeavored to meet them. He knew her mind well enough. She was not going to call off the wedding. That wasn't what this was about. Lillian Burkett was going to marry Whitney Hoyt, and she would be at his side when he began making his moves in earnest. But first she had to rage. She had to generate this secret and then slip it into her pocket. Over the course of their marathon weekend the lawyer warned Lillian that Whitney Hoyt was going to come to control her, that he was going to dull her edges. If he were to achieve his goals, he counseled, this was inevitable. He told her further that if she wanted to share in those goals, she would have to accept the costs. An honest look at how things had been going since her engagement to Hoyt would have revealed to the young beauty that she had already begun to pay some of that price. But Lillian was not particularly interested in taking honest looks.

Six weeks later Lillian Burkett married Whitney Hoyt. The reception was held at the Pierre Hotel. After the toasts and the speeches and the endless series of first dances, the newly minted Lillian Hoyt sought out her lawyer friend, who was seated at one of the large tables holding forth to an audience of beautiful people.

Lillian called him away from the table, as she had something she wanted to tell him.

"State secret," Lillian crooned, bringing him close so she could whisper hotly in the man's ear. "Guess what? It looks like we're going to have ourselves a baby."

The lawyer pulled back. "That's great, kiddo. You and Whit might as well get that dynasty under way."

Lillian was already shaking her head. Her violet eyes lit with mirth.

"You and me." She put her finger to her lips. "State secret."

Chris Wyeth was speechless. A rare moment in the young lawyer's life.

CHAPTER 57

On her way to Katonah, Megan put a call into headquarters to get the sniffing under way for any trace of Robert Smallwood's high school friend Jonathan Cole. Technically, Megan knew that she should be passing the name along to Armstrong. Nonfamily were the FBI's charge. Of course, there was the possibility that Armstrong had picked up the name already on his own. If Cole was still living anywhere in the area, the FBI would want to talk with him. It wouldn't be too pretty if Armstrong were to make his way to Jonathan Cole only to find Megan already sipping tea with the man.

Megan terminated her call and squeezed down on the accelerator.

Screw pretty.

Philip and Judy Resnick lived in a quiet tree-filled neighborhood just under half a mile from the Katonah train station. The house had been built in the thirties, a two-story colonial with a two-car garage, an oversize bay window, and an ancient elm dominating the front yard.

The Resnicks were expecting Detective Lamb, and they led her through the house to the stone patio off the kitchen, where a perspiring pitcher of lemonade sat on the outdoor table. As the three settled in, a newly clipped poodle made the rounds, anointing knees and ankles with her runny nose.

"Maggie!" Philip Resnick snapped. The dog cowered, and then accepted Judy Resnick's silent invitation to come over for a vigorous head rub.

Philip Resnick poured the lemonades. A crow passed low just as Megan began to speak, preempting her with its resounding *caw-caw.* Megan waited until the bird had plunged into the trees.

"I can't tell you how sorry I am about your daughter. I'm sure the last thing you want right now is to talk with the police. I appreciate your co-operation."

Judy Resnick spoke first. She was somewhat birdlike herself, though hardly of the hearty crow variety.

"This is just so perplexing. Are they really positive it was Robbie?"

"There's very little question at this point," Megan said. "Everything seems to be pointing to your nephew."

"And he has . . . they're saying he has *kidnapped* Senator Foster's daughter? It's just so hard to believe."

Philip Resnick spoke up. "We had one of Foster's signs in the front yard last fall. He's been a good senator as best I can tell."

Judy Resnick was still grasping for some clarity. "What could Robbie possibly want?"

"That's the problem, we don't know that yet. He hasn't contacted anyone." Megan took a beat. "I need to ask. When was the last time you had contact with your nephew?"

Judy Resnick answered. "We were asking ourselves that same thing. It was several days after Joy's funeral. Robbie called us to see how we were doing. It was . . . well, at the time it seemed like a sweet gesture."

"What do you need from us, Detective?" Philip Resnick asked. "We don't want to see Robbie hurt, but if he's responsible for what you're saying, we want him in custody. Clearly he needs help."

Megan assured the couple that no one was planning to harm their nephew. "Trust me, there are a lot of eyes watching this case. All caution will be taken, but first we have to locate him. I'd like to pick your brains a little, if that's all right."

Judy Resnick was practically buffing the poodle's head by now. "Of course."

Megan pulled out her notebook.

"As you can imagine, time is of the essence here. If your nephew has abducted Senator Foster's daughter, we need to determine what he has in mind. Obviously, we need to know where he might be holding her. Any patterns of Robert's that you can identify for me would be helpful. I've just come from speaking with your son. His picture of Robert sounds pretty close to the classic loner. Does that sound accurate to the two of you?"

Judy Resnick glanced at her husband before responding. "I don't think I would describe Robbie as completely antisocial."

Philip Resnick cocked an eyebrow. "Jude?"

"Well, I wouldn't." She turned to Megan. "Maybe you could say square peg, round hole. It's difficult to fit in when . . . when you don't fit in."

She paused and again looked over at her husband.

Megan prompted. "In what ways would you say your nephew didn't fit in?"

"Well, his size was certainly a factor," Judy Resnick said. "When he was little . . . when he was young, Robbie was always being mistaken for being older than he really was. When a person is expecting a three- or four-year-old to behave like a six-year-old and he doesn't, sometimes the child absorbs some unfortunate messages. Like a sense of ineptness. Or disapproval. This is all very amateur psychology, I realize, but it makes sense to me. Personally, I thought maybe he'd end up being an artist of some sort. He used to keep a sketchbook with him all the time."

Her husband cut in. "Let's remember the drawings, sweetheart. Robbie was not exactly the next da Vinci."

Judy Resnick looked annoyed. "That's an awfully high standard, don't you think?"

"You know what I mean." Smallwood's uncle addressed Megan. "The boy couldn't draw. I mean, no better than I can draw, and I can't draw. He was very inward. I think his scribblings were partly so that he didn't have to talk to people."

"Robbie liked to read," Judy Resnick jumped in. "He devoured all sorts of books. He even read poetry. Soon after Robbie moved in with us he discovered Shakespeare. Imagine. A fourteen-year-old boy. But you know the type, don't you? They're the ones who sit quietly while everyone else is chattering away, and then suddenly they come out with a comment that shows that they have been hearing everything. Robbie observed people. He was always processing."

She paused. It seemed to Megan that the woman was expecting her husband to interject. But Philip Resnick remained silent. The woman continued. "I guess I'd have to say he judged people, too."

Megan asked, "How so?"

"By the time he got to high school Robbie's sense of himself was . . . how would you characterize it, Philip?"

Philip Resnick was ready with a reply. "Superior. The boy felt he was superior to everyone. It could get quite tedious. He was constantly going on and on about how stupid everyone was. And how weak."

Megan consulted her notebook. "What about a Jonathan Cole? Your son told me that he remembered Cole as one of Robert's closest friends."

Philip Resnick made a snorting sound. "Eddie Haskell."

"Excuse me?"

"The show *Leave It to Beaver*. Maybe that's before your time. Eddie Haskell was an ingratiating phony. A classic kiss-up. 'You look so nice today, Mrs. Cleaver.' 'I trust Mr. Cleaver is doing well?' That kind of crap. That was Jonathan Cole. His name wasn't even Jonathan. It was John. He took it on as a pretension. That's your Jonathan Cole."

"And your nephew was close to him?"

"They hung around together most of high school. I guess Robbie didn't find him 'weak' and 'ignorant' like he did everyone else. Cole was just one of those sarcastic too-clever kids. Sarcastic."

Megan asked, "Was Robert ever violent?"

"You mean did he drown cats and blow up frogs with firecrackers?"

"You tell me," Megan said.

Philip Resnick passed the question over to his wife. "You tell her. Does Robbie have a temper?"

Megan felt she was being forced to read between the lines with this couple. It seemed they were working some things out between them. Or perhaps *not* working them out.

"I wouldn't call it volcanic," Judy Resnick said evenly. She pulled her lemonade glass closer but did not pick it up. She ran a finger along the condensation. "I've seen Robbie throw a few tantrums in his time. His expectations about people are not always reasonable."

"So, there's anger."

"Well, it makes sense that there'd be some anger. My God, look what became of his parents."

"What can you tell me about that? What was Robert's relationship with his parents? His mother was your sister?"

Judy Resnick nodded her head. "Robbie was terrifically ambivalent about his mother. On the one hand, he adored her. Physically, Vivien was quite a beautiful woman. But my sister was not the most loyal of wives."

"She had affairs." Megan didn't bother making a question of it.

"Yes, she did."

"And your nephew knew this about his mother?"

"At least on some level, I believe he did."

"And this is why her husband murdered her? Because she was sleeping around?"

Judy Resnick's voice tumbled to nearly a whisper. "It was horrible what he did to her."

Philip Resnick spoke up. "You have to understand something about Ray, Detective. Ray was very much a beta male. Nice enough guy, in his way, but pretty ineffectual overall. Killing Vivien was probably the one true assertive moment of his life."

"Don't you mean *first* assertive act?"

"What do you mean?"

Megan put her index finger to her head and cocked her thumb.

The man got it. "Oh."

Judy Resnick quietly folded in on herself.

The Resnicks had no sense of whether or not their nephew had maintained contact with Jonathan Cole. Judy Resnick recalled that after graduating from high school Cole had attended Brown University and that Smallwood had visited him there several times. Smallwood himself had attended Hunter College but had dropped out before the end of his freshman year and immediately taken his job at the museum.

"I don't need to tell you what a waste that has been," she said to Megan as the three made their way back through the house. "Robbie has been hiding from life in that museum. A man with his brains and his potential should be a curator, not a security guard. It's tragic."

Megan left the couple standing at the front door and returned to her car. As she turned the ignition she saw Philip Resnick lowering himself onto the stoop and burying his face in his arms. Megan pulled her sunglasses from the visor and put them on. She reversed the car and swung the wheel, backing to the edge of the driveway's semicircle so that she could exit the property forward. She was shifting into drive when she saw Judy Resnick hurrying over to the car. Megan stopped and rolled down the window.

"I just thought of something," Judy Resnick said. "The house. On Shelter Island."

Megan pushed her sunglasses up onto her head. "What about it?"

"It was the place Robbie always seemed most happy. You know how beach places can be. Especially for a child. It's such an escape from the real world. I was just thinking. If Robbie made a conscious decision to . . . to do what he did to Joy out there specifically, at the house . . . or maybe it wasn't even conscious. But you're telling us that he also took Senator Foster's little girl out there?"

"We know he was there. We're only assuming the rest."

"You were asking if we could recall anything like a pattern in Robbie's behavior. Well, isn't that a pattern? Going to the house to murder Joy and then taking this little girl back out there?"

"That's a good point," Megan said. "But I don't think we're going to see your nephew pop up there a third time."

"No, no. That's not what I'm suggesting. It's not the beach place. It's *about* the beach place."

CHAPTER 58

Christine pulled a plastic pass card from the sun visor of Jenny's car and fed it into the metal slot out the driver's side window. The yellow swing arm in front of the car pitched up swiftly forty-five degrees, shuddering to a stop, and Christine pulled onto the King's Hook peninsula. Beside her, Lillian released a barely audible sound of relief. Christine knew this much: Her mother's story had exhausted them both.

Christine steered the car slowly along the narrow roadway, bordered on both sides by the gray waters of Long Island Sound. Several hundred feet from the gate, the first of two parking areas appeared on the right. On the left, the boulders and grass gave way to the thin white stretch of sand that comprised King's Hook Beach. A select group of local residents paid hefty sums annually to the King's Hook Beach Association for the privilege of baking their well-oiled bodies each summer on the sandy white strip of beach. The limited number of users' passes available were highly cherished documents in the region, often passed along from one generation to the next and not infrequently the subject of rancor in property settlements during local divorce proceedings.

Christine pulled into the parking area and killed the engine. She checked the rearview mirror. The parade of news vans and other vehicles that had been trailing Christine and her mother ever since they cleared her father's front gate were pulled up short at the gate. She watched the Greenwich police cruiser that had accompanied the parade move past the vehicles and stop at the yellow swing arm. Christine released her own sigh. It was doubtful that any members of the media were in possession of the prized user's pass for King's Hook Beach. She and her mother were again on private property. Safe harbor.

Since concluding her tale, Lillian had fallen into an unaccustomed silence. She sat quietly now in the passenger seat, looking impassively out over the gray water. Christine took the opportunity to study her mother's profile. She shuddered inwardly, noting the astounding resemblance to her deceased brother. The similarities between the two had also gone well beyond physical appearance. It was there in the similar displacement of their hearts, their need for a form of affection that never quite appeared. In Lillian's case, her ability to accommodate that absence had been sharper than that of her son. Her passion for survival had proved more keen. Or possibly more desperate.

As Christine stole a look at her mother, the revelations concerning the sailor's assault and the circumstances surrounding Peter's conception hit her, and she realized for the first time in her life just how unkindly she had always treated this woman. And how selfishly. In reality, Lillian's tough little heart was a bundle of fractures and fault lines, damage that was achingly evident in the very bigness of the woman's habitual dismissal of them. Granted, much of Lillian's damage had been self-inflicted, the result of her own petulance and foolishness and immaturity. But where had *those* come from?

Christine was stunned at her own capacity to condemn. Nobody puts in a request for suffering. It simply happens. Brothers die. Mothers disappoint. Husbands lie. Who was Christine to exile anyone? Who knew what behaviors Christine might be manifesting in the future as a result of the multiple tragedies that were unfolding right in front of her? How cruel it would feel if her less-than-perfect responses to her own calamities were to provoke the sort of judgment and anger that her own mother had been forced to endure for most of her life. Christine felt ashamed. And with the feeling came something else. It was relief. The absolute last thing in the world she would have expected.

Christine reached over and pried her mother's hand from her lap. It felt as cold as chilled glass. Lillian's bottomless gaze rode back in with the next small wave, and she turned a wan smile to her daughter. Christine squeezed gently on the fingers.

"Let's walk."

The rain had let up considerably. It was no longer a slashing attack but had reduced more to a light silver sprinkle. After crossing the road to the slender strip of beach, both Christine and her mother removed their shoes. The sand was cold at first, but after several minutes a natural numbness set in, leaving just the resistant texture of wet sand through the gaps between their toes.

As they made their way silently in the opposite direction of the mainland, Christine was cognizant of the news vans still backed up behind the restrictive yellow gate. No doubt she and her mother were being filmed. No doubt more fodder for the meaningless tape loops. Such was the fishbowl they inhabited, hopscotching from behind one locked gate to another.

The beach itself ran just less than a mile, after which the sand came to an abrupt end at a wooded area at the far end: the hook end that gave the peninsula its name. Christine was keenly aware of what resided back in the dense pines. Six grand stone houses, built several generations in the past. The oldest of the properties, a dark sprawling dwelling that seemed almost to rise up from the earth itself, was particularly familiar to Christine from the days of her childhood. The large stone house had been the original family home of the Wyeth clan, built by Chris Wyeth's father in the 1930s, soon after he had purchased the slender overgrown peninsula from its cash-strapped owner. Wyeth's convivial parents had enjoyed opening their home to visitors, and Christine and her brother had always thrilled at the prospect of an afternoon at the big house on King's Hook. The two never tired of losing themselves in the mansion's endless labyrinths of rooms and hallways while the grown-ups gathered in either the great living room or out on the pine-needled patio to drink and laugh and argue and do whatever it was that grown-ups did. There were canoes and badminton and, seemingly, always a litter of new kittens with which to play. The Wyeth home was where both Christine and Peter learned to swim. The massive black boulder at the edge of the water—appropriately tagged Courage Rock—loomed large and daunting for years until the day that Peter had dared his first leap. After the deaths of their parents, Chris Wyeth's brother and his family had moved into the house, while Wyeth himself eventually took up residence at his large sun-drenched property several hours away on the south shore of Long Island.

As Christine and Lillian made their way along the sand, Lillian remained several feet in front of her daughter, her focus very much on the thickly pined acres at the end of the beach. For her part, Christine could not shake—didn't want to shake—the invisible presence of her brother. It was almost as if the revelation of Peter's true parentage might serve as the portal for bringing him back from an exile into which he had been unwittingly plunged. No such luck, of course. No third set of footprints was miraculously appearing in the sand.

Abruptly, Christine halted in her tracks.

"Did he know?"

Lillian slowed and then stopped. Reluctantly, she turned to face her daughter. The raw wind picked up her hair.

"Did who know?"

"Peter. Did he know this? Did you tell him?"

Lillian's head moved almost imperceptibly. "I never told him."

"Did Chris?"

"I made him promise he never would."

The wind gusted, and a buckshot of sand slapped against Christine's face. "But you told Whitney. You don't even have to say; it's obvious he knew. All the crap he threw at Peter . . . it all makes so much sense now. That's why he hounded that poor boy! He was really hounding you."

"I don't disagree."

"You don't *disagree*?" Christine's voice pitched harshly against the wind. "How about maybe you *do* something! Did that ever occur to you? You stood by while that man punished you through your own son, and then you watched as that poor unloved boy just withered away and died."

"Peter was not un—"

"He *died*! He's not here anymore! All he wanted was a little love from his father, and the poor thing didn't even know he was looking in the wrong place. I don't know if I've ever heard of anything so cruel."

Lillian remained silent. Christine waited for her to speak, not knowing what it was she expected the woman to say. She'd already said plenty. Perhaps the best thing would be for her to go completely mute for the remainder of her visit. It seemed to be Lillian's specialty: open mouth, wreak havoc.

As Christine stood bracing against the wind, a fresh thought popped into her head. More accurately, it erupted. Rising up from a place where in all likelihood it had always existed, merely waiting for its moment.

"I'm not Whitney's, either."

The words did not come out as a question. Christine's voice was so small the wind nearly took them away. But Lillian heard them. Her hands came together, and she brought her fingertips to her lips.

"Oh my God. It's not just Peter. It's me, too."

Lillian's eyes closed. Her head tipped forward. It was impossible to tell if she was praying or presenting herself for execution.

CHAPTER 59

Megan Lamb would have preferred taking the Taconic State Parkway north and then cutting over to the west, but the first available cutover was well beyond her destination. Besides which, Megan didn't much like the name of the cutover. Pudding Street. How much pedal to the metal could a person expect to use on something called Pudding Street?

A call came over her radio as she passed the village of Yorktown. Megan lifted her transmitter and thumbed the switch.

"I read. What've you got?"

What they had was substantial. Robert Smallwood's car had been located. Megan's foot involuntarily squeezed down harder on the accelerator.

"Where?"

The car had been located on a residential street near the train station in the town of Huntington, on the north shore of Long Island. It had been parked legally, and it might have remained there unnoticed through the weekend except for part of a large branch on a nearby tree that had broken off during the recent storm and landed on the car's hood. When the Huntington police showed up and ran the license plate number, bells went off in the system.

Nice, Megan thought ruefully as she crossed the Taconic. *An act of God. Everybody's getting in on this one.*

Megan was told that there was no sign of Robert Smallwood or Michelle Foster. But the car was still being licked clean by the police. If the girl had spent any time at all in the vehicle, some trace of her would arise.

The FBI was descending on Huntington. Immediate speculation was on the nearby train station. Abandoning his car within sight of the station strongly suggested that Smallwood had opted to continue on via the rails. This was not necessarily a good sign. If he was traveling with Michelle it was difficult to imagine the girl cooperating placidly with the stranger, especially after so traumatic an abduction. The only imaginable way it seemed Smallwood could have boarded a train in public view would have been if the child was locked away in a large roller or duffel bag of some sort. And if she wasn't with him, where was she?

Megan goosed the speedometer up another inch.

She hit Route 9 and took it north. To her left, the Hudson flashed through the trees. Occasionally the trees opened up and the broad expanse of the river revealed itself. She spotted the Circle Line boat moving south, back toward Manhattan after its day trip upriver to West Point. Otherwise the river was essentially empty.

The massive granite outcropping on which the West Point Academy was built came into view on the far side of the river. Most of the academy's buildings were constructed of the same gray granite, which lent to the impression of an earth-forged fortress rising up from the bank of the river. The original West Point fortress had been built at this part of the river, where it narrows, making it ideally suited for wreaking havoc on unwelcome ships. Megan recalled hearing how chains would be stretched from the fortress to the far shore across the narrow portion of the river, submerged several feet so as to remain unseen. With a full head of steam— more accurately, wind—a ship could possibly overcome the chain and snap it. But traveling at more subdued speeds, the wooden hulls would experience serious damage. At the very least, the craft would be slowed down as it contended with the obstruction, making it an easy target from the rocks above.

Across the river from West Point was the village of Garrison, a collection of homes cast so disparately about the woods as to barely qualify for the term *village*. Several artisans selling ceramics and watercolor renderings of the area occupied a few low-roofed buildings adjacent to the train station; this was the extent of commerce as far as Garrison was concerned. Only fifty minutes north of Manhattan by train, the rural suburb was light-years away by any other standard.

Robert Smallwood's grandmother lived in Garrison. She occupied a white neoclassical-style farmhouse dating back to the eighteenth century and located at the end of a quarter-mile unpaved driveway roughly three miles inland from the river. Following Judy Resnick's instructions, Megan left Route 9 and began making her way along a narrow serpentine road leading up the steep hill next to the tracks. The hill was thick with trees, and a welcoming chill moved into the car the moment Megan began her ascent.

Megan removed her sunglasses and tossed them onto the dashboard. She glanced at her gas gauge, making a mental note not to pass up the next opportunity for fuel.

A call came in over the radio. It was Brian Armstrong. Headquarters was patching him through.

"Where do we stand, Detective?" Armstrong asked brusquely. "What's your progress?"

Megan took a beat. Her natural response to the man's curtness was not going to be helpful. Megan had her own experience with losing a partner in the process of a criminal investigation. By all available evidence, Agent Armstrong was conducting himself with a hell of a lot steadier hand than Megan had done under similar circumstances. A *hell* of a lot. Even though Megan's experience was several years in the past, her default whenever the matter threatened to rise into her mind was to shove it back in the black bag and stuff it out of sight.

Megan asked, "You've heard about the car?"

"Roger. Got that one. Looks like he got straight on the first available train out of there."

"Any witnesses?"

"Not yet."

"The conductor?"

"I said not yet."

Megan took a beat. "What are you thinking about Michelle? Do we see Smallwood dragging her around with him onto a train?"

There was a crackle over the radio. "I don't," Armstrong said. "We're going with the Foster girl being kept somewhere. I think Smallwood is traveling solo."

"Shelter Island? She could still be there."

"We've got a team out there. We're combing the whole island."

Megan backed off the accelerator to better navigate an S curve, just missing an oncoming car by several inches. The blare of its horn faded quickly. Armstrong continued.

"We're looking for freshly dug holes. It's sandy enough soil, a man Smallwood's size could make quick work of it."

"I don't like it. It's missing logic. Why would he kill her?"

"It's what killers do." Armstrong did little to mask his sarcasm.

Megan pressed. "He's not killing merely to kill. He had a specific reason for going after his cousin. On some level the woman pushed a major button."

"And Marion Mann?"

"I don't know. Maybe she pushed the same button. I'm just saying Michelle Foster was taken for a reason. It has to do with the senator. That's his target. Michelle is simply the means."

There was a pause on the radio. "Look, I don't want to think she's dead, either. Another option is that he stashed her someplace else before going out to the island and now he's heading back to her."

"Why would he do that?"

"I don't know. We'll have to ask him when we find him."

"Shit!"

Megan slammed on the brake. The rear of the car fishtailed as a zigzag of rubber appeared on the road.

"What happened?"

"Nothing. I just missed a turn," Megan reversed the car and took a left onto another country road, in accordance with her instructions. "Look, I'm heading for a talk with Smallwood's granny. It was she and her husband who bought the Shelter Island place way back when. According to Smallwood's aunt, he and his grandmother always got on well together. She says the grandmother speaks his language. Maybe she can shed some light on his thinking."

"That would be nice."

Megan had no choice but to drive more slowly. The narrow road was little more than a series of blind curves.

"By the way, I've got a name to pass on to you," Megan said. She gave it to him. "A buddy of Smallwood's during high school and possibly into college."

The radio crackled again. "Cole. Yeah. I got that one already. But thanks."

"Good. Anything come of it yet?"

"Negative," Armstrong said. "Mr. Cole's a goner. He died three years ago. A lover's quarrel. In this case, a boyfriend."

"Cole was *killed*?"

"Yeah. His boyfriend shot him."

"Whoa." Megan braked and let the car drift to a stop. She couldn't follow Judy Resnick's directions and keep up this conversation at the same time. "Where'd you get this?"

"One of Smallwood's old high school teachers. She seemed up on all the alumni news."

Megan realized she was staring out the windshield at a deer. The animal was standing just off the roadway in a clearing no larger than a child's wading pool. The deer was stock-still, its large black eyes fixed on the motionless vehicle.

Armstrong continued, "Apparently Cole's boyfriend shot the guy while he was taking a bath."

Megan jerked in her seat, and the deer's head jerked up. "A *bath*?"

"Yeah. Cole was blown away while he was taking a bubble bath, then his boyfriend turned the gun around and offed himself. Right there in the bathroom. At least it was easier to clean up for everyone else."

Megan was barely hearing the agent's ramblings. She was peering out the windshield, tracking the deer's brilliant white tail end as the animal bounded deep into the trees.

CHAPTER 60

"**H**e's *here?*"

Christine was holding on to her mother's arm to steady herself while she wiped the wet sand from her feet and put her shoes back on. The two had reached the end of the beach.

"He is," Lillian said.

"How do you know?"

"How do you think I know, darling? I called him before I left Denver and asked if he could come up to see me. He told me his brother and the family are away on vacation and that the house is empty. With all that's going on with him right now he thought it would be a perfect time to slip away."

Christine darkened. "What you're telling me is that you tricked me into coming out here."

"Let's not start that. You and I both agreed this was the only place where the jackals couldn't follow us."

"You tricked me," Christine said again. "Why did you call him in the first place?"

"Don't be so mean, Chrissie. I called the man because I wanted to see him while I was East. Simple as that. I do have that right, do I not?"

Christine had an urge to take off running across the sand and plunge into the chilly water. "Of course you do," she said evenly. "What I'm asking is why you felt compelled to drag me into your little reunion."

"No one's dragging you anywhere."

"Does he know that *I'm* here?"

"He knows I was hoping I'd finally find the nerve to tell you all this. We discussed it at length when I spoke to him from Denver. He said that with all his current hullabaloo he was not so impressed with my timing."

Christine was surprised to hear herself laugh. "Timing has never exactly been your strong suit, Mother."

A light twinkled in Lillian's violet eyes. "There are some who would argue that point, sweetheart."

As the two approached the massive stone house, Lillian explained to her daughter that it was Chris Wyeth who had informed Whitney that he wasn't Peter's biological father.

Christine asked, "But why in the world would he tell him?"

"It's another long story." Lillian slowed her steps. Her eyes cast about the large silent house. "Whit and Chris have such a peculiar history. The news about Peter was a large part of why your . . . why Whitney dropped his plans to run for the White House that year. Why we took off for England."

"Was he separating you from Chris?"

Lillian considered the question. "Honestly? There was nothing to separate at that point. Anything between Chris and me was long over by then."

"So why did he tell him?"

"It just came out one night when the two were together. Whitney was being Whitney, and I think Chris had just finally had enough of him."

"That's one very serious sucker punch."

They had stopped some fifty feet from the house. In the subdued light peeking in through the thick pine cover, the structure lacked definition. Moss and lichen tempered the stone, giving the place a sense of something that had risen up gradually from beneath the ground. Christine turned to face her mother.

"So then, what about *me*? I've always been Whitney's little princess. He was always smearing me in Peter's face. When he learned the truth about Peter, he must have immediately asked you about me."

"He doesn't know."

"But that doesn't make *sense*. He must have at least suspected."

The breeze was stirring the pine trees and Lillian hugged herself against its sudden chill.

"Whitney could not get me pregnant, darling," Lillian said flatly. "It's . . . this is a horrible thing to tell you. He was never tested for this, at least not in my time with him. After Peter was born, trust me, I felt so guilty, all I could think about was bearing Whitney his own child. But it just wouldn't happen."

"So you turned back to Old Faithful."

Lillian's shoulders sagged. "Please. Don't be like that. I didn't turn back to Chris simply to get pregnant."

"But that's what happened."

"Yes. That's what happened."

Lillian reached out to touch her daughter, but Christine stepped clear.

"But when Whitney learned about Peter, he must have suspected me as well."

"Of course he did. Whitney asked me point-blank if the same was true with you. And I denied it. I'm a good liar when I have to be. I said you were his, Chrissie, and that there was no question about it. He wanted to believe me. Deeply. That's the thing. When a person wants to believe a lie—"

She cut herself off. A light had come on over the front door. Lillian gazed up at the buttery glow, then turned a beatific face to her daughter.

"Oh, look. I think someone's home."

CHAPTER 61

Doris Smallwood was hanging Japanese-beetle traps around her vegetable garden when Megan pulled in next to the elderly woman's eleven-year-old Plymouth. The sense of a property slowly losing the long battle against overgrowth of ferns and wildflowers and tall grass was mirrored somewhat in the image of the property owner herself. Doris Smallwood wore her body heavily. The nest of frizzled gray hair could have been a bramble of untouched weeds. She was dressed in a pair of faded khaki shorts, a worn blue oxford shirt, and a pair of red rubber boots. Not that Judy Resnick would have thought to warn Megan—and certainly hadn't—but the detective nonetheless wished she had been prepared to encounter a woman who stood easily over six feet tall, even bent as she was with the gravity of her eighty-three years on the planet. As Megan killed the engine and got out of the car, the large woman made her way over from the far side of the garden, wielding one of the yellow traps as if it were an old-fashioned train lantern.

"Lost?"

"Mrs. Smallwood?"

The woman nodded and Megan shut the car door.

"I'm Detective Lamb with the New York City Police Department. I'd like a little of your time, if I may?"

"New York City?" The mocking tone was only slightly disguised. "That's quite a wrong turn, Miss."

"No wrong turn." Megan said. "I'm here to talk with you about Robert."

"Robert?"

"Your grandson."

"I know who Robert is."

Megan sensed that she was on delicate ground. "It's very important, Mrs. Smallwood. I don't know if you've been following the news. This concerns the daughter of Senator Foster. She's missing, and we have reason to believe your grandson has information on where she might be. Time is of the essence, ma'am."

"You don't have to 'ma'am' me."

The phaser was definitely set on *hostile.* Doris Smallwood lifted the yellow trap. "You want to help me with this?"

"What is it?"

"It's for Japanese beetles. You ever seen those? They're no bigger than your little fingernail. Copper-colored. Real shiny. You could mistake them for good brass buttons. Except brass buttons don't eat holy hell out of leaves and vegetables. I've got to hang one up in each corner of the garden."

"The fact is, Mrs. Smallwood, I need to locate your grandson right away," Megan said. "I don't really have time right now."

The large woman continued to ignore her visitor's urgency. She held up the trap again. "You see, there's a plastic bag goes with each of these. Black bag. By midsummer there'll be over a thousand of the beetles in each of the bags. What you do is you pour sex scent in there. They can't help themselves, they dive in and then just start piling up on top of one another. The ones down below suffocate. The ones on top gradually sink down below."

Megan sensed she was being toyed with. "Could we maybe go inside, Mrs. Smallwood? Or have a seat out here somewhere?"

Doris Smallwood stared at her for several seconds. "You help me hang this one, and we'll have your talk."

She turned around and started back over to the garden. Megan followed. Some fifty feet or so past the garden, past a decaying trestle long ago captured by vines and weeds, stood a small barn sharing the property's general sense of neglect.

They stopped at the near corner of the garden. The woman had been pounding a long wooden stake into the ground with a rubber mallet. A metal hook was screwed into the stake, near the top. She picked the mallet up off the ground and handed it to Megan.

"Here. See if you can sink it a little farther."

Compliance seemed to be the currency, so Megan humored her. Her angle was a lot less effective than the considerably taller woman's, and she had the feeling that Doris Smallwood was having her wield the mallet primarily to emphasize the fact. Megan pitched upward on her toes and landed the mallet solidly several times on top of the stake. The ground was moist from the recent rain, and the stake sank obediently. Doris Small-wood tested the spike and made a satisfied sound.

Megan lowered the mallet. "Mrs. Smallwood, this is official police business I'm on here. I'd really like us to go inside now, if that's okay with you."

"Of course," the older woman said. "The name was Land?"

"Lamb."

"Right. Baby sheep. Well, come on."

Whether the inside of the house looked like it was in the state of fading away or of resurrection from an era of neglect would depend on the mind of the observer. Megan leaned toward the former, if only because her assessment of the owner fell in that direction as well. With some silver and brass and wood polish and an astute eye, an antiques dealer could have seen a mother lode in the stuff that was crammed in the front room alone. A fifteen-foot-long, rough-hewn wooden dinner table sat in the middle of the floor. Doris Smallwood asserted that the table had originally come from an Italian monastery, circa the late 1700s.

"You could fit eighteen bald men around that piece," she said, cutting loose a husky laugh. She pointed to the table's claw feet.

"I used to be your basic domestic slave. When the children were in their teens I went on strike. One day I got down on the floor and gave those claws a layer of red toe polish and I gave it a full two weeks to see if anyone noticed. Not a soul said anything. That's when I started my strike. If that's how much attention people were paying to my work around this place, I was wasting my valuable time."

"How long did the strike last?" Megan suspected she knew the answer already.

"It's still on." There was a touch of pride in the answer. "My husband's dead. My son's dead. My other children don't come visit. I've only got to please myself now, and it turns out I just don't care. As far as I'm concerned, I'd be happy to just lie down next to the squash and beans one day and sink on down into the ground."

The Louis XIV chair that Megan lowered herself onto tried to throw her to the ground. An unmoored spring pushed at the faded upholstery just under Megan's thigh. Doris Smallwood settled into the colonial rocking chair. It creaked. Or the floor creaked. Something creaked. She threw Megan her hardest look yet.

"What exactly are you accusing my grandson of?"

"I told you. We're trying to find Senator Foster's daughter."

"What does Robbie have to do with that?"

"Mrs. Smallwood, are you aware that a Suffolk County detective and an agent with the FBI were shot to death on the doorstep of your family's house on Shelter Island?"

The woman did not answer immediately. Her eyes remained on Megan as she rocked forward to pick up a wooden ruler from the floor and used it to reach an area in the middle of her back.

"I don't watch the news," she said curtly.

"The evidence is very strong that your grandson is responsible for those murders." Megan decided to leave out the presumption of Robert Smallwood's culpability in the killing of his cousin.

"That's a ridiculous accusation."

"I'm afraid it's not. The point is, your grandson is very sick. A woman was also killed in connection with the abduction of Michelle Foster."

"I see. So now Robbie is shooting anything that moves?"

"In fact, that victim had her throat slit. Have you spoken with Robbie recently?"

"Why would he do any of this?" she demanded. "You don't know Robbie. He's a kind, moral man. He's got higher standards than most of the people you know."

"He needs help."

"Oh. He needs help? Is that what you're here for? You're trying to locate Robbie so you can get him some help? You'll have to excuse me, but I don't buy that. I don't know where Robbie is, but if I did, I'd give him that car out there and tell him to drive it to Mexico."

"Your grandson has a—"

The woman wasn't finished. "Are you even aware of the life that boy has led? I'm telling you, he's a sweet young harmless man. His mother turned out to be nothing more or less than a whore, and his father had all the backbone of a jellyfish."

"Robert killed his parents," Megan said.

"Jesus Christ!" The ruler rattled to the floor as Doris Smallwood pushed herself up from the rocking chair. For a moment Megan feared she was about to be attacked by the old woman. "He did not kill anyone! Ray killed that slut, and then he killed himself, useless coward that he was. What are you trying to do, pin every last thing on that poor boy? I want you out of here! This instant!"

Megan held her ground. "You need to hear this. Something sets your grandson off. His best friend from high school died the exact same way as his mother. In the bathtub with a bullet to the heart. And just like with your daughter-in-law, the man's partner also wound up dead on the bathroom floor. It was made to look like a murder-suicide."

The elderly woman's face was crimson. "You give me that gun on your hip, young lady, and I'll show you murder-suicide right now! You are trespassing on my property. I want you back in that car and out of here by the count of ten!"

Megan rose from the chair with deliberate slowness.

"We're going to ignore that threat to a law enforcement official," Megan said evenly.

"*Pig!*"

"It wasn't my intention to upset you. I just want to repeat, your grandson is extremely dangerous. He's—"

"Get out!"

Megan produced one of her cards and set it down on the table.

"If Robert contacts you, please be smart about it. If you can find out where he is, you'll be doing him a huge favor by letting us know. Call me. I promise you, he will not be harmed. You have to remember, there is a child involved here."

Doris Smallwood was finished with conversation. She remained standing in front of the rocking chair, glaring. Megan passed through the door and into the mudroom.

As Megan passed the garage and turned to see over her shoulder if the old woman had moved to one of the windows to watch, her attention was snagged by a pair of tire tracks in the puddled mud in front of the garage door. Doris Smallwood's Plymouth was parked off to the side some ten to fifteen feet from the garage. The paneled wood of the garage door was set off the ground by no more than a few inches, and it was clear that the muddy tire tracks continued on under the door and into the garage.

Megan noted that none of the Plymouth's tires showed signs of mud on their treads.

Checking again to see if she was being spied on—she wasn't—Megan slipped quickly to the far side of the garage, where she couldn't be seen from inside the house. She continued along to the back of the garage, where there was a door that sat slightly crooked on its hinges. She tried the handle. It was unlocked.

Stale air met her as she slipped into the garage. It was dark inside. She nearly collided with a large rusted coil of garden fencing just inside the door.

A car was parked in the garage. Megan snatched the pen from her pocket and crouched down in front of the car to scribble the license plate number down on her hand. They were New York plates, set to expire the following January.

"Hey!" The harsh voice sounded from the direction of the house. *"Where are you?"*

Megan backed swiftly out of the garage, still in her crouch. She heard the heavy sound of Doris Smallwood coming down off the steps onto the grass.

"Where the hell are you?"

Looking about, Megan spotted a flash of yellow off near the far rear corner of the vegetable garden. Remaining in her crouch, she crab-walked swiftly across the grass. The garage remained between her and the side of the house. As she neared the stake that she had earlier pounded into the ground, Megan swept her hand down and grabbed the rubber mallet. She continued on to the other corner of the garden, and picked up the stake that was lying in the grass and poised the sharp point of it on the ground. As Doris Smallwood appeared from around the garage, Megan was already pounding away at the stake.

"What the hell are you doing?"

Megan lowered the mallet. "Oh, I thought I'd help out a little more before I go. Just trying to salvage the reputation of the NYPD."

She picked up the beetle trap and hung it deftly on the hook. Doris Smallwood remained where she was, with her hands on her hips.

"Are you done now?"

Megan released the mallet and started for her car, conveniently keeping the garden between her and the old woman.

"You should try to chill out, Mrs. Smallwood," Megan said as she reached the car. "It's just a little friendliness. It won't kill you."

She got back into the car and backed out of the driveway. Doris Smallwood remained planted to the ground.

Back on the road, Megan called in the license plate number, putting a top priority on it. As soon as she had rounded a curve and was out of sight of the old lady's driveway, she pulled over and killed the engine.

Her imagination ate up the minutes. Primarily, she envisioned the car in Doris Smallwood's garage springing out of the driveway at full getaway speed.

The radio finally crackled. Megan jerked in her seat.

"What've you got?"

"The vehicle is registered to a Holly McGregor. The address is 282 New York Avenue in Huntington, Long Island. A Kia Sephia. Black four-door. Flagged here as a 411."

"What's the date on that?"

The answer came back.

"That's yesterday," Megan said.

"Correct."

Megan closed her eyes. Her heart slammed hard against her rib cage. "Very good," she said evenly into her transmitter. "Get Captain Bell on the line here."

"I believe Captain Bell is—"

"I don't care if he's making love with the queen of Kashmir, get him on the line. *Now!*"

CHAPTER 62

It was the embrace that did Christine in.

Chris Wyeth stood in the doorway, looking relaxed, wearing a black sweater over a white T-shirt, along with a pair of slightly faded jeans and white Converse sneakers, no socks. Upon seeing the two women he broke into a warm, welcoming grin.

"Girls."

Christine remained frozen, flat-footed, as Lillian stepped up into the doorway. The two old friends came together like a set of tumblers within a lock. They held the embrace five ... ten ... however many seconds. Christine saw the cool act collapse and a shudder pass through Chris Wyeth's body. Tears appeared in his eyes. It wasn't until Lillian's body jerked slightly and she sounded a deep sob that Christine's heart kicked in.

My God, she thought, *this is my mother and my father.*

Putnam County Police and New York State Police coordinated beautifully. Within forty minutes of Megan's conversation with Malcolm Bell, the intersections of all secondary roads and lanes within a six-mile radius of Doris Smallwood's property, including the Bear Mountain Bridge south of Garrison, had been manned. All officers had a full description of the black Kia and its likely driver. On Megan's heads-up, the same information concerning the cantankerous woman's Plymouth was also transmitted. Train traffic, both northbound and southbound, had been suspended and Routes 9 and 9D leading into and out of Garrison had been sealed off to unauthorized traffic. The process was overkill, of course. There was only the single driveway available for a vehicle to exit the Smallwood property, and Megan's eyes were locked on it. But the matter concerned a United States senator's—and possibly imminent vice president's—daughter, as well as a fallen federal agent. There could be no precaution sufficient to qualify as overkill.

Outside the arts center in Garrison, three federal SWAT units were gathered, their members poring over topographic maps of the area. The Smallwood house was marked with a red O. The small barn behind the house was awarded the X. The red light on a black metal box in the command van began to blink, and several seconds later a dozen satellite photos called up from the previous winter's area mapping began to emerge soundlessly from the brushed nickel slot on top of the equipment. The barn, the house, the patch of earth designating Doris Smallwood's vegetable garden, even a semblance of the weed-choked trellis, all were clearly visible in the satellite shots. The photographs came out in duplicate. Each pair was numbered and one copy of each was circulated to the leaders of the various SWAT teams. The duplicate copies were pushpinned to a large corkboard, which had been secured to an aluminum tripod.

Those who worked in Garrison's small mercantile strip adjacent to the train station—not to mention anyone who happened to have found themselves in the area when the SWAT units moved in—were effectively being held against their will by U.S. government order. William Pierce, the FBI director, along with the top officials at the Justice Department, was present via secure radio transmission. An argument between FBI and Justice over the use of helicopters in the opening phase of the operation had inadvertently been broadcast over external speakers from the command van until the belated flipping of the mute switch.

The coordination all sorted out, dispersal began. Camo-clad SWAT team members piled into the four vehicles taking them to their drop-off points. As the vehicles headed off, a blue step van arrived carrying twenty-five plain pizzas and two cases of bottled water—compensation for the civilians who were being detained on-site for the duration of the operation.

Agent Brian Armstrong cadged a slice before getting into his vehicle, folding it neatly lengthwise as he slipped behind the wheel. Before biting into the pizza he picked up his transmitter and flicked a pair of switches on the radio.

"Do you want a slice of pizza, Detective?"

The radio crackled, then the voice of Detective Lamb sounded. "Are you kidding?"

"Just checking," Armstrong said, chuckling. "I'll be there in eight minutes."

"Roger that," Megan radioed. "I'm timing you."

CHAPTER 63

Christine's head was in her hands. She was addressing her father, her *real* father, but at that precise moment she could only manage to direct her words to the floor.

"So . . . Michelle is *your* granddaughter. This whole thing . . . I'm sorry, this has me in serious circles."

Christine found the room they were in intimidating. It felt vast. The ceiling was too high, the oak walls were too dark, the wine-colored floor-to-ceiling draperies were too much fabric; it felt like a room more comfortably inhabited by giants. The cavernous fireplace sealed the deal, being constructed of the same rough-hewn stone as the house itself and practically the size of a small car.

Christine and Lillian were seated together on the couch, while Wyeth occupied a chair opposite them. His elbows were on his knees and his hands hung loosely, one of them dangling a bottle of beer by its neck.

"Nobody is proud of what happened, Chrissie. And I hope you know that your mother's not to blame. You're not to lay any of this on her. I'm the culprit in this show. If you need someone to get angry with, get angry with me.

"The important thing is, I want you to know that the FBI is doing everything in its power to locate Michelle and get her safely back to you. Trust me on this. You and Andy have the resources of the entire United States government at your disposal on this."

Christine raised her head from her hands and glanced up at the dark beams of the distant ceiling. It wouldn't have completely surprised her to see a cloud of bats swooping down from the shadowy corners. "I have a question."

"Fire away."

"Lillian tells me that you were the one who told . . . who told Whitney about Peter."

"That's correct."

"But you must have known what that would do to him. Why did you tell him? Why then? Everyone knew he was leaving the governorship to make his run for the White House. Were you purposefully blindsiding his candidacy? Was that it? Did you threaten to go public about Peter?" She turned to her mother. "Please tell me that's not what the two of you were doing."

Her voice had risen sharply, but her words dispersed swiftly. Lillian remained silent. Wyeth answered.

"That's exactly what happened," he said simply. "But it wasn't your mother. It was my call."

"But . . . *why?* Whitney had been your mentor. All those years he helped you so much and you pay him back like that?"

"It was necessary."

"No! What was necessary? Stabbing him in the back?" She shot a look at her mother. "Again?"

Wyeth snapped, "Leave her out of it!"

"Oh, I don't think so! She's smack-dab in the middle of the whole fucking mess!"

Wyeth's beer bottle sounded like a gunshot as it hit the stone floor. Glass and foam everywhere. Wyeth was on his feet. His finger stabbed in the direction of Christine's face.

"You listen to me. Whitney Hoyt is a dangerous man. I'm telling you, his sense of entitlement and his disdain for civil liberties wherever and whenever they cross his own notion of what's necessary to shape this country . . . Chrissie, it's not enough just to say that ice runs in that man's veins. For Christ's sake, you grew up in his household. You should know. Look how he treated your brother. And your mother! Whitney doesn't just identify enemies, he delights in undoing them. A Hoyt administration would have been an administration of witch hunts and hate mongering. The man is like a Caesar. He believes completely in centralized power, and all the better if he's the one at the center. Whitney disdains people. He doesn't think there are enough intelligent people around to run a church bazaar, let alone an entire country. You might think I'm joking, but I'm not. Whitney scared the hell out of me. So yes, dropping the truth on him about Peter was as hard a blow as I could have possibly landed. It was completely tactical. Of course, I had no guarantee that he could be stopped politically. But you better believe I made it clear just how savagely I would spin the information."

"So, you sacrificed Peter for the good of the country. *That's* what you're telling me?" She turned to her mother. "And you approved of this? Knowing full well what you were condemning Peter to?"

Wyeth answered. "I told you, this was my call."

Christine wheeled on him. "Then what about *her*? What about my mother? You condemned her as well! She had to live with the man. He dragged her off to London just to get her away from you."

Lillian spoke up. "That's not true, Christine. I've already told you."

"What about when you did come back?" Christine asked. "What about Whitney's second crack at running for president?"

"You know perfectly well what happened. Your brother died."

"Right. He died, and you went completely nuts."

Wyeth snapped. "Stop that! This is *my* son we're talking about. You might want to think about that for a moment. No matter what you might think about how all this came about, I had to stand by while Whitney drank in all the support and love over the passing of *my* son. I didn't have the luxury of public grieving. And meanwhile your mother had to button her lip, plus face the fact that that poor mixed-up boy went to his early grave not even knowing who his real father was. And you're right. You saw what happened. Your mother grieved herself right to the brink of suicide."

"Which certainly put the kibosh on any plans of Whitney's running for president."

Wyeth was disgusted. "Oh, please. Don't start blaming your mother for *that*. The woman was hardly acting on an agenda."

"But *you* were! I'm sorry, but I'm just not buying this purity act of yours. Whitney got knocked down a second time, and instead of him, *you* ran for the damn nomination."

"As I'd always planned to do. And I lost. All's fair in love and politics."

Christine managed a harsh laugh. "You can say that again."

Wyeth glared at her, then moved over to the cavernous fireplace. For a moment Christine thought he was going to step right into it. Above the mantelpiece hung a formal, full-length oil portrait of Wyeth's father and mother. Wyeth stood a long moment looking up at the portrait. Finally, he turned back around.

"Do you know why I'm resigning my office?"

Christine expected him to continue, but when he remained silent she answered, "Because your past caught up with you."

Wyeth waved his hand dismissively. "That's smoke. You of all people should know how many politicians there are with unsavory nonsense. The real question is, how did my particular unsavoriness surface? And why did it surface when it did? And while we're asking questions, *who* managed to get hold of that dusty old information and see to it that it broke all over Washington like a bloody egg?"

This time he did answer his own question. He held up two fingers.

"Two people. Whitney Hoyt. Bill Pierce."

Wyeth moved away from the fireplace and stepped back over to where Christine was sitting.

"Whitney Hoyt's single lifelong obsession was to one day become president of the United States, for the reasons I have just laid out for you. Anything less than the brass ring would be considered a failure. I helped him fail, not once but two times. And let's add in the fact that his wife and I have shared the sort of relationship that Whitney is incapable of knowing."

He shared a look with Lillian, then continued.

"If Whitney didn't already hate me before I made it to the White House, even if only as the vice president, he surely loathed me afterward. And it would not have been too difficult for him to convince his pal Bill Pierce to loathe me as well. Bill's a vindictive prick, if you'll excuse my bluntness. He and I have never got along. And my God, Christine, the thought of Pierce at FBI *and* Whitney in the Oval Office? For that matter, I can tell you, he'd have put Pierce at the head of the Justice Department, I'm sure of it. He'd have made that son of a bitch attorney general, and then let me tell you something, this country would have *really* been cut off at the knees. You can take that one to the bank."

Christine frowned. "But he's still head of the FBI. That doesn't sound so safe."

A twinkle came up in Wyeth's eyes. "Not to worry. I didn't completely waste my seventy-five days in office. John Hyland is no fool. Pierce will be boxed out. Count on that as well. It's just a matter of gathering the political support."

Christine looked from Wyeth to her mother.

"You're driving at something."

Wyeth nodded slowly. "Andy."

"Andy? What about Andy?"

Wyeth started to reply, but Lillian stopped him. "Let me." She reached over and took Christine's hand. "Andy's in trouble, sweetie."

"What do you mean? What sort of trouble? What are you talking about?"

"Chris told me about it when we spoke on the phone."

Alarm moved into Christine's voice. "What is it? Is this something to do with Michelle?"

Wyeth had retreated to his chair, sidestepping the spilled beer and the bits of glass. "Tangentially," he said. "At least I assume that's what's happening."

"Tell me."

Wyeth settled back in the chair. "Chrissie. Whitney couldn't make it into the White House. His chances had long passed. But he still had Andy. I can't even tell you how I know this is true, but it is. I know it. Whitney worked it. He worked it like a master. The day I handed in my resignation to the president, Hyland informed me that Whitney had told him that he'd had the goods on me all along. He had the evidence he needed to cripple me and he could have made it public any old time he wished to. He'd simply been holding on to it. Whitney could have scuttled my chances for a spot on the ticket right at the beginning."

"Why didn't he?"

"Simple. Whitney didn't get me pulled off the ticket because that would have only succeeded in achieving the goal of revenge. And revenge simply wasn't going to be enough for him. Instead, Whitney decided to game the system, which he has done perfectly. Or nearly so. He waited until after I was sworn in and was finding my legs in the office. He gave me two months, and then he dropped the dime, as they say. He and Bill Pierce and their entire little network of loyalists. They nailed me. For what in today's political world practically passes as a misdemeanor, but that doesn't matter. They nailed me, and I'm gone. I hang up my hat on Monday. And so, what then? A vacancy. Interesting. Who is going to replace the disgraced Mr. Wyeth as the second-most-powerful man in the world?"

Christine barely recognized her own voice. "Andy."

Wyeth nodded. "Whitney has micromanaged your husband right up to the threshold of the vice presidency." He laughed harshly. "No one ever said Whitney Hoyt can't run a hell of a campaign once he sinks his teeth into it. I fully suspect he's been cooking up my downfall and Andy's rise for quite some time. It's pretty clear. He and Bill Pierce systematically plucked off the other candidates one by one until the only one left stand-

ing was your husband. And I'm afraid they've got him by the balls, Christine. That's the simplest way to put it. I have reason to believe that Whitney has caught Andy up in a very nasty little trap."

"I don't understand. What kind of a trap?"

"Let me try to explain. Andy came to me several weeks ago. Or rather,
I should say he called on me. In a panic. Something had gone . . . something had happened. Neither one of us knew it then, but the trap had already been snapped. And let me tell you something. I consider myself a
pretty smart egg, and I know for a fact that Andy is a smart cookie, but for
the life of me I don't see how the hell he can get himself out of this thing.
Even if he were to gnaw off his own leg to get himself free, he'll still be
bleeding too much to survive."

Christine felt herself getting light-headed. She thought about Andy
and the wrenching disclosures he had made to her just several hours earlier. She felt as if the knife that Andy had plunged into her chest was still
embedded there. She was afraid to draw another breath.

Wyeth continued.

"I think Andy's dancing as fast as he can to keep you and everybody
else in the dark. They've got him. He can't make a single move unless it's
one they want him to make. If he didn't love you so much, Chrissie, that
would be the case. I don't know if you understand what I'm saying. But
Andy loves you, and he loves Michelle. And because of that, he's screwed."

Christine's gaze traveled between Wyeth and her mother, then fell to
her lap. Her eyes clenched shut. Air seemed to be rushing wildly into her
lungs. It raced through her entire body like a wind blowing through a
freshly cleared-out house. And it felt good.

Her eyes popped open.

"He told me."

Her voice was so soft the others were not certain they'd heard her correctly. Wyeth spoke. "He *told* you?"

"Yes. He told me everything. I know it all."

Wyeth shared a look with Lillian. "Well, that's perfect, Chrissie. That's
good news. You see it, don't you? You're no longer leverage."

But Christine had closed her eyes again. The winds were still whipping
about inside her. No doors. No windows. Unobstructed, they blew freely.
More freely than they'd blown in ages.

CHAPTER 64

Andy clicked the touchpad and paused the images on the screen. He felt completely empty, as if everything physical within his body had been vacuumed out, leaving him a hollow fragile shell surrounding space. With the lightest tap the outer shell could shatter instantly into countless minute particles.

Andy lowered the screen of the laptop and addressed the man seated across the desk from him.

"You might want to do something about that smirk, Paul. It makes you look twice as smug as you already are."

The comment served only to deepen Paul Jordan's expression.

"I have to say those are some awfully nifty moves you've got there, Senator. And the lady didn't appear too unhappy, either. Bravo."

Andy's voice remained even-toned. "You're talking about a woman who was murdered in cold blood."

"Well, yes. But things did appear to be fairly hot just before that, wouldn't you say?"

Andy lunged across the desk, catching Whitney Hoyt's personal secretary firmly by the lapels of his jacket. Jordan pulled back, dragging Andy with him, and the two toppled to the floor.

Andy was no brawler. He attempted to dig his thumbs into the man's eye sockets—maybe the son of a bitch would never have the chance to see *anything* ever again—but he didn't even get close. Jordan *was* a brawler. Or at least he had been, back in the day. Paul Jordan's left jab had once helped his team take home the trophy at the ABA Championship Finals at the Crystal Palace. The moment the two hit the carpet Jordan rolled deftly away from the senator and pounded his fist sharply into Andy's face, followed by a swift jab at Andy's windpipe. Andy rolled to his side, gasping for breath, and Jordan popped to his feet. He brushed himself off and ran a hand through his mussed hair.

"You need to be a bit more . . . skillful with your rough stuff, Senator," Jordan said, slightly winded. "Not everyone's a willing young lady, you know."

Andy was still coughing uncontrollably on the floor as Whitney Hoyt stepped into the room.

"What the hell's going on?"

Jordan indicated the computer on the desk. "It appears our friend didn't find the programming to his liking."

"Don't be an ass, Paul! Is he all right?"

"He'll be fine."

"For Christ's sake, I hope we can do better than this. Make yourself useful, Paul. Pour us some fucking drinks." Hoyt directed himself to the man on the floor. "Andrew, listen to me. We don't need to be thugs about all this. Are you all right?"

Andy had gotten himself to his hands and knees. He was drawing deep lungfuls of air. "I'm going to kill this bastard." His voice was strained and raspy.

"Enough. I hope we can dispense with the alpha show. The both of you."

Andy got shakily to his feet. He stood leaning against the desk as he continued sucking in air.

"Where did you get that tape?"

Jordan paused in mid-pour. "It's not a tape. It's a file."

Andy ignored him. He was addressing himself to Hoyt. "How did you get ahold of that?"

"I didn't 'get ahold' of anything, Andrew. I hope you don't take me for a bottom-feeder. I commissioned it."

Hoyt moved over to the armchair and lowered himself into it. He held up a hand and Jordan delivered a drink into it, then handed a second glass to Andy, who accepted it wordlessly.

"What do you mean you 'commissioned' it?"

"I financed it," Hoyt said. "I arranged for your little tryst with Miss Resnick to be recorded for posterity."

The scotch slashed at Andy's throat. "So you knew about Joy as well?"

"That's correct. I guess I failed to mention that the other day."

"Christ. What did you do, pay her off to set me up?"

"Not at all," Hoyt said.

"Then how the hell did you know where we were going to be that night?"

Jordan spoke up. "Unfortunately for you, your lady friend wasn't always very kind to the hired help."

"What's that supposed to mean?" Even as Andy asked the question, he understood. Marion Mann.

"Paul had a number of conversations with Miss Resnick's assistant," Hoyt said. "Have you ever heard Paul's southern accent, Andrew? It's quite convincing; I think you'd be impressed."

Andy felt the blood coming into his face. "What did you two do? Once you didn't need the woman anymore you *killed* her?"

Hoyt shook his head adamantly. "We had nothing to do with that. Absolutely nothing. This is God's truth, Andrew. This was never about murder. At least not from our side. Paul extracted what we needed from Miss Mann, and that was that. All the rest of it—all this bloodshed—this is not on my hands. None of it."

"And I'm supposed to believe you?"

"Believe what you will. All I was looking for was your performance on that machine there." He indicated the computer. "And let me tell you something, the price for capturing you and your friend in Technicolor went sky-high the moment that lunatic smashed his way in and did what he did. This is the truth, Andrew. That development was in no way part of the plan. That was a case of extremely bad timing. For you. For me. Certainly for Miss Resnick. The only people advantaged by that gruesome act were the ones who had ahold of that file. Obviously, once they saw what they had, the value of what they were holding went way, way up. I don't even want to tell you what I had to pay just now to finally get the damn thing."

"What about Michelle?" Andy demanded. "Where is she? If anything happens to her, Whitney, by God you're going to see some fucking bloodshed. The both of you."

"I promise you, Andrew, I have no idea where Michelle is."

"This son of a bitch has her. Joy's cousin."

Hoyt continued shaking his head slowly. "I don't know a thing about that man."

"Who the hell are these Russians? Is that who you've been dealing with? For God's sake, who's blackmailing me here, Whitney? Them or you?"

"I just explained that," Hoyt said, calmly taking a sip of his drink. "I was paying for the services of certain people—"

"*Aleksey Titov!* I know your fucking 'people,' Whitney. I know who you're in bed with."

Hoyt glanced over at Jordan, composing himself with another sip of his drink.

"Paul handled the negotiations. I certainly wasn't going to get involved in that. As I already said, the complications set in when this gorilla came crashing onto the scene and turned your private little party into a blood-bath."

"And all this was for what? Explain this to me. Was this all just so that you could get me in your pocket?"

"Persuasion 101," Hoyt said. "You've been around long enough to know this, Andrew. If you want someone to do something, the most effective method is to give them a compelling reason *not* to say no."

Andy slammed his glass down on the desktop. The brown liquid spilled onto his hand. "Jesus Christ, Whitney! What the hell am I sup-posed to *do*?"

Hoyt was unmoved by the violence. "Stop being dramatic. You listen to me. You're my son-in-law. You've got a stunning career in front of you so long as you don't blow it. I don't want to see you flame out, son. I want you to reach your highest potential."

"And making . . . *files* like this is going to do that?"

"Reining in your weakness is going to do that. Plus having something very potent with which I can call you on the carpet if need be."

"Call me on the *carpet*? What you mean is blackmail."

"I mean persuasion, Andrew. Influence. I don't really care what you call it."

"Well, I fucking call it blackmail."

"Then call it blackmail. It's just a word."

Andy glared across the room at his father-in-law. "Okay. Fine. Got it. You're coming in loud and clear, Governor. You've got me with my pants down in every sense of the term. You've got your dirty little movie. You've got me racing as fast as I can away from the scene of a crime. Bravo, mae-stro. Job well done. The whole world's proud of you, Whitney. So, now what the hell do you plan to do with it?"

Hoyt looked authentically confused. "*Do* with it? Not a thing, I hope.

It's my fervent prayer that not a soul outside this room ever lays eyes on this sordid thing. I mean that in all sincerity."

"So, I accept Hyland's offer, and the whole 'sordid thing' remains stashed safely away somewhere?"

"Precisely. And when I die, it's yours to do with as you please."

"Sweet."

"Come on now, Andrew. How onerous is this, really?"

Andy glowered at his father-in-law. "Is there anything else, Whitney?"

"What do you mean?"

"You know what I mean. You corner me into accepting the vice presidency, and then what? Once I'm in the White House, you start cornering me there as well? You just said it yourself. The expiration date on this damn thing is the same as your own expiration date. Your grip on me lasts as long as you draw breath."

"I respect you, Andrew," Hoyt said. "In all this silliness, let's not forget the basics here. I think very highly of your political instincts. I agree with the great majority of the stands you take. I don't see any real trouble ahead on that front."

"A great majority."

"Yes."

"How big of you. So what about those areas where you and I maybe don't see eye to eye? What happens when you want a favor from me and I don't want to give it? Come on, I'm not a fool. You're literally drooling over the prospect of pulling the strings on the vice president of the United States any old time you wish. A fine fucking way to run the country, Governor, I have to say. Nice nasty stuff, Whitney. I'm real proud of you."

Hoyt said nothing. He made a deliberate show of his silence and a deliberate show of finishing up his drink. He held up the empty glass, and Jordan took it from him. Whitney rubbed his thin fingers over his jaw and settled his gaze on Andy. The eyes were stunningly vivid; it appeared nearly as if the eyes of a younger, hungrier animal were looking out from a misappropriated facade.

"Of course you're not a fool," Hoyt said, lowering his voice. "You're extremely smart. That's part of your perfect package. But I do have to say, I'm disappointed in you."

Andy knew that he shouldn't take the bait, but he did anyway. "Why's that?"

"Because you're so shortsighted, son, that's why. Maybe *that* really is your basic flaw. You're pretty good with the big picture in general. In your way. But I guess you really do fall down when it comes to the *bigger* picture."

The phone on the desk rang.

The sound jolted Andy, but Hoyt waved a hand. "Jenny will get that."

The ringing ceased in the middle of the third ring. Hoyt took a deep breath, then let it out slowly.

"Andrew. Think about it. Why in God's name do you think a person of my ambition and my intelligence and my understanding of the way the world operates would give two flying hoots in hell about pulling the strings of the vice presidency of the United States? Seriously. Think about it. That's exactly what we call shooting low. That's not a *big* picture."

Jordan piped up. "He's not getting it."

Hoyt ignored him. He was focused on Andy.

"Chris Wyeth lasted two months. Two. Now the bastard's on his way out, and you're in. You've got to wake up, Andrew. You are the next vice president of the United States. Let that sink in. It's monumental, of course. In its way. But for goodness' sake, don't let yourself get too settled in. By this time next year, John Hyland is already going to be pasting clippings into his scrapbook. Hyland's gone, Andrew. Just like Chris. He simply doesn't know it yet. Veep schmeep, son. You're the next *president* of the United States. That's the bigger picture. *That's* the old man's vision. Now do you see how this works?"

Andy saw. He saw clearly. He slouched against the desk. "You think you're a kingmaker. You and your stooge here. What the hell is *he* going to be? The next secretary of state?"

"Don't be foolish," Hoyt said. "Chief of staff would be the most logical. Isn't that what we last thought, Paul?"

The son of a bitch was not kidding.

"Andy!"

The cry came from out in the hallway. A second later the door opened, and Jenny Hoyt practically fell into the room. She seemed not to notice the tableau of tension.

"Andy! Whit! They think they've found her! Michelle! There's about to be a raid!"

Andy pushed off the desk. Jordan came forward as well, and the two met in the middle of the room. Andy stiff-armed the Brit in the chest, never breaking stride. He strode past Whitney and past the trembling Jenny.

"Andy?"

As Andy hit the hallway, he began running. He didn't know where to.

CHAPTER 65

Michelle Foster stood at the edge of the hayloft. She knew it was called a hayloft even if there was no hay in it.

Back when Michelle was in kindergarten her teacher had once taken the class out to the country for a daytime Halloween party. Her teacher's brother was a farmer, and *his* hayloft was *filled* with hay. Not only the loft, but down below the loft a gigantic nest of loose hay had been piled up for the kids to jump into. The children had all worn their Halloween costumes, and the brave ones had climbed the thick wooden ladder to the loft and then leaped into the large pile of hay. Over and over and over. Michelle had been Tinker Bell that year. She wore a silver jumpsuit under a silver skirt, and her mother had fashioned a set of silver wings using white coat hangers and silky material. The funny part was that Michelle had been told to remove the wings before she jumped into the hay pile. They might bend, or worse, they might injure her. Michelle had told her friends that if she hadn't removed the wings before she jumped she would have flown all around the inside of the barn.

"Mommy doesn't want me to show off," she had explained. "She says it's not fair to other people who can't fly."

So the wings had remained with Michelle's regular clothes in a paper bag near the barn door, and her mother had stood with the other mothers clicking away with her camera, taking shot after shot of the falling children. The Little Mermaid. Dracula. Some hobbits. Spiderman. Simba. Snow White. Derek Jeter. Harriet the Spy. Down they all came. Little shrieks. Falling bodies. Costumes billowing. Landing safely. Michelle's mother filled her camera with the images. When that part of the party ended, Michelle stood patiently while her wings were reattached to her costume, then she dashed off to join her friends for pumpkin ice cream, leaping as she ran but of course not taking flight. Her mother caught her with the camera in one perfect shot. Both of Michelle's feet were off the ground. The wings were flapping out to the side. She was flying.

This barn was dark and filthy. The only light that entered came in through gaps in the walls and through some broken places in the roof. But even the light leaking in remained stingy and narrow.

There was a wooden ladder in this barn, too. But it was down on the floor. There was no pile of golden hay for Michelle to leap into. There were parts of a machine. There was a long metal trough, partly rusted. An oil puddle. An old stove. Just junk. If she dropped into that mess, it would eat her up.

Michelle's face was sore from all the gray tape that the giant kept putting over her mouth when he didn't want her to call out.

Her throat was sore from all the times that he did let her call out. But her mommy and daddy did not come rushing to save her.

Her eyes were dried out. Her stomach hurt. Even when the stinky piece of cloth wasn't over her nose and mouth and making her groggy, she could still taste the smell, and it was upsetting.

The hayloft was large. She could move around freely. But there was no way to climb down. There had been rain outside earlier, and some of it had come inside the barn. The floor of the hayloft was slick in spots, and now the air smelled like wet laundry.

Michelle remembered her kindergarten wings. If she had them now she might have tried to use them. She knew it was make-believe, but she wanted to believe it would have worked anyway, and so she let herself imagine that she could fly right through one of the holes in the barn's roof.

As she stood peering over the edge of the hayloft, the barn door slid open. The small wedge of light on the floor grew swiftly. And then a shadow stepped into it.

It was the giant.

He came into the barn and lifted the heavy wooden ladder and placed it against the floor of the loft. Michelle backed away. Except for the gray tape and the stinky cloth, the giant had not been mean to her. In fact, he'd been repeating over and over that she was a good person.

Her knees buckled when she saw that he had the glass jar with him. The stinky cloth was inside the jar. She backed herself into the far corner of the hayloft.

The giant spoke. "We have to go."

Michelle's protest sounded like the mews of a kitten. "No. Please."

But he was already unscrewing the lid of the jar. He had a blue paper mask with him that he slipped over his nose and mouth. Now he looked scarier. He was muttering under the mask, but Michelle couldn't understand what he was saying. She only knew that if she had her coat-hanger wings she might fly right past him. But she didn't have them. She only had her arms, and right now, they were useless.

She was crying even before she had actually smelled the stinky cloth that was floating toward her face.

The two cars sped off the King's Hook peninsula. The trooper who had remained at the security gate fishtailed in his U-turn, stamped down on the accelerator, and switched on the lights and sirens. The news vans lagged far behind.

Lillian phoned the house as the mini-caravan approached Whitney Hoyt's property. Jenny answered.

Lillian asked, "Anything?"

"Not yet," Jenny said.

Lillian glanced at Christine. "Get the gates open, please. My driver here is definitely not going to slow down."

As the vehicles came within sight of the Hoyt driveway, the paired iron gates were sliding off to the sides. Jenny Hoyt's car flew past the collected media and through the gate.

Followed by Chris Wyeth in his car.

The state trooper eased to a stop just in front of the gates. He turned off his siren. Behind him, the news vans lurched to a stop.

The trooper flipped off his flashing lights.

The two halves of the iron gate slid silently back together.

CHAPTER 66

"*That's* the plan?"

Megan was seated on the hood of her car, her feet up on the bumper. Agent Armstrong stood just off the roadway, his arms crossed tightly.

"If the old lady can be extracted, we extract her."

"You haven't tangled with this particular old lady," Megan said. "She might be a little less extractable than you think."

"It'll either be simple or it'll require force. Either way, she comes out."

"And if Michelle is in there somewhere while we're laying it all over this woman?"

"If that's the scenario, we'll move in. You're not to worry about that."

Megan gave him a crooked look. "This is Smallwood's grandmother. We drag this woman out by the hair, I don't think Smallwood is going to stand by biting at his hangnails. He has killed *eight* people. And that's just what we know of."

Armstrong had donned his sunglasses, even though the area where the two were wrangling was fully shaded by a high canopy.

"It's our operation, Detective," Armstrong said. "We're past pissing time. Do we need to get your superior in on this? We've got twenty-three men ready to go. Christ's sake, you can hardly say you're being marginalized here. You're the fucking point person."

She knew he was right. The plan held plenty of risk, but all other options would require a willingness to dig in and allow time to become a factor. That wasn't going to happen.

The clean version of the plan made sense. Draw Doris Smallwood off her property one way or another, then establish through her where Smallwood and Michelle were located. The house? The barn? Somewhere else? Together? Separated? Once they had Smallwood's location pinpointed, the SWAT teams could move in and chemically disable the subject. Textbook all the way.

"We didn't exactly part on loving terms," Megan said, slipping down off the hood. "I wouldn't be surprised if the woman pulled a shotgun on me."

"You'll be wearing a vest."

"The rest of my body thanks you very much."

Armstrong's exasperation boiled over. "For Christ's sake, are you a fucking law enforcement agent?"

Megan held her tongue. Anything less and the operation was shot. "Suit me up," she said curtly. "I'll go grab the old lady."

Armstrong stood down somewhat. "Thank you." He pointed to the man in the front seat of his car, which was parked behind Megan's. "Curt will get you wired up. We'll hear everything. Outside the house is preferable, of course. But if she'll only talk to you from inside, we're listening."

"Your boys can pounce if necessary."

"Correct. But persuade her if you can. Try not to pull the badge on her. Try that sweet talk of yours. If Smallwood's listening, he'll be less suspicious. But if you have to cuff her and drag her, then cuff her and drag her."

"This woman is a bear," Megan reminded him.

"Shit. You can handle a little old bear, can't you?"

Megan arrived by foot this time, leaving her car at the end of the rutted driveway, blocking it. She paused as the house came into view and scanned the visible windows. She detected no movement.

"Nothing," Megan muttered. "No one's outside."

The fiber microphone affixed under her collar required no unnatural volume on Megan's part. The technician who had wired her up had told her that he'd be able to hear her swallow.

Armstrong had agreed not to transmit through the transparent earpiece Megan was wearing unless absolutely necessary. What the detective needed was her focus, not a voice chattering in her ear. Even so, the lack of even an affirmative grunt through the earpiece rattled her. The Kevlar vest was bulky, exacerbating her already rapid breathing.

"I'm heading to the door."

Megan was keenly aware of the house dominating her vision as she approached it. It seemed as if its walls were stretching sideways and the roof growing higher, the entire structure expanding and cutting off her view of all else. Megan was also aware of swallowing hard as she reached the stoop and rapped her fist sharply against the door.

"Mrs. Smallwood! It's Detective Lamb! I'm sorry to bother you again! I need a word with you!"

No response.

"Friendlier," Armstrong whispered in her ear.

You fucking try friendly, Megan thought. She knocked on the door again. "Mrs. Smallwood! This won't take a minute! Please!"

"That's better."

"Shit." Abruptly Megan stepped back from the stoop.

"What's up?"

Megan's eyes played swiftly over the windows again. "Nothing," she murmured. "Except I just remembered that Smallwood's known to have a fairly crude way of answering the door." Armstrong said nothing. Which said plenty. Megan continued, "I want to check the barn."

Armstrong protested. "No! If he's in there you're completely exposed. We don't want you stumbling into him. That doesn't do any good. Get the lady. Follow the plan, Detective. We know what we're doing."

Megan didn't care for the implication. But now was not the time to stand there arguing into her collar.

"No response to my knocking," she said tersely. She remembered all of a sudden that her transmissions with Armstrong were being recorded. *Use manual-speak,* she reminded herself. "I'm going with a verbal warning and then entering the location."

Armstrong had picked up on the tone. "Roger that."

Megan knocked again, and again called out. "Mrs. Smallwood! I left state property behind in error! I'm coming inside to retrieve it!"

A lie, but sufficient cover if she needed later to justify her entering the private home without a warrant or invitation.

The door was unlocked.

Megan moved through the mudroom and into the dining room. "Empty," she said softly. "No one yet."

"Weapon?"

Despite her queasiness, Megan smiled. She unholstered her weapon. "Definitely."

Logic said that the woman was still in the house. The fact that she was not responding to Megan's calls suggested either unwillingness or inability to respond. Doris Smallwood seemed far too voluble a person to simply opt for clamming up. This was not the woman's style. Smallwood was here. Megan gave Agent Armstrong a nice solid swallow to groove on.

"Commencing room search," she whispered. "First floor. Dining room clear."

The search proceeded swiftly. Rooms. Closets. Behind large furniture. "Negative," she murmured with the conclusion of each room.

Armstrong and Megan had discussed the matter of the house's basement and attic. The decision had been made that Megan was not to pursue either option. Both were considered too remote and too dangerous. Barring the easy removal of Doris Smallwood from the house and her cooperation in identifying Smallwood's location on the property, the waiting SWAT teams would have to resort to an upscaled siege. Not the preferred option, but there it was.

The possibility of the elderly woman's vanishing had not been covered, but Megan swiftly went over the territory in her mind. If the woman was not on the first or second floor but was still in the house—presumably now with her grandson—they had to be in either the basement or the attic.

Or the barn.

Or anywhere else.

Damn. This operation was methodical, but whether it was brilliant or bogus was still anyone's guess. Megan felt vaguely like a bug on a string being lowered into a pit of spiders so as to get a good read on their hunger level.

As she headed for the second floor, the old wood steps had a lot to say. Naturally. The lighter Megan landed her feet, the more robust the snap and the creak.

The hallway at the top of the stairs was unlit and cold. She counted the doors. Seven. All closed. It was lady's choice.

Megan pushed open the door nearest her. "Bathroom. East side." She gave the room a quick look. "Empty."

She moved on.

"Looks like the master bedroom. No one. Closet empty. Nothing under the bed."

She continued.

"Unused bedroom. Trashed. Junk. Old furniture. Clear."

"Closed door . . . hallway closet. Clear."

"Small bedroom. One bed. Empty. Closet clear."

"Another hallway closet. Nothing. Got one more door at the end of the hall."

Doris Smallwood was in the bedroom at the far end of the hallway. She was lying on the twin bed farthest from the door. She was lying on her side, the large expanse of her back facing Megan. The hinges on the door had certainly announced Megan's entrance, but there was no movement from the woman on the bed. Megan whispered hoarsely into her collar.

"I've got her. The grandmother. Back bedroom. North end. She appears immobile."

Her earpiece crackled. "Immobile? Is she alive?"

"I'm checking now."

Megan crossed swiftly to the bed. "Mrs. Smallwood?"

Megan reached out and placed a hand on the woman's shoulder. When there was no movement, she tugged, and the woman shifted like a large sack of oatmeal. She rolled heavily onto her back.

"Mrs. Smallwood? Are you—"

The eyes popped open, and Megan's head jerked back. More startling than the sudden movement was the thin grin that spread wickedly across the woman's face. Megan had less than a second to realize that the smile was not aimed at her. She noted a shift of the light on the peeled wallpaper next to the bed.

Megan spun. But it was a spin into blackness. Her gasp was choked by the coarse blanket that instantly enveloped her. Before she could respond, her arms were pinned to her sides by something strong wrapping swiftly around her small body and yanking her tight. She jerked her shoulders impotently as her assailant grunted hotly, right next to her ear. Her feet were leaving the floor; her ribs were being crushed against an unyielding surface. Megan's next attempt at breath brought a mouthful of rough wool, simultaneous with a violent blast against the side of her head. Then another. Sparks exploded in the dark, and Megan's head dropped limply to the side.

CHAPTER 67

Megan Lamb had no notion of direction as she slipped back to partial consciousness. Her immediate sense was that her head was in misalignment with her legs and with the rest of her body. She was being jostled. She was being carried. A fire seemed to be blazing at the base of her neck. She sucked desperate breaths of hot air.

She was still wrapped in the blanket that had been brought around her like a net, and she was doubled over across her assailant's shoulder. His grunting kept rhythm with the bouncing.

Then she dropped.

She landed on a hard surface. A floor. The fire at the base of her neck raced into her entire skull, and Megan panicked she might be sick. She'd choke. She needed air.

"Robbie?"

It was Doris Smallwood. The voice was distant. The answering voice—a man's—came from right next to her ear.

"Not now!"

"But—"

Megan heard a familiar metallic twanging sound. The spring mechanism on a classic attic trapdoor. She sensed the faint sealing off of an attic door swinging closed. She pressed her chin toward her throat as hard as she could and prayed that the fiber microphone was still in place. She whispered so softly she could barely hear her own words.

"The attic. The attic."

Megan braced for a swift reaction from her assailant. It didn't come. She dared again.

"Attic!"

An instant later the blanket came off her face. A rush of air raced into her lungs. She felt as if her head was about to break into pieces.

She was lying on the floor of the attic, her body still encased in the blanket. Above her, the raftered ceiling slanted off to the sides. Robert Smallwood stood between Megan and the ceiling, his feet planted on either side of her head. He was winded from carrying the detective up the steep ladder.

A hissing sounded in Megan's ear. It was Armstrong. "Weapons? Is he armed? Is the girl there?"

Megan tensed, but Robert Smallwood could not hear the FBI agent's tinny voice. Megan cleared her throat. Under the circumstances, she came out with a decently commanding tone.

"Where's Michelle?"

Armstrong whispered again. "Is she there?" She heard the agent addressing the SWAT teams. "Stand by. Mark for ready."

Megan spoke up again. "Robert, where is Michelle? Tell me she's safe. Where is she?"

The earpiece hissed. "Does he have a weapon on you? 'Please' means no. 'Don't hurt me' means yes."

Megan glanced to her side. The attic—what she could see of it—was filled with boxes and furniture. Her mind raced. *What the hell means* maybe?

"Please," she said, enunciating as clearly as she dared. "Robert. We just want the girl back home with her family. Please."

The voice sizzled in her ear. "Good . . . good."

Megan continued. "She's just a little girl. Nobody wants to see her hurt. She's only—"

Smallwood exploded. "Who says I hurt her?" He brought a hand to his face and wiped it across his mouth. "I didn't hurt anybody. Who the *fuck* said I hurt her?"

"No one. Nobody said that, Robert. I just—"

"I *saved* her!" He swooped down and grabbed hold of Megan's shoulders through the blanket. With a sharp jerk of his hands he rattled her head against the floor. "She lives with *pigs*! She lives in a pig family!"

He shook her again, snapping her head even harder against the floor. Spittle was flying from his mouth. His thumbs tightened on Megan's shoulders and he dragged her up almost to a sitting position. His large round face looked poised to devour her.

The earpiece crackled. "Positions! Positions! We're close to go!"

She saw her.

The girl was seated in a cane chair in a corner in the far end of the attic.

Megan spotted her over Smallwood's shoulder. She was secured to the chair. A strip of duct tape covered her mouth, and another one was over her eyes. Megan called out.

"Michelle! I see you! You're safe!"

Armstrong yelled. "Positions! The girl is a yes! Megan, where is she? Give me a position!"

Smallwood was shaking her again. Megan shouted. "Stay in the corner, Michelle! You're fine! Stay back there! In the corner! Just—"

Smallwood rose, hoisting Megan with him. "Shut up!"

"*Go, go, go, go!*"

Robert Smallwood lurched forward, propelling Megan backward. One of his hands closed over the detective's face, and she felt the transparent listening device fall free of her ear. She heard a loud pop. An explosion. Megan's feet left the ground as the force of Smallwood's huge body drove her backward. As a second explosion sounded, the two crashed against the side of a wooden trunk and landed on the floor, the wind knocked from both of them. Smallwood buried his head in the detective's chest, and instinctively, Megan clutched at it. A cloud of pumpkin-colored smoke blossomed out of thin air and enveloped the two of them.

CHAPTER 68

The entire operation was captured by the news helicopter that hovered high above the farmhouse.

From seemingly nowhere, dozens of olive green–clad figures emerged and moved in on the farmhouse, racing in all directions. Simultaneously, four black vans sped up the unpaved driveway, two of them cutting off and veering to either side of the house while a third bounded across the grass toward the rear, stopping just short of the barn. Additional figures poured from the vehicles. Together the rescuers looked like a swarm of ants descending eagerly on the farmhouse. Half the figures melted away into the house itself while the remaining ones took up positions on all sides. As swiftly as the activity had ignited, stillness abruptly set in.

This lasted all of a minute.

Poof!

A yellowish cloud appeared from within the house. And then another, followed by yet another. The smoke burst from the attic. The frozen figures outside the farmhouse surged forward and disappeared inside just as a fourth smoke cloud exploded from the small windows. In less than a minute the combined smoke had effectively blocked most of the farmhouse from sight.

Two other vehicles arrived, one of them an ambulance. It was the sight of the ambulance that brought a cry from Christine Foster, who was watching all this unfold on the big-screen television in Whitney and Jenny Hoyt's den.

"Michelle!"

Andy was seated right next to Christine, squeezing her hand so tightly her fingers were nearly white. "She's fine, she's fine, she's fine. Everything's going to be fine." His expression belied the certainty of his mantralike muttering. Standing directly behind Christine, rubbing her daughter's back, Lillian was finding it difficult to take a single decent breath.

Whitney Hoyt stood next to the room's large bookcase. The phone was at his ear, as it had been since even before the images began coming in on the television, but he was not currently saying anything into it. Hailey Jordan was present. She sat in a straight-backed chair, her ivory-skinned hands folded one atop the other in her lap. Jenny was near the diminutive Brit, perched on the edge of a maroon ottoman, chewing on her lower lip.

And the resigning vice president of the United States sat in the room's bentwood rocker, pivoting his attention between Whitney Hoyt, the scene unfolding on television, and Paul Jordan, who stood near the window furiously jabbing at the keys of his BlackBerry. Had a mother ship suddenly appeared outside the window and drawn the urgently transmitting man into its bowels via an ether beam, Chris Wyeth would not have been all that surprised.

Whitney suddenly called out. "They've got her!"

He jammed the phone even tighter against his ear and bent partway forward to hear better. All the others in the room had swung their attention over to him. Christine and her husband rose from their seats in perfect tandem. It was Lillian who spoke into the charged silence.

"Whitney?"

Hoyt looked up at the others. He looked old. Old and tired. Lillian spoke again, softly, almost as if she was addressing a baby.

"Whitney? Tell us."

"She's alive," Hoyt said. "That's all they know."

All eyes shifted back to the television, where little remained to be seen but the merged clouds of rusty-colored smoke and the occasional dark figure scuttling in or out of the cloud.

Then one of the figures moved swiftly out from under the cloud, making a beeline for the ambulance. It was possible to make out two tiny stick-like legs dangling from the figure's arms. Christine's hands covered her mouth.

"Michelle! My baby!"

The rear door of the ambulance was already open, and the figure vanished inside. The door closed. The top lights began to spin. And the ambulance began to make its way down the driveway.

Christine turned to embrace her husband. But he was no longer standing next to her. She watched—amazed, confused, and oddly exhilarated—

as Andy crossed to where Paul Jordan was still hammering away on his BlackBerry, seemingly oblivious to what had just taken place on the flat screen. Andy strode over to the window and, with a move as fluid and seemingly effortless as capturing a handful of air, sent his fist solidly into the face of the unsuspecting man.

CHAPTER 69

On the direct orders of President John Hyland, FBI director William Pierce instructed the New York office to conduct raids on the home and business offices of one Aleksey Titov.

Mrs. Titov was at home when the agents arrived at the house brandishing their warrants. She gave the agents an earful. When this seemed to have no effect, she got her husband on the phone and gave him an earful. He hung up on her.

Boxes of files and papers were removed from both locations. Agents flipped through every book and magazine and checked every CD and DVD. They searched through drawers, kitchen cabinets, all the furniture and cushions and pillows, and patted down the Titovs' clothes hanging in the closet.

All computers were removed, including the one used by Titov's petulant wife. She nearly caused bodily harm to the female agent who slipped the flat monitor under her arm, but settled instead for a string of invective so creative she nearly had the agents diving for their notebooks.

At the conclusion of the search, FBI technicians in both locations swept the rooms with a powerful electromagnetic device. Aleksey Titov—at his office—cried foul.

"What the hell is *this* doing?" he demanded.

"It's a wipe," the technician explained calmly. "If you've got any computer files or digital camera files or anything else like that lying around somewhere, they're blank now."

Titov was furious. "I will have your ass in boiling oil, you son of a bitch!"

The technician laughed at the short man. He directed his device toward the mobster's crotch and moved it in small circles.

"Oops. Sorry."

A senior official of the Justice Department met with President Hyland in the Oval Office. The official's most recent—and final—report was already on the president's desk. For several months the official had been detailing collusion between two key members of Justice and several named personnel at the FBI with regard to the stalled investigation of several businesses located in the Brighton Beach–Sheepshead Bay area of Brooklyn, New York. The Justice Department official had agreed to serve as a mole and had positioned himself to participate in a secret operation designed to obstruct, stall, and ultimately eradicate the racketeering investigation. For reasons that the mole had been unable to uncover, some person or persons at the FBI were specifically identifying Aleksey Titov as a person to *un-target*.

President Hyland thanked the man for his good work and his loyalty.

"It appears that Mr. Titov was being promised a free pass so long as he provided certain services for certain individuals," Hyland explained vaguely. "This racketeering investigation was used as leverage."

His visitor asked, "Do we know where these promises were coming from, sir?"

"We do," Hyland said. "And that information is classified. We're going to do the country the favor of not making a big noise about it. Nobody wants headlines out of this. I certainly don't. I've had enough headlines the past two weeks as it is."

"Yes, sir."

Hyland added, "Not to worry. Free passes for the offenders are not being provided. We just prefer to handle this in-house."

The president thanked the official again and bade him a good afternoon.

It was a little after three o'clock when William Pierce's letter of resignation was delivered to the White House. Hyland's secretary brought it in to her boss.

"What do you know," Hyland said, looking up from the document. "Apparently, after an illustrious career our friend Mr. Pierce wants to spend more time with his family."

Hyland's secretary beamed. "That's very sweet, sir. I'm so happy for Mrs. Pierce."

"What are the rules, Liz? Can we buy the director a set of matching luggage or something nice like that in thanks for his years of service?"

"I'm not really sure, sir. It would be a beautiful gesture, though."

"Hell, I'm the beautiful-gesture president, Liz. Haven't you picked that up yet?"

"I hadn't. I'm sorry."

"Why don't you go buy yourself a big box of chocolates," the president said. "Compliments of the United States of America. We have power, I say let's use it."

"Right away, sir."

CHAPTER 70

Chris Wyeth met privately with Whitney Hoyt.

Former mentor, former protégé. Former friends.

The meeting lasted less than forty minutes. Having spoken extensively with Andy Foster the day after Michelle Foster's rescue, Wyeth entered the meeting with the full knowledge that the former governor had been setting the stage for John Hyland being removed from the office of the presidency before the end of the year and Vice President Andy Foster subsequently performing his constitutional duty by stepping into the post. When Wyeth broached the topic, Hoyt refused to give it any credence. He scoffed at the idea. Wyeth had never expected Hoyt to come clean with him. That would have been expecting a minor miracle.

On the other hand, Wyeth did come clean with Whitney Hoyt. Ten minutes after his arrival, Wyeth pulled some file folders from his briefcase and set them on his rival's desk. One of the folders included black-and-white photographs of the accident scene near Port Jervis when Jenny Hoyt's first husband had driven his car off the narrow road that zigzags high above the Delaware River. Another folder contained a copy of the official police report on the accident, including interviews with witnesses, as well as the analysis of the blood alcohol level found in Roger Mead at the site of the crash. The level had been extremely high, no particular surprise to anyone who had known Roger Mead. The report's conclusion had been that Mead was too inebriated to maneuver his vehicle along the multiple serpentine curves of Route 97 and that he had crashed through a low stone wall and remained trapped in his vehicle as it tumbled down five hundred feet of shale and brush, coming to rest roughly fifty feet from the river below.

Hoyt looked up irritably from the report. "And why am I looking at this?"

Wyeth continued to lay papers out on the desk, making a deliberate point of moving the framed photograph taken of Whitney and Jenny

Hoyt on their wedding day out of the way. One of the folders contained the medical examiner's report on Roger Mead's cause of death. The ME's report essentially ascribed Mead's death to any of a number of fatal causes. Broken neck, collapsed lungs, severe head trauma, loss of blood—take your pick.

Wyeth picked loss of blood.

He directed Hoyt's attention to a series of written reports compiled by two independent investigators that Wyeth himself had hired within twenty-four hours of hearing the news of Roger Mead's car crash.

"What can I tell you, Whitney? I guess I've just always been a very untrusting person when it comes to you."

In an interview conducted by one of the investigators with an attending physician in the emergency room where Roger Mead had been taken, the doctor had admitted noting an especially clean slice running along the victim's neck. It was the very lack of raggedness that had drawn his attention. The victim had been badly battered during the tumble down the steep hill. The physician's statement was that a slashing piece of metal or shard of broken glass would have likely left a very different wound on the victim. Even so, the driver had been drunk, his car went off the road, and the man was most certainly dead. Broken neck, collapsed lungs, and all the rest. End of story.

Hoyt studied the physician's report with an expression of casual interest then let it drop back onto his desk.

"This is all very ghoulish and boring, Chris. And I don't mind telling you that if this is the level of conversation from you I've been missing all these years, I'm finding it hard to feel much regret."

Wyeth gave the man his smile. "Oh, I've had a few sparkling conversations over the years."

"My loss, then." Hoyt indicated the papers strewn about on his desk. "Is there any point to all this?"

Wyeth answered, "I think you know there is. Of course, I don't ever expect you to admit to it. If through some extreme fluke Roger Mead had managed to survive all of those traumas on the way down the hill, his severed jugular would have surely sealed the deal."

He began collecting the folder and files and photographs together.

"It's all here, Whitney. I'm not going to sit here and lay it all out for you, because I know full well you already know it. And I'm not saying your man wasn't extremely clever. He was. Paul Jordan knows how to run an operation, no question about it. Even after he went down to the crash site to make sure that Mead had been killed, he kept his cool, didn't he? One quick slice and then he vanishes into thin air. All so that his boss could then go ahead and begin publicly courting his new lady love. Fine stuff, Whitney. A superbly organized campaign. We're all so proud of you and your trained monkey. He's been quite the asset, hasn't he? No wonder you felt comfortable sending him off to gather dirt on Andy."

Wyeth slipped the materials back into his briefcase and clicked it closed.

"Do you know what Paul Jordan is, Whitney? I'm sure you've heard this term. For all his stiff-upper-lip bullshit, he's a garbage collector. That's all he is. He collects garbage. And then he comes here and dumps it on your desk, and the two of you pick through it to see what kind of crap you can find. Very commendable, Whitney. It's a fine legacy. Governor. Ambassador. Garbage trawler."

Chris Wyeth gave an almost wistful look to his long-ago comrade. He dropped his anger down a notch.

"Christ's sake, Whit. It's all just check and checkmate bullshit, isn't it? Same old, same old. We're two old wannabes fighting a stupid useless cold war right here."

"I haven't admitted to anything," Hoyt said stiffly.

Wyeth picked up his briefcase. "I don't need you to. I have a story I could tell and some documents to wave around, and that's all I'd need. People would listen. They eat this stuff up, as you well know. Whatever legacy you think you've been crafting all this time, it would be gone in a single news cycle. I wouldn't even have to prove anything. I'd only have to accuse. Beautiful thing, isn't it?"

"You think you're being very clever."

"It doesn't matter what I think. You made me immune. *My* legacy is sealed, thanks to you. You've already dumped me out of office, and you can't hurt me anymore. But I can hurt you, *friend*. Hurt you like the truly deluded son of a bitch you are."

He paused. A good shooter always pauses before squeezing the trigger. A trace of a smile moved across the deposed vice president's face.

"And listen closely. If I ever catch wind of any smut against Andy coming to the surface, or if any sort of whisperings about John Hyland start making the rounds..." Wyeth raised the briefcase and rattled it. "Your Mr. Jordan will go down for murder. And so will you. Do you know what you need to learn, Whitney? Although it's probably too late to do you any good. You need to learn to keep your hands in your own pockets. Stop messing with other people's lives, Governor. Mess with your own; that's yours to screw up any old way you wish. But let other people screw up their own lives. That's the real American way."

Not another word was spoken. Wyeth could feel his old friend's eyes on his back as he left the room and made his way down the hallway. Like two red lasers. Skittering about. Seeking out the soft spot.

CHAPTER 71

The waitress brought Megan's breakfast to her. Her usual. French toast with sausage. Refill on the coffee.

"Thanks, Dolly."

Dolly came as close to touching without touching the bandage on Megan's head as possible. "What happened to you? Your brain explode from thinking too much or something?"

The waitress knew Megan well enough to take her sneer for a smile.

"That's as good a reason as any," Megan said.

Dolly frowned. "Seriously. You okay?"

On the small television set next to the kitchen, a segment on a morning show was comparing ultraexpensive designer wedding dresses with identical knockoffs that come dirt cheap by comparison. A pair of sexy blond twins were modeling the two wedding dresses. The show's hyperkinetic hostess buzzed around the models like a bee that can't decide where to land.

Megan grunted. "Can we turn that thing off, Dolly? I'd hate to put a bullet in your TV."

"Sure thing." The waitress crossed to the television set and switched it off. Megan winced a smile. She took a grateful sip of her coffee and closed her eyes.

The little girl was safe. Michelle Foster was back with her mother and father, shaken by all that she had been put through, naturally, but by all early indications capable of moving past it. Of course, time would tell. If in about twenty years from now somebody started picking off museum security guards . . . not so good.

But for now she seemed fine. The little girl had given the detective a huge hug around the neck just the day before when Megan had dropped by the Fosters' apartment at Senator Foster's insistence so that the family could thank her personally for her part in the rescue. After the hug, the sweet little girl had burst into tears.

The girl was safe, and the kidnapper was in custody. Such a collection of charges were being filed against Robert Smallwood, Megan figured the man would be dead of old age before all the sentences had even been passed. The media were all over the story, of course, and Malcolm Bell was pleased. He had caught up with Megan at the precinct house soon after her return from the Fosters' apartment.

"I'm just curious how this 'hero' business sits with you, Detective?"

Megan's response was terse and immediate. "It doesn't. I guess it sells papers, but that's not the business I'm in."

Bell said, "There's nothing wrong with a little shine on your badge now and then. It's good for the morale."

Megan looked slowly around the tiny restaurant. She'd always liked the fit of the place. Some years back, in fact, when she had been on forced leave from the department, Megan had even carried a few of Dolly's shifts, to give the waitress a little more time with her son. Megan picked up her fork. The French toast and sausage looked good. The coffee was freshly brewed. The inane yabbering of the morning show was now turned off, and the restaurant was blissfully quiet. The forecast was calling for highs in the low seventies, cooling air being pumped in from the Great Lakes. Big smiling sun. Clouds like popcorn. An open day stretched in front of her, and her brother was having her over for dinner that night. Track it up, down, and sideways, and all was pretty damn right with the world.

So why did Megan Lamb just want to cry?

CHAPTER 72

The stream of well-wishers into Senator Foster's office resembled Free Pie Day at the State Fair. The senator's key assistants, Greg and Linda, shuttled visitors between the front office and Foster's private office continuously.

"Representative Heidt is here to see you, Senator."

"Senator Dulev would like a word."

"Sir? Chairman Riechers is hoping you could give him a minute."

Several of the visitors took Senator Foster in a full embrace. In some cases, there were tears. Some even brought a copy of his book with them, hoping that he would be willing to autograph it for them. To a person, the visitors expressed heartfelt relief and joy over the safe return of his daughter. Only a few displayed the crassness of bringing up their intention to introduce new crime legislation as a result of the Foster family's recent ordeal. The senator from New York handled these potentially awkward moments with his customary aplomb. Today, of all days, he was not going to be knocked off his game.

The closest Andy Foster came to missing his stride was about forty minutes before the swearing-in ceremony, when a bulldog of a man, accompanied by a pale nervous woman, appeared at the office door pushing a ruby red wheelchair in which sat Lindsay Packard, Senator Foster's former intern. Her left leg was elevated and bound up in a plastic cast. Lindsay introduced the senator to her parents, and both she and her mother blushed as Tom Packard sputtered his apologies for his behavior over the phone with the senator the evening of Lindsay's accident.

"I . . . we're both fathers," Packard said. "We've each got our little girls. I just . . . I guess it's easy to overreact."

Senator Foster assured the man there were no hard feelings. At Lindsay's request—she was a bit embarrassed about asking—the senator posed for a photograph with the family. Andy parked himself behind the wheelchair, flanked by Tom Packard and his wife, and smiled broadly for the camera. He gave his former intern a peck on the cheek before she and her parents trundled off.

At a quarter to eleven, Christine appeared. She was wearing a brand-new outfit she had picked up shopping with her mother. She kissed her husband lingeringly on the cheek.

Andy asked, "Where's Michelle?"

"She and Emily are with Lillian. I left them in the rotunda. The girls are trying to get the statues to speak."

"Please," Andy said. "There's enough yabbering around this place as it is. The last thing we need are the mighty ones weighing in."

Andy turned to his aides. "That's it for visitors, Linda. Tell them happy hour's over."

He escorted his lovely wife into his private office and closed the door behind them.

Christine stood with her arms crossed and her chin dipped slightly, considering the framed photograph on the wall. Out the window, the crowds both on and around the front steps of the Capitol appeared highly restive and excited.

"I suppose you could turn this one into a dartboard."

The photograph she was referring to had been taken seventeen years before, when Andy had made his first run for statewide office. Then ambassador to Great Britain Hoyt had been back in the country for the annual meeting of the U.N. General Assembly and had taken time out to make a campaign appearance with his daughter's boyfriend. Christine had taken the photograph of "her two men" at a rally in the Bronx. Both the candidate and the ambassador had donned Yankees caps for the occasion, and Christine's photograph captured them at a moment when they'd been glancing at each other, both clearly exhilarated by the moment.

Andy was at the window, his hands in his pockets. On the Capitol steps, a large American flag was being unfurled. He pulled his attention away from the activity and considered the photograph. What was striking about the image was the commonality of the two men's expressions.

"It's depressing to think that the final judgment on a person's entire life is going to be based on his absolute worst moments."

Christine turned from the photograph. "That depends on who is doing the judging, don't you think?"

"I'm thinking about history's judgment."

"I'm sorry, I just don't find that so important."

Andy asked, "Is that because we won't be around to hear it?"

"Not at all. It's because what you're calling history is really just another snapshot, don't you think?" She indicated the photograph. "It's like this. That's history, it took place. It happened to be a good moment. Then along came the next moments, and the ones after that. And in this case, a lot of those weren't so good. So which history is being judged?"

"I can't pretend that's a different Whitney," Andy said. "I've tried."

"Why does it have to be a different anything?" She tapped her finger against the photograph. "It's a good moment."

"A good moment of a bad man."

Christine wasn't having it. "I'm fatigued with *bad*. Flawed. He's deeply flawed. Last time I checked, there was a lot of that going around."

Andy pulled his hands from his pockets and placed them lightly on his wife's shoulders.

"I am so sorry, Chrissie. I am so, so, so sorry."

Christine's reply was barely above a whisper. "I know you are."

"I'm never going to ask you to forgive me."

"I think that's a smart plan."

Andy gave her shoulders a squeeze. "You're an angel. I mean it."

Christine reached out and ran her hand down her husband's tie, smoothing it against his shirt. "Well, that's sweet of you to say. I'll tell you what, though. We should let history decide that one."

"I thought you just said—"

She silenced him, placing her fingers on his lips. Her eyes played over his face. "I say a lot of things, Andy. Most of it happens to be brilliant, of course, but not all of it. You'll just have to sort through it yourself."

Andy always felt he was good at reading his wife's expressions, but Christine had managed to find one he'd never seen before. It was a kaleidoscope. On the steps outside, the flag was waving furiously. The general movement was decidedly in the direction of the doors at the top.

"We'd better get going," Christine said. "I'd hate to miss democracy in action."

Christine sat with her mother and the two girls in an area in the gallery reserved for special guests. Michelle and Emily were fidgety. Christine and Lillian took turns patting the girls on the leg and hushing them. They might as well have been urging tadpoles to stop swimming.

The chief justice of the Supreme Court delivered the oath of office. Seated in the front row was President Hyland, along with his wife and their three children. It had been at Hyland's urging that the ceremony was being conducted in the Senate chamber and not in a more intimate setting at the White House. His new vice president was a product of the Senate. The people with whom he had worked were all gathered here. It was here he would preside as president of the Senate. The country was going to be handed a vice president who had not been offered up to them in the election, and Hyland wanted the matter handled as openly and publicly as possible. He had informed his new political partner that after the swearing-in he wanted to hear a podium-pounding, roll-up-the-sleeves-and-get-to-the-people's-work barn burner of a speech.

"We're rebooting this administration," Hyland had said to him in their brief meeting. "Not to disparage Chris Wyeth, by any means, but I want them to like you *more*. For the one day at least, it *is* a popularity contest. So damn it, be popular."

"**I** do solemnly swear that I will support and defend the Constitution of the United States against all enemies, foreign and domestic; that I will bear true faith and allegiance to the same; that I take this obligation freely, without any mental reservation or purpose of evasion; and that I will well and faithfully discharge the duties of the office on which I am about to enter: So help me God."

Senator Mitchell Cutler of Colorado lowered his right hand. The chief justice caught it on the way down and gave it a vigorous shake.

"Congratulations, Mr. Vice President. Good luck, sir."

The chamber erupted into applause and cheers. Cutler's wife turned to her husband, and the two embraced. President Hyland was on his feet, and in no time so was every single person in the room.

"**W**here's Daddy?"

Michelle looked up at her mother. Her own view of the main floor was hopelessly interrupted by the big people all around her.

Christine was clapping vigorously. "He's down there, honey. I can't see him right now, but he's there."

Her hands came together over and over. The huge smile refused to leave her face. She had no control over it, any more than she did the tears that flowed freely down over her cheeks.

Christine sat near the Reflecting Pool with her camera, watching as Michelle and Emily played a game nearby with ice-cream cones. The idea of the game was to swap the cones back and forth as swiftly as possible, slurping a speed-bite from each cone before passing it right back. Christine knew full well where the game would lead. And it did. Within thirty seconds, one of the cones failed to complete a clean handoff, and down it went, landing on the pavement, ice-cream side down.

The girls thought it was the funniest thing in the entire universe.

The steps of the Lincoln Memorial were dotted with tourists. From deep in the marble shadow, the gaze of the sixteenth president of the United States directed itself past the steps, past the Reflecting Pool and the Mall, ostensibly off into an endless future of possibilities for freedom, harmony, peace, happiness. Or something along those lines.

Christine focused her camera on the two laughing children, their faces a picture of pure delight. She didn't shoot. A strong breeze kicked up and was moving along the water of the Reflecting Pool, turning its ripples back on themselves. Christine lowered her camera. By the time the breeze reached her, her eyes had closed. A serene expression graced her face.

ABOUT THE AUTHOR

RICHARD HAWKE lives in New York City. He is the author of *Speak of the Devil* and *Cold Day in Hell,* and under the name Tim Cockey is the author of the award-winning "hearse" novels. Visit his website, RHawke.com.

ABOUT THE TYPE

This book was set in Requiem, a typeface designed by the Hoefler Type Foundry. It is a modern typeface inspired by inscriptional capitals in Ludovico Vicentino degli Arrighi's 1523 writing manual, *Il modo de temperare le penne*. An original lowercase, a set of figures, and an italic in the "chancery" style that Arrighi helped popularize were created to make this adaptation of a classical design into a complete font family.

NS